BRANCH

	DATE DUE	
	RECEIVED	
	AUG 2 6 1999	
	By____	

BRANCH

SEA CHANGE

SEA
CHANGE

James Powlik

DELACORTE PRESS

Published by
Delacorte Press
Random House, Inc.
1540 Broadway
New York, New York 10036

Delacorte Press® is a registered trademark of Random
House, Inc., and the colophon is a trademark of Random
House, Inc.

Library of Congress Cataloging in Publication Data

Powlik, James.
    Sea change : a novel / by James Powlik.
        p.   cm.
    ISBN 0-385-33399-4
    I. Title.
PR9199.3.P725S33   1999
813'.54—DC21   98-33242
                                                          CIP

Manufactured in the United States of America
Published simultaneously in Canada

September 1999

10 9 8 7 6 5 4 3 2 1

BVG

For my mentor and colleague, Dr. Alan Lewis,
who posed a challenge, then opened the door

And my friend, Mr. John Boom,
for making the impossible possible

And my father, Roger Powlik,
for all the rest

DISCLAIMER

The setting and locations in this story—aside from Juniper Bay, Washington—are real. The scientific and military programs, methods, apparatus and organisms are authentic to the extent that they complement this dramatization.

SEA CHANGE

*The second angel poured out his bowl on the sea,
and it became like the blood of a dead man,
and every living thing in the sea died.*
—Revelation 16:3

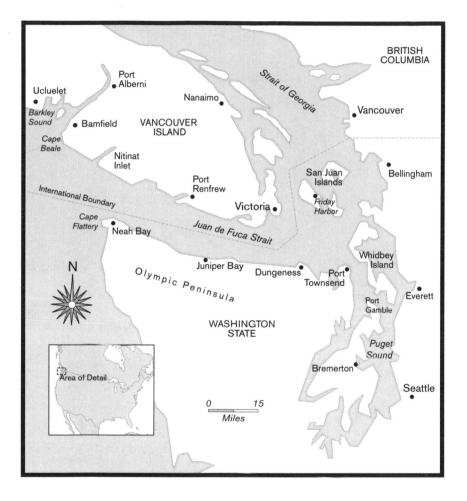

BRITISH
COLUMBIA

Ucluelet

Port
Alberni

Nanaimo

Strait of Georgia

Vancouver

*Barkley
Sound*

Bamfield

VANCOUVER
ISLAND

Bellingham

*Cape
Beale*

Nitinat
Inlet

Port
Renfrew

San Juan
Islands

Victoria

*Friday
Harbor*

International Boundary

*Cape
Flattery*

Neah Bay

Juan de Fuca Strait

N

Olympic Peninsula

Juniper Bay

Dungeness

Port
Townsend

Whidbey
Island

Port
Gamble

Everett

WASHINGTON
STATE

*Puget
Sound*

Area of Detail

Bremerton

Seattle

0   15
Miles

PROLOGUE

Alan Peters had always enjoyed the serenity of inner space. As a boy, he had been fascinated by magazines like *Popular Science* and *True Adventure,* publications that described a future where humans would live underwater, leaving behind the encumbrances of the terrestrial world to pilot personal submarines, reside in dome-shaped habitats, and grow crops on the seafloor. Swept away by the Artist's Conception of Life Underwater, he devoured the stories of shoreline nature writers like Rachel Carson or ocean explorers like William Beebe and Jacques Cousteau.

Later, growing up in northern California, the ocean was his playground, a handy after-school facility for body surfing or fishing. He could hardly endure the passing of the years and months until his sixteenth birthday, when he could legally take a registered course in scuba diving. Two nights a week for two months, Peters shivered at the bottom of a community center swimming pool in Salinas with rented dive gear and a smile so broad he could hardly keep his lips sealed around the mouthpiece on his regulator. He had taken his first steps toward the promised land pictured in those timeworn magazines, leaving behind, if only temporarily, the world of the air breathers. Since then he had gained thirty years in age, a hundred pounds of flesh, and more than four thousand dive hours, but had never lost the thrill of diving: of flying nearly weightless through an alien environment. The silence, the slower, more deliberate movements, and the submerged vistas that unfolded below him had never lost their attraction.

Now, floating twenty feet below the surface, immersed in liquid night, Peters adjusted the angle of his waterproof light and returned to his work. The water was an unpleasant fifty degrees, but his drysuit kept him warm enough. At the current rate of harvesting, he would be here another half an hour, adjusting his buoyancy slightly as the twin cylinders on his back lost their compressed air pressure.

Nothing at all was visible beyond the illumination from his light, not that he would have taken the time to notice his surroundings. His every effort was focused on the outcrop before him and its healthy growth of abalone. As his knife removed each calcified piece, he transferred it to a large mesh collection bag dangling from his weight belt. He had established an almost mechanical rhythm, concentrating on the profits to be had from the task at hand but lulled enough by its tedium to allow his mind to wander.

A final, stubborn abalone came free from its attachment, and Peters placed it in the bag, already filled nearly to the top. He'd expected Ricky to be back from the surface by now and assumed his partner had stayed topside to watch over their catch while Peters finished up for the night. He tried, unsuccessfully, not to speculate that Burgess might have headed for home without him, leaving him, literally, holding the bag. Such was among the many hazards of freelancing with a human eel.

On land, Ricky Burgess habitually looked pallid and haggard. His skin was pockmarked and creased from years of problem acne as a child, and he tried to cover this dermatological horror with a thin, ragged beard. He seemed to Peters to be perpetually angry, clenching and unclenching his jaw muscles as he spoke and nervously smoking his cheroot cigarettes. When drinking, he liked to preen his widow's peak and brag that, as an extra on the television series *Gunsmoke,* he had been shot "dead" by James Arness on three separate episodes. There was the suggestion that Burgess had a prison record. And that he had been discharged dishonorably from the military. And that he had had intimate relations with the teenage daughter of his (former) common-law wife. Burgess denied none of these things with the vigor of an innocent man.

A jack-of-all-trades, Burgess was a fellow dropout from the mainstream, who supported himself throughout the year using any number of cottage industries, from drying kelp to small-engine repair to shoveling snow to growing hemp. He considered himself, alternately, a survivalist, a businessman, and the unofficial mayor of Galiano Island, where he and Peters lived. The seclusion of Galiano enabled local denizens like Burgess and Peters to follow their unregistered interests, and the local constabulary allowed them to operate peaceably, provided they remained appropriately discreet. That had always suited Burgess just fine, thank you, and in time, Alan Peters found it suited him as well.

It was two summers ago, at the Hummingbird Pub, that Burgess first told Peters about his plan to expand his enterprises into aquaculture. With dramatic sincerity, he confided to Peters that he wanted to farm abalone. He said he wanted to hire local kids to dig the beds while they—he and Peters—turned a profit with the local seafood markets. He had applied to the government for a permit, was declined, then declared that the abalone market in the Galiano area was overfished anyway. To hell with permits, he said, pressing his index finger into Peters's chest as he always did when making a point while half-pissed. The unemployment line was full of guys who rolled over and died just because they let the government tell them what to do, right? Damn right.

After that, Burgess began spending his free time—of which he seemed to have an endless supply—journeying farther and farther afield to find natural abalone banks that they could work as "freelance harvesters." By the start of that summer, they had discovered Nitinat Inlet and the sizable abalone that grew there, feeding on kelp in turn nourished by nutrients upwelled in the area and the highly oxygenated water delivered from the northeast Pacific. The fact that the banks were a part of reserve land that was owned by the Salish Indians was an incidental consideration. As far as Burgess was concerned, profit margins did not recognize the treaty rights of First Peoples. Their land rights, if they deserved any at all, ended on the dry side of the tide line.

"Is that at high tide or low tide?" Peters asked, enjoying any opportunity to stoke Burgess's perpetual ire.

"That's at the frickin' *parking lot*," Burgess spat, his tobacco-stained teeth catching the light like the fangs of a wolf.

Nitinat was the third abalone site they had harvested in as many nights. The calm conditions helped to improve the underwater visibility, as the waves were minimal and the sediment load from the river was reduced. The long hours underwater left Peters aching with deep-seated fatigue, even though years of diving had made his body thick with muscles and his lungs as tough as horsehide. Peters remained impressed that a wretch like Burgess could even keep up with him.

Peters turned away from the outcrop and drifted with the current for a few yards. With each inhalation, his regulator dispensed air into his lungs with a thin, metallic hiss. With each exhalation, the discharge of bubbles from the side of his regulator thundered past his ears with all the cacophonous rumble of a subway train.

The light revealed only a few sickly strands of kelp atop a submerged gravel bar. British Columbia, renowned for its breathtaking marine life, was apparently hiding her treasures. Then Peters turned his light toward the surface and illuminated thousands of tiny planktonic creatures suspended in the water, all awaiting daylight to return to the surface and resume photosynthesizing. He paused to toy with the willowy form of a jellyfish no larger than a dime. The creature gracefully pushed itself up in the water column, then slowly drifted downward, feeding on anything unlucky enough to get caught in its tentacles lined with minuscule but effective stinging cells.

Peters swung the light through a wider arc in the darkness, still trying to locate the mooring line of the boat. Swimming slowly amid the sediment stirred up by his movements—conserving energy and keeping his bearings—Peters moved in an outward spiral, gradually increasing his search area. If he couldn't find the anchor soon, he'd have to head for the surface and use his light to find the boat. The current could displace him as much as a half mile downstream. He hardly felt like swimming back on the surface or calling any attention to them by hollering for Ricky.

A thin scraping sound reached his ears from somewhere to his right. He pointed the light in that direction and moved forward cautiously. After a moment, the light found the source of the noise—the anchor from Burgess's boat had come loose and was scraping slowly along the gravel bottom. The conditions on the surface had evidently worsened, or at least grown windier. Peters cursed Burgess's irresponsibility again and imagined he was too busy topside trying to light a joint with his cold-numbed fingers to notice that the mooring had come loose.

Then something else caught his eye. At first Peters thought it was only a trick of the light, maybe a reflection of the moon passing through the water. But it grew more distinct as he slowly rose toward the surface. Thin, ethereal strands of some material that looked almost like spider webs or a vast sheet of transparent plastic. It *felt* like . . . nothing at all. He was rising right through this strange-looking underwater cloud, which didn't seem to consist of anything visible to the naked eye. It was some kind of microorganism—maybe a bloom of some kind of Protozoa. He knew that sulfur-producing bacteria sometimes colored the water white and had seen it many times in stagnant water in California. He made a note to consult the books in his home library for a description of such a phenomenon.

Peters reached the surface. His head came out of the water, and he could see that the waves had increased as the tide was beginning to come in. He spit out his regulator and let it gurgle in the water beside him. Filling his lungs with night air, he nearly retched from the unexpected foulness around him. The air smelled like rotting fish, thick and laden with ammonia, and utterly unlike what it had been when he started his dive. He coughed, spluttered, looked around, and tried to ascertain whether the wind had somehow changed direction. A full moon had risen over the trees lining the inlet, illuminating the water all around him. Twenty yards away was the familiar aluminum hull of Burgess's boat—the pseudo-philosophical moniker LIFE'S A GRIN painted on the stern in well-weathered and virtually illegible letters. The boat was rolling lazily back and forth in a backwater eddy without an obvious occupant or a concern in the world; Ricky tended his boat like he tended the rest of his slipshod life.

"Ricky?" Peters called out. "Hey, Dick?" Peters looked from the boat to the surrounding water, but Burgess was still not anywhere to be seen. The porch light of a cabin a quarter mile away was the only sign of habitation.

He paddled closer to the boat, looking around for any sign of his partner. Suddenly, from inside the hull came a series of loud thumps, followed by a loud *clank!*—unmistakably the sound of a scuba tank falling out of its rack. He could hear the rivets in the thin hull buckle and bark; it sounded as though something was thrashing around down inside the gunwales. A raccoon? A mink?

"Dick?" Peters repeated, growing angry.

As Peters reached the boat, Burgess's arm flew up over the gunwale, scratching frantically at empty air. In the light, Peters could see that Burgess's flesh had been . . . scalded? The skin was blood red, swollen, and bubbled away from the bones in the hand.

"Help me!" Burgess screamed, a hysterical, high-pitched yelp that rang out to the trees on the nearby shore. *"Jesuschrist help me! I'm burning up!"*

Peters swam over to the boat's small, makeshift dive platform and struggled frantically to haul himself aboard. The boat rolled freely back and forth, taunting him, repeatedly escaping purchase by his cold-numbed fingers.

"Help me! Helllp meee! Ohfuckingchrist—" Burgess cried, then screamed again.

Peters's drysuit caught on an exposed bolt and tore open from shoulder to elbow. Frustrated and growing frantic, he dropped his weight belt and quickly shrugged off the straps of his vest. Standing, he trained the light down into the hull.

"Dick? What's going on?" Peters called out.

Burgess, or what was left of him, was writhing around in the bottom of the boat. He was half out of his drysuit, and his exposed upper torso was riddled with fresh, leaking sores. As with his hand and arm, the skin on his chest and stomach appeared to have burst—appeared to have *liq-*

uefied—falling away in bruised chunks from its supporting skeleton. Below the waist, his legs remained limp, only twitching as his arms and head thrashed wildly.

"What happened?" Peters gawked, hauling himself over the transom and moving along the debris-strewn hull to help Burgess. *"What happened?"* The smell of gasoline was thick and cloying. In his thrashing, Burgess had kicked the fuel line free of the outboard motor and gasoline was draining into the bottom of the boat.

"The water," Burgess moaned. "There's something in the water. Dammit, it *burns!*" Burgess rolled over to look at Peters, and his eyes widened in terror. "Oh shit, it's got you, too!"

Peters only now became aware of a burning sensation on his cheeks and neck. He wiped his forearm across his chin and it came away bloody. He could only stare at it, transfixed, and wonder what his face must look like.

"Get us out of here. Get us to shore. Shit, *look at me! Looook at me!*" Burgess screamed.

"Hang in there, buddy, I ll get us in," Peters said hollowly. His movements were too slow, slipping out of his conscious control. He was reacting in third person.

The boat slammed into an outcrop. The rudder scraped bottom as the water temporarily retreated, then the next wave slammed into the side of the hull. Peters lurched to his feet, reconnected the fuel tank, and primed the motor. Leaning on the steering wheel to brace himself against the rocking of the waves, he turned the key in the ignition, then cursed as nothing happened. He tried again, producing only a clicking noise.

"Get it off me! *Get it off me!*" Burgess moaned from behind him.

"We'll get you to a hospital, buddy. You hang on," Peters said. Then suddenly, an angry red light glowed behind him. Incredulous, Peters whirled and saw Burgess holding a lit emergency flare in one hand. A *road* flare! What the hell was that doing on a boat?

"Ricky, *don't!* The gas—"

"Have to. Get if *off* me—"

With the next swell, Burgess's body rolled over and the flare spilled into the greasy pool in the bottom of the boat. Peters saw the slick erupt in flame, consuming Burgess immediately. In the split second he had to think, Peters turned away and threw himself over the side. As he hit the water, the flame reached the fuel tank of the boat, and the stern exploded with a thunderous *whump!*

Cold water poured in through the tear in Peters's suit, followed immediately by the same intense burning sensation he had felt on his cheeks. Images of Burgess's torn body fueled the terror rising in Peters's throat as he tried to swim away from the burning boat. Flotsam and assorted pieces of debris rained down on him as the boat settled in the water, then rolled over on its side. The boat crashed against the rocks to his right, groaning as the water twisted it on its keel. Peters's foot came down, momentarily, on solid ground before he was upended again.

He was floundering in a rip current, ignoring the futility of fighting against the flow of water as it dragged him back from shore. As his suit filled with water, it threatened to drag him to the bottom. He allowed himself to sink through the strongest portion of the current, then kicked out violently with his legs, struggling to move laterally along the shore and out of the rip. Another wave tumbled over him on the shallow bottom, peppering his blistered skin with sand and gravel as it rolled him over into the surf.

Peters tried to stand, tried to focus his eyes. The burning on his flesh was incapacitating, drawing the air out of his lungs. The next wave pushed him up onto the shore. His chest slammed heavily into a gravel bar, and he scrambled to find a handhold before the return water dragged him back into the swash. Lying face down, he coughed up the last of the water he had swallowed, feeling it burn as it returned past his throat and nasal passages. The next wave pushed him a few feet closer to dry land before abandoning him for the last time.

"Oh Christ. Jesus Christ," Peters moaned, the words gurgling in his bloodied throat. He rolled over on his back, gulping at the salvation offered by the cool air, then coughing it back out as his lungs convulsed. He could feel the water trapped inside his torn drysuit continue to irritate his skin where it pooled around his joints, crotch, and limbs. He lacked any strength to pull it away.

My arms. Why can't I move them? Why can't I move my body—?

With a forced effort, Peters got his arm to respond. The limb, hung with shredded neoprene and flesh, twitched and jerked spasmodically as he clutched it to his side and brought it up to his face. His fingers touched the point where his right eye should have been, coming away coated with jellied viscera. He could not yet know it, but he would soon lose sight in both eyes as the blood vessels there ruptured and the extent of the nerve damage revealed itself. Losing consciousness, struggling to draw air across the shredded lining of his lungs, Peters looked back at the tree line, trying to guess exactly where he was.

To his semi-conscious amazement, he saw a young Indian boy squatting on the rocks only a few feet away. The boy's skin glowed a fiery orange, reflecting the light of the burning boat.

Peters could only manage to blink at the boy.

The boy blinked back.

1

The horizon was a featureless gray line in every direction from the R/V *Exeter* as the ship cruised directly west, out of sight of any land. Except for drifting cloud formations, the view had not changed for ten days. Stretching nearly one-quarter of the way across the North Pacific, the 50th parallel of latitude was known as "Line P" on an alphabetically assigned sampling grid devised by researchers of JGOFS—the Joint Global Ocean Flux Study. Twice each year, survey ships returned to these same positions for up to five weeks at a time, sampling the ocean's temperature, salinity, microscopic fauna, and trace elements to evaluate their cycling and recycling in the sea. Through careful repetition, a model was being devised to determine what the ocean contained, how it continued to evolve, and what predictions could be made about its behavior. Those who believed, and appreciated, that the ship would soon turn back toward solid ground affectionately knew Station P24, the end of this line at 150 degrees West Longitude, as "Papa."

Standing just over six-foot-two, William Brock Garner had learned to duck his head slightly whenever passing through one of the *Exeter*'s hatchways. He was muscular in an understated way, with toned limbs and a naturally athletic stride that suggested more than his infrequent participation in beach volleyball, pick-up basketball, or a Sunday morning jog. Garner's eyes were a sharp, crystalline gray, capable of flicking from compassionate to predatory with a single blink. His features were handsome and defined, smooth except for two minor but noticeable imperfections: a slight curve to the slope of his nose and a small scar that cut across his eyebrow in the shape of a lazy-*S*. Both were souvenirs from an abbreviated but respectable career in the U.S. Navy that saw him retire early at the rank of Lieutenant Commander.

Another place, another time. Same ocean.

Garner glanced at the depth meter as he moved from the main lab to the afterdeck: 3,520 METERS/11,550 FEET, roughly the average depth of the oceans worldwide. Having long ago passed over the continental shelf that bordered the North American continent like a submerged geological hoopskirt, the *Exeter* was now cruising at 13 knots two miles above the ocean floor, the closest point of solid earth. Anything tossed overboard would take more than ninety minutes to free-fall to the bottom.

A massive A-frame boom painted industrial yellow centered the stern of the *Exeter,* the ship's frothy wake stretched out behind it. Nearly as massive and colorful in his orange exposure suit was Sergei Zubov, the *Exeter*'s chief science assistant. At the moment, Zubov's gaze shifted repeatedly between the winch and a gleaming, five-foot-diameter sphere that gently bobbed against its restraining cables fifteen feet above the deck. The result of Garner's painstaking design, the sphere was an automated plankton sampler. In the previous hundred years of formalized ocean study, there had probably been as many designs for "the definitive plankton sampler," and several had survived the test of time. Many found Garner's elegant but temperamental design unpalatable, if not utterly ridiculous; the rest regarded it as revolutionary. Zubov had subscribed to the latter group the first time Garner brought the gleaming beast aboard the *Exeter*. While that first impression had ebbed after countless adjustments, blown circuits, and frustrated profanity, Zubov now watched over Garner's invention like the tireless parent of a brilliant but habitually sick child.

The lower hemisphere of the device was cast from weighted titanium, nearly smooth despite its full array of infrared sensors and microfocus cameras designed to count and identify microorganisms in their natural habitat. The equator of the instrument contained openings to a cadre of specimen chambers that automatically captured parcels of water for later analysis. (That the arrangement of the chamber ports resembled a grinning mouth and eyes when viewed from the front wasn't just a functional decision by the device's inventor.) Finally, the top of the sphere renounced all symmetry, blossoming into an ungainly bouquet of instruments for recording temperature, pressure, light, and conductivity as the device was towed through the euphotic zone, the light-penetrated surface waters of the ocean.

Some said the instrument looked like *Sputnik* on a bad hair day, but Garner selected a more obvious nickname for his brainchild: the Medusa sphere. In the search for vindication, the Medusa supported its mythological moniker. The first several attempts to sample with the device had produced no useful results. After each failed attempt, Garner would bring the instrument back into its deck housing and meticulously check each of its connections to the computerized controls in the lab. Zubov then had to ensure that the instrument was precisely redeployed so it would fly properly as it was towed through the water.

When Medusa did work—had a good hair day—the sphere had to be paced through its sampling regimen under precise parameters over several miles, despite adverse sea conditions attempting to thwart this arrangement and its house-of-cards fragility. If all went right, Medusa could provide more data in a single tow than any two dozen alternatives. The samples were cleaner and more precise and could be processed more efficiently than with any other sampler ever built. But if one thing went wrong, the trial was lost and the entire sampling schedule could be delayed or canceled completely.

The learning curve of such attempts was especially annoying to the *Exeter*'s crew, who were at sea for two hundred days a year and had hosted an unending series of neurotic, obsessive, and (usually) far-from-seaworthy scientists and their brittle equipment, whose racks of Pyrex glassware and schizophrenic electronics did little to earn the respect of those accustomed to gear grease and pig iron. If for no other reason, Garner and Zubov should have been natural adversaries, but Garner proved to be a very crewman-like scientist and Zubov was a very scientific crewman.

Following countless nights shared on a storm-swept deck, inventing new expletives about Medusa or complaining to the bottom of a bottle of liquor smuggled on board, the men had established an effective system of communication. More than that, Garner trusted implicitly Zubov's accuracy in deploying Medusa, so much so that Garner could concentrate on the processing of samples rather than their collection. With the majority of his NSF—National Science Foundation—and NOAA—National Oceanic and Atmospheric Administration—research funds invested in a sphere of titanium and PVC flying through space some two hundred feet below them, peace of mind only vaguely covered the ease that Garner felt. For his part, Zubov knew that getting the samples was virtually all that could justify the expenditure of effort. Besides, as he often immodestly reminded Garner, ensuring that the right numbers got collected was his job.

"Fucking *whore*," Zubov cursed as Garner approached. "The damn sensor array keeps getting caught up." Zubov was two inches taller than Garner and outweighed him by a hundred pounds. With his coal black eyes and coils of shiny black hair flowing down into a thick, matted beard, Zubov reminded Garner of a younger, larger, but more tapered version of Luciano Pavarotti. Zubov had been born in the Ukraine, leaving the rest of his natural-born family there and defecting to America only months before his hometown near Chernobyl rose to global notoriety. Now a permanent U.S. citizen, Zubov retained little evidence of his homeland beyond name, appetite, and a stalwart dedication to duty. Occasionally, only when he was drunk and rarely for more than a few syllables, his accent would slip its Americanized clarity and provide an echo of an almost-forgotten former life. The subtle departure in character often surprised those who didn't know Zubov well; for friends like Garner, former lives were simply another reason to go to sea in the first place.

Sweat trickled down Zubov's forehead as he wrestled with Medusa, leaning his enormous bulk against a guide wire and pulling at the device once more.

"She'll be fine once she's in the water," Garner assured him.

"She'll be fine when she gives me a friggin' heart attack," Zubov grunted.

"No, that'll come from the extra bacon you had at breakfast."

"Thanks, Mom," Zubov said. "At least, I've always considered you a *mother,* Brock." With a final tug, Medusa lolled back to her correct position.

"Good. We've got two minutes to get her—"

"She's ready now," Zubov assured him, then spun his finger in the air, signaling the boom operator. With that, the A-frame tilted toward the transom on its hinged footing, gradually moving the instrument out over the stern. "Whoa. *Whoa!*" Zubov barked into the radio. "Take it back a bit. No, the *other* back, you sonofabitch. A bit. *Whoa!* Sixteen degrees. Then let it out to two-five-oh."

"At three knots, for six minutes," Garner reminded him. "Not two, not four. For six minutes."

"Screw you," Zubov grumbled.

"Were you abused as a child?"

"I'm being abused as an adult. Go back to your room."

Garner's "room" was his assigned bench space in the ship's main lab. He waited for Zubov to confirm Medusa's correct position below them, then switched on her electronic sensor array. Numbers began scrolling through his software program, and Garner liked what he saw. He tripped the first two sampling bottles, then radioed Zubov to take Medusa to the next depth. "Looking good, Serg. So far this one's a keeper."

Within minutes, a computer program Garner had written for Medusa began determining the health of the ocean with clinical accuracy Instantaneously, calculations of nitrate and phosphate concentrations were compared to light levels, water temperature, salinity, and trace-metals content. These results were compared to the resident plant—phytoplankton—and animal—zooplankton—constituents suspended throughout the water column, their density, and species composition.

Once Medusa brought her bottle samples back up to the *Exeter,* Garner could compare the actual community structure of the sea beneath them with the calculated or estimated predictions. Comparing these results across depth strata, Garner could produce a real-time snapshot of the ocean's fundamental, ubiquitous, and complex cycling of energy.

Medusa would determine how rapidly and how efficiently oxygen, nitrogen, and carbon dioxide were being exchanged between the ocean of water beneath them and the ocean of air above. By tracking the vertical migration of the plankton through hundreds—even thousands—of meters, Medusa could estimate how rapidly carbon, trace metals, and any number of pollutants were being drawn out of the surface waters, and whether enough life-sustaining nutrients were being resupplied from the colder depths below. If the ocean could be considered the lungs of the planet, the fully functioning Medusa could measure this exchange, or flux. Medusa could determine Mother Earth's rate of breathing.

In the abstract, the concept seemed simple enough to grasp, however unlikely a pursuit for a quick-witted kid raised in the heart of the Iowa grainbelt. On his infrequent visits to his extended family, Garner would try to explain what, exactly, an oceanographer did and what his own "ocean research" was all about. Searching for a useful analogy, Garner would draw comparisons between counting plankton and harvesting wheat. From a known amount of nutrients, oxygen, and sunlight came a predictable crop, whether it be cereal grains on land or microscopic life in the sea. These crops recycled nutrients with the atmosphere and with the earth, absorbed pollutants, and supported higher life-forms with harvesting and consumption. The crop remaining to be gleaned indicated the potential to support life once again.

But every now and then, unfavorable conditions, a blight, or a pest would find the crop and it would crash or die out. Sometimes the disturbance would replace old life-forms with new ones. Replace the grass in a field with weeds and you still had energy being recycled—growth, death, and decay, the conversion of energy. What needed further evaluation was whether the decrepit "crop" could support life, and what the quality of that life might be. It was these occasions that most attracted Garner's attention. For all the simplicity of a bacterium or a virus or a toxic phytoplankter, it was such microscopic menaces that determined the health, resiliency, and viability of the most fundamental units of the ecosystem and thus determined the fate of all organisms living within it—first within the ocean, but ultimately all over the globe.

In short, work as important as they were doing in JGOFS needed to be explained to the widest possible audience. This had inspired within Garner the philosophy that, no matter what the price tag, no matter how shiny the toys or how pretentious the academic jargon, any research that could not be encapsulated and explained to a reasonably bright eight-year-old probably wasn't worth doing. In response, Medusa often mocked even this straightforward credo.

As Garner now watched, the readout from his sampler began to go haywire. The data from the inorganic samplers—trace elements, oxygen, pH, temperature, salinity—continued as before, but suddenly the organic numbers fell to zero on all channels.

Zero? thought Garner. Though midocean plankton assemblages were usually far less dense than coastal populations, the only thing that would cause the readout to fall to zero so suddenly was a loss of electrical power. But a loss of power would have killed the inorganic readings, too.

"Check the wiring at your end," Garner radioed to Zubov. It was unlikely that one of Medusa's sensor leads had come loose. But if one of them had, it would mean hauling the sampler back to the surface, turning the *Exeter* around, and starting the tow all over again. Garner cursed under his breath and worked the muscles of his jaw in quiet frustration. First, an unexpected storm had halted all sampling on the *Exeter* for eighteen hours. Now, a serious breakdown or failure in Medusa's operation would mean more delays. If the delays were too time-consuming, Garner might lose the rest of his allotted time to use the A-frame and the *Exeter*'s deck crew. A mysteriously sick child was a taxing and expensive ordeal. Short-circuiting on one JGOFS cruise meant a three- to six-month delay until the next one, which could add as much as another year to his doctoral program. An entire season's worth of data, or two, could be lost by a single irreparable mechanical or electronic failure.

Zubov called back diagnostic readings from Medusa's deck controller. The outputs seemed normal, but that would mean the sampler had passed through a region of absolutely no life in the middle of the ocean.

Then, before Garner could even contemplate the impossibility a lifeless hole in the ocean, the organic channels came back up.

"What did you just do?" Garner asked Zubov.

"Nothing," Zubov replied. The only thing that had changed was that the *Exeter* had progressed five cables—roughly six-tenths of a mile—farther west. Medusa was operating normally once again; life had suddenly "returned" to the sea.

Ten minutes later, the organic channels dropped off again, then returned a few minutes later as they had done before. Garner scratched at his dark hair and gnawed at his lip as he looked at the readout. Intermittently, the sphere was working fine—perfectly, in fact—then suddenly and inexplicably, the organic channels would be lost. He called Zubov into the lab and both men plotted the dropouts against the *Exeter*'s cruise track.

According to what they had both come to know from past experience, Medusa was working better than on any previous cruise. The latest changes in Garner's design were holding up, and the inorganic data was, at first inspection, accurate. The biological information between the inexplicable black holes in the tow—phytoplankton and zooplankton density, species composition, and dissolved organic matter—was also within the expected range.

"But look here," Garner said, comparing the real-time data plot to the ship's course. "Every time we pass this one corridor"—using a set of dividers, Garner defined the area to be about a half mile wide but an indeterminate length—"it's like there isn't a single thing alive down there."

"So what is it, a dead zone?" Zubov speculated. They were both familiar with the increasingly common phenomenon of "dead zones," temporary areas of depleted oxygen that could grow to encompass hundreds, even thousands of square miles. Dead zones were thought to be caused by pollutants, namely excessive nutrients, and would literally suffocate anything too immobile to move out of them. But they were temporary phenomena and usually localized on the seafloor. The open ocean was far too dynamic to support such conditions for any length of time.

"Like that," Garner said. "Only the oxygen sensors check fine, and this thing isn't fluid." He thought for a moment, searching for the right descriptive term. "It's like there's a hole in the ocean. A biological sink, fixed in time and space. An abiotic stasis."

Zubov looked back at him and chuckled. "An *abiotic stasis?*"

"I just made that up," Garner admitted. "But it fits."

"Brock, you start talking like that and NSF really will pull your funding. Then you can go study your abiotic stasis with an afinancial stasis."

They had no choice but to cancel the tow, haul Medusa back to the surface, and compare the electronically transmitted data with the samples collected at depth by Medusa's water bottles. Quickly siphoning some water from the rack of bottles, Garner inspected the samples by eye, then under a high-powered microscope, and finally in a high-resolution particle-counter in the *Exeter*'s auxiliary lab. Within an hour, he had confirmed that nothing was wrong with Medusa. The samples taken from inside the "abiotic stasis" were absolutely devoid of either microscopic or macroscopic life.

Garner and Zubov deployed Medusa again, over the same patch of ocean, and received the same result.

"Serg, *look* at this," Garner pressed.

Zubov knew Garner, knew that he had never been prone to drama or exaggeration. *A hole in the ocean,* he had said, and that was exactly what it looked like. "These plankton numbers are the lowest I've seen anywhere, and we're sticking to the same grid as on every other JGOFS cruise," Zubov said.

"The sampling grid doesn't affect the fluid within it," Garner said irritably. "In a few hours the system should equilibrate on its own. An abiotic stasis isn't possible, but that's exactly what we've got."

"You're sure?" Zubov asked.

"You know I am," Garner said.

"I know you are, too," Zubov agreed. "But I also know you can't be." Claiming there was a stabilized lifeless region in the middle of the ocean was like claiming that there was a permanent sand dune in the middle of the Sahara Desert.

"So either there's a big biological hole out here or your fussy little toy is on the fritz again," Zubov said. "Which do you think the guys holding on to your funding are gonna believe?"

2

The screaming began just after midnight.

At first, David Fulton thought he was dreaming and, from the depths of his sleep, simply misinterpreting the sound of the breeze in the forest canopy high above them. Then he felt his wife's body become rigid in her sleeping bag, and he knew she had heard something, too. As the next shrill cry split the darkness, Karen sat upright, her head pressing against the roof of the tent, its nylon hung low with accumulated condensation.

"It's Caitlin," she hissed, vocalizing Fulton's own realization as she swatted him awake. In a sequence of rapid movements, she rolled forward, grabbed their lantern flashlight, and pulled on her hiking boots as she ducked through the door flap. Fulton kicked out of his own sleeping bag and scrambled after his wife.

Fulton exited the tent to see Karen's bare legs kneeling outside the girls' tent, crazy silhouettes of his family cast by the beam of the flashlight flicking quickly around inside.

"What is it? What is it, honey?" he could hear Karen asking Caitlin, trying to convey comfort but not quite concealing the rising fear in her voice. "Oh my goodness, *look* at you. What's the matter, precious?"

Instinctively, Fulton glanced around their campsite, looking for signs of an intruder or a wild animal. All around them, bordering the clearing, towering conifers shifted restlessly in the wind coming off the beach. The embers from their campfire still glowed a dull orange, abandoned less than an hour ago when he and Karen had finished the last of a bottle of burgundy and gone to bed. Damp clothes swung lazily from a line strung between two trees. A neat row of shucked clamshells, souvenirs from the beach and precisely arranged by six-year-old Caitlin—David Fulton's only child—and nine-year-old Lindsay—Karen's daughter from a previous marriage—sat along a large, smooth-topped stump they had used as their dinner table. The sound of retching returned his attention to the girls' tent, and the next thought he had was *food poisoning*.

Karen called out to him for a towel, which he located and handed to her as he knelt down and leaned inside the tent. The smell of vomit overwhelmed him. He saw Lindsay cowering against the far end of the tent, covering her mouth and nose with her hands. He saw little Caitlin, curled up in a fetal position in her sleeping bag, clutching her stomach and wailing between convulsions. Karen was attempting to wipe Caitlin's face with the towel, but Caitlin vomited relentlessly onto the weatherproof floor of the tent. Dark green and grainy, the fluid oozed thickly downslope into the corner. Fulton smelled feces and realized that the violent reaction was not limited to one end of his little girl.

Something was turning his daughter inside out.

Caitlin's skin was cold and slick with perspiration. Her eyes were flat and dull, staring ahead at the light from the flashlight. She was shivering, quaking from head to toe as Karen plied her for any kind of information.

"My legs hurt," she whimpered. A gurgling sound grotesquely punctuated the mucus drying around her tiny mouth. Karen quickly wiped it away.

"They hurt? What do you mean 'hurt'?" Karen pressed. "Like a cut? A burn?"

"Pins and needles . . ." Caitlin whined, then trailed off, shaking and moaning.

"What is it, Mommy?" Lindsay asked, wide-eyed. "What's wrong with her?"

Fulton told Lindsay to find some warm clothes and get dressed, told Karen to get Caitlin up and wrapped in something dry, then scrambled back to their own tent for his pants, car keys, and the few valuable items they hadn't locked in their Pathfinder. Karen carried Caitlin to the four-by-four, and Fulton helped them into the backseat, where his wife could better cradle the little girl. Climbing behind the wheel, Fulton picked up the cellular phone from its cradle on the center console, punched in the number for emergency assistance, then waited, breathing heavily while the device confirmed that they were out of range. Hell, they were sixty miles from the nearest good-sized town. He strapped Lindsay into the passenger seat, turned the key in the ignition, slammed the vehicle into reverse, and backed to the access road, only vaguely aware of where he was going or how they were going to get there.

For several miles, the road to the remote campground was little more than a muddy, rutted break in the dense forest. Gravel chattered against the undercarriage of the vehicle like antiaircraft fire, and mammoth potholes swallowed the thick tires, several times threatening to wrench the steering wheel out of Fulton's hands. Battalions of unkempt, over-hanging boughs rose up in the bouncing glare of the headlights, slapped against the side mirrors of the vehicle, and scratched past the windows and roof like arboreal goblins. Twice the Pathfinder slid off the track and collapsed the soft shoulder of the road, fishtailing dangerously close to the tree trunks that lined their path.

Caitlin had stopped coughing and had grown quiet. Fulton repeatedly glanced over his shoulder to glimpse her ghostly reflection in the light from the dashboard. Karen gently rocked the little girl, whispering words of comfort to her, then repeated the words, louder, to Lindsay in the front seat.

Halfway back to the town of Port Alberni, their path mercifully widened into the Sarita Main access road, owned and "maintained" by the largest logging company in British Columbia. From the drive in, Fulton knew the road was well traveled by all kinds of trucks, graders, and medieval-looking logging equipment. The company employees traveled at excessive speeds, headlights on against the silty dust that rose up and clogged the air for several minutes after they passed. Worse, the largest of these trucks were often encountered in the wrong oncoming lane as they navigated the twists and turns and sought the most level track on a road that resurfaced itself daily.

Thirty minutes later they hit pavement for the first time in a week, and Fulton pressed more speed into the vehicle. It took nearly another forty minutes for Fulton to reach Port Alberni, then, thankfully, the route to the hospital was clearly marked. Fulton sped past the red sign indicating the emergency room and parked in the nearly deserted lot. He retrieved Caitlin from Karen's protective grasp and rushed his daughter inside. The six-year-old had always been small for her age, and bundled up and lying so quietly in his arms, she seemed almost ethereal, lighter than air. He couldn't take his eyes off her as the automatic doors slid back to admit them into the harsh, sterile glare of the reception area.

The on-duty nurse listened to his rapid-fire description of the symptoms as she paged an orderly to retrieve Caitlin and printed her name on the top of a patient chart. Caitlin was loaded onto a gurney and quickly wheeled down the corridor. Karen's eyes grew wide as she tried to follow but was gently restrained by a second orderly.

"Goddamn it, I'm not letting her out of my sight!" Karen shrieked at the orderly, then the nurse. "I'm not letting her go until we know what's *wrong* with her!"

Fulton wrapped his arms around his wife and held her tight as she began to sob. Lindsay stood between them, wrapping her arms around her mother's waist. The nurse prompted him for Caitlin's date of birth, age, allergies, insurance, and other particulars. From down the hall, they could hear the sounds of Caitlin moaning, and then a doctor talking quietly to her, before the door to the examining room was closed.

"Home address?" the nurse asked.

"When can we see her?" Karen demanded. "When can we *be* with her?" His wife's concern had grown ferocious.

"Seattle," Fulton said to the nurse.

"Seattle, Washington?"

"No—Seattle, *Egypt,*" Fulton snapped.

"So you're American," the nurse said, as if that explained his sarcastic hostility. Fulton watched as the nurse wrote SEATTLE, WASHINGTON on the form, slowly and deliberately, further emphasizing that they weren't from around here. *What's the matter? Just glimpse your first black bear? Caught with your pants down after setting up camp above a rising tide? Oh no, just panicked to high hell and ready to sue the entire nation of Canada over a bad case of the trots in a six-year-old.*

"Could you please hurry?" he said, the frustration rising in his voice. The nurse glanced up at him. "Please. Just hurry," he repeated.

Eventually, the Fultons moved to the waiting room, taking a seat on orange plastic chairs that afforded them a view of the reception desk and the corridors beyond. Twice more a second nurse came out to ask them questions. Did they know where Caitlin got the abrasions and cuts on her feet? From running barefoot on the rough sand beaches, of course. What did they have for dinner? For lunch? Did Caitlin have any food allergies? Drug allergies? Neurological disorders? *Neurological disorders!* Neither Fulton nor his wife could imagine how that possibility had come to be considered.

A dozen times in the next hour, Karen returned to the reception desk, asking what the delay was. Asking to see her daughter. Each time she returned with more festering anger; then Fulton would try it himself, with no better luck. Lindsay had begun to occupy herself at a small play area intended for children half her age. A VCR wired to a TV set played cartoons at a low volume. As Fulton watched, a trio of squirrels appeared on screen and began taunting a little girl with a song he recalled from a childhood nursery rhyme:

If you go out in the woods today / You better not go alone

The irony of the lyrics stung, but David Fulton wasn't thinking about going out in the woods, today or ever again, until someone told them what was going on with Caitlin. He wasn't thinking about the damage to the Pathfinder, or how their "adventure vacation" had suddenly run amok. He was no longer a tourist in a foreign country trying too hard to make this the Family Vacation of a Lifetime and maybe throw his marriage a life preserver in the process. He wasn't the managing partner of Fulton Architects, an appreciating gem in the increasingly crowded crown of the Emerald City. Not the eleven-hours-a-day, eleven-months-a-year workaholic or infrequent churchgoer. He was, simply, a father—first, last, and only—nearly blind with worry that his child was terribly sick.

The swinging doors opened and a doctor finally approached them, an athletic-looking woman with striking blue eyes and long curly hair drawn back in a loose braid. She introduced herself as Dr. Ellie Bridges in a measured tone of voice that was neither clinical nor dispassionate; it was simply resolute. Fulton would later evaluate her expression as professional and well rehearsed, if only to reduce the need for painful words. Through a growing fog, Karen's hand found David's forearm and squeezed tightly as her own realization dawned, detonating the panic.

Their daughter was dead. Caitlin was dead, and in Fulton's throat, the words to demand an explanation died with her. The numbness began at the base of his skull. Darkness crushed in on him from every angle as he heard his wife shriek and clutch desperately at her surviving child.

The walls of the architect's world began to collapse.

3

R *ed sky at night, sailors' delight. Red sky at morning, sailors take warning.* The precise origin of that nautical wisdom was lost to Mark Junckers, but it never failed to come to mind whenever he saw traces of scarlet on the horizon. He knew that weather patterns tended to move from west to east in the Northern Hemisphere, so a red sky in the morning meant that overcast conditions were pushing in from the west; in the evening, the setting sun reflecting on cirrus clouds in the east meant that the storm had passed and clearer weather was on its way. This morning, it was the eastern sky that drew his attention as he ambled down to the public dock and freed the mooring lines of the *Pinniped*.

Warning or not, Junckers paused to take in the spectacle with appreciation, tilting a tin cup of instant coffee to his lips. After pressing a Creedence Clearwater Revival CD into the boat's stereo system and selecting the track number for "Fortunate Son," he started the auxiliary motor of the thirty-five-foot sailboat and turned away from the dock, headed toward the rising sun.

This was the third summer for Mark Junckers—the Junkman, as

most of his friends called him—as a visiting researcher at the Bamfield Marine Station, making the pilgrimage from Stanford to study the resident sea-lion populations of Barkley Sound. Each year he arrived on Memorial Day weekend to begin teaching a three-week undergraduate course in marine mammals to thirty marine-biology students. For the rest of the summer he could concentrate on his research, filming, measuring, weighing, and radio-tracking families of *Zalophus californianus,* the California sea lion. Sixteen hours a day clambering over boulders and the emerged gravel bars that accessed the rookeries had left his body hard and tanned; three months of such self-imposed isolation left his hair long and sun-bleached, his beard more than a little unkempt, and his eyes filled with a look of "crazy, faraway happiness," as at least one of his past girlfriends had called it.

Junckers pushed his sunglasses up on his hawkish nose and squinted. His eyes—narrow and deep-set, innately nervous, suspicious eyes as his teachers had teased since grade school—read the waves coming in from the Pacific, and he adjusted the mainsail. He stripped the T-shirt from his long, gangly torso and slathered himself with sunscreen. Part of the day's intent would be to redefine the odd-looking tan lines that currently ran around the base of his neck and the top of his shoulders. The marks had been produced by the limits of his life jacket during three days of the previous week as he paddled around the northern edge of Barkley Sound in a borrowed sea kayak. While Junckers rarely considered his research to be work, neither was it idle recreation. He knew the long days of summer were beginning to dwindle and had forced himself to take a much-needed vacation-within-a-vacation. Of course, he continued to watch sea lions and otters whenever they crossed his path—a biologist in Barkley Sound was always tempted back to work, at least with one eye—but for the most part he enjoyed his time alone with the waves, a couple of Robert Heinlein novels, a hibachi, and some beer.

Three days ago, a wet, windy storm had blown through the sound from the west, driving him to the shelter of Ucluelet. Junckers found a shower behind the town Laundromat, washed his tangled, wavy blond hair, and found an accommodating barstool at the dockside pub. His career, his life, had been on no defined schedule since leaving the Navy, with the possible exception of making tenure someday. Even that was no longer the ultimate livery of intellectual freedom it had been for earlier generations, so for now the wind, the waves, and his ever-intriguing *Zalophus* would suffice nicely.

Sailors' warning or not, the sun that day was well above the horizon and growing hot by the time Junckers had brought his sailboat the twenty miles across the sound. He steered the *Pinniped* through Coaster Channel in the Broken Group Islands, a formation that roughly centered the 170-square-mile inlet, then angled the sails for Bamfield. Approaching Satellite Passage, the marine station was now directly ahead, facing back at him with its panoramic western view, sunlight scattered on the waves before it like diamonds on a sea-blue carpet. Off the *Pinniped*'s starboard bow, along the southeast shore of the sound, sat the Deer Group Islands, where his stepfather still maintained a cabin atop a lone windswept promontory. Charles Harmon, Yale alumnus, now professor emeritus of the University of Washington. Internationally renowned expert on marine pathogens and infectious fish diseases; domestically renowned as a cold and indifferent bastard, at least from Junckers's own experience.

What his mother had ever seen in such an overbearing yet reclusive personality escaped him. Maybe it was the security that a tenured professorship offered—to Harmon's generation, thirty years ago—or maybe it was just the exquisite scenery and solitude of his "summer home" on Helby Island, three thousand plus miles from New Haven. Junckers began exploring the tide pools along Harmon's beach when he was five years old, dragged along by his older stepsister, Carol, Harmon's daughter from his first marriage. At the time, Professor Harmon was far too busy traveling to conferences in Athens or Brest or La Jolla to give lectures to his children about what they discovered in their own backyard. But ultimately, something besides fish diseases must have been infectious about their father's vocation. Both Junckers and his stepsister had taken up careers in marine biology. Carol's bioacoustics work with humpback whales was still cited as groundbreaking. Junckers had gained some recognition for his own work as well, but if the old man was ever impressed, he hadn't ever shown it. If Junckers had ever felt driven to surpass the old man in his own research career, he had long ago forgotten this desire.

Junckers turned his binoculars to a small rock reef about half a mile off his starboard rail—Wizard Islet. The breakwater was little more than an accumulation of gravel, scrub, and storm debris, yet on any given day there could be up to fifty sea lions clustered there, entire extended families basking on the wave-washed beach. Oddly, none could be seen today.

Junckers brought the *Pinniped* around, circling the islet to confirm what he had seen. There were no sea lions on the gravel bar and none in the water. While the heat might keep them off the rocks, they could usually be seen in the water, their sleek, dog-like heads bobbing in the swells as they repeatedly dipped and dived, perhaps playing polo with a strand of bull kelp.

Junckers turned the boat and headed south, the *Pinniped* actually passing below the old man's cabin. He lifted his binoculars again and trained them on the beach before scanning the shore up to the main house. If the old man was home, he was either sleeping or reading indoors to avoid the heat. In recent years, it exhausted Harmon just climbing up to his home from the dock, though the man was far too proud to admit he should seek a more convenient retirement home.

Arriving at Diana Island a few minutes later, Junckers saw several maritime birds—oystercatchers and red knot—foraging high on the rocky shore, but again, no sign of otters or sea lions.

His puzzlement now bordering on concern, Junckers dropped his sails and drifted alongside a pair of local charter fishermen, their charges dangling lines out over the breakwater in search of halibut or cod as "the locals" talked. The area fishermen generally regarded the station's researchers with a mixture of incomprehension, ridicule, and disdain, but these fellows knew Junckers and liked him well enough to listen to his oddball questions. Junckers asked if any of them had seen any sea lions in the area, either that day or the day before. They thought for a moment, shook their heads, and went back to their cooler of Hamm's beer.

Junckers cruised another mile south using his outboard motor before dropping anchor and securing the *Pinniped* fifty yards from shore. He stripped to a pair of faded gym shorts, pulled on a wetsuit, and dived gracefully over the side. The shallows were unseasonably warm this year, not only because of the summer sun but also as a result of the past year's El Niño event. Noted by researchers for at least the past century, the periodic disruption of the ocean's surface waters occurred irregularly every three to seven years. A single El Niño event lasted only eighteen months, but the global pre- and postcursor events—a back-and-forth sloshing of warm surface waters across the Pacific Ocean in the absence of the typical trade winds—could extend this interval to as long as three years. The passing storm might even have increased this effect, driving the warmer surface water over the cooler layers below, downwelling the latter to the bottom.

Junckers swam to shore at a leisurely pace, pulling himself onto a rugged outcrop shaded by a stand of century-old fir trees. He smoothed his long hair back from his face and drank in the taste and smell of the fresh sea air of the open coast. He could just discern Cape Beale two miles farther south, a forbidding extension of land pointing westward across the open Pacific to Japan. The *Pinniped* bobbed dutifully offshore, awaiting his return. She could wait a little longer.

With the agility of a mountaineer, Junckers began climbing over the boulders packed into the intertidal zone, his bare feet gripping the broken rocks where he stepped. Fifty yards along the shore, he passed by the entrance to a sea cave formed through centuries of relentless wave erosion. He and Carol were still in their pre-teens when they had first discovered this cave with its sheltered rock benches and a natural chimney system that ran up through the cliff face. As adolescents, they had turned the spot into a kind of clubhouse and had come out to this spot countless times over the years for overnight camp-outs, drinking and drugging with their friends, or simply to defuse the daily stresses of life, school, or the old man—which were inevitably and inextricably related.

Junckers stepped out to where the bedrock cut deeply into the island, forming a narrow but very deep surge channel. During rough weather, waves could be funneled into this region and amplified with amazing force, exploding on the shore at the other end and even pulling down trees with their greedy fingers. Today, however, the weather was calm and the water sloshing below him was an inviting aquamarine color.

A mischievous grin spread across his face, and he leaped out into the air with a defiant whoop before plunging twenty feet into the surf below.

Momentarily disoriented, he let the next wave carry him the length of the channel, a surfer without a board. When he felt the water beginning to retreat, he flung his arm out, searching for a handhold. His fingers clutched and held something that felt like a softened log. As he blinked the salt water from his eyes, his hand came back bloody.

Struggling against the current, he stood in the shallow water and saw the bloated carcass of a sea lion, a large male with most of its side eaten away. Behind it was another. And another. Climbing out of the water, fear rising in concert with his disbelief, Junckers counted twenty-two bodies, including three sea otters, *Enhydra lutris.* Every one of them was dead, their wounds no longer bleeding. He wondered if they had gotten tangled in a drift net or some other abandoned fishing gear. But there was no sign of the net, and the wounds were too indistinct to be lacerations. They looked like ulcerated bruises, emerging through the wall of the belly and throat of the sea lion and inflaming the animal's face.

The sight of so many ravaged animals compacted into the end of the surge channel was numbing, mortifying. Still, his objective mind persisted, searching for a rational explanation. He recalled the pods of beached whales he had occasionally witnessed. Some researchers believed mass beachings were caused by parasites or chemical toxins that disrupted the whales' ability to navigate properly. Junckers knew of one case where more than a hundred dolphins had been killed by toxic phytoplankton in Mexico's Sea of Cortez. In Florida, manatees had also been killed by toxic plankton blooms, popularly (if sometimes incorrectly) known as red tides. If sea lions were subject to the same kind of thing, Junckers had never heard of it. None of those carcasses had shown these peculiar, crescent-shaped sores—too small to be from cannibalism or shark bites, too symmetrical to be natural lacerations, and too haphazard for even the most wasteful of poaching techniques.

Moving quickly, he struggled to haul as many of the animals as he could above the high-tide line. He returned to the *Pinniped,* loaded his dinghy with field-sampling equipment, and rowed back to the surge channel. He worked for the next six hours, drawing blood and tissue samples, recording each animal's size and gender, and describing the extent of the injuries into a microcassette recorder. He gagged several times on the smell coming from the bodies, even though most had only just begun to decompose. Taking a deep breath, he cleared his throat and continued recording his findings.

The sun had set by the time Junckers finally docked the *Pinniped* at the marine station. His eyes burned, he guessed, from the prolonged exposure to the sun and saltwater, and a dull ache throbbed in his temples. He stripped off his wetsuit, rinsed it in fresh water, and hung it on the railing outside the dive shed before walking up the ramp to the shore, clad only in his shorts and shivering slightly. He put the small box of samples in his lab cubicle, grabbed a clean shirt and some sneakers, and hiked up to the small, pressboard cabin he shared with two other postdoctoral students.

The small black-and-white television was on as he came in the front door, flickering over one of the one and a half stations Bamfield received with an antenna, but both his roommates had evidently gone down to the town's only pub. Junckers considered joining them but instead showered and went downstairs to the kitchen. Despite his fatigue, he felt restless and irritable, which he attributed to the gnawing in his stomach. His nose began to run and his sinuses throbbed.

There was a message from Carol, written in his roommate's familiar, scratchy handwriting. Big sister was just checking in, wanting to know if he was "working hard" or "hardly working" under their father's watchful eye. Junckers thought again about calling the old man, but decided it could wait until morning. Harmon would expect him to have a series of necropsies on the sea lions at least *theoretically* diagrammed before bothering him with the issue. Then of course there would be the paperwork involved in tagging and disposing of a protected species.

Junckers fixed himself a heaping plate of scrambled eggs and toast, leaving a return message on Carol's machine as he chewed and swallowed the food down. He relayed a brief description of what he had found that afternoon and asked if she had ever seen or heard of similar injuries on beached whales.

He then called Brock Garner, a buddy from his Navy days. Conveniently, and in part because of that association, Carol had become Garner's wife, then within a few years, Garner had become her ex-husband. More easily impressed by the old man's prowess, Garner had become a keen student of toxic plankton blooms in the meticulous world of Charles Harmon. Though still working on his doctorate in oceanography, Garner was probably sharper on the subject than the old man and would certainly relish scooping his mentor if there really was some kind of nasty bug out there.

Although he had used it a hundred times, the phone number for Garner's live-aboard boat in Friday Harbor, Washington, now somehow slipped Junckers's mind. He looked it up in his address book, then twice dialed it incorrectly. He tried again, pressing the numbers on the phone slowly and deliberately.

Garner's machine answered after the third ring. Junckers relayed what he had seen that afternoon, his account growing somewhat convoluted and halting. He signed off by inviting Garner up to Bamfield for a working vacation, to be marked by a bottle or two of Irish whiskey and a few pounds of steamed prawns with the Junkman.

Hanging up the phone, Junckers was left unfulfilled by breaking his news to a pair of answering machines. His throat was dry and tight as he swallowed. He still had time to return to the lab and properly preserve the samples he had collected and could dash off more detailed e-mails to Carol and Garner later. First he needed to share his discovery with a live human being in verbal shorthand. He dumped his dishes into the sink and went to collect his wallet from his bedroom, energized by the prospect of some thirst-quenching draft and a captive-by-default audience.

As he reached the top of the stairs, the pounding in his temples began to flare. Junckers scrunched the muscles of his face several times, blaming the discomfort on his excitement, the sun, and too much time squatting over the dead animals—and not necessarily in that order. He stopped to get some aspirin from the medicine cabinet in the bathroom.

His fingers felt clumsy as he struggled with the tamper-resistant vial, and the buzz of the fluorescent bulb on the ceiling was unusually loud and irritating.

It wasn't until he swung the cabinet door closed and glimpsed his reflection in the mirror that he saw the trickle of blood coming from his nose. The dark crimson color curled down from his left nostril, as thick and ominous as a red sky at morning.

Then, before his fascination could wane, he began to tremble.

4

For the past five days of Garner's lengthy sampling regime, the mysterious hole in the ocean had continued to appear intermittently but increasingly predictably on Medusa's organic readouts. It coincided with nothing on the inorganic channels. Other than slightly higher than usual concentrations of copper, there was nothing at all remarkable about the ocean around it. The "abiotic stasis" extended along the eastward surface current for an undetermined distance toward shore, but tapered at its westward end, nearer the *Exeter*'s wake, as if collapsing upon itself. That was an encouraging sign. The dead zone was apparently temporary after all, but what they were witnessing with their sampling instruments still defied description. Given the dynamic, fluid environment in which it lived, plankton distribution was notoriously erratic or "patchy," and the deck crew of the *Exeter* could only surmise that they had discovered the Mother of All Bald Spots. The question was, if the entire organic content of this patch of ocean had been displaced, where was it?

An hour later, the *Exeter*'s bridge crew broke in on the three-way radio conversation between Garner, Zubov, and the winch operator.

"Hang on a minute, boys," the thick brogue of Peter McRee, the *Exeter*'s first mate, crackled on their headsets. "I've been watching a freighter off the starboard, and her bearing isn't changing."

"Well, tell her to change course. We're towing," Zubov said.

"She ain't gonna move for little ol' us," McRee replied. "She doesn't have to. It's her right-of-way." At sea, the rule of thumb for right-of-way was that the smaller vessel lost out, and the *Exeter* was barely a quarter of the size of the approaching freighter.

"What's going on?" Garner called up from the lab. From his position, he couldn't see out any of the ship's portholes, but he could see Zubov move to the gunwale and scowl at what he saw.

"You're not going to believe this," Zubov said. "Or maybe you will. There's always something coming along to jerk us around."

"What is it?" Garner asked again.

"Come on back," Zubov said.

Garner returned to the afterdeck and followed Zubov's gaze off the port bow. The shape of a freighter was unmistakable, an alien and strange blight on the unbroken horizon. She was still two miles off but clearly on a collision course with the *Exeter*.

"Unbelievable," Zubov spat. "Not another goddamn ship around for a thousand miles and they want to play bumper boats with us."

Garner turned and trotted nearly the entire length of the *Exeter*, climbing three flights of stairs as he made his way to the bridge. As McRee looked on, the captain, a stocky and impressively fit man by the name of Robertson, studied the freighter through his binoculars.

"How long has she been out there?" Garner asked.

"Practically since we started the tow. An hour or so."

"And we haven't strayed off course?"

Robertson gave him a patient look, one reserved for the science crew and their quaint concerns. "No, we haven't gone off course, Brock. She should have passed clean in front of us, but she's been limping along on that same tack like we're not even here."

Limping was an appropriate description for the approaching vessel, which seemed to be listing slightly to starboard, moving steadily at only a few knots. Garner's thoughts returned to Medusa, which was working better than ever before. "So we're going to have to break again?" He knew the answer but prayed he was wrong.

McRee tried the radio again. "Attention freighter *Sato Maru*. This is the United States Research Vessel *Exeter*. We have sampling gear in the water and cannot alter course at this time. Please adjust your course to port, one-five degrees." They watched the freighter creep steadily closer with no response from the radio. "Ah shit," McRee cursed, flipping a toggle on the ship's radio, reconnecting himself to Zubov at the stern. "Cancel the tow, Serg. We're gonna have to break it off."

Zubov's reply was quick and slightly annoyed. "No luck?"

"Not unless you speak Jap-an-easy," McRee said. "Get all the gear out of the water, and we'll come around for another pass." He flipped the radio off and turned back to the captain.

Robertson was still studying the foreign ship. "Response or not, I don't like the looks of her at all."

"D'you think she's a derelict?" McRee asked.

"I doubt it," Robertson said. "Too expensive to ditch her way out here, salvaged or not." He lowered the binoculars and scratched at his neatly clipped beard. "Try hailing her again, and if there's no answer, I want you to go over and have a closer look," he finally said to McRee. "Take Garner and Zubov and some emergency provisions with you."

"Sir?" Garner queried the unusual selection of landing-party members.

"McRee can represent the *Exeter*. And it looks like you're out of business for a while anyway," Robertson said. "Besides, when Serg finds out the tow is canceled, I don't want to listen to him getting all cranky about it until we can come around again. As he's apt to do."

"Sure. In the meantime, maybe we can arrange a little cultural exchange," McRee said to Garner, adding a slight bow to illustrate his sarcasm. "Let's trade 'em a VCR or two for the Ukrainian version of Godzilla."

Zubov used the outboard motor to reverse the Zodiac from the stern of the *Exeter* and pulled the inflatable boat around in a wide arc, headed for the silent freighter. The bow of the small craft hopped erratically up and down as Zubov steered it into the oncoming swells. Garner gripped the rubber cleat mounted on the pontoon to keep his balance. Across from him, McRee did the same.

They crossed the half mile to the *Sato Maru* in minutes, drawing alongside and locating the drop-down loading platform. The side of the huge ship towered more than sixty feet above them, and the slight list to starboard seemed to magnify the effect. Looking up, it wasn't hard to imagine the rusted vessel exhausting its useful life and rolling over on them.

McRee hopped over to the landing platform, dropped it down with a loud *clank*, and fastened the Zodiac's bow line to it. Garner passed him the sparse collection of gear they had brought along—flashlights, a first-aid kit, field radios, flares, and a pistol. As Zubov switched off the motor, McRee directed his light into the dark recesses of the hull. "Hello? Anybody home?"

"How many are *supposed* to be home?" Zubov asked, hefting himself onto the platform.

"If her hold's full, maybe eighteen. Maybe two dozen. Fewer if she's empty, but you don't run a ship like this empty if you want to stay in the black."

"Ship of opportunity?" Garner asked.

"Could be." McRee nodded. "She ain't fitted for anything industrial."

"What about her list?" Zubov said.

"Looks like they tried to flood, or purge, the ballast but got hung up halfway. If there's any damage to the hull, it's too far below the waterline to see."

"I don't see any storm damage," Zubov remarked. "Remember that blower we passed through? It came out of nowhere. When was that— five days ago? A week?"

"She isn't exactly a wooden galleon," McRee said. "This thing could drive over the *Exeter* without getting a scratch. Not that we'd notice a scratch on this rusted-out piece of shit."

As if in reply, Zubov wrinkled his nose as he stepped inside. "*Jee-sus.* What's that *smell?*"

"Rot. A lot of rot from a lot of different cargo," McRee said. "Brings back memories of my days as a longshoreman."

"Really? I thought it was your cologne," Zubov quipped.

"Just for that you can check out the engine room and the hold," McRee said. "Brock and I'll check out the bridge. Radio us if you find anything."

As Zubov began to make his way laterally through the hull, Garner and McRee followed a set of ladders up six flights to the main deck, then up another stairwell inside the superstructure. The latter part of their climb took them past the corridors of crew cabins. Garner paused and knocked on the first cabin door before searching inside. The room was unused and deserted, as were the next three. Below, Zubov made certain they could still hear his muffled complaints.

In the next cabin, Garner found the first two bodies.

The stench in the room was overwhelming, a combination of stale air, gangrenous flesh, and assorted bodily fluids. The two crewmen, both Asian, were still in their bunks and covered with several layers of blankets. Their mouths and chins were coated with a dried film of saliva and mucus, and one had apparently voided himself in his bed. A quick inspection of the cabin's private head showed that it, too, had experienced some heavy use.

The scene was eerily similar in the next room, and the next. Another body was found in the galley, bathed in the light of an opened and leaking refrigerator. The rotted remains of the last meals—assorted vegetables and seafood—had yet to be thrown overboard, as was usual for table scraps.

"This is incredible," Garner whispered, playing his flashlight over the man.

"Dropped in his tracks," said McRee. "No sign of injury or struggle."

"Not outside his own body, anyway," Garner agreed. He trained the flashlight on the remains of the last food to be prepared on the kitchen's cutting board. "No way to tell if this stuff went bad before they died or since. Food poisoning isn't usually fatal."

"Spewing like that might be, though," McRee offered. "Christ, he's a mess. Reminds me of this flatlander we took out on the *Exeter* once. He got *so* sick—"

Garner raised a hand, cutting him off. "Thanks, Pete, I get the picture." Garner was used to McRee's irreverence under the worst of conditions, but the wholesale death they continued to discover set a new benchmark for "worst."

On the next deck, they inspected the officers' quarters, room by room. In all, they counted thirteen bodies, including the captain, who had apparently died in his bunk. Climbing the last flight of stairs, they came to the bridge. The lights of the abandoned control panel winked on and off, their full significance occluded by their Japanese markings. From what McRee and Garner could discern from the indicators, the throttle had been left on SLOW AHEAD, which would explain the vessel's awkward tack. Moving against the oncoming swells, the *Sato Maru* was left to struggle along in a northwesterly direction at only a few knots.

"What have we got here?" McRee mumbled, then turned to Garner. "Some kind of virus? You're the friggin' biologist here; you tell me." His eyes widened. "Oh shit—did we just step into some kind of quarantine situation?"

"It looks like they had plenty of food and fuel," Garner said.

Robertson's voice came over the radio from the *Exeter,* the crisp, electronic crackle disrupting the lifeless air on the bridge.

"Radio's working, too," McRee muttered, then picked up the microphone to talk to Robertson. Meanwhile, Garner located the ship's log, which was largely indecipherable. From what little Garner knew of the language, it looked as though the last entry had been four days ago.

As McRee got off the radio with the *Exeter,* both he and Garner heard a muffled thud followed by the sound of clanking metal. At first they thought it was Zubov, then they realized the noise was coming from above them, on the roof of the wheelhouse. The noise came again, unmistakably the sound of a heavy chain sliding along the deck.

"What the hell is that?" McRee said, looking up. "The Grim Reaper?"

The two men stepped outside and climbed a short ladder to the next deck. There, huddled between two deck-mounted water tanks, was one of the ship's crewmen. He wore a thick sweater and looked to be about twenty-five, decidedly overweight, with a greasy complexion. A heavily rusted chain had been padlocked around his neck, then locked to the base of one of the tanks. The crewman looked like he had been there for several days and, curiously, did not look at all relieved to see Garner and McRee.

"Speak English?" McRee asked. The man nodded, but admitted his English was poor. Though hard to understand, he answered their questions willingly, staring sheepishly at the deck as he did so. He gave his name and said he was the ship's first mate. The captain had taken ill and left him in command one day out of Seattle. They were preparing to meet a severe storm head-on when the crew had mutinied and decided to take the ship's cargo for themselves. The mate had tried to stop them and was taken prisoner. There was a struggle on the bridge, and by the end of it, he was chained outside. His captors had not returned to check on him, and the deathly silence was the only clue something was wrong. Once he had grown too weak to continue shouting to be released, the mate had assumed the mutineers didn't know how to run the ship alone or were still deciding among themselves what to do next. The mate said he had been asleep and awoke to see the *Exeter* off the freighter's starboard bow.

The way the mate told the story—dispassionate, continually looking away, remaining purposefully vague on some facts and repeating others several times—was hardly convincing. It suggested none of the trauma or frustration an innocent man would experience while imprisoned on an open deck. Both Garner and McRee had the sense that the mate was lying about at least some of his account.

The mate said he knew his crewmates had taken ill, but appeared genuinely stunned and saddened that they had actually died. As for what caused their demise, he had no more clues than McRee and Garner. He said he interacted little with the others and stayed mainly in his own cabin or out on deck, even before the mutiny. The ship's refrigerator had stopped working, and most of the perishable food had begun to spoil. Although the mate usually ate the same provisions, he had eaten only snacks from his shore leave since their return voyage began. The tank he was chained to was part of the ship's drinking-water supply, and he had been sipping from its spigot, with no effects of his exposure more adverse than a mild sunburn and dehydration of his body and pride.

"See if you can find something to cut him loose," Garner said to McRee.

"Brock, he's *locked up,*" McRee said, clearly still suspicious of the mate's tale. "There's probably a reason for that."

"If ever there was, it's over now," Garner said. "Whatever's passed, he's still a human being and lucky to be alive."

As McRee went to find some tools, Garner sat down across from the mate. "You saw the others while they were sick, right?" he asked. "Before the mutiny?"

The mate nodded. "They get sick very quick. Very bad." He went on to describe the symptoms he had seen in the captain and some of the others.

"You worked alongside the others who were sick?" Garner asked again. The mate nodded. He had, but only for a while. By the time of the mutiny, he had confined nearly everyone else to their quarters below. "And you feel fine? Not at all sick like the others?" The mate agreed. If it was some kind of virus, it didn't appear to be airborne, contagious by inhalation or external contact, though direct ingestion could not be ruled out.

McRee returned a few minutes later carrying a large fire ax. As the mate pulled back on his tether, Garner wrapped the most rusted portion of the chain around a cleat. McRee smashed the broad end of the ax head down onto the chain several times, until the battered links eventually parted. The mate was free from the ship, but the chain was still locked around his neck until they could find some chain cutters. The three men returned to the bridge. Garner gave the mate some water from their field kit and cautioned the boy not to guzzle it all at once. The boy took the bottle gratefully and took a seat in the vacant captain's chair.

The radio crackled again. It was Robertson, asking for clarification on McRee's last transmission. As McRee pressed, the mate eventually told them the name of the ship's operator. He gave them a contact number for his uncle, the company's managing partner in Hokkaido. "You've got some explaining to do, son," McRee said. "To your uncle and to us." McRee glanced at Garner as he turned back to the radio. "I swear, if we catch some goddamn Asian flu because this little punk can't keep his crew in check—"

"I cannot tell my uncle this," the mate said. "It would be a disgrace."

"I think it already is a disgrace," McRee said. "A disgrace that this situation was allowed to go on this long. I think it's a good thing we came along when we did."

McRee talked to Robertson for another moment, then called Garner over to the radio. "Robertson wants your advice," he said.

"Tell him it looks like the crew died from some kind of food poisoning," Garner said. "Our friend here appears to be fine, and if what he said is correct, I don't think we need to be worried about a quarantine. Just to be safe, have Robertson send someone over with some laundry bleach and a clean change of clothes for each of us." Rinsing in a mild bleach solution would help to contain any virus to which they might have been exposed. Garner knew he was only speculating, but the options available to them were limited and their resources even more so. "We've got to scrub down before we leave. Then we'd better contact the owners and have them come out and claim their property."

Behind them, neither Garner nor McRee saw the mate watching their every move. His eyes moved from them around the bridge, reacquainting himself with the room as he had last seen it—on the night of the storm. The American intruders were both at the radio, along the far wall. Across from him, the ax now sat on the chart table where McRee had set it down. The mate began to move, as quietly as possible, coiling the abbreviated length of chain around his hand as he stepped down from the captain's chair and moved toward the chart table. Neither of the intruders turned to notice him.

The mate reached the table, then knelt down on the deck, reaching his arm underneath it. After a moment of searching, he found what he was looking for: his gun, exactly where it had fallen on the night his crew had jumped him. The mate crept back and took his seat in the captain's chair. He heard one of the intruders tell the other ship to contact his uncle and shame began to boil within him like a hot iron. Now the intruders were discussing the cargo and whether others would come to look at the ship.

His command was over. In truth, it had never really begun.

Closing his eyes, the mate put the barrel of the gun into his own mouth and pushed it against his palate. With a single constriction of his finger, he would no longer care what his crew, or these intruders, or his uncle, or anyone ever thought of him. . . .

The gunshot banged loudly in the confines of the bridge. Garner and McRee whirled around to see the boy's head recoil from the headrest of the captain's chair, the back of his skull sprayed with bright red blood. As they watched, the mate's body pitched forward onto the floor, the gun skittering back under the chart table, following the awkward slope of the deck. The spent shell rolled across the deck and came to rest against Garner's foot.

Garner and McRee gaped in shock at the spectacle before them. McRee was the first to find words. "What the hell was *that* for?" he said.

"His uncle," Garner speculated. "We were talking about reporting this, and the kid probably opted for death before dishonor. Don't ask me where he got the gun." Garner stooped and retrieved the weapon. "It was his last bullet, too."

" 'Death before dishonor,' what a convenient bitch," McRee said. "The rest of us have to do it the other way around."

A moment later, Zubov joined them on the bridge, wheezing hard from his climb up the stairs. "It's friggin' hot down there, and the smell is unbelievable."

"What did you find?" McRee asked.

"A dead guy in the corridor. Looks like he just collapsed in his tracks." If he expected to shock the other two men, he didn't succeed.

Then Zubov saw the fallen first mate, blood still trickling from the fresh wound. "Who's this?"

"Ship's mate," McRee said. "He just blessed us with his *jisatsu*. Suicide. What about the hold?"

"Full of timber from the West Coast of Canada. Dry goods from Seattle. A few crates and a couple of cars, including a cherry new Corvette."

"They're carrying anything they can, for a price," McRee said.

"Tell me about it. This thing is a rolling garbage dump. There're barrels and discarded containers down there that look like they haven't seen daylight since World War Two. To top it off, they've got all their bulk provisions down there."

"And the hull?"

"The port ballast is blown; starboard is partially flooded. The load's secure, but it looks like they didn't know if they wanted to go up or down or some combination of the two. The engines are greasy as hell but seem to be okay. It's damn hot down there, too."

"They could have shut down the ventilation to cut off an airborne contaminant," Garner speculated.

Zubov shook his head. "What d'you mean, 'airborne contaminant'?"

McRee nodded at the fallen sailor. "Except for this guy, the entire crew seems to have died from some kind of illness, or poisoning."

"Fuck *me!*" Zubov said. "Don't *tell* me that! I was practically *wading* in that shit down there." The big Ukrainian pushed at the mate with his foot, stepping around the body and stooping to examine it. "Oh shit, did you see his *face?*" he said. "It's all marked up."

"A pretty ugly outbreak of *Acne vulgaris,*" Garner offered.

"*Acne vulgaris?*" Zubov repeated. "Is it contagious?"

"Only through cheeseburgers and pubescent hormones," Garner said. "*Acne vulgaris* is the bacteria that causes zits."

McRee laughed as Zubov flushed. "How do *you* feel?" he asked Zubov.

Zubov considered this for a moment. "The goddamn stairs just about killed me, but otherwise fine."

"So far this doesn't look like anything worse than food poisoning," Garner said. "Unbelievably ugly food poisoning, mind you, but probably not contagious."

"What about this airborne contaminant you mentioned?" Zubov pressed. "Why'd they shut down the ventilation?"

"Serg, it's a very old and very crappy boat. Chances are it shut itself down. Or it wasn't working in the first place," McRee said. "Either way, we've done about all we're gonna do," McRee finished. "It ain't our property and we ain't taking this girl home."

Garner retrieved some plastic bags from their field pack and fashioned them into makeshift filtration masks for the three men to wear over their noses and mouths. It took nearly another hour for them to figure out how to level the ship by balancing her ballast tanks, then attempt to power-down the freighter's nonessential operating systems, leaving it as safely "parked" as possible atop two miles of water. After a cursory search of the rest of the ship, the men received the delivery of bleach and extra clothes from the *Exeter,* located an outlet hose, stripped down, and scrubbed themselves thoroughly.

"I haven't been this clean since . . . since . . ." Zubov began.

"Since I've known you," McRee teased. "You might as well know, Serg, this whole thing was cooked up to call attention to your personal hygiene."

Garner couldn't share in the jocularity. He toweled himself dry and hoped they were taking enough precautions. The bleach rinse should help sterilize them, but the microbe responsible for all this—if it was a microbe—would need a field lab to isolate and identify it. So far, the unbalanced young mate was their only indication that the pathogen wasn't a "slate wiper," as a virologist friend of Garner's called a bug with one hundred percent lethality. What they had witnessed in the past twenty-four hours was as chilling as it was perplexing. First an inexplicable dead zone, then a ghost ship miles from the nearest human traffic until the *Exeter* had unwittingly come along. The combination of clues suggested nothing Garner could yet imagine, but the pieces in and of themselves were already troubling. Without the time for further investigation of what was going on out here, the fact that the ship's mate and the three members of the makeshift landing party were apparently unaffected was Garner's only tangible reassurance.

"Whatever you do, don't touch anything, and get back to the Zodiac right away," Garner advised.

As they dressed, they heard a new sound coming from outside and climbed up to the main deck to investigate. It was a helicopter, looking as obvious and alien against the featureless horizon as the freighter had a few hours earlier. From the deck of the *Sato Maru,* Garner, Zubov, and McRee watched it come closer and hover near the *Exeter* as it apparently radioed the bridge. Though it would have been a tight fit on the *Exeter's* small helipad, the helicopter did not try to land on the research vessel. Instead, it turned and angled toward the freighter.

It couldn't possibly be someone representing the *Sato Maru,* not this quickly. The helicopter itself looked fast, and its nose and cabin were rounded in the characteristic fashion of European manufacturers. Indeed, as it drew closer, Garner identified it as an Aerospatiale Dauphin, made in France. As such, out here the craft was close—if not dangerously close—to its maximum flight range.

McRee squinted to make out the large gold letters printed on the matte brown fuselage. *"The Nolan Group?"* he read. "Never heard of them."

"They're an environmental consulting firm, based in Seattle," Garner said. "Pretty big. *Very* expensive. Sort of an ecological think tank."

"Think tank, my ass," Zubov sputtered. "They run half-hour infomercials on late-night TV." He put on a wide, plastic grin, like a wax rendering of a game-show host or a pretentious funeral director. " 'Hello, friend. I'm Bob Nolan, president and CEO of the Nolan Group. If you've got an oil spill, toxic waste, or emissions problems, we can help. Let my overpriced A-team of eco-guerrillas-for-hire sell you a bunch of equipment you don't need, for problems you don't even *have.* Together we can make this a better world for everyone. Especially . . . for the children.' " Zubov broke the caricature long enough to let out a loud, prolonged fart. "Yeah, Bob, I've got an emissions problem for ya, right here."

"Well," Garner grinned, as McRee broke out laughing, "I didn't say it was a very *deep* think tank."

"And is the head lifeguard there still banging your ex-wife?" Zubov asked.

"As far as I know," Garner said, the sting of the remark not completely hidden.

" *'Especially . . . for the children.' "* Zubov laughed, reprising his impersonation of Bob Nolan. Then he noticed the look on Garner's face and backed off. "Ah, don't worry about it, man. He's doing it to all his clients, too."

Garner knew Zubov's tirade against Nolan wasn't based on any personal experience. In fact, none of them had ever met Honest Bob in person. Garner had found some excuse to decline a handful of social invitations since Carol's marriage to the chief eco-guerrilla and his millions inherited from Nolan Timber Products. Zubov's insults derived from the kind of jealousy and disdain most legitimate researchers had for corporate grandstanders like Nolan, whose capped teeth and tanned face seemed as enduring as his supply of capital and high-priced toys. Zubov simply had a bad case of helicopter envy.

"It looks like a turd," Zubov said, as if reading Garner's thoughts. "A giant, flying turd."

The sleek shape loomed above them like a surreal locust, slowly gliding directly overhead, then settled down easily on the expansive open deck. Beside the pilot, the single passenger removed his headphones and climbed out. He approached the scientists with his head ducked out of the path of the rotors and his open hand extended, waiting to be shaken. The updraft pulled at his necktie and the fringes of his tailored Italian suit, so that the visitor's posture looked comically "like Groucho Marx," as Zubov indiscreetly observed.

"Doctor Garner?" the man asked, his thinning hair tossed around into a reddish splash on his high forehead. "Doctor William Garner?"

"Brock Garner," Garner corrected him. "And I'm not a Ph.D."

"I'm Darryl Sweeny, Mr. Nolan's executive assistant. I have an important message for you from Carol Harmon. An emergency. She'd like you to come with me back to the mainland."

Garner cocked his thumb toward the *Exeter*, still shouting over the roar of the helicopter. "I'm sure she knows we have radios on board, for just such an 'emergency.' Besides, we've got a situation of our own here." Garner knew this was only partially true. There were plenty of others aboard the *Exeter* who could supervise the transfer of the *Sato Maru* and file the report of her discovery, many of them more essential then himself. Maybe he was feeling a little helicopter envy, too.

The man glanced up at the pilot through the windshield of the helicopter. The pilot responded by winding his hand quickly forward in the air: *Hurry up.* "We'd better get going, sir," the man said. "We leapfrogged here from a Nolan research vessel three hundred miles out. This thing's been modified for long-distance flight, but we're still getting close to our point of no return on fuel."

Sweeny held out a small white envelope with THE NOLAN GROUP letterhead printed in the corner and W.B. GARNER written on the front in Carol's handwriting. "She told me that she wouldn't accept no for an answer. And that, when you heard the news, you'd want to be on your way as soon as possible."

The envelope fluttered in the wind from the rotors as Garner took it. He slit the envelope open, withdrew a single sheet of paper, and read Carol's brief note.

"Mark Junckers is dead," Garner said. Already moving toward the open door of the helicopter, he handed the note to Zubov. "I have to go," Garner shouted over the noise of the engine. "Mind the shop and I'll call you in a couple of days, okay?" Stunned, Zubov nodded in agreement. He was familiar enough with Medusa's sampling regimen to carry out the rest of Garner's work if he had to, as it now appeared he did.

The helicopter began to rise from the deck even before the door was closed, Garner shouldering his way into a seat belt in the rear compartment. Moments later, it was little more than an indistinct speck above the horizon, returning to the mainland.

5

The shrill ring of the telephone on Ellie Bridges's bedside table awoke her with a start. It was not quite eleven o'clock in the morning and less than two hours since she finished her night shift at the hospital and collapsed into bed.

"Hello?" Ellie said cautiously. None of her friends would think of calling at this hour, and this was not the first call of the morning.

"Ellie? Don Redmond," the caller said brusquely. Not hello. Not good morning, sorry to wake you. Don Redmond, the hospital's administrator, telephonically beamed into Ellie's bedroom. She reflexively sat up in bed, pulling the covers with her.

"Hi, Don. What is it?"

"I need you to come in for a meeting with the hospital's legal counsel," Redmond said. "I assume you know why."

She did.

"I'll see you at eleven-thirty, then," Redmond said.

Redmond and the legal advisers met Ellie in Redmond's well-appointed office, shook her hand, poured her a cup of coffee, then spent the next four hours interrogating her. They asked about Mark Junckers and then focused on the circumstances surrounding Caitlin Fulton. The girl's father was bringing a lawsuit against the hospital that included Ellie among its defendants. The hospital lawyers assured her that, provided she was found innocent of any malpractice, she would be fully covered by the hospital's insurance. If she was found negligent, she would be responsible for her own legal fees and could possibly be asked to resign from the hospital, pending the outcome of the case.

Lawsuit. Defendants. Resign.

Ellie drank the tepid remains of her coffee and asked for another cup.

Ellie Bridges could still recall the day she decided she wanted to be a doctor. It was her sixth birthday. An aunt from a shady branch of the family tree gave her a toy doctor's kit as a gift. Inside the molded black carrying case was a veritable cornucopia of healing potential, from an assortment of Band-Aids to a vial of sugar "aspirin," a cardboard thermometer, and a plastic stethoscope. Ellie adored that kit and spent most of the next year meticulously examining the family dog, diagnosing then curing an unending series of make-believe illnesses that would have killed a lesser canine.

Now, at thirty-two, three years out of med school and working in the emergency room of the hospital in Port Alberni, she felt she had finally lost her love for medicine.

Perhaps that wasn't exactly true—the love affair had been on the ropes for some time—but the events of the past week had effectively flattened her professional motivation. Before that she had only been in a pressure cooker for the past eighteen months as part of her routine emergency-room duty, working eighty, ninety, sometimes over one hundred hours in a single week.

Port Alberni was an island town of approximately 19,000 residents that depended upon the logging and fishing industries for its lifeblood. It commemorated its claim as "The Salmon Capital of the World" with a Labor Day weekend festival and boasted commercial and charter fishing for sockeye, coho, chinook, and tyee salmon throughout the year. The

round-the-clock pulp and paper mill and its support industry were probably the most dependable source of emergency patients to the hospital,
ranging from the poison ivy, broken bones, and rolled trucks of the bush
crews to the amputated digits, scaldings, and eye injuries from the mill.
Beer hall drunks, boating accidents, and teenage auto wrecks had long
been stalwarts of any mid-island hospital, but increasingly, the number
of battered spouses, drug overdoses, and racial disputes with the local Indian bands had contributed to Ellie's nightly workload. The ER of the
town hospital managed to keep its bedlam controlled and professional,
most of the time, but Ellie had started to lose sight of why that might
ever fully satisfy her.

She found herself wondering increasingly whatever had become of
the "perks" a medical doctor should expect as a reward for her professional commitment and ten years of university. Where was the comfortable home? Ellie rented a two-bedroom flat above a fish market with
leaky plumbing, battalions of carpenter ants, and, for as much as she was
ever there, rarely more than condiments and a few Diet Cokes in the refrigerator. Where was the heavyset European sedan? She drove a ten-
year-old Honda Accord with a coat hanger for a radio antenna and three
of its four fenders rusted through and held together with duct tape. Ellie's world rotated, predictably and unfailingly, between her bed, the
gym, and the hospital, with the hospital increasingly becoming an uncomfortable place to be. Where was the retirement plan and six-figure
income? Ellie had taken the job in Port Alberni because, first, the hospital was hiring, and second, it offered what the smaller centers called "isolation pay." She booked ER shifts whenever she could because she
needed the overtime. Most of her paycheck went to repay her student
loans. *Stick with it, darling,* her parents still needed to console her. *Eventually, all that hard work and those long hours will pay off. You still get to
practice medicine. You still get to make a difference for your fellow man.*
Even after ten years, Ellie still needed to hold on to such vacuous plati-
tudes. She was far too intelligent, by now too experienced, to believe any
portion of her callow, Pollyanna daydreams about a career in health
care—not really. But it wasn't until lately that she realized how jaded,
how anti-Pollyanna she had become.

While her marks in premed were outstanding and her medical-school evaluations well above average, it had taken Ellie far too long to choose an area in which to specialize. First she considered pediatrics, then (as though in rebellion) she dabbled in geriatrics. She worked as a resident at Shaughnessy Hospital in Vancouver, then at a free clinic in the slums of the city's East Side. As an intern, she worked part-time at an upscale dermatology clinic in West Vancouver, assigned to a semi-retired widower named Stanley Melnyk who insisted on being called Doc.

Ellie spent her days examining and treating Melnyk's predominantly elderly and overtly vain clientele for all manner of skin blemishes, only a fraction of which posed an actual health risk. The majority of her work was cosmetic—the removal of moles, keratoses, warts, and boils with cryotherapy or curettage. When Doc Melnyk was in the office, which wasn't often, he would spend at least a portion of his day napping at his desk and punctuated his examinations with a pull from a flask of vodka he kept chilled in the specimen freezer. After drinking, Melnyk's eyes took on a glassy, unfocused shine and he held a leering grin on his face. Drunk or not, Melnyk complimented Ellie again and again on her "striking beauty" and several times had tried to "collegially" embrace or clumsily paw at her. When the vodka had inspired him to expose himself to her in the privacy of the examining room, Ellie tendered her resignation. This was not helping people. This was not practicing medicine. This was in the days before sexual harassment claims were even reasonably considered, let alone legally *en vogue*. It was probably such dissatisfaction that eventually drew her to the ER, the most dramatic example of practicing medicine she could imagine.

She recalled the stereotypical image of a Lady Doctor she had concocted as a little girl and hadn't fully relinquished until her first necropsy of a human cadaver. The lady doctor with the practical but stylish bob haircut, the single strand of June Cleaver pearls, and the effortlessly trim figure, pausing to give a lollipop to a sick child or to prescribe pain relievers to a grateful senior citizen. Husky adolescent patients and hospital orderlies surreptitiously lusting after the shapely legs exposed beneath her pressed white lab coat. Starting every day with a bagel and a Starbucks latte and leaving the office at 5:01, maybe 4:59, stopping at

Safeway or the crafts store as she drove her Mercedes home to her rug-gedly handsome husband and adoring 2.3 children. Martha Stewart with a stethoscope.

The reality for Dr. Ellie Bridges was that she couldn't afford dry-cleaning, let alone pearls, she rarely had the time or need to shave her legs, and her headache had become permanent. In stark contrast to her creative and vigorously promiscuous college days, men were now simply the reason for the second set of rest rooms along the hospital corridor. The erstwhile-yet-comely lady doctors portrayed on the colorful bro-chures in the ER's waiting room belonged to some other species. The day-to-day reality of Ellie's job—the geysers of bodily fluids, the unend-ing parade of battered and broken unfortunates, the endless night shifts, and the repeated trial-by-fire—left her feeling like a blood-soaked extra on a tired old episode of *M*A*S*H*.

Today she realized she had never liked *M*A*S*H*.

Ellie flushed as she sat in Redmond's brushed-leather guest chair, facing the panel. She fought back tears—of fear or of anger, or both, she didn't know—and started to again describe her actions with Caitlin Fulton and Mark Junckers. Redmond lifted his hand, cutting her off.

"You'll have plenty of time to tell us your side of the story as, or if, this thing progresses," Redmond assured her. "I'm sure the lawyers on both sides will be interviewing everyone on staff that night."

Ellie looked at the floor, her eyes roving, her brow knitted in concern. It was not the look of a negligent physician but, rather, a professional searching her memory for a missing clue, anything overlooked that might have led to Caitlin's death. Damn David Fulton for spiriting the girl's body away so quickly; there was no way for her to even go back over the physical evidence.

"Ellie," Redmond said, moving around his desk and sitting on the corner, facing her. "I'd like to say this kind of thing is uncommon, but it isn't. Accidents happen, and every lawyer out there wants a piece of it. You're a good doctor who's had a bad week."

"I lost two patients," Ellie said, still searching for answers. In the past three *years* she had lost perhaps only twice that number. No, not perhaps. Exactly five. She remembered each of them by name and circumstance.

Now she would have to remember seven.

The catalyst for Ellie's frustration, her professional gridlock, and the fatigue exceeding even its usual heroic levels began less than a week ago. As usual, Ellie was the attending physician on the 12:00-to-8:00-A.M. shift—hospitals called it the third shift, not the *graveyard* shift, thank you—when a frantic man came in. An architect and his wife, from Seattle, clutching desperately at their sick little girl.

Sick was an understatement. The child had severe diarrhea and had vomited until her stomach was completely empty, then she began vomiting blood. Then she had gone into shock and respiratory arrest. Her tiny body's systems began shutting down, one by one. Ellie and the attending staff desperately addressed each new emergency; this was hardly their first fire drill, and the team worked as an effective, professional unit. Ellie nonetheless managed several glances at her senior RN, Bonnie, looking for assurance. In addition to ten years of ER experience, Bonnie had four children of her own and could always be counted on as a source of moral support under the most harrowing conditions. But even Bonnie's eyes showed fear as they worked on this little girl. This one was going to hurt, and they both knew it.

Ellie looked at the child, so fragile, so pale. Six years old, the same age Ellie had been when she discovered the attraction of medicine.

A lifetime ago.

Ellie was still shaken as she returned to the waiting room and delivered the news to Caitlin's mother, father, and sister. Once again, this was something Ellie had necessarily become practiced at; it was the lack of a definitive cause of death that left her unnerved, stepping awkwardly through an explanation to the Fultons. Enraged, they denied Ellie's request for an autopsy on the basis of "Canadian incompetence," then proceeded to raise holy hell right there in the ER and began making threats to sue the hospital and end Ellie's career. Ellie heard them out, applying as much compassion as she could to the situation, then helped the Fultons with the paperwork to have their daughter returned home.

Ellie took a deep breath, said a prayer for little Caitlin, then tried to forget the memory of that horrible night.

Seventy-two hours later, again on the third shift, a pair of graduate students from the Bamfield Marine Station brought their roommate into Ellie's ER. The man—Mark Junckers, they said his name was—was laid out on the attending table, his breathing almost too shallow to detect. He was also bleeding from the eyes and ears, his limbs twitching of their own accord. He was conscious, reacted to her touch, but could not speak. She immediately placed Junckers on a respirator and reviewed his case with the two friends. He had apparently been out in Barkley Sound for a few days' vacation, then returned home while his roommates were out. They returned home to find Junckers prone and nearly catatonic on the bathroom floor. He had not fully revived or spoken a single word on the entire way into Port Alberni. It had been two hours or so since he had begun bleeding from his nose, mouth, eyes, and ears. The nasty burn on his leg, they said, was the result of his walking into an ill-placed propane heater in the Bamfield pub. It was still far from healed and looked as though it had recently been infected. She studied Junckers's face, handsome in a gangly sort of way. A man in the prime of his life, obviously fit, no history of epilepsy, diabetes, or anything else on the questionnaire his friends filled out.

For the second time that week, Ellie found herself and her crew of attendants trying to revive their patient, struggling to get any further information out of him. Once again, they lost the battle. Junckers's body shut down, sliding first into pulmonary arrest, then into nothing at all. He was pronounced dead less than an hour later.

Another deep breath, another prayer.

Ellie stayed at the hospital until 9:00 A.M. to confer with the hospital's chief cardiologist. Comparing the patient's symptoms, observed or relayed, Junckers's death was posthumously attributed to an idiopathic ventricular fibrillation—a sudden, fatal flutter of the heart rhythm, followed by massive hemorrhaging. The condition was linked to a defective gene, and of the 300,000 such cases each year, about ten percent had no prior history of heart trouble. The physicians had no way of knowing if the genetic anomaly ran in Junckers's family, but they quickly found out. In the rush to get Junckers to the hospital, his friends had neglected to even notify Charles Harmon, who then had to be contacted to admit Junckers.

Ellie had returned home after that shift, popped two Sominex, and tried to sleep. Her phone rang less than twenty minutes later. It was Charles Harmon, asking for more details on his son's death. In her sedative-induced fog, Ellie relayed the symptoms and the conditions as she knew them. As she began relaying the symptoms, Harmon's tone changed, less that of a grieving father and more that of a pragmatic pathologist. It struck Ellie as oddly cold that a father would be so dismissive of the victim and so interrogative of the cause. Odder still that Harmon would demand his son's body be returned to Bamfield, without autopsy, for immediate burial. She did all she could do at that point and referred Harmon to the hospital's medical examiner.

Still perplexed, Ellie hung up the phone and tried to sleep, eventually succeeding.

An hour later, Don Redmond called.

"Two patients. Out of how many?" Redmond asked. "A couple hundred emergency cases this week alone. Ellie, I've looked at your billing, and you've been working a helluva lot of hours. I know, it's the job. But maybe you need—"

"I can't *afford* to cut back," Ellie started to protest.

Redmond raised his hand again. "I understand, Ellie. It isn't easy the first few years. But pushing yourself through longer and longer hours is just asking for more trouble."

"I can't afford a lawyer," she continued.

"As we said, it won't cost you a penny," one of the lawyers interjected. "Provided you're not found at fault."

"It won't happen again," Ellie said, looking directly at Redmond.

"You can't promise something like that," Redmond said. "None of us can. But if you ask me, you'll be able to cope with all this if you take some leave."

"I can't *afford* to take leave."

"Well, you're going to," Redmond said. "Payroll's up on the six-teenth, and I want you to make that your last shift. I don't want to, but I have to. You can take two weeks' leave, or I can suspend you without pay. Your choice."

6

Hearing the sound from above, Carol Harmon craned her neck upward and used one arm to shade her eyes against the setting sun. The Nolan Group helicopter appeared over the trees surrounding the Friday Harbor Marine Laboratory and lowered itself to the nearly deserted parking lot. When she saw Garner return her wave, the tension that had been roiling inside her began to lessen. Garner climbed down from the Dauphin with his familiar, easygoing smile, looking every bit as if he had *planned* to be flown in from God-knew-where just to hold her hand, reminding Carol, for the hundredth time, exactly why she had needed to call him.

To Garner, his ex-wife looked as beautiful as ever. Married life, the second time around, was treating her well. What Garner considered her natural beauty had only increased since his first glimpse of her, eight years ago. The strained expression was a more recent acquisition.

"Thank you," Carol said, as soon as Garner stepped out from under the whirling rotors. She threw her arms around his neck and hugged him with an intensity that revealed the understatement of her words.

Behind them, the gilded brown helicopter lifted from the ground and headed south, toward Seattle. Garner cradled Carol in his arms. "I didn't have much of a choice," he said with a weak smile. "I only wish we could have taken the *Exeter* in that fast."

"I know. I know how much you hate to fly," she said.

"It's not the flying; it's the altitude," Garner said.

"Ordinarily the two go hand in hand," Carol teased. She wiped a tear from her eye and kissed his cheek. "Unless you're an albatross." She knew Garner had struggled with varying degrees of acrophobia his entire life. At its mildest, he would develop a headache and a mild sensation of vertigo. At its worst, it could drive him to his knees, seeking the stability of the low ground, and even cause him to black out. The malady had held him back on the Navy's career ladder and had propelled him toward acoustical intelligence. It was in the latter posting—working at a high-level naval facility in Newport, Oregon, listening for the signatures of Soviet submarines, earthquakes, or bellyaching whales—that Garner had first met Mark Junckers. Mark had eventually introduced Carol to Garner. They were married six months later, divorced three years after that. In the conflicting mixture of causes and effects, Carol was uncertain whether Garner considered his fear of heights an auspicious quirk or a decided liability. Treating it with levity seemed to help.

As testimony of his own sense of humor on the subject, *Albatross* was the name Garner had chosen for his live-aboard sailboat, which he kept moored near the Friday Harbor lab for most of the year. The Junkman had given him the idea to buy the boat the year they left the Navy, then promptly bought one of his own, outfitted it almost identically, and christened it the *Pinniped*. The similarities of the two boats were not lost on Carol as Garner escorted her down the dock and onto the deck. Tears welled up in her eyes once again, and she slumped onto one of the *Albatross*'s benches. "Brock, it's been one hell of a week."

Garner ducked below deck to retrieve two beers from the refrigerator, returned, and gave one to Carol. "Week? You mean there's more?"

"There's always more," she said, accepting a bottle and rolling the chilled glass along the back of her neck. "Being a woman in science isn't getting any easier. I'm on at least a half-dozen committees, loading up my lab with too many wanna-be Jacques Cousteaus and Eugenie Clarks, publishing my butt off, and still having to fight for every penny of funding in the ever-dwindling pot." She paused to take a drink. "And now this."

Garner sat across from her in the cockpit and studied her face. It was difficult to believe that the wife of Bob Nolan could be lamenting anything in limited supply, particularly money. She was a bioacoustician by training and a specialist in the study of the behavior and vocalizations of free-ranging whales—a high-profile and "sexy" field, if not a well-remunerated one. Garner's own background in acoustics had been far more utilitarian and ultimately less interesting to him than the study of biologics. Perhaps Carol was still avoiding the temptation of soft money to retain her objectivity—or rebuff political inferences among her colleagues that she had fallen back on some less objective route. The loss of her stepbrother was something she clearly couldn't be objective about. Garner studied her reflective gaze and felt the sense of helplessness.

"What happened? What did Mark get himself into?"

"That's what I hope you can help me find out. He left a message on my machine. It was late and he must have been tired—he was stuttering and repeating himself, searching to find the words to complete his sentences, but still very excited."

"Excited about what?"

"Maybe *frightened* is a better word. He said he found about two dozen sea lions washed up on one of the islands in Barkley Sound. Otters, too, though the two don't usually frequent the same areas. Apparently, they all had these peculiar, crescent-shaped lesions. He asked me if I knew of any parasites or diseases in marine mammals that might do that."

"Did he say which island?"

"No. As I said, he was kind of warbling in and out, without specifics. His speech was kind of slurred, almost like he had been drinking. But he wanted . . ." Her voice trailed off, and she took a moment to regain her composure. "He said he wanted me to call him back for the details. Always the little brother with a precious new discovery."

"Still trying to impress the old man," Garner offered. He knew the relationship between Charles Harmon and his children—between

Charles Harmon and *everyone*—was strained, at best. At times the Junk-man was utterly consumed by his need to impress his stepfather, though Garner had come to wonder if Charles Harmon was even capable of be-ing impressed.

"He said he didn't want to bother Dad until he had his facts straight," Carol said. "The next thing I heard, his roommates had found him on the bathroom floor."

"You said it was some kind of heart attack?"

"That's what the hospital said. I haven't been able to get ahold of the doctor on duty when they brought Mark in."

"A heart attack. In a healthy, thirty-nine-year-old man," Garner of-fered.

"That's all they said they'd know until the autopsy report comes back from Victoria."

They spent the rest of that night preparing the *Albatross* for the trip to British Columbia, packing her hold with equipment signed out from the University of Washington lab and checking her lines and sails. Garner could tell that Carol was anxious to get going, to see Mark for herself, if nothing else, but she assured him she would be more comfortable taking the *Albatross* and appreciated the distraction afforded by the prepara-tions.

Garner found the message from Mark left on his own answering ma-chine, but it left fewer clues than those Carol had already provided. Garner replayed the tape three times, until he noticed the effect the Junkman's voice was having on Carol. Finally, he removed the cassette from the machine and suggested they drive into town for provisions.

It was after dark when they returned to the marine lab. Garner used his key to let himself into the main office and radioed the *Exeter* to see if there had been any further unusual developments with the transfer of the *Sato Maru*. Zubov was asleep, but McRee was on third watch and re-layed that both men appeared fine and that the freighter's owners would arrive at Papa in the morning. If whatever killed the freighter crew was a virus and it acted as quickly as the mate had claimed, it had apparently passed by the time the *Exeter* discovered the derelict vessel. McRee agreed that no further pieces had been revealed to complete the puzzle and said he'd radio either the *Albatross* or the station at Bamfield if any-thing more developed.

Returning to the *Albatross,* Garner and Carol talked for another two hours, Garner relaying the latest news about Medusa's successes—and failures—and Carol talking about her cetacean research with a genuine passion. Both of them spoke of the Junkman with reverent affection, finding it difficult to speak of him in the past tense. Neither of them even once mentioned Charles Harmon or Bob Nolan, the other men in Carol's life having been displaced by her grief for Mark.

They agreed to leave for Bamfield at dawn. Although the cabin of the *Albatross* was accommodating, Garner wasn't used to sharing the space with another body, much less the piles of crates, boxes, and watertight plastic bins he had stowed there. The couple had to squeeze past each other several times as they prepared for bed, with each movement re-quiring a calculated rearrangement of the decor.

"It reminds me of that video game," Carol remarked. "You know, *Tetris?* The one with all the stacking boxes?"

"It reminds me of our first apartment," Garner quipped. Carol roared with laughter as she stepped into the head to freshen up, leaving him mo-mentarily alone with his reminiscing. She reappeared a moment later, a towel draped over her arm and her toothbrush protruding from her mouth.

"What is it?" she asked, noting Garner's bemused expression.

"Nothing," Garner said, indicating the double-tiered berth. "It's just that, if I ever imagined us sleeping together again, I never thought it would be on bunk beds."

"No?" She winked. "Well, then, I hope you'll at least let me go on top."

She made no attempt at modesty as she packed her towel away and pulled off her shorts and cotton shirt, exposing a long, naturally athletic body, evenly browned by the sun and capably toned by countless sets on the tennis courts. She seemed smoother, in the way that the wealthy typi-cally are. When she was a graduate student struggling for her share of the rent, she was still pretty but invariably unkempt, her nails chipped and her limbs covered with abrasions and bruises from her fieldwork.

Now her skin was unblemished and almost radiated the effects of a healthy, energetic lifestyle. For all her lamentations about "the rigors of being a woman, a scientist, and generally misunderstood," it hadn't begun to noticeably erode her exterior.

She noticed his lingering appraisal as she pulled on a T-shirt. "Yeah, I know it's inappropriate adult behavior, but I'm too tired for modesty." With that she hoisted herself into the upper berth and made a point of leering at Garner as he undressed himself. "Besides, it's not like we haven't seen each other naked before. Right?"

Garner smiled at her candor and took momentary assurance that Carol was coping well with the loss of her stepbrother. But as he reached for the light, he saw Carol still watching him with tears silently coursing down her cheeks. As Garner drew close and undressed himself, she reached out her hand and caressed his cheek, noting the nondescript gold stud Garner had in his left earlobe.

"I see you're still wearing an earring," she said. "I remember when you had that little hoop and grew a beard to go with it. You still looked like the world's youngest pirate."

"I shaved the beard just after I got rid of the parrot," Garner said. "I'm slowly growing out of my swashbuckler phase. Kind of a twelve-step program for rogues."

"Thank you again. Thanks for coming," she said, emotion rising to her eyes. "I don't think I could handle this without you."

"It was nothing," he assured her. "The hardest part of the trip was trying to get a conversation out of that little guy who delivered your note."

"That's Darryl. He's a bit . . . ."

"Constipated?"

Carol giggled. "Yeah. I hadn't thought of it that way—but yes. Exactly."

"And if Darryl is as hard as this thing gets, we're both going to be just fine. The real adventure begins tomorrow. First light. Remember what Mark would always say when he took us out sailing?"

"Red sky at night—"

"Sailors' delight."

"Red sky at morning—"

"Sailors take warning."

As he took Carol's hand in his own, her resolve melted away completely and she began to sob. He held her, standing there alongside her berth until her tears had subsided. After a moment she spoke in a small whisper.

"But there was no warning, Brock. If it had to happen, if it was his time, then fine. I just wanted the chance to say good-bye to him, you know?"

7

As Carol loosened the lines and stowed them carefully on deck, Garner started the *Albatross*'s small outboard motor and left the San Juan Islands under power. Once they were on the outer coast, Garner raised the mainsail against a convenient westward wind. Carol brought up two bowls of granola and peaches in milk, ate one, then took the wheel from Garner as he had breakfast.

"I guess you won't get the chance to race the *Pinniped* to Hawaii," she said wistfully. For years, Junckers had been challenging Garner to a race across the northeast Pacific, possibly rendezvousing with Carol as she studied humpback-migration routes off the coast of Maui. Given their respective research interests, it wasn't practical for either man to operate a "floating laboratory"—in the Junkman's case, his study animals were too large; in Garner's case, the equipment was. But each had chosen a sailboat as a live-aboard abode for very similar reasons. In a way wholly unlike any motor-driven craft, sailboats allowed their operators to become *of* the sea, to travel *within* the water, *because* of the water, steered by its natural inclination. Motors might be more effective for making time, making headway, or simply making noise, but none of these advantages had ever appealed to Junckers or Garner. To motor was to use a watery highway; to sail was to be embraced by the sea.

"He would have kicked my ass, and he knew it," Garner admitted. "So would you."

"It runs in the family," Carol said. "Some parents push their kids to become lawyers or medical doctors. Daddy wanted sailors, so he got sailors."

"Have you talked to him at all?" Garner ventured.

"Oh sure. He knew all about Mark's death, but of course I was the one who had to do the reaching out and make all the funeral arrangements."

"Will he be at the funeral?"

Carol kept her eyes on the horizon, mimicking its placidity. "You know Charles Harmon," she said. "Charles Harmon doesn't make plans in advance. Charles Harmon keeps his own agenda."

By noon they were passing the broad mouth of Juan de Fuca Strait, named for the Greek navigator with an oddly Spanish name. The forty-mile separation of land was the nautical gateway to Seattle and the Olympic Peninsula to the south, and to Vancouver and the Lower Mainland of British Columbia to the north. It was also the predominant shipping channel to the entire Pacific Northwest, and the *Albatross* shared her tack with dozens of charter vessels, sailboats, and freighters. The latter reminded Garner of the *Sato Maru,* and he took his first opportunity to relay to Carol what they had seen.

"What do you think it was?" she asked.

"McRee and Serg had some colorful theories," Garner said. "Everything from a bad batch of smuggled heroin to a suicide pact. I think it was food poisoning, assisted by some pretty awful living conditions."

"You *think*? You weren't worried about a possible quarantine?"

Garner turned his hands palms up and shrugged. "The *Exeter* was more worried about a lawsuit. Their job should have been finished once they reported finding the vessel. Why? Do you think I might have contaminated Darryl on the ride in? Given him mono or something?"

"Or something," Carol said, unimpressed with Garner's bravado. She rolled over on her stomach and adjusted the straps of her bikini top against the sun's rays. "All these new diseases in the world, and you're dashing around like some Indiana Jones of the sea."

"At your insistence," he reminded her. "Remember, I kissed you, too."

"Great. Blame me for bringing some kind of monster virus to shore."

"I'll let you know the moment I sprout any fangs," Garner said. He knew Carol was only half joking with the remark, and it was the serious half that preoccupied his mind for the rest of the trip. Despite McRee's notion to call in only unusual news, Garner would radio the *Exeter* again in a few days and see what had become of the ghost ship. He would also have to retrieve the latest list of obscenities from Zubov about Medusa's operation.

Carol stretched out on the foredeck and set to proofreading a draft chapter of a textbook Garner was writing. By the time she finished her critique, the *Albatross* was approaching Barkley Sound.

"Very good," Carol said, tucking the manuscript back into its folder. In all the time Garner had known her, the only comment she had ever made on his writing was "very good." At least one of them was consistent in their efforts. "Now, are you ready for my contribution to show-and-tell?" she asked.

Garner was, keeping one eye on the water and the other on Carol as she quickly unpacked one of her storage cases. She extracted a sleek black laptop computer and booted it from its battery supply. Loading a software program she had designed and written, she called up a map of the Queen Charlotte Islands, off the northeast fringe of Vancouver Island. The map included labels for several pods of killer whales, which Garner recognized from Carol's past research. At one time, she had been recording and cataloging the sounds that family groups of whales used to communicate with each other.

Carol clicked on the northern portion of the map, opening a window with a picture of a killer whale. The sound of the whale song, eerily familiar, came out of the computer's built-in speakers. "It's been known for some time that whales communicate within their travel groups and that different groups have slightly different sounds." She clicked on the southern portion of the map, revealing a second group of whales, with a distinctly different sound. "And where these groups cross paths, the communication is some combination of the two." She then clicked on the center of the map, and the resulting sound did appear to be some hybrid of the north and south dialects.

"Interesting," Garner said.

"Interesting, but known for some time, without any details. Some research is already disputing it as really true. But watch this."

She then called up a second screen on the monitor, which translated the sound of the whales' song into a waveform representation. "By comparing the amplitude, frequency, and complexity of these sounds, we can begin to filter them for common components."

"Words. Language," Garner offered.

"Exactly. Which has also been done, with some success."

"But no one knows what the words are." Garner had retained an interest in whale communication—biologics, as sonar operators knew them—through his own experience at Newport. He saw from Carol's expression that he had played right into her hands. "Until now?"

"Until now," she said. "The problem in looking at natural populations is that there's no way of knowing what their experience really is. Are they hungry? Afraid? We know they're talking, but about what?"

"So you controlled their experience?"

"We used the controlled experience of orcas in captivity. Recent inductees to injured whale facilities and transplants to aquariums. We compared what they talked about to what we knew they had done and what we were asking them to do."

"Let me guess: all they said was *Let me out of this place!*"

"Among other things, yes."

Garner watched as Carol's fingers flew across the keyboard, typing in coordinates to compare two waveforms, one from a captured whale in San Diego, another isolated from a pod in the Chukchi Sea. "If anyone had ever thought to do this before, they didn't have the database that I've got after ten years of recording. Even if they did, they didn't have my software program, and they didn't have processors sophisticated enough to track all the audible and subsonic factors necessary to determine whether the sounds actually matched." The next screen showed a side-by-side comparison of the natural whale's sound with those of the captured animals. The waveforms were merged together, then compared for similarities.

"Watch this," Carol said. "Here, where we got the Zodiac too close to the whale, versus here, where the Jet Ski in the aquarium show came too close. A virtually identical vocalization from one whale to the others, which we can interpret as 'Danger, move away.' And here, when they're feeding, an identical series of clicks to the surrounding whales, saying—"

"Soup's on."

"Sure, or whatever their idea of soup is. And here, the sound of the whale in its holding pen is a near-perfect match with this one, a whale stranded off the coast of Monterey. That's your 'let me out of here' signature."

"Amazing. So how come the Navy isn't interested in this?"

"Who said they aren't? By now I've probably got a higher security clearance than you."

"Probably. In terms of sex appeal, this certainly has Medusa beat." At his request, Carol replayed the waveform comparison for him again. "Amazing," he repeated.

"Well, convenient," Carol said. "The more matches in complexity we find, the closer we come to an acoustical road map of whale communication. It just takes the patience to listen." The tutorial finished, she folded her arms in satisfaction. Garner had no doubt she possessed the resolve to employ that patience.

"And all that on a laptop," Garner said, marveling at the technology.

"A twenty-thousand-dollar laptop," Carol corrected him, with a grin.

"You're pretty proud of yourself, aren't you?" Garner teased.

Carol nodded vigorously. "Oh yeah."

"So you admit to a few sunny breaks in the harried world of the intrepid female researcher?"

"Okay, so it has its perks," Carol admitted with a smile. "I've earned them."

It was at that moment that Garner figured the appropriate gesture would be to say something like, *You sure did,* then reinforce that sentiment with a warm embrace. But as Carol instead turned away and began packing up the computer, he was reminded that she didn't seek his approval, or affection, any more than she ever had.

He steered into the southeast corner of Barkley Sound, then up Trevor Channel, piloting a course between Mills Peninsula—which sheltered Bamfield from the open sea—and Helby Island—where Charles Harmon lived in self-imposed isolation. Given the choice of either destination, Carol elected to moor at the Bamfield Marine Station. She surmised, correctly, that the people there would know more about Mark's funeral arrangements than would her father.

The Junkman's body was placed in a modest pine box painted a garish yellow by Carol herself. She felt it was a casket with enough kitsch to appeal to her stepbrother's bohemian sensibilities in the afterlife. A small group of the Junkman's friends loaded the box onto the *Albatross* and followed Garner's boat north to Tzartus Island, where the family retained a small plot of land in an alpine meadow overlooking the sound. As the box was lowered into the ground, Garner could see Carol's gaze fixed on Helby Island, peering through the dense foliage to where her father's cabin perched on its rocky promontory. Seeing her anger and disappointment, Garner slid a comforting arm around her.

"He'll come," he said. "Eventually and in his own way."

"Families aren't supposed to be built on eventualities and 'own ways,' " Carol grumbled, reminding Garner again of how much her sensibilities had strayed back to the traditional since joining, if only by marriage, the fast track of the independently wealthy.

No Nolan Group helicopters appeared to deliver flowers from President and CEO Bob or redemption from Charles Harmon. Present, however, was Saunders Freeland, the station's research coordinator and—in Garner's estimation—a more appropriate father figure for the Junkman on such an occasion. As Sergei Zubov did on the *Exeter,* Freeland made certain the station's researchers were provided with the resources on hand, or he tracked down whatever they needed from Vancouver, Victoria, or Seattle.

Freeland showed his mood, his emotions, his history through the character lines creasing the leathery skin at the corners of his eyes. Wiry gray hair topped his ruddy complexion and blended irregularly with a longish, grizzled beard more suited to a Yukon prospector than a research coordinator. A slight paunch betrayed his affection for Irish stout and the patty melts at the Bamfield coffee shop. His back afflicted with severe arthritis from years of cold-weather fishing on the Grand Banks, he walked with a stiff-legged but urgent shuffle.

Each time Garner ran into Freeland, which never seemed often enough, the man seemed a little better preserved by his continued exposure to the elements—meteorological, chronological, bureaucratic, or otherwise. Looking at the slightly stooped, weathered figure with the elfish face, typically dressed in a flannel shirt and dungarees held up by a belt with a tarnished rodeo buckle, no one would ever have guessed that he possessed the hands of a skilled mechanic, had the intellectual latitude of an artisan, held a Ph.D. in molecular biology, and retained several patents in biotechnology. Enthusiastically inspired by too much liquor at one of the station's regular mixers, the Junkman had once called Freeland "a better carpenter than Jesus Christ," and Freeland had a hand-built cabin to prove it.

Also akin to Zubov, Freeland made it his job to make certain the scientists could do *their* job. He had a logistical stake in every study performed at the station and looked after its visitors, particularly the graduate students, with a fatherly interest—coaching them along with a never-ending series of cantankerous advice and guiding admonishments. Freeland truly loved his job—he just didn't like anyone to know it.

"The Junkman was like the nagging, pain-in-the-ass son I never had," Freeland said when he saw Carol at the funeral. Carol embraced him, then he shook Garner's hand warmly. "Brock here's the nagging, pain-in-the-ass son I *did* have," he said with the same backhanded sentiment. "Ten months a year for three years."

"Two years," Garner corrected him.

"Felt like three," Freeland said, clapping Garner on the back. "But it was all worth it in the end, huh? Lookit you kids, out there making a name for yerselves."

"We started here," Carol said.

"Some start, some end," Freeland said, then realized the significance of those words. He looked at Carol again, fixing her eyes with his. "The work's important, y'know, but this"—he lifted his arms and gestured to the surrounding scenery—"this, *life,* is more important. I get paid to help you damn kids get your research done, but . . ." His voice hitched and trailed off. As Freeland composed himself, Garner saw tears well up in the man's eyes for the first time ever. "But I like to think I can help keep ya alive, too. It gets pretty rough up here." The tears had begun to drizzle from Freeland's eyes as he held on to Carol, comforting her. "I am sorry. Junkman's gonna be a big loss for us all. You make sure your tight-ass pop knows that, huh?"

As the services began, the small, intimate congregation bowed their heads away from the majestic view. Only the sea breeze and the ruminations of those who could find words to speak aloud broke the silence. Then the displaced ground was shoveled back atop the yellow box. Apart from the memories that the mourners carried, a simple granite stone became the only reminder of the Junkman's existence.

8

By the time the *Albatross* returned to the marine station from the funeral, Carol's disappointment with her father's behavior had grown into abject anger. She left the boat and climbed the hill from the dock with long strides, quickly outdistancing the rest of the group. Garner moored the *Albatross* beside its sister ship and followed Carol up the stairs at a reluctant pace.

Constructed in 1900 by work crews of the Canadian Pacific Railway, the trans-Pacific cable station at Bamfield once provided a critical link in the communication network of the British Commonwealth. Anchoring the easternmost end of the longest continuous telegraph line in the world—4,000 miles—the station facilitated the passing of messages from Fleming Island in the mid-Pacific through Canada to the United Kingdom. Bamfield was selected both for its extreme western location and its isolation, away from shipping traffic and the electrical disturbances endemic to urban areas. A victim of the inevitable shift in technology and strategic importance, the cable station was replaced by a more modern facility in Port Alberni in 1959. The trans-Pacific station itself was burned to the ground in 1963 in an administrative move to reclaim the land and reduce the taxable value of the buildings.

A consortium of five Western Canadian universities surveyed and purchased the 190-acre site in 1969, and in 1972 established the first incarnation of the Bamfield Marine Station. As a research facility, the station retained little of its original Victorian charm. The original building—three stories modeled after the princely hotels CPR work crews were more accustomed to building—had included a hotel-caliber kitchen and such amenities as open fireplaces, a billiards parlor, a library, and a hospitality staff for visitors. Now a scattering of functional timber-and-pressboard buildings, slung low against the seasonal winds and driving rain, dotted the landscape on a promontory overlooking Barkley Sound. Among the more modern luxuries were a tennis court, laundry facilities, and an assortment of coed dormitories and faculty cabins. Each summer the station hosted undergraduate and high-school classes; a small contingent of researchers used the facility throughout the year.

Built within a four-story concrete foundation nestled into the side of the cliff face, the main station housed the research laboratories, classrooms, and staff offices. Adjacent to the visitors' entrance on the topmost floor, a mural of the original cable station paid homage to the former grandeur of the site. On one side of a modest atrium, the station retained a small but amply stocked library; on the other was the main reception and the office of the director. This was where Garner eventually caught up to Carol.

With her shoulders back and every muscle in her body tensed, Carol had effectively cornered her intended target: Charles Harmon. Raymond Bouchard, the station's director, looked trapped behind his massive desk, a prisoner of domestic war as the Harmon family argument began.

Carol's tone was crisp, defying either retort or escape by the two men. "Where were you?" Carol asked her father, her hands already balled into fists at her sides.

"I assume you're talking about the funeral," Harmon said, attempting, unsuccessfully, to placate his daughter with his drooping, blue-gray eyes and pretending to adjust the level of his hearing aid. He moved slowly, folding his hands neatly over the pearled top of a walking stick, the posture in which he usually presented himself during conversations. Despite the heat and his location in the middle of the British Columbia wilderness, the professor emeritus still wore a collegiate wool suit with a shirt buttoned to the throat. Going without a necktie, as he currently did, was evidently Harmon's idea of casual summer dress.

"I am talking about *Mark's* funeral," Carol spat. "Your stepson has died and you can't even be bothered—"

"Yes, he *is* dead," Harmon said. "But no one seems to know why, including you, for all your fretting. What Dr. Bouchard and I were just discussing is, possibly, *why.*"

Garner stepped into the room behind Carol, and Harmon deflected his attack accordingly. "Mr. Garner, good to see you again. I see Carol still recalls her past mistakes in times of distress."

"Mark was a good friend, Charles. Probably my best friend," Garner said.

"Yes, of course he was. For a moment I thought you might be up here chasing one of your mythical red tides. I thought you would have learned your lesson from your miscalculated warning to Washington State in—when was that, 1991?" Harmon shared a mildly bemused look with Bouchard.

"I wasn't aware of any more-accurate calculation models that would have disputed my predictions," Garner said coolly, though Harmon's barb had reached its intended target.

"Common sense would suffice," Harmon said, the thrill of the hunt momentarily rising to his eyes. "The common sense of experience, not the unbridled effervescence of hysteria."

Bouchard cleared his throat, attempting to do the same to the air. "We've all made mistakes Charles," he said. "Even Mark." The station director was reclined in his usual pose, angled back in his office chair with his legs crossed and his hands clasped behind his head. Garner noted that Bouchard perpetually had the look of a doughy catalog model for L.L. Bean—rugged, but not weathered enough to scuff his Rockport hiking boots or lose the crease in his khaki slacks.

"What is that supposed to mean?" Carol challenged him. "According to the autopsy, Mark died of a heart attack."

"A ventricular fibrillation accompanied by a significant disruption of the central nervous system," Harmon said as if reciting the autopsy report of a stranger.

"Fine. How does that equate to 'making mistakes'?"

"Oh, come now, darling," Harmon scoffed. "Mark's lifestyle was his own undoing."

"Lifestyle?"

"Of course. He was certainly well acquainted with recreational drugs. He tried LSD, he tried hashish—he told me that himself. He could have been an excellent organic chemist."

"He was a stupid kid! That was ten years ago, at least!" Carol exclaimed, but her outburst had no effect on her father.

"The damage was done, Carol. Long ago. That is what we were discussing when you barged in here. He died *of* an undetected heart flutter and thoracic hemorrhaging, but he also died *because* of his own stupidity and recklessness." As ever, Harmon enjoyed erudite word emphasis to infer the ignorance or quaint incomprehension of his audience.

"You insensitive bastard!" she hissed.

"That was long ago as well," Harmon said calmly. "My insensitivity didn't kill Mark."

Carol gaped at this remark. "I'll bet you believe that, too. Don't be so sure."

Garner placed a hand on Carol's arm, restraining her. "Doesn't it strike you as a little odd that Mark would be in apparently ideal health, years since his last experimentation with drugs—I can promise you that, too—and then he suddenly dies, only hours after he discovered some diseased sea lions?"

"Where is the proof of that, Mr. Garner?" Harmon said. "Where are these specimens he says he found?"

"Has anyone looked?"

"Yes," Bouchard said. He had been following the exchange like a tennis match. "I've had some students out checking the area around Mark's registered field sites. If he did find some dead animals, we'll have to report them to Fisheries and Wildlife. But as you know, there are hundreds of nooks and crannies all along this peninsula."

"And if something *is* found, is anyone going to be allowed to inspect them?" Carol asked, her temper cooling. "Will they be checked for parasites, or rabies?"

"Of course," Bouchard said offhandedly.

"Ray?" Carol pressed. "*Will* they be inspected? Will they be looked at by anyone who knows what to look for? At least two of the best people in the world for that are right here in this room." Of course, she was referring to Garner and Harmon, and the men exchanged a glance.

"And they're both welcome to join the search," Bouchard said. "You, too."

You, too. Carol instantly resented the tone in Bouchard's voice. *Yes, even you—a woman—can come along.* The station director's chauvinism was legendary among any of the women researchers who had crossed his path, administratively or otherwise.

"What about the possibility of domoic acid, or okadaic acid, or DMSO from a plankton bloom?" Garner said. "Either of those might produce vascular or neurological seizures."

"Of course, in *theory*—"

"That's a start," Garner said.

"A foolish one," Harmon said. "You're trying to dredge up another completely unnecessary scare, Mr. Garner, and I won't have it. I thought you two weren't up here for professional reasons. 'Here just to mourn a brother and a good friend.' Yet that boat of yours is packed to the gunwales with equipment, and now you're speculating about a marine pathogen. Right here under my nose and against any likelihood—"

"It's about as likely as a drug overdose, ten years overdue," Garner shot back.

"—against *any* likelihood of that being the case," Harmon finished. "We've looked. We *are* looking, for anything out of the ordinary. The surface temperature is a bit elevated—phosphate, too—but salinity and dissolved oxygen levels are completely normal. If there was anything noxious out there, we would have found it. Any number of fish would have found it, and we would have found them floating belly-up in the sound."

"You're checking nitrogen levels, too? Nitrate?" Garner asked.

"Especially nitrate," Harmon said. They both knew that plankton blooms, particularly those of toxic dinoflagellates, were nitrate-limited. An increase in the available nitrate in the water opened the door for the explosive growth of certain species.

"It's not unknown for marine mammals to succumb to toxic plankton," Carol offered. "A plankton bloom in the Sea of Cortez killed more than a hundred fifty dolphins in the space of a week."

"That's right," Garner agreed. "And there have been at least three cases of manatees dying from blooms in Florida."

"In stagnant, unflushed, over-nutrified waterways ideal for supporting plankton blooms," Harmon concurred. "But the same cannot be said for the exposed, well-mixed conditions we have here."

"There is a case to be made for natural causes, Carol," Bouchard said, resurrecting the notion that Mark was somehow responsible for his own death. "Irresponsibility happens to all of us." He nodded at the elder Harmon. "Even to this crusty bastard, someday."

"Thank you for that vote of confidence—I think," Harmon said, and the two members of the Old Boys' Club shared a brief chuckle.

Seeing the flush rise in Carol's cheeks, Bouchard increased the sincerity of his attempt to placate her. "We may never know what killed those animals, even if they're found. You know that. It could have been oil jettisoned from a fishing boat. Hell, they might even have been attacked by a rogue shark."

"A shark!" Carol gasped. "My God, Mark has studied sea lions for years. Are you saying he can't tell the difference between a shark bite and diseased tissue?"

"As we know, misdiagnoses aren't impossible, even from 'experts' like Mr. Garner here," Harmon said. "As we also know, marine toxins aren't usually lethal to human beings, and then only when consumed directly. Mark's autopsy showed no indication of gastric distress, and there was nothing remarkable in his stomach contents. Not that the boy would ever afford himself the luxury of a decent meal."

The dispassion in Harmon's voice as he paraphrased Mark's autopsy report struck Carol as ghoulish and callous. She wouldn't have stood for that from a total stranger; the fact that it was spouting from their own father enraged her further still. "Poor, penniless Mark, huh?" Carol spat at him, her angry voice booming in the small office. "Spent every nickel he had on drugs, I suppose. Dropped every dollar into *that fucking sailboat* you *made him buy*!"

"Darling . . ." Harmon said, waiting for his daughter to calm a bit. "I am only saying that, sometimes, things are exactly as they seem. Thinking otherwise is just a foolish waste of time."

"Most things that involve dealing with you are," Carol said, then turned and shouldered past Garner as she left the room.

Soon after nightfall, Carol retired to the *Albatross* and collapsed on her bunk. Allowing her some privacy, Garner walked down the pier and stepped aboard the *Pinniped* with the reverence of entering a shrine. The familiarity-yet-dissimilarity of the vessel, his own belongings supplanted by the Junkman's, provided an eerie sense of comfort. Above the chart table, Garner found an old photograph of his friend from years earlier. One corner of the photograph was marked by a trace of lipstick in the shape of a woman's mouth, possibly that of his girlfriend from last summer—a biochemist from the University of Calgary. The Junkman's tanned and unshaven face beamed his maniacally happy smile at the camera from under a battered straw hat. It was a smile Garner had known for twenty years, from his first day at the Naval Academy in Annapolis, when a cautious Iowa farm boy first met his cocky, gregarious roommate born to a Yalie in New Haven, Connecticut. It was a smile that had carried them through Tibet and other parts of Southeast Asia, on vacation after leaving the academy, where the Junkman began to craft the philosophy and reputation his stepfather would forever remember and condemn. It was the smile that introduced Garner to Carol, stood by them on their wedding day, and kept them all close in the years after their divorce.

Garner let his mind wander where it dared through those years. Watching his friend's eyes light up when the hydrophones in Newport picked up the vocalizations of a whale while they scanned channel after channel in search of Soviet submarines. Garner knew that the Junkman's love of the sea, affection for whales, and interest in sea lions derived from those graveyard shifts and the natural history books he devoured by the armload. Returning from their post-graduation travels, Mark had gone on to get his Ph.D. on the ecology of pinnipeds, though snubbing the old man's distinguished alma mater. The one time the three of them had ever worked together was on an expedition Carol had been invited to join to the Canadian Arctic. While Mark snapped roll after roll of film of the resident seal populations, Garner had assisted in the collection of zooplankton samples, work that eventually inspired the prototype for Medusa.

Released from the Navy but unclaimed by a university, Garner struggled to find a doctorate program that would let him develop his master's work on plankton systemics, including the groundwork for Medusa. As Carol's career began to skyrocket, Garner's own future in marine research was less certain. Adding to this stress, a brief fellowship for Garner in Charles Harmon's lab ended with "political differences" and marked the beginning of the end for Garner's marriage to Carol. As a dumbfounded divorcé, Garner dropped out of polite society to drive a taxi and drink himself into a painless stupor. Once again, it was the Junkman who found him, gave him a kick in the ass to correct his course, and told him to rejoin the scientific ranks, for the immodest purpose of Saving the World. Garner listened and, notwithstanding the blackballing Harmon had given him, was now less than a year away from completing his dissertation on part of the JGOFS research out at Papa and his development of Medusa.

Alone in the empty cabin of the *Pinniped,* Garner looked again at the photograph and the crooked grin that stared so arrogantly back at him. "All right, I'll admit it," Garner said. "I owe you a lot, you cocky sonofabitch. Beginning with an explanation of what killed you."

The Junkman's time-frozen expression challenged him to search for deeper answers to the meaning of life. And, perhaps, to search for meaning in death as well. *You're not done yet,* it seemed to say. *Prove it to me.*

Eventually, Garner made his way back to the *Albatross,* silently crawling into the bunk beneath Carol without turning on the light. Before he drifted off to sleep, he reviewed the events of the past three days, since

Nolan's helicopter had plucked him from the deck of the *Sato Maru*. It was not serendipity that drove Carol and him apart. It was not fate alone that brought Mark to those sea lions and moved Mark to call them for support. It was not entirely a coincidence that the old man still didn't believe their theories. He was glimpsing a pattern that was neither simple nor random.

Even the word *plankton* derived from the Latin for *tending to wander*. It was a description equally applicable to Garner's entire life. Each time it seemed he was progressing toward some meaningful destination, another wave—another favor, another distraction, another Charles Harmon—seemed forever willing to drag him back into the maelstrom of uncertainty. If for no other reason, that was why Garner hated funerals and was uncomfortable at most reunions. Any forum that allowed him to ruminate too much was, in general, maddening and, specifically, something to be avoided.

Bridges burned. Chasms uncrossed. Regrets. Mistakes. The San Juan Islands in 1991 represented all of these. Charles Harmon wasn't the only one who remembered Garner's passionate predictions of the red-tide-that-wasn't. Garner had been so confident of his model, which mathematically suggested an outbreak of several toxic species of microorganisms known as diatoms, that he had convinced Washington State to adopt an unprecedented preemptive—rather than reactive—approach to researching the problem and protecting its coastal shellfish industry. Florescing in large enough quantities, the diatoms could produce lethal levels of domoic acid, a potent neural disrupter that acted vigorously on brain tissue. Accumulating in shellfish feeding on the diatoms, the domoic acid could in turn produce permanent brain damage in anyone eating the contaminated shellfish. The economic and environmental implications were not to be ignored, and some $12 million in state funds was committed, enough to, predictably, raise the hackles of public-health officials with passionate concerns of their own.

Equally predictably, when the media got hold of the decision out of Olympia, there was an immediate knee-jerk response from the general public. Chambers of commerce, resort owners, restaurateurs, and legislators alike demanded to know the "real-world basis" for Garner's dire predictions. There were uninformed, mob-like assertions that state funds were being channeled away from education, highways, and "legitimate health care," even though those funds came from different sources than disaster relief or prevention. However unjustly—in actuality, he never saw any of the program funds beyond his modest consulting fee—Garner was labeled as "The $12 Million Man," focusing the public's anger even further. They called for him to be personally audited. They first accused him of fraud and embezzlement, then later, as discretion spiraled further from reality, they threatened to scuttle the *Albatross*. Alone in his own defense, Garner could only defer to his model and tell them all to wait on the wind and the water, and wait for the diatom bloom worth $12 million in public fear insurance.

So they waited, and the bloom never came.

Eventually, only one of Garner's prescriptive concerns came to pass: when diatoms failed to bloom in sufficient numbers to prove toxic to the local shellfisheries, his career was suddenly the only thing in jeopardy of foundering. Indeed, one of the few times in his professional life that he had steadfastly followed his convictions, his gut instincts, it had nearly cost him his career. Only the continued academic fascination with Medusa's potential—the empirical eyes, ears, nose, and mouth of Garner's mathematical models—had managed to keep him in oceanography at all.

Now, years later, Harmon wasn't the only one still unimpressed with Garner's demonstrated skill at intellectual survival in academe. Conversely, Garner couldn't deny that a large part of his professional drive was still an overt attempt to earn the respect of the Old Boys, who, despite their lack of social graces, had been single-handedly responsible for crafting Garner's field of occupation and preoccupation.

In the silence of reflection, there came the nagging wonder of whether it was even possible to know if a choice had been the right one, or if being right even mattered at all. It called to his mind a passage from Euripides' *Hecuba*:

Do we, holding that the gods exist, deceive ourselves with insubstantial dreams and lies, while random careless chance and change alone control the world?

The conundrum of a 2,400-year-old Greek play, no closer to resolution in Garner's planktonic, chance-ridden life. It was something far easier to ignore, buried under an all-consuming career, a call to duty, or unwavering devotion to a friend in need. The answers Garner sought remained just out of his reach, not unlike the end of his dissertation, the end of his marriage, and the end to the restlessness that haunted him. Out of reach, but closer now, among friends and the puzzle the Junkman had left for them all.

Maybe chance had brought them all back to this place. But this time, for whatever reason, it felt more like home.

9

You can take two weeks' leave, or I can suspend you without pay. Your choice.

The numbing events of the past week still drummed in Ellie's mind as she worked her last shift—a sixteen-hour, second and third shift doubleheader—before her suspension took effect. She was about to take her dinner break when a twenty-two-year-old was brought in from a motorcycle accident. Both the boy's hands were smashed, and his femur was broken so severely it had torn through the skin of his thigh. Ellie barely had time to sedate the boy and stabilize the wounds when she was called back to the reception area. A sweaty, obscenely overweight millworker who reeked of draft beer was storming around the waiting room, kicking at chairs and demanding to see a doctor about a massive, bloody cut over his left eye. By the time Ellie finished suturing the wound, the police had arrived. They clapped handcuffs on the man and drove him down to the RCMP detachment for questioning about a domestic dispute earlier that evening. No lollipop needed there. No gratitude expressed or inferred.

Then, miraculously, a cease-fire. Midnight in the ER, the last few hours before her enforced vacation, and all suddenly fell quiet.

Ellie took the opportunity to step out the main doors of the receiving area and let the cool night air soothe her frazzled nerves. She inhaled, drinking deeply with her lungs, appreciating even the smell of wood pulp that perpetually blanketed Alberni. On a bad day, the air smelled like rotten cabbage; tonight it was more akin to wet paper grocery bags. It had been much worse before they shut down the Kraft mill in 1993. The first time Ellie caught a whiff of this place, she had asked for a modest increase in the proposed isolation pay.

Her head hurt, her bones hurt, her *hair* hurt. She was exhausted, but she had come to prefer working all night to working all day. At night the world was quieter, the white noise of six billion people abated, and she could finally hear herself think. The third shift was her favorite, even if it meant dealing with more drunks, domestic-violence cases, and the primal lunatics who always seemed to come out around a full moon, like tonight. She had birthed her first child during the third shift. Extracted her first bullet. She had also lost Caitlin Fulton and Mark Junckers on the third shift, and this third shift might be the last one she would ever work at this hospital.

Ellie was about to go back inside when a set of headlights flashed around the corner, washing over her as she stood outside the emergency entrance. A moment later, the vehicle, a muddy, rusted Ford F-150, lurched to a stop at an angle across the driveway. Ellie stepped forward to the driver's-side door. There was an elderly Indian at the wheel, turned toward his passenger. Ellie tapped on the window and was about to explain where the vehicle should be parked, when she saw the Indian in the bed of the pickup.

She saw two men in their late forties, early fifties. Seeing the tattered scuba gear, her first thought was that the men had nitrogen narcosis—the bends. If that were true, they were wasting valuable time. The divers would have to be airlifted to the hyperbaric chamber at CFB Esquimalt.

Then, looking at them more closely in the half-shadowed driveway, she saw how their skin had been blackened and blistered. She pulled a penlight out of her pocket and shined it into the back of the truck. The bodies looked badly burned.

The driver of the truck swung out of the cab and looked at her without saying a word, as if the condition of the two divers explained everything. A little boy no more than seven or eight climbed out after him, coughing wet, hacking coughs and wiping a hand over his runny nose. His eyes were rimmed with red, and it seemed as though he had been crying.

"What happened?" Ellie asked, shining her penlight on the larger of the two divers, the one still moving. Bizarrely, though his skin had been blistered and bubbled, the equipment he wore looked virtually untouched by heat or any kind of corrosive fluid. It was as though he had hemorrhaged from the inside out.

"There was a boat fire," the Indian said, his voice slow and blunt. "These men were poaching abalone on the reserve. My grandson here saw them." The boy nodded vigorously in agreement.

"Where?" she asked.

"Down in Nitinat," the Indian said. "The boy says they started screamin' and hollerin' in the water, then their boat exploded."

"Nitinat?" Ellie said. "What are you doing *here*? Victoria is closer." Even as she asked the question, Ellie knew the answer. Vancouver Islanders, those outside of Victoria and especially the Indians, preferred Alberni to the larger centers like Victoria or Nanaimo. "You treat us better," the Indians had often remarked. "At least, you treat us like people."

Ellie called inside for a pair of gurneys, then moved around the truck to look at the smaller man. She gasped at what she saw. His face, arms, torso had all been badly burned, but there was much more damage to the body than that. His skin, muscles, tendons, all of the soft tissue had begun to slough from the bones. The man was like a skeleton, draped in his own viscera. His equipment *had* been scorched; his drysuit and equipment had in several places melted into his flesh.

"You said this happened in the river?" Ellie asked the little boy. "They were screaming *before* their boat caught fire?"

The little boy nodded again. "Yes, missus," he said. Any further details were cut off by another bout of coughing.

"But you're okay?" she asked. More nodding.

"Do you think there was something in the water?" Ellie asked. "Something corrosive—like an acid, I mean?"

"I wasn't in the water," the boy said.

"You didn't get wet when you dragged them out?" Ellie asked the Indian.

"They weren't *in* the water," the Indian said. "Their boat run aground, and this here fella crawled right up onto the beach." Beside him, the little boy again nodded in agreement. He clutched at his grandfather's jacket and wiped his nose on it.

The gurneys arrived and Ellie coordinated the orderlies as they moved the divers out of the truck. The Indian had no idea who the men were, and neither carried any identification. As relayed to her, the site of the accident was left purposely vague by the Indian. "It was on reserve land. Our land" was all he would divulge.

The boy started coughing again. Ellie stooped and asked him to say "Ahhh." The boy complied, and Ellie shined her light into his mouth. The back of the boy's throat was extremely inflamed. "Since you're here, why don't you let us look at that, too?" she said. "Has he had this cough for long?" Ellie asked the grandfather.

"He wasn't sick before tonight," the Indian said.

"But the inflammation looks quite advanced—"

The Indian cut her off. "Missus, we got no insurance to stay here."

"What a coincidence." Ellie smiled. "After tonight, neither do I. So let's have a look at your boy anyway."

Behind them, the nurse called out that the diver had been prepped for examination. Ellie referred the boy to the attending nurse and told the Indian she would get back to him as soon as possible. "As soon as possible" was also too prevalent in her dialogue with patients. She knew that, in all likelihood, the boy and his grandfather would be long gone by the time a sore throat made it to the top of the ER's queue.

"We'll do what we can," she said. "That's all I can promise." More boilerplate.

In the end, for the third time in a week, Dr. Ellie Bridges found she could do very little. The smaller man was likely dead before he was loaded into the truck. The larger man made several painful attempts to breathe once he was brought into the ER but was dead within minutes. If Ellie had needed to administer CPR, she would have had a difficult time of it. Most of the man's mouth, throat, and thoracic cavity had been eaten away.

The attending nurse, a large, pillowy woman with thirty years' experience, suddenly burst into the examining room. "It's the boy," she said.

Ellie bolted down the corridor, following the nurse. They reached the boy just as an orderly set him on an examining table. The boy was racked with coughs and strained against an apparent constriction in his lungs. The next savage cough produced a spray of blood, and the boy doubled over in the fetal position. The boy's grandfather wore a mask of fear and concern. What was happening?

Ellie found she knew, and she didn't know. Her unit set to work on the boy.

Over the next hour, they would all relive the horror of Caitlin Fulton. With the same result.

It was after 5:00 A.M. when Ellie finally shuffled back toward the staff room, rolling her head from side to side in an unsuccessful attempt to relieve the muscles in her neck. She found the coffeepot still on its burner and the last half ounce of caffeinated sludge someone had carelessly left to cook onto the bottom of the yellowed glass bulb. Instead, she fished some change out of her pocket, plunked it into the vending machine, and pressed button C2. A Snickers bar dropped into the machine's gullet, and she fished it out like a strand of June Cleaver pearls from an oyster.

A pair of nurses sat at one table, gossiping and complaining about the latest hospital staffing regulations. Ellie couldn't help but overhear them begin to edit the tone and context of their ruminations as soon as Ellie, a doctor, entered the room. Not wanting to participate or be reminded of what was wrong with the medical profession, Ellie merely said good morning to the women as she peeled the wrapper off her chocolate bar, then stepped back into the corridor. Finding herself alone, she slumped into the nearest available chair.

No more tonight, she prayed silently. *Please, no more* . . .

ER physicians learned early not to dwell on the one that got away. To look for some miraculous abatement in the flow of blood, vomit, human suffering, and unbridled stupidity that flowed through this place on a nightly basis was only futile. But the sight of those two divers flayed open on the attending table before her, the third incident in less than a week, was too much to simply block out. It was horrifying.

Now she would remember nine. Ten, if she counted the second diver, the one who was DOA. The Indian had driven at least fifty miles out of his way to deliver the divers and the boy directly to her on her last shift.

She felt cursed.

She thought again about Mark Junckers. And about Caitlin Fulton. And now the little boy. What were the odds there? Three catastrophic respiratory and neurological failures in the same ER, under the same doctor, in the same week. All of them in otherwise healthy people, two of them children? What could do that? What could kill so suddenly and catastrophically, yet apparently select its victims?

The Fultons had been unaffected. Junckers's friends from the marine station had been fine. The old Indian was the healthiest of them all, even though he had carried the divers to his truck. Their blood was all over him, yet it was the boy, a bystander at best, who had gotten sick.

He wasn't sick before tonight, the Indian had said about the boy. Not sick before he watched "the screaming in the water." If it was a chemical spill or some kind of virus, why was the grandfather unaffected? What on earth could it be?

Forget about practicing medicine. Forget about diagnoses and cures. Forget about keeping a patient *alive,* for God's sake. Ellie Bridges's life had taken a sharp departure from reality—even her interpretation of reality. Where could she turn for clarification? Her colleagues? The RCMP? Don Redmond? Ellie couldn't imagine there being an expert to consult about something this strange, this mortifying.

That shift, she decided she wanted out. For the first time in her life, she wanted to run away and hide from something instead of trying to make sense of it.

She wanted to run but had absolutely nowhere to go.

She closed her eyes for a moment, then, fearing she would fall dead asleep, stared instead at the fluorescent bulbs mounted in the ceiling. Each lighting panel was two-toned, with a bright, bluish fluorescent bulb installed in parallel to a pale orange, natural-light fluorescent. The rationale was to make the lighting in the hospital more natural, less like a 7-Eleven, yet still bright enough to see. They claimed it was more natural.

Nothing in this place seemed natural any longer.

She dropped her eyes to the community bulletin board on the wall across from her. For a moment her eyes remained unfocused, not seeing anything but a colorful collage of mixed paper. Then, one particular notice, printed on bright yellow paper and tacked over the top of several others, caught her eye.

BEACH CLOSURES IN THE BAMFIELD AREA?
7:00 P.M., AUGUST 19
VOLUNTEER FIRE DEPARTMENT HALL
COME LEARN THE FACTS!
COME SPEAK YOUR MIND!

10

The two days following the funeral were long and disappointing for Garner and Carol. They spent a total of twenty hours exploring the areas around Mills Peninsula and Grappler Inlet, looking for any sign of the Junkman's sea lions or any other carcasses. Wizard Islet, Sanford Island, and Helby Island all had at least some marine mammals occupying their coastal rookeries, though only an expert like Junckers could tell if their population was in any way depleted. Saunders Freeland helped them with their search for the first day before having to leave on a supply run to Vancouver. Charles Harmon stayed in his cabin, neither venturing outside nor calling for a boat to pick him up and deliver him to the marine station, as he usually did.

At the end of the second day of searching, Garner asked to use the radiophone in the assistant director's office. The space was small and crammed with files of every description, but it offered him some much-needed privacy as Garner called the marine operator and was patched through to the *Exeter*. McRee was on watch and answered the call from the ship's bridge.

"How did you make out with the *Maru*?" Garner asked.

"She's fine," McRee said. "Her owners sent a replacement crew out lickety-split. They got her powered up and sailed off over the horizon."

"That's it? No further information on the crew?"

"Nope. The ship was operational; it's just that there was no one left alive to run it." For all his lack of emotion, McRee could have been reading a prepared statement.

"Pete, you don't have to bullshit me," Garner said. "How can you just brush off what we saw out there?"

"Robertson doesn't want us to see anything," McRee said. "NOAA doesn't either. Screw the facts; turn the ship over to its owners and look the other way. Nobody owns the water out here, and no one's set up to police it. We can't afford to do anything but go back to business as usual."

"And you and Serg are still fine? Your health is fine?"

"Hell, yeah. Zubov's got the usual bug up his ass—in fact, the bug up his ass has a bug up *its* ass—but otherwise, we're fine. I think we're out of the woods of contagion, assuming we were ever there."

From Medusa's inexplicable failing to the sudden loss of the Junkman, it was as if the normal parameters of life and death had been thrown for a loop. There couldn't possibly be a plausible connection between Medusa's electronic myopia, Junckers's "heart attack," and whatever had happened aboard the *Maru,* but the ironic concurrence of these things unnerved him. The sailors had probably succumbed to severe *E. coli,* staphylococcus, or salmonella poisoning; the Junkman probably did just have a freak heart attack, though the suggestion it had anything to do with drugs was utterly ridiculous. Charles Harmon's only contribution to his stepson's funeral was to ensure that the body was returned to Bamfield and buried quickly, without further comment or investigation. That in itself might have been disconcerting, were it not the selfsame way Harmon dealt with any emotional issue. Conversely, it was Garner's tendency to formulate patterns from apparent chaos that now went into overdrive. Stretching that ability to the limit suggested daunting odds and, more frightening, a scale of impossible magnitude. The pieces were still scattered, and so, too, was Garner's confidence.

Garner could hear Robertson direct a question to McRee from the background. The mate excused himself to answer his captain. The radio clicked, then went silent as Garner waited. He recalled the sight of the *Exeter* next to the *Sato Maru,* both ships moored on an endless blue carpet. He imagined the *Exeter* now cruising for home, headed due east along the JGOFS Line P on the fringe of the Alaska gyre. He picked up a pen, found a blank piece of paper, and sketched a rough map of the area and its currents from memory. Anything in the water where the *Exeter* met the *Sato Maru* could easily be carried to shore by the local surface currents. Countless millions of salmon did exactly that each year as they returned from the sea to their coastal rivers to spawn, but Papa was much farther west. Papa was hundreds of miles from Bamfield, with nothing but open water in between. A lot could happen to a salmon, or a freighter for that matter, over that kind of distance.

When McRee returned, Garner asked, "What do you suppose the odds would be of a contaminant from the *Maru* reaching the mainland? Anywhere in the Pacific Northwest, I mean."

"You mean something like an oil spill?"

"Something like that, yeah."

"Landing where you are? From Papa?" McRee asked. "Virtually zero."

"But if she was coming from Seattle . . ."

"Well, then it'd depend where she lost the contaminant. But even if it were over the shelf, the surface currents would take it south or north, or to the bottom. Either way, there'd be massive dilution. It would have to be a motherly big amount, and even then I doubt you'd ever detect it."

"Yeah, that's what I'd figure, too," Garner said, not completely closing the issue in his own mind. "Is Sergei there? I'd like to ask him about my sampling."

"He's here somewhere," McRee said. "Hang on." Garner waited as he was patched through to his friend in the *Exeter*'s main lab.

"The good news is, Medusa's working fantastic. Better than I've ever seen," Zubov said. "The bad news is, you're gonna lose your data set for this cruise. I've gone over the numbers and you haven't got enough stations to compare with last year."

The news troubled Garner, but it wasn't unexpected. He'd gambled on taking Medusa out to sea again before she was ready—gambled, hell, he had to go; the calendar had forced his hand—and lost an entire summer season.

"And the other bad news is," Zubov continued, "your 'abiotic stasis' is gone, at least according to Medusa. Closed over completely. Good-bye, *Science,* hello, *World Weekly News.*"

"So we'll never know if it had something to do with the *Maru,*" Garner said.

"Or if it was ever there at all," Zubov said. "After you left I took some of the *Maru*'s bilge water and ran it through Medusa to find out."

"And you found nothing?"

"Actually, I found *everything.* Diesel fuel, food waste, fecal coliform bacteria, leachate from her cheap copper plating. The hull of that pig was like a floating landfill."

"But still no side effects with you or Pete?"

"Nothing. Certainly nothing like we saw with the crew of the *Maru.*"

"Oxygen levels? Nitrate?"

"Oxygen, nitrate, pH, salinity—all normal," Zubov confirmed.

Garner winced. The "phenomenon" they had witnessed had to be a problem with Medusa after all. Garner looked at the crude map he had drawn, trying to process everything he had heard in the past two hours. Frustrated, he scribbled over the diagram and tossed his pen aside. "When do you think you'll be back?" he asked Zubov.

"That depends on Christopher," Zubov grumbled, mentioning one of the researchers on board who was known for being inconveniently temperamental. "He wants to do some repeat sampling at some of the inshore stations. Since we got nothing off the shelf, Robertson figures it might be worth his while. We haven't got another cruise scheduled for a month, so the only thing we're missing back home is downtime."

"A week, then?"

"A week. Maybe five days till we're back in Everett. Why, do you miss us?"

"I miss my girl. Schizophrenia or not, I could have some work for her here."

Zubov chuckled. "You don't know when to give up, do you? You can't launch Medusa from that little rowboat of yours."

"That's right, I can't. I'd need a ship like the *Exeter*. In fact, I'd need the *Exeter*."

"At ten thousand bucks a day, who's gonna bankroll it?"

"What if I said Bob Nolan?" Garner asked.

"What if I said you're full of shit?"

"Maybe I am. Nolan hasn't shown his face around here yet, and I get the feeling Carol doesn't particularly miss him."

"Trouble in paradise?" Zubov said.

"Indifference in paradise, I suspect," Garner said. "I'm trying not to care whether they're actually in love, but it would be nice to get some Nolan dough behind this little beach party."

"When are you opening the keg?" Zubov asked. "Do you need cups?"

It was Garner's turn to laugh. "Just get Medusa back here in one piece in case we need her."

"Don't worry," Zubov said. "I'll get your baby home from the prom by midnight, with her panties still in place."

"You've been out to sea too long, Serg," Garner warned.

"You should try it sometime," Zubov said. "The boys and I are worried you might be going soft on us."

Garner thought of the *Exeter* cruising through thirty-foot swells out of sight of any land and compared it to the suffocating stacks of paper surrounding him in the darkened office. "Tell them they're probably right. The first sign of senility is when you start seeing holes in the ocean."

That night, Garner did what he always did when a puzzling new question took hold of him, germinating in his mind, gaining real estate in his cerebellum until he could think of nothing else: he went to the library. The library at the marine station was small but highly specialized, housing a collection of tomes dedicated to marine science and ranks of file cabinets filled with papers and abstracts detailing the geology, biology, chemistry, and meteorology of Barkley Sound and the Pacific Rim National Park. The facility was quietly efficient, constructed and stocked—at least in its infancy—by the vehement demands of Charles Harmon. Carol and the Junkman often joked that Harmon only lobbied for the library to be built in order to have a safe harbor in which to house his own literary discards. Over the years, as the bookcases, tabletops, stairwells, and floors in Harmon's cabin filled to overflowing, the number of "acquisitions" ferried over to the library had increased accordingly. This was the house of knowledge built by Father Charles, and Garner felt it in the pages of every dusty tome.

Two hours later, Carol found Garner sitting at one of the large round study tables next to the wall of picture windows that looked out over the sound. She had spent every free moment since arriving in Bamfield talking to her brother's friends and acquaintances, trying to collect sentimental details about how the Junkman had spent his last few weeks. Since their argument with Harmon, Carol had been instrumental in coordinating graduate students, technicians, support staff, or anyone else who could spare a few hours into a series of impromptu field-study teams. When there continued to be nothing obviously wrong with the fish or marine-mammal stocks in Barkley Sound, she ordered them to begin taking water samples. So far, all had come back empty-handed, but only a fraction of the sound's extensive coastline had yet been searched.

She looked exhausted as she entered the library, hands stuffed deep into the pockets of her field jacket.

"How goes the battle?" Garner asked.

Carol slumped into a chair across from him and pulled a stack of flyers from her inside pocket. She dropped the sheaf of bright yellow paper on top of Garner's handwritten notes.

" 'Come speak your mind'?" Garner chuckled as he read the bulletin aloud. "That won't take long for some of the minds around here."

"Tell me about it," Carol sighed.

"A little premature, don't you think?" Garner asked. "I mean, lacking any more evidence . . ."

"We're lacking *time* as well," Carol said. "And resources. And information. Right now I don't care if we actually do close the beaches, I just

want to get everyone together in one room and find out what they've
been seeing out there. The commercial fishermen, the charters, anybody.
Everybody. See if anyone else has gone missing or turned up dead."

Garner smiled. "Sounds like you've taken a page out of Honest Bob
Nolan's Big Book of Marketing."

"When in doubt, rouse them out," Carol said. "I've got Mark's roommates sticking these flyers in every bait shop, convenience store, and gas
station between here and Nanaimo." Garner could almost visualize the
battle map Carol had no doubt drawn for her fact-finding campaign.
Bulleted lists. Media outlets. Tapping the pulse of the local fishing community. The motivation of grief and frustration was a tool she had come
to use expertly. "What about you?" she asked, nodding at the splash of
two dozen books and research journals opened on the table between
them. "Find anything?"

"I found too much," Garner said, rubbing his eyes and stretching the
kinks out of his back. "They've got monographs and textbooks here I
can't even get in Seattle. Half of them were donated by Charles, and the
rest were written by him." Garner patted a thick, comparatively new-
looking tome at his elbow. "This is his book on practically every recorded red tide this area has ever seen. It goes back to Captain Cook's
records in the late seventeen hundreds, through the first Spaniards to
land here and the reports of the Catholic missionaries, right up to that incident in Kingcome Inlet two years ago. I think of us speculating on the
potential for a red tide right now, then I see this book and think, 'Man,
it's *done*. Find something else to worry about.' He documents over a hundred accounts of local shellfish poisoning or toxic plankton blooms, but
not a single victim with Mark's symptoms."

"Sounds like you're letting that World Renowned Authority thing
creep back into the equation. If Professor Charles Harmon says the sky is
blue, then so it shall be."

Garner studied his ex-wife's expression. "Maybe that's preferable to
clouding the issue just to prove your point in a family dispute." Despite
her marketing savvy, Garner wasn't convinced that the furor of a public
lynching was yet in order.

"That doesn't sound like the young hell-raiser I married."

"No, it's more like the cautiously apathetic pain in the ass you divorced."

"In a word, yeah."

"We still have to stick to the evidence we have, which isn't much. After two full days of looking, we haven't even located the last place Mark visited, much less a dead animal or even a water sample with elevated phytoplankton levels."

"We will."

"Maybe so, but it won't be a bloom of any of the usual microorganisms that can bloom in this area and cause health problems. *Pseudonitzschia* produces domoic acid, a potent neural disrupter that sometimes affects humans or sea birds." *Affects* was an understatement, and they both knew it. A cumulative concentration of domoic acid from tainted shellfish could cause irreversible brain damage; *Pseudonitzschia* was, in fact, one of the toxic diatom species Garner's model had predicted in the San Juans. "*Heterosigma* can paralyze fish, and *Chaetoceros* or *Dictyocha* might shred gill tissues, but the water conditions just aren't right for those species to bloom. *Vibrio* bacteria can cause food poisoning from undercooked oysters, but the symptoms aren't nearly this pronounced. *Alexandrium* has been known to cause paralytic shellfish poisoning, but if anything, its levels are lower than usual out there." He nodded toward the large windows overlooking the sound, now showing only a reflection of the library itself as darkness had fallen outside.

"You said there'd never been anything causing these symptoms recorded here. . . ." Carol chewed at her lip as she leafed through her father's book. "But what about other parts of the world? Could all this be from the introduction of an exotic species here?"

"Of course. No question, with all the international shipping traffic. And people can fly halfway around the world in a few hours."

"So of all the things you know of, anywhere in the world . . . ?"

"Some of Mark's symptoms are consistent with those of *Pfiesteria piscicida* or *piscimortua,* a nasty little dinoflagellate found in estuaries on the East Coast of the United States."

Carol's eyes glazed over. *"Pfiesteria piscicida?"*

"A single-celled microbe. A protist with a pair of long, thin filaments used to move itself through the water."

"Is it a plant or an animal?" she asked.

"A little of both. They have chloroplasts, like a plant, but respond to other stimuli like an animal. Like most dinos, it's a tough little bug—a thick, armored cell wall when it's moving around and a dormant cyst stage when things get too rough. Given a warm, stable water mass, they can multiply to astounding levels. About five dozen species are known to be lethal, if encountered in sufficient amounts."

"Sufficient amounts?"

"A few hundred million cells per liter. Some species of dino produce neurotoxins ten thousand times more lethal than cyanide. A single concentrated drop could kill a human being."

"And even though it's only found in the Atlantic, this *Pfiesteria* is a candidate for what happened to Mark?"

"I didn't say that," Garner said. "You asked me to throw common sense away."

"I've never heard of *Pfiesteria* before."

"Neither had most people until the late eighties. Fisheries biologists had been tracking fish kills along the shores of the mid-Atlantic states for years and attributing them to low levels of dissolved oxygen. Then a couple of researchers in the southeast U.S. isolated and described *Pfiesteria*. It represented not only a new species but a new genus and taxonomic family. Actually, it's probably been there for hundreds or thousands of years, but nobody took an interest in it. It was overlooked or misidentified in plankton samples, known by another name or an undescribed species complex. But for now it's *Pfiesteria*."

"What makes it so special?"

"Well, for one thing, it produces at least two different kinds of toxin. The first is water soluble and acts as a powerful neurotoxin to paralyze its prey. It can even become an acidic aerosol, suspended in the air. The second is fat soluble and corrodes the connective tissue of the flesh while lowering the prey's resistance to disease and infection."

"Like AIDS?"

"Like that, but in a far more aggressive way. What's more frightening is that while most dinos secrete these toxins as metabolic by-products or as a defense against predators, *Pfiesteria* seems to be a predator itself. With the right stimulus, it can come out of its dormant cyst stage and actually attack its prey."

"Which is what?"

"Fish, mainly. Menhaden, pike. Some people have attributed *Pfiesteria* to more than a billion fish deaths in North Carolina alone."

"But why now, all of a sudden?"

"The coastal waters are becoming more polluted with runoff from local industry—fertilizer and animal waste from hog and chicken farms, mostly. The nutrient levels are going through the roof, which makes for ideal bloom conditions. The warm, stagnant waters of Carolina estuaries provide an ideal breeding ground for beasties like *Pfiesteria,* but it's been found from Delaware to the Gulf of Mexico. Why not? It's all affected by the Gulf Stream. There's certainly enough pollution on the Eastern Seaboard to keep it fed, and enough shipping traffic to move the seed beds around."

"And now you think it's come here?"

Garner held up his hand. "I'm *not* saying that. I'm saying *Pfiesteria* is a good candidate for what happened to Mark, but he hasn't been to the East Coast in at least ten years—"

"About as long as he's laid off drugs," Carol said sarcastically.

"—and I would guess it's virtually impossible for *Pfiesteria* to survive here. For one thing, the water's too cold. We're a long way north, and the water is well mixed, too. I don't have to tell you that high levels of pollution aren't a factor here, either."

"We also know last year's El Niño still has the sea surface temperature much higher than usual."

"That's true, and *theoretically,* yes, if somehow some *Pfiesteria* had found its way here in the past few months, then *theoretically,* yes, it might survive."

"You don't think so?"

"No, I don't. For one thing, *Pfiesteria* attacks fish. It responds to fish-oil secretions in the water, suffocates them, then strips their flesh to the bone. If *Pfiesteria* had become established here, we wouldn't have to be searching the coastline. The fishermen would have discovered it long ago."

Carol began to protest this assumption, and Garner stopped her again. "Secondly, even though Mark's description of the sea lions sounds similar to *Pfiesteria* damage, there's absolutely no evidence that *Pfiesteria* is lethal to marine mammals."

"What about humans?"

"Nothing conclusive. When the *Raleigh News and Observer* broke the story about *Pfiesteria*, it produced the expected public hysteria. Everyone from Chesapeake watermen to lab technicians began coming forward with reports of lesions that wouldn't heal, memory loss, trembling, and other neurological disorders."

"Let me guess: the tourism office convinced the public it was all a mass hallucination."

"To a point, yes. To make matters worse, when fish were removed from the area, the *Pfiesteria* disappeared as well. With the culprit gone, most of the illnesses reported in the short term were thought to be psychosomatic. However, years later, there are some legitimate health effects that can't be explained by anything but exposure to *Pfiesteria*."

"So it's still possible—"

"No, Carol, it isn't. Mark may have had similar symptoms, but we don't know that. He didn't mention any dead fish and probably wouldn't have a clue about seeing evidence of *Pfiesteria*. Most importantly, whatever he did come across killed him within hours. *Pfiesteria* attacks—humans, at least—very slowly, over a much longer interval. Days, at least. Months in some cases. If something in the water did kill Mark, it acted more like a filovirus or morbillivirus. Like Marburg or some kind of Ebola of the sea. If *that's* really what's out there, we wouldn't have to look very hard to see the effects."

Carol was clearly distressed at the lack of a culprit on which to focus her anger. "Stick to the evidence at hand, right?"

"Until we find those carcasses, or others, yes."

"So humor me. Why don't we look again in the morning?" She leaned across the table and took his hand in hers, holding on to him, as if trying to stave off another wellspring of grief.

"Hey? Do you feel lucky?" she asked after a moment.

"Yeah, I do," Garner said. And sitting alone in the silent library with his once-precious love, he did.

11

"The smallest organisms in the world are among the most deadly," Charles Harmon said as he paced, slowly and haltingly, across the makeshift stage in the Bamfield fire hall. "I know because I've seen them and I've seen their effects. I've been studying them for more than fifty years."

Standing before the crowd assembled in rows of folding chairs, Harmon was completely at ease. A mixture of faces—ranging from the eldest of the town's fishermen to the scrubbed, cherubic expressions of the first-year coeds from the marine station—hung on his every word. Their eyes flicked only occasionally to the world-renowned professor's face as he described the images projected on a large screen behind him. Narrating with practiced ease, Harmon moved smoothly through a seemingly unending series of deadly, bizarre, yet elegantly beautiful microorganisms, from marine viruses to bacteria, diatoms, and dinoflagellates.

Despite Carol's protests, Bouchard had insisted that Harmon's lecture be positioned to lead off the public debate, evidently hoping to quickly short-circuit any "unfounded" public concern. It was an effective maneuver; after the dazzling array of photographs and micrographs, it would be doubly hard for the audience to perceive any sort of threat from these minuscule creatures, especially when accompanied by a lack of physical evidence beyond the Junkman's death.

Harmon showed a table listing every toxic plankton bloom on record in the Barkley Sound region, then systematically dismissed the species involved as irrelevant to the current concerns. He punctuated this point by marking a large X in the air with the tip of his cane.

"So much for the station distancing itself from the issues at hand," Garner muttered to Carol.

"If there's going to be any disinformation spread here, you can bet that Bouchard wants to be doing the spreading," Carol replied.

Harmon finished his lecture and thanked the audience for their time and attention with a warmth he seemed to reserve only for passing strangers. As the lights came up, he took a seat at a long conference table facing the room. He was flanked by Bouchard and Brad Davis, the station's assistant director and a visiting professor from the Scripps Institute of Oceanography. Joining them at the table was the head of the local fishermen's union and the town council, as close to an elected mayor as the town possessed. There was no local constabulary and, beyond the Coast Guard, usually no need for one. Garner and Carol had taken seats in the front row of the audience. For all their apparent interest, the audience seemed a little intimidated by the master academician and sat mainly toward the back of the room. Like Carol, they were here to see what kind of information there was to share but had little of their own to contribute to the discussion.

Carol recognized two reporters and a columnist from the Port Alberni newspaper in attendance. She had specifically contacted them to raise awareness about the hearing. Though alternative opinions were conspicuously absent among the panelists facing the room, the audience included a majority representation of the Bamfield town council, the National Parks Service, and several commercial and charter fishermen. Carol also recognized several of the local Ohiat and Salish Indians. If anything unusual had been washing ashore, they would be among the first to know. She smiled at the effectiveness of a single ream of yellow paper flyers. All the players had been brought to this single room, and on the basis of the information raised, she hoped, some valid recourse would be revealed.

Either that or this social powder keg needed only a match for the fireworks to begin.

Harmon first addressed a question asked by one of the reporters, his voice rumbling over the table microphone set before him.

"I can tell you without hesitation that we do not have the conditions for a red tide this season," Harmon said, his tone as flat and reassuring as that of a commercial airline pilot. "I've had my graduate students out sampling the beaches the entire length of the peninsula. The surface temperature is a bit high—"

"What about that?" the reporter asked. "There are reports that the sound is still being influenced by that unusually strong El Niño event last year."

Harmon released a slow, patronizing chuckle. "There you go with El Niño, the latest *cause de rigueur* of all meteorological phenomena."

Bouchard shared Harmon's amusement. "In the past year I've seen 'El Niño' blamed for everything from the availability of lettuce to the price of four-wheel-drives."

"Although the water temperature is a little high, the salinity and dissolved oxygen levels are completely normal for this time of year," Davis said.

"According to the Pacific Weather Office, Barkley Sound has been affected by all three El Niño events in the past ten years," the reporter said. "Three events, with each one stronger than the last."

"We've had El Niños before—a dozen since fifty-one—and we'll have them again," Bouchard said. "We have detailed records going back thirty years. Some are stronger, some are weaker, but no algal blooms have been correlated with them in this area."

Garner knew this to be true, in part. While algal blooms were rarely correlated with elevated water temperature alone, prolonged calm conditions and hot weather *combined* with a general warming of the surface waters provided ideal bloom conditions. "And that is very much what has happened this summer," Garner said to the room. "According to Environment Canada, only one significant storm front has passed through Barkley Sound in the past month."

"Yes, two weeks ago," Harmon said. "I keep a rain gauge at my cabin and record the weather and tide conditions daily. These 'conditions' you suspect have something to do with a red tide began *after* that storm, when the stable conditions had assumedly been broken."

"What about that?" the second reporter raised his hand. "What about the reports that several marine mammals had washed ashore near here, apparently killed by an unknown marine pathogen?" The question was remarkably learned and forcefully delivered for a small-town newspaper reporter. From the corner of his eye, Garner caught a sly grin slip across Carol's lips.

Bouchard fielded the question. "We've had no confirmed reports of that. Once again, all the water samples we've taken have been completely normal, especially with regard to dissolved oxygen, which we would expect to be depleted during a bloom."

"*Dissolved* oxygen levels are only going to affect water-breathing organisms," Garner spoke up again. Bouchard, like most marine biologists, tended to adopt a kind of tunnel vision toward the organism alone. The organism's environment—various water properties and how they were interrelated—rarely crept into the discussion.

"Besides," Carol added, "as mammals, the sea lions would be taking their oxygen from the air. Whatever killed them was most likely in the water."

"I see the answer to your question depends on which 'Dr. Harmon' you're asking," the elder Harmon responded to the reporter, grimacing in Carol's direction as he did so. "I concur: these reports appear to be completely unfounded. No carcasses have been found."

"Marine mammals are protected in the park," Bouchard said. "If anyone discovered any carcasses, they should have reported them to Fisheries and Wildlife."

"What about poachers?"

"What about the *fish,* fer chrissakes," one of the fishermen boomed from his reclined position on a frail-looking folding chair. "I hear all this talk about whether the water is safe, and it seems to me the best way to know that is the same as it's ever been: look at the fish stocks."

A second fisherman spoke up. "Exactly. I ain't seen nothing wrong with the catches this year."

"And you aren't *gonna* see anything wrong with them," said one of the town council members. "Not with the peak of the charter fishing season three weeks away." Several members of the audience applauded this sentiment.

"That's an extremely dangerous philosophy," Garner said.

"August and September alone are responsible for more than two-thirds of this area's annual income from tourism," the council member said. "If you close that down, most folks in this town aren't going to survive the winter, financially."

"And what if there *is* something out there?" Garner said. "What if there's some kind of toxic microbe out there—a *Chaetoceros* or a *Heterosigma* bloom, a *Vibrio* bacterium, or something more deadly than we've ever seen? If the salmon run goes through it, or it contaminates a shellfish bank, the entire fishery could be wiped out."

"But we're *not* seeing any effects on fish stocks," Bouchard said. "And we haven't seen any cases of shellfish poisoning."

"I have," said a woman's voice from the back of the room.

Garner turned and could just glimpse the petite woman who stepped forward. Even from his position across the room, he could see that her eyes were the bluest he had ever seen, framed by a mane of long, curly hair swept over one shoulder of her denim jacket. It looked as though she had arrived late. She was short of breath and a healthy flush glowed on her smooth cheeks. But she wasn't in the slightest bit embarrassed or apologetic for her interjection. If she was a stranger to Bamfield and its denizens, the set of her jaw didn't show it.

"Who are you?" Bouchard said for the benefit of the room.

"My name is Ellie Bridges," Ellie began. "I'm a doctor in Port Alberni." Then, as if it could not be more obvious, she added, "I'm here to find out what the hell is going on out there."

———

For the next fifteen minutes, Ellie held the crowd of thirty people transfixed as she recounted her experience with Caitlin Fulton, Mark Junckers, the abalone divers, and the Indian boy. As she relayed the information, the condition of these patients and their symptoms, Carol hung on Ellie's every word. For his part, Charles Harmon showed less interest than boredom. Carol shot her father an angry look that said, *Shame on you.* His dispassionate return conveyed, *What difference does drama make at this point?* Even as she spoke, Ellie noticed this silent exchange. The others in the room were apparently too impressed or too intimidated by Harmon's obvious scientific knowledge to interfere. A possible exception was the oceanographer from Friday Harbor, who, despite the commotion, had not escaped her notice.

Ellie finished her impromptu lecture by pulling a folded piece of paper from her jacket pocket and holding it up for all to see. "This is a letter from the little girl's father. It's part of a lawsuit now attempting to charge me with negligence and malpractice. At first I couldn't believe it, but now I don't know what to believe. We've got people dying of symptoms I've never seen before. Symptoms that no doctor I know has ever encountered. I'm here to find out if anyone in this room has."

Once again, it was Garner's turn to speak out. "Six days ago, I was on a research ship that found a Japanese freighter adrift at sea. All fourteen men on board were dead, from apparent food poisoning. We didn't see the kind of ulcerations Dr. Bridges has just described, but the stomach and respiratory disorders sound quite similar. The lone survivor said that whatever it was, it killed the men within twenty-four hours."

From where she stood, Ellie's eyes again found Garner's in the crowd as he relayed what he had seen. It was the first hint that there were other victims. The first suggestion that she wasn't imagining things. Garner had seen the same horrors and was willing to believe her. He exuded a raw confidence that gave Ellie her first feeling of hope.

"If this 'thing' killed everyone so quickly, then why was there a survivor?" Harmon asked, breaking the unspoken connection between Garner and Ellie.

"I don't know," Garner admitted. "It may have been because the

crewman avoided the others and kept to himself. He was locked up for
days outside the ship. He didn't share their food. He was also overweight
with a larger body size than the others."

This also struck a chord with Ellie. She thought of the two children
who had been so racked with symptoms and the smaller of the two abalone divers, the one who had the flesh virtually stripped from his bones.
Whatever this thing was, it killed smaller individuals first.

A concerned murmur had begun to spread among the crowd, and
Harmon tapped on the head of the microphone with his pencil to draw
their attention. "Mr. Garner, you said this freighter was at sea?" Garner
nodded. "Where exactly was that?"

"Downrange of Weather Station Papa, about six hundred miles out."

"Six hundred miles out," Harmon repeated. "Across open sea." He
turned his attention to Ellie. "And your patients came from Nitinat—the
divers and the Indian boy—and somewhere around here—my stepson,
correct?"

Ellie said it was, then admitted she had not found out where the
Fultons had been camping, but suspected it was near the Pacific Rim National Park.

"And you expect us to blindly accept that these cases—spread across
hundreds of miles of open ocean and fifty miles of broken shoreline—are
all related?"

"I only said the symptoms were suspiciously similar. . . ." Ellie said.

"Confusion, irregular heartbeat, slurred or incapacitated speech,
numbness, respiratory failure, that sort of thing?" Harmon offered.

"Yes."

"The same kinds of symptoms associated with stroke, heart attack,
even hypothermia?"

"Yes."

"And in my stepson's case, consistent with a ventricular fibrillation,
which is what you put in your report," Harmon said.

"Yes," Ellie admitted. She could sense another meeting with Redmond coming on.

"What about the blistering?" Garner said, coming to her defense.

"She said the skin had practically liquefied on their bones. And the lesions she mentioned sound similar to what Mark said he found on the sea lions."

Harmon's eyes focused on Garner. "I said these cases are too far apart to be related to a toxic algal bloom." To him, there had suddenly ceased to be anyone else in the room. "And if you are ready to assert, Mr. Garner, that a species of toxic dinoflagellate somehow crossed hundreds of miles of open ocean, killing some and sparing others, then vanishing into oblivion, then I would love to hear your estimation of the species responsible."

Garner had no answer.

"Dr. Harmon is right," Bouchard suddenly interjected. "While superficially these cases may appear similar, I think it is unreasonable to start throwing them all together in the same stew pot." He glanced in Carol's direction. "Perhaps that is one of the problems with promoting these kinds of discussions without substantive proof."

Carol fumed. "What do you call what we've just heard? Imagination?"

Bouchard was unruffled. "I'd call it a single unfortunate incident inconclusively linked to some kind of possible—and I emphasize *possible*—shellfish contamination," Bouchard said. "Even if someone walked in here right now with a rotten clam, that wouldn't justify canceling the entire fishing season or closing our coastal parks."

"Ray, I can't believe you're willing to overlook the potential for bioaccumulation of a potentially deadly pathogen," Carol said.

"In plain English, please," one of the reporters complained.

"What she's saying is, while the toxin may not be directly lethal to fish, there's the potential for it to accumulate in their tissues to such an extent that it becomes lethal to higher organisms," Garner explained.

"Meaning humans," the reporter pressed.

"Meaning that none of the deaths reported here has been linked to the consumption of contaminated fish," Charles Harmon said. "End of discussion."

"Can you really afford to use that kind of reasoning?" Garner said. "What if that seafood gets harvested—harvested by some of the hard-working people in this room—and those people start getting sick? What if that harvest gets to market and people begin dying by the hundreds or thousands?"

Brad Davis was eyeing the reporters with bureaucratic nervousness as he ignored Garner and addressed Ellie. "Dr. Bridges, I'm sure we all appreciate your dedication to your patients—"

"Nonsense," Harmon bellowed. "I'd say the potential for a malpractice suit, irrespective of the potential cause of death, adds a high degree of *subjectivity* to Dr. Bridges's attempt to raise public concern." He was acutely aware of the reporters as well, and he paused to let their scribbling pencils catch up. "I only hope your invited guests are wise enough to see that. From what I've witnessed here today, I might just file a malpractice suit of my own."

"That's a totally unfounded accusation," Garner shouted above the rising din.

"Is it?" Harmon said, once again training Garner in his sights. "Is it so unusual for a public health official to raise a public furor over some obscure but potentially hazardous condition, which just happens to lie within their own jurisdiction?" He waggled a knobby finger at Carol. "My own bloody son-in-law does it for a living!" In her seat, Carol reacted as if slapped. Her father continued, "And while I'm pointing fingers, Mr. Garner, I understand the National Science Foundation is about to cancel the ill-spent funds directed at your—what's it called?—'wonder ball'? I imagine that some timely and widespread attention like this could postpone that decision."

"What is your goddamn problem!" Carol suddenly exploded, glaring at Harmon. Garner moved quickly to intercept her as she lunged toward the stage. "Why are you all so apathetic about this!" she screamed. "People are *dying!"*

Carol's angry outburst and the sudden exchange of bitter mudslinging prompted Bouchard to call an impromptu coffee break. Garner looked in Ellie's direction several times as he tried to console Carol, wanting to speak with the doctor in private, but the doctor was surrounded by the reporters present. She spoke easily and openly with them, never once losing her composure. Pending malpractice suit or not, she seemed determined to relay exactly what she had seen as objectively as possible.

A few minutes later, the reporters approached Garner and Carol, plying them for technical details and asking a few more questions for clarification. As they ambled away with their notes, one of them said, "Remember that movie about the shark, where the hook line was: 'Just when you thought it was safe to go back into the water . . .'?"

"Yeah, now the fuckin' *water* can kill you," the second reporter remarked.

"An' you don't even have to be in it," the first agreed.

Carol overheard the exchange as well. "Looks like we had some effect on them," she said. "Even if they do bastardize the facts to sell papers."

"In the present case, that might not be such a bad thing," Garner said, then shook his head in resignation. "Remember when *sensational* meant something was really good?"

Carol saw her father yawn and flash his wristwatch at Bouchard. Bouchard responded by reconvening the group and calling for one more Q&A session, provided everyone kept their emotions in check. It was quickly apparent from the amount of fidgeting going on that no one had expected the hearing to proceed in this manner. Ellie's arrival had muddied the waters considerably, but for the most part, the audience seemed to hold on to its conviction that there was no cause for alarm.

The second reporter, the one who had obviously been primed by Carol, restarted the discussion. "Dr. Harmon—Charles—you just showed us how simple an organism a virus is—really nothing more than a strand of DNA with a protein coat and a tail to move it along. These diatoms and dinoflagellates don't seem much more complex."

"Yes, they are beautiful in their simplicity," Harmon agreed, apparently relieved that the lynch mob had stepped down from the gallows, at least for the moment. "An elegant, purely functional design virtually untouched by natural selection."

"Be that as it may," the reporter continued, unimpressed, "doesn't that make them even more susceptible to some kind of mutation?

We've seen you dismiss other species known to cause red tides in this area, but couldn't we be dealing with some kind of potent new strain here?"

"Oh *Jay-sus,* boy," one of the fishermen said, throwing up his hands. "That's all we need now. Some kinda superbooger in the water. Prob'bly dreamed up by th' Chinese or th' Russians just to put us out of business!" The belligerent outburst met a mixture of hoots and laughter throughout the room. Both Garner and Carol recognized the man's homegrown Bamfield dialect, a mishmash of prominent Newfoundland brogue, displaced slang from Holland or the Netherlands, chewing tobacco, and laziness.

"Another example of a completely unfounded public hysteria," Harmon said. "The real threat isn't in the natural potential of these microbes, but in how you, the media, use your sound-bite intellect to peddle it to the public."

The first fisherman rolled his head back and scoffed. "You academics really crack me up. It's all about keeping your research money coming in. But for what? We got our salmon. Our halibut. Who gives a rat's ass about *shell*fish out here? Or sea lions?"

"We do!" Carol said. "You've heard it here, from your own"—she stopped short of saying *kind*—"colleagues. The health of these stocks provides an indication of the health of the entire ecosystem."

"Well, then, I h'ain't seen any indicators. Not from where I'm standin' every day of da week. It's the commercial fish stocks that feed this town. If you all got a problem with your 'protected species,' then you deal with it yourselves."

Ellie glared at the man. "What will you do when your own children begin getting sick? What will you do if your fish start dying by the thousands?"

"I h'ain't seen none of that," the fisherman repeated. He jabbed his finger first at Bouchard, then at the Wildlife officer, who had so far added nothing at all to the dialogue. "But I *yam* tired of you people and your *theories,* tellin' me how much I can harvest. If dere's anything wrong wid my kids, it's that they're gonna starve to death if their daddy can't get out on da water."

"Ed is absolutely right," the union leader said. "The economic health of this entire area is determined by the quality of the water out there."

"Folks," Davis said. "We're on your side here. I come from Southern California, and believe me, pathogens of any kind are not the problem up here. As natural systems go, it's probably the most pristine temperate system on the planet."

"I agree," Harmon said. "This entire get-together is fueled by unfounded ecological hysteria." He looked again at the reporters with disdain.

Ellie was nearly trembling with anger. She couldn't believe how quickly she had been dismissed. "I have medical evidence of a young girl who died in my arms from gastric hemorrhaging," Ellie said to Harmon. "If what I've just heard is correct, your own son suffered massive hemorrhaging after handling contaminated marine mammals—"

"And virologists are now finding hemorrhage-inducing viruses in large mammals," Carol added. "Herpesviruses that can destroy an elephant from the inside out in a few days or outbreaks of bovine or porcine encephalitis."

"All speculative," Bouchard interjected, speaking clearly into the microphone. "We haven't found any evidence linking Dr. Junckers to marine pathogens." He fixed Ellie in his gaze. "And with all due respect, Dr. Bridges, neither have you."

"Maybe so, but my boy never did anything to deserve that." For the second time, a new voice entered the conversation. All turned to see an elderly Indian standing near the back of the room, his arms folded across his once-proud chest. Only Ellie recognized him.

"The men she's talking about were found by my grandson off the Kleekatch Rocks," the Indian continued. "He said he saw them blow up their boat trying to get away from something in the water. I believe him. I believe there was something very bad in the water there."

"Something," Harmon said, rolling his eyes. "A phantom. A killer microorganism unlike anything described by science."

"Since when does 'not described by science' mean that something can't exist?" Carol shot back.

"What happened to these men is not so different from a story carried by our people," the Indian continued. "It was passed down from the time of the first white settlements. One of your Roman Catholic missionaries fed some shellfish to the children, but it made them very sick. Many of them died. The rest of the Indians refused to eat it and forced the missionary out of the area."

"I am aware of that lore," Harmon said. "In fact, as a postdoctoral student I did an anthropological assessment of the account and attributed it to an outbreak of *Alexandrium* or *Pseudonitzschia*—I showed you the slides of them. These are species that can cause severe illness, particularly in small children, but the effects aren't lethal. Ulcerated skin is not at all consistent with either species."

"But would be consistent with a dino like *Pfiesteria*," Garner interjected. He pronounced the genus again—"Fis-*teer*-ee-ah"—and spelled it for the benefit of the reporters.

"Only if you're a fish," Harmon said. "And immersed in a stagnant estuary on the Eastern Seaboard." He shared a bemused look with Bouchard. "My goodness, we're really cleaning out the cabinet of Caligari today—from El Niño to killer viruses to *Pfiesteria*. What's next? Bigfoot?"

Bouchard couldn't resist the opportunity to interject. "While we appreciate the motivation of you people to 'think globally and act locally,' that does not mean taking everyone else's problems and dumping them here!" He laughed at his own comment, and several others in the room did as well.

Carol bristled at the director's tone. *You people.* Who the hell did that mean? Activists? Scientists? Bouchard was drawing battle lines that didn't even exist.

"Brock, *tell* him," Carol said to Garner.

The attention of everyone was suddenly drawn to a loud *clang!* from the back of the room. They turned again to the old Indian, who had picked up one of the thin metal chairs and slammed it against the concrete floor to regain the attention of the group.

"If I can *finish* my story . . ." the Indian said with steely resolve. "I will say, yes, I am certain these men found something in the water. Something that also made my grandson very sick. I took him with me to the hospital, and then he died. The doctors said every one of his internal organs was bleeding. They said parts of his brain had turned to liquid."

"That's right," Ellie said quietly.

"Was anyone else affected?" Harmon asked.

"We went back the next morning," the Indian continued. "We looked around, waded in the water, but we found nothing."

"Nothing," Harmon repeated, less convincing this time. "There, you see?"

Bouchard took the microphone once again. "Well, obviously this is disturbing news." He coughed nervously several times. "But if there are any health issues at stake, perhaps it should be of more concern to the Indians of Nitinat, not the fishermen here."

This raised a furor from several of the other Indians present. "What's the matter, Professor? Killings on reserve land don't interest you none, eh?"

"The potential for an outbreak of *Pfiesteria* there is equally remote," Harmon said. "And, scientifically, I would hope we've all learned something from Mr. Garner's little rain dance in the San Juan Islands in ninety-one." Harmon's use of *scientifically* was intended to jab Garner; the mention of *rain dance* as a slur purported to do the same to the Indians. Harmon was an equal-opportunity offender.

Bouchard leaned across the table toward the reporters. "He's talking about Mr. Garner's misdiagnosis of a harmful plankton bloom in Washington State. The beach closures cost the local economy a fortune, based entirely on his incorrect predictions."

"Thank you for encapsulating the event so succinctly," Garner said. "I was beginning to think the actual situation was more complicated than that."

"No more complicated than what we've got here," Bouchard said.

"Even if there were 'something in the water,' as it has so precisely been defined," Harmon said to Ellie, "you've just suggested it's a massive event, or several localized ones, involving a completely exotic species. The probability of that is infinitesimal."

"We have an old saying in environmental management, especially in

the ocean," Bouchard said with a placating smile: " 'The solution to pollution is dilution.' "

The first fisherman got to his feet, his rubber boots squeaking on the
polished cement floor. "Then it's settled. There's nothing out there hurt-
ing the fish, so we ain't closing nothing." He looked at the Indian who
had lost his grandson. "Sorry about your boy, mister, but it h'ain't happened around herebouts."

"That's so foolish," Ellie said. "You can't take the attitude that whatever you can't see can't hurt you."

The fisherman stopped and glared at her. "Listen, lady, my job is
dangerous enough. There's plenty enough I *can* see that's out to hurt me.
If it h'ain't the weather, it's the government and their quotas. If it h'ain't
that, it's the bank holding the title on my boat, or the guy next door with
a bigger boat who's gonna go out tomorrow whether or not you tell him
there's 'something in the water.' "

"Hear, hear," one of the town council members said, and several
voices in the audience agreed. A show of hands was called, and the motion to keep the fishing banks open was passed by a vote of thirty-nine to
four.

As the crowd began to file out of the room, the fisherman stepped
past Ellie. Pausing, he indicated David Fulton's letter, still clutched in
her hand. "Thanks for nottin', *Doctor*. You said your piece; now go
back to Alberni and leave us to making a living the only way we know
how."

Darkness had fallen by the time Garner, Ellie, and Carol left the fire hall.
They began walking back to the station as various vehicles dispersed
from the parking lot. Ellie explained that the rear axle of her Honda had
fallen off less than ten miles along the logging road from Port Alberni;
she'd had to hitchhike the rest of the way with the owner of the Bamfield
general store and was now stranded in town. As they walked, Carol offered Ellie a bunk for at least that night, and Garner said he would show
her around the station.

After a quarter mile, Bouchard pulled up behind them in one of the BMS pickup trucks. Charles Harmon was in the passenger's seat.

"Need a lift?" Bouchard called through the open window, indicating the open bed of the truck.

"Screw you, Ray," Carol hissed. Bouchard shrugged, and they watched the pickup pull away, its taillights disappearing around the next bend in the gravel road.

"Another hit for organized environmentalism," Carol said. "And I use the term 'organized' lightly. Unless the environmental movement can learn to wear a suit once in a while and coordinate its efforts, economics is going to win out every time."

Carol's sudden corporate posture surprised Garner. "If you're so interested in making a difference, why don't you drag some of Bob's resources up here and do it yourself?" he asked.

"I've *tried*!" Carol suddenly shouted. "I've phoned him every day. I've *told* him what we need up here, but—" She fell silent, once again stopping short of talking about her husband. "I've already asked him," she finished.

"Then ask a little nicer," Garner said.

"I've tried, but he's a businessman, too," Carol said. "The Nolan Group doesn't operate on IOUs."

Ellie tried to ease the tension by drawing a deep breath and gazing up at the surrounding trees. "It really is beautiful here," she said. "I suppose the isolation helps keep it that way."

"The isolation itself is nice, too," Carol said.

"At least for the first six weeks," Garner said. "After that, the comforts of civilization take on a Zen-like appeal. There's a reason why the hikers who finally get to this place are willing to spend six bucks for a cheeseburger."

"But the red tides are free," Ellie said.

"Depends who you ask," Carol grumbled.

"It sounds like you've been working in a war zone at the hospital," Garner said to Ellie. "Some of the symptoms you described sound like PSP—paralytic shellfish poisoning—or ASP—amnesic shellfish poisoning. But some of the symptoms don't. Maybe Charles is right. Maybe we are falling back on what we 'know' and looking for facts to fit our accusations. So far there's still no evidence of a harmful bloom."

"*But,*" Carol began, "if we could get more-specific information on these victims—autopsy reports, the exact time and location of possible exposure—then we might be able to determine whether we've got widespread contamination."

Garner winced at Carol's speculation. That was one thing Harmon *was* right about. If all the victims Ellie had seen and the crewmen on the *Sato Maru* were somehow linked by the same toxic conditions, that would mean thousands of square miles of the Pacific were contaminated. There would be no need to go looking for the symptoms; they would all be immersed in an aquatic pandemic of unimaginable proportions.

When they reached the marine station, Carol showed Ellie their cabin and the bunk she could use. Ellie thanked her for her hospitality and said she would probably try to find a ride back in the morning. She didn't even have a change of clothes with her and would have to arrange for the Honda to get towed back to Port Alberni.

Yet as pragmatic as she appeared to be, Ellie seemed to be making polite excuses, and Garner suspected that she was in no particular hurry to get back to the hospital. He convinced himself it was for purely therapeutic reasons that he invited Ellie for a moonlight cruise on the *Albatross,* though he sensed a deeper therapy in her cool blue eyes.

"Be careful of those moonlit cruises," Carol said to Ellie, giving her a friendly nudge. "That's how he collects wives." She was teasing, but a strain of jealousy was evident in her voice. She knew that her ex-husband was an expert sailor in the dark.

Ellie followed Garner down to the dock and helped him loosen the lines on the *Albatross.* Within minutes they were cruising past the main station and turning toward the Broken Group Islands in the middle of the sound. Garner couldn't help but notice the calm in Ellie's face as they crossed the water. She seemed to be enjoying herself tremendously, watching as thin wisps of cloud drifted across the moon. He realized that for the first time in weeks, maybe even months, he was enjoying himself as well.

"You seem to know your way around," Ellie said, watching the ease with which Garner navigated the sound.

"I've been coming out here since Carol and I started dating. At first it was to see Charles. Then Carol was studying the gray whales coming down from Alaska."

"You never caught that bug? Whales, I mean?"

"I guess I did, but there were other, more attractive bugs to be had. I was fascinated by how something as big as a whale could be supported entirely by something like zooplankton. So while Carol went off in search of the perfect whale song, I started puttering with plankton nets and bottles. Saunders helped me get started with the research that eventually led to my plankton sampler."

"Saunders?"

"Saunders Freeland, the station's research coordinator. He's down in Vancouver picking up some supplies, or the hearing would have *really* been a circus. It would have made it on pay-per-view. I can tell you, he'd have some choice words for Bouchard's cover-your-ass approach."

"So Saunders thinks there could be a toxic bloom out here, too?"

"I don't know," Garner said. "But if he ever gets it into his head, I guarantee we'll find one. He's a one-man support staff, from carpentry to boat repair, and even a little advice on molecular biology if you need it. Today we're thick as thieves; back then, I think he just felt sorry for me, left in the wake of the wonder woman of whales with nothing to do."

Ellie drew her hair back from around her face, retying her ponytail with practiced ease. "And what's the story between you and Carol now?" she asked.

Garner laughed at the abruptness of the question. "The story? I guess that would depend on whom you ask. Most of our friends would call our story *War and Peace*."

"At least it ended in peace, then, right?"

"She's doing well for herself. Being with Nolan gives her the stability she needs to do her work. She knows the bills will be paid, so she can concentrate on applying her research."

"I know a few starving artists who would dispute that," Ellie said. "They'd say if they ever sold a really expensive piece, something that really set them up for life, their creativity would just wither. Still and all, I guess it's a welcome dilemma."

"Carol's pretty good at staying focused. She could have had all the support in the world from Charles Harmon, but she refused to accept his view of the world. Nolan is a little more compromising, and less of a dictator than Charles."

"She looked furious at the hearing tonight," Ellie said.

Garner laughed again. "That's just her politics talking. Carol would never admit it, but she really likes pushing the buttons of guys like Bouchard and Charles as a means to whatever end she thinks will help save the planet."

Ellie withdrew for a moment, and Garner asked what was on her mind.

"Semantics," Ellie said. "I was thinking how—however we go about it—you, me, Carol, her husband, all of us do what we do under the banner of Saving the Planet or Making the World a Better Place—all capital letters. But the planet's been here for five billion years and probably will be for another five billion. It doesn't need saving; it'll survive whether we abuse it or not. We could consume the entire ozone layer, block out the sun, or replace the atmosphere with ammonia, and somehow, some kind of life would survive. Life always finds a way. So what we really mean to do is save a planet that's capable of sustaining *human* life and maybe some of our cuddly cousins at the top of the food chain. We want to preserve a planet that appeals to us, always assuming we were the ones meant to rule the roost."

Garner agreed, though he had never heard the sentiment expressed quite that way. "So much for nobility," he said.

"You don't think saving human lives is a noble pursuit?" Ellie asked.

"I do," Garner said. "I've just never been in the position to find out."

"I have," Ellie said. "But I'm still not sure I'd use the word *noble*."

Ellie fell silent again. She noticed a small brass plaque set into the boat's gunwale and traced her finger around its engraved lettering:

ALBATROSS—FRIDAY HARBOR, WASHINGTON
W. B. GARNER—OWNER & OPERATOR

"So, what's the 'W' stand for, Captain?" she asked.

"William," Garner replied. "After my father."

"And 'Brock'?"

"After Major-General Isaac Brock, leader of the Upper Canada forces in the War of 1812. He had fifteen hundred men to protect half a million Loyalists from the advancing American militia. Apparently a master tactician with no official government support but a ton of resourcefulness. He allied with Tecumseh's Indians, held the line against invasion from the south, and probably prevented a second War of Independence in the bargain. That's noble enough for me. Maybe even noble enough for William, too."

Garner noted Ellie's surprise at this sudden wellspring of obscure history. "Dad was a fanatical military buff," he explained.

"And you prefer Brock?"

"Dad was more of a military buff than a family buff." Garner shrugged, unwilling to elaborate. "I guess I try to distance myself from the association. Saunders is about the only one who ever calls me 'William' or 'Will' anymore."

"Why's that?"

"Mom passed away during my first year at Annapolis and I don't have any siblings. But Saunders figures a man should put up with his given name. He says if he had to go with *Saunders* his whole life, then *William* can't be half-bad." It was Garner's turn to reflect. "Then again, Saunders didn't know William. But I suppose it's one way he could substitute for the real thing."

"Sounds like it worked," Ellie mused.

"Hell, he could call me *Saunders* if he wanted to," Garner admitted. "At least, he's earned it." Even in the near darkness, Ellie could see the appreciation in Garner's eyes.

Eventually, they cruised back to the station. The water was flat calm under the hull of the *Albatross,* and her topside was cast in the light of a breathtakingly clear moon. "It's a beautiful night," Ellie said. "Can we stay out here for a few minutes?"

Garner agreed and switched off the engine. The *Albatross* glided silently through the dark on her own momentum. They were halfway to the station, the Junkman's grave receding into the pitch-blackness behind them; directly ahead, the small array of station lights beckoned them home. Eventually.

"Listen to the silence," Ellie whispered. "So peaceful. Hard to believe so many people have died out here over the centuries. Sailors. Missionaries. Indians. Fishermen. Students. Did you know they called this place the Graveyard of the Pacific?"

Ellie's question recalled in Garner's mind the image of the *Sato Maru* aimlessly listing along its uncompleted course, and he shivered despite the warm breeze.

Unfettered by the concentrated lights of civilization, a thousand stars twinkled above them, painting a celestial ceiling. As if summoned, a meteor shower blazed briefly across the sky as they gazed upward in appreciation. Ellie asked Garner to point out several constellations and recall the names for her.

"I once had a boyfriend who was a pilot and big into celestial navigation," Ellie said. "He told me about how the first mariners couldn't find their way from east to west, even though they could go north and south by following the pole star."

"You mean 'sailing down the latitude.' "

"That's it. They'd have to sail down the coastline to a known latitude, then stay on it as they made their way across the ocean in a straight line."

"That's right," Garner said. "Until they developed a reliable seafaring clock, navigators couldn't determine their ship's longitude. So they found a known latitude and kept in line by keeping the pole star at a constant elevation above the horizon."

"Sounds like kind of a limited worldview."

"A little two-dimensional," Garner agreed.

"It sounds like your research is a little like that clock. That it will open new doors for research. Instead of pulling a net in a straight line through some vast unknown, your Medusa sphere will allow a three-D picture of all the life in the area."

"The microscopic life, anyway," Garner corrected.

"Still, that's pretty impressive."

"I like to think so." Garner shrugged with an immodest grin, equally impressed at the doctor's level of immediate understanding. "Are you sure you don't want to give up the medical game and come work in my press office?"

"Actually, I do," Ellie said. "If some single organism out here is responsible for what I've seen this week, I want to help find out what it is. There's no way I can just sit at home for the next two weeks, waiting for someone else's version of reality." Her eyes were deadly serious as she looked at Garner. "If this thing is as dangerous as you say, I want to help you kill it."

12

They returned to the station long after midnight. Garner admitted he was exhausted just as Ellie said she was just waking up; it was third shift for her. Since she had decided to stay in Bamfield for a few more days, Garner sent her off in the direction of the library, then lapsed into a restless sleep aboard the *Albatross*.

It was still dark when he awoke with a start, momentarily confused as to where he was, or why. His mind immediately turned to Medusa and Zubov's latest word from the *Exeter*. The combination of the spoiled sampling regime and Garner's own departure from the ship would definitely mean he would lose this season, unless he could salvage something useful from the data. He made a note to check the numbers Zubov had given him against the sampling figures from the previous two summers. He also tried to remember if he'd kept any plankton samples from Papa in his lab space back at Friday Harbor.

Then another thought brought him upright in his bunk. He quickly dressed and climbed up the ramp to the dock, breaking into a run as he headed for the stairs to the station and vaulted them two at a time.

The third floor of the marine station was dedicated to the research and teaching laboratories. Two rows of cubicles lined either side of the main lab. Ranks of pipes of every description crisscrossed the ceiling, while a spotless tile floor belied the facility's rustic locale. A large rack of seawater tables stood in the center of the room and was occupied by various ongoing experiments. At one end of the room sat an ice machine, an industrial-sized sink, and a small office containing a scanning electron microscope. The opposite wall held a bank of storm windows facing west onto a panoramic view of Barkley Sound.

As the station's permanent research coordinator, Saunders Freeland's was by far the most cluttered of the modest work spaces. Next to it sat the cubicle once used by Mark Junckers. In its appearance, Mark's small office paid homage to Freeland's own disheveled brilliance, possessing a filing "system" utterly baffling to anyone but its proprietor. Encouragingly, nothing seemed to have been removed from the office for several weeks, let alone in the past few days. It was exactly as Junckers had left it, Garner hoped.

Intact were his friend's notes and files from that summer, his field kit, and his wet-weather gear. Significantly, there remained several plastic bags and test-tube-sized vials containing water, tissue, and blood samples. The last specimens the Junkman had collected and perhaps the clue to what had killed the group of sea lions he found. The samples should have been labeled with date, location, and other details, and though Junckers's published research was renowned for its meticulousness, his field notes were in dire need of a coherent recording system.

Garner was equally disappointed to find that many of the tissue samples that needed refrigeration or preservation in buffered formaldehyde had been left untreated. Whatever his intent, Junckers hadn't lived long enough to return to the lab and properly prepare them. Now, some eight days later, most of the specimens had long since begun to decompose, hampering any sort of close inspection. If Freeland hadn't been down in Vancouver for the past few days, he would have spotted the samples and properly fixed them himself; as it was, they were probably a loss.

Struck with the thought that Junckers would have left some physical evidence of his mysterious find, Garner spent the rest of that night with his eyes focused into his friend's stereomicroscope. He donned gloves, safety goggles, and a respirator, then slowly peeled open the samples one at a time, examining them with a trained eye. Articulating the scope's specimen stage slowly back and forth, he carefully passed over each scrap of sea-lion tissue in a grid-like search pattern. Even in their decomposed state, the epidermal cells retained signs of massive hemorrhaging and lysis before death, leaving them to burst open into a nearly indiscernible liquid mass. As Garner worked in the silent, half-lit lab, the stolid words of the Indian at the town meeting crept back to him:

Every one of his internal organs was bleeding. They said parts of his brain had turned to liquid.

By daybreak, Ellie and Carol had located Garner and joined him in the lab. He had found nothing indicating a concern for contamination and now retained only his latex examination gloves as he processed the samples. Fighting eyestrain after his hours at the bench, Garner gladly stepped aside to show each of them the material passing under the microscope's objective lens.

"There are hardly any white blood cells," Ellie remarked.

Carol agreed. "If it was hit by some kind of virus, there should be more leukocytes as it fought off the infection."

"Unless the sample was taken after the white blood cells lost the battle," Garner said. "With a severe lysis of the white cells, eventually any infection could spread throughout the body unchecked. Once the host is dead, or removed from the vicinity, *Pfiesteria* retreats to a vegetative cyst stage."

Garner pushed his chair back and indicated a series of lists he had scrawled on a nearby whiteboard. He had drawn separate columns for VICTIMS, SYMPTOMS, LAT./LONG., and POSSIBLE PATHOGENS, then tried to connect them in series with arrows indicating their common aspects.

"Looking at the bigger picture, there are some definite similarities to a *Pfiesteria* bloom, except that the victims so far are apparently human beings and marine mammals, not fish."

"Indulge us with your speculation, then," Carol said in a fair imitation of her father.

"If all these cases are related, we can't possibly be dealing with a single toxin," Garner said. "The symptoms are bizarre and very diverse, but we can divide them into two distinct groups. The first group—the little girl, Mark, and possibly the crewmen on the *Sato Maru*—indicates exposure to some kind of fast-acting, degenerative neurotoxin. This would help explain the acute nervous disorders, chills, and failure of the gastrointestinal tract. The two poachers from Nitinat show an entirely different set of symptoms—severe irritation, corrosion, and sloughing of the skin. Ordinarily, I wouldn't relate the event to the rest of these, except that the tissue damage appears to be quite similar to what Mark found among his sea lions, and we see it here under the scope.

"Nitinat is also quite a ways down the coast, but no farther south than the *Maru* was west of here. It's also possible the *Maru* encountered something much closer to shore than where we found her. *Pfiesteria* shows us that the two distinct groups of symptoms are not impossible from the same source, but the distance involved leads me to think we have three distinct but unrelated cases."

"That's based on location," Ellie said. "Except for the poachers, we still don't know the exact location of any of the victims when—or if—they were exposed to something."

"True, but I'm inclined to side with Charles Harmon on that. The odds of concurrent outbreaks of an exotic species are long enough; the chances that something like this could originate offshore and somehow reach land are infinitesimal."

"But not impossible," Ellie pressed.

"Not impossible," Garner admitted. "The *Maru* was six hundred miles out, and there's a gap of six to eight days between the night the storm hit the *Maru* and when Caitlin Fulton was exposed."

"Three or four miles per hour for the bloom to reach shore," Carol estimated. "A reasonable surface current in a storm."

"And a path right past where we were towing Medusa," Garner added. "But for these cases to be related, we'd have to be dealing with an abundantly toxic organism that thrives in these water conditions, which don't appear to be especially unique. If it's a dinoflagellate or a diatom, the bloom would have to remain remarkably stable in strong current and wave conditions or somehow disperse its toxins through the air. In either case, I don't think we'd have to look too far or closely to see the effects."

"The beaches would be knee-deep in dead fish and marine mammals," Carol said.

"Without some kind of field evidence, I'm afraid all we have is some kind of theoretical science fiction," Garner said.

A new voice suddenly entered the conversation. Loud and well-defined, rough-edged with distinctly cantankerous overtones, it reached them over the top of the cubicle's open partition. "Well, then, I guess you can either pack up your schoolbooks and go home, or get your arses out there an' look for yerselves."

Freeland was back. And looking at the mischievous twinkle in his eye, it was hard to imagine someone like Bouchard ever standing in his way once his mind was made up.

"So what is it?" Freeland said, his hands in the pockets of his dungarees. "Are you gonna bend to those assholes upstairs, pack up that rowboat of yours, and head home scratchin' your head? Or are you gonna talk to Grumpy Ol' Freeland here and let him help you look under a few stones?"

They spent the next hour briefing Freeland on what they knew about each of the victims and the outcome of the spurious town meeting. As he listened, Freeland began mentally compiling a list of equipment to begin a more extensive search of the immediate coastal area.

"What about cell concentration?" Carol asked. If there was a high enough concentration of *Pfiesteria*—or anything else—to do this to a group of sea lions, wouldn't there be traces of the little bastard in the tissues or the blood?"

"I thought so," Garner said. "But not only do these samples show a distinct lack of any sort of parasite infection, they show a lack of *anything*.

Even the most carefully collected field samples are bound to contain some kind of microscopic life—insects, zooplankton, even larval fish. I've seen tap water with more organic content than these samples."

"Have you tested the water for pollutants?" Ellie asked.

"I tested for abnormal levels of nitrate and phosphate. Salinity and dissolved oxygen levels are within the normal range."

"Sounds like the more concentrated the toxin or toxins become, the more lethal and severe the symptoms become," Freeland said.

"Amazingly severe," Garner agreed. "I've never heard of any natural toxin working so quickly. Even with a positive identification, I have to agree with Charles's skepticism—plankton blooms just don't act this way. Whatever it is, it's long gone, even under the electron microscope. This thing vanishes like a phantom as soon as it's done its damage."

"If it didn't, those gloves of yours wouldn't have done much good," Freeland said. "We'd be carting you out of here by now."

Garner turned to Ellie. "What's the latest on the autopsy of the Indian boy and the poachers?"

"I talked to the medical examiner's office in Victoria this morning," she said. Without any identification, the poachers' bodies were released to the province. In the case of the boy, Ellie had pleaded with his grandfather to allow a proper autopsy to be performed on at least one of the victims. "I asked them to send us blood and tissue samples from the bodies. I also faxed them the micrographs of *Pfiesteria* you showed me in that textbook."

"How long before we hear something?"

"Later today or tomorrow. Graham—the Chief Examiner—owes me a favor or two, so he's putting in some overtime for us."

"In the meantime, we can prep some of these samples for the electron microscope and take a closer look at that tissue corrosion," Garner said. "Maybe we'll get lucky and find some signs of our little predator."

"This waiting around is too frustrating," Ellie said. "While we're talking about this, the only ones who've done any real looking are Harmon's graduate students."

"Those kids couldn't find sand on a beach if Father Charles told them it wasn't there," Freeland said.

"Carol and I have done some looking in the most likely spots—embayments and places with localized upwelling," Garner said. "But there's no point in going back out there until something new turns up, or until we locate the place where Mark found these sea lions. Without some fresh carcasses we're working as blind as bats."

Carol suddenly looked up from the blood sample she was inspecting for the third time. "Bats—that's it! There was a cave over on Diana Island where Mark and I used to go as kids. It was cut into the cliff near a surge channel on the western coastline, so low that the opening is covered with water at high tide." She grew quiet, awash in memories. "I was with him the day he found the cave. I guess I always thought of it as our clubhouse."

Garner now remembered the spot as well. Carol had taken him up there for a few adult-oriented picnics. It was therefore of little surprise that he had not immediately recalled the scenery.

"Have you checked there?" Freeland said. "Has anyone?"

"I doubt it," Carol said. "You can't even see it from offshore. But now that I think of it, it's probably the best place to start."

Freeland seemed relieved at the shift in the group's momentum. They were going to turn over some stones after all. "Then it's settled. It's pouring rain out there right now, but I'll reserve one of the station's boats and we can head out later, or first thing tomorrow."

"Let's take any masks and respirators we can scrounge as well," Garner said. "If this thing is still out there, I don't want to take any chances."

"If we do find something, we'll be scrounging a hell of a lot more than respirators," Freeland said. "We'll need the help of everyone available on staff."

"I don't think Daddy will buy into that idea," Carol said. "And he's got Bouchard tied around his finger. We'll never get their consent to tie up the station's resources on what he thinks is a goose chase."

"We'll see what he says once we find the goose. Besides, who says we need their endorsement?" Freeland scowled. "With the money your husband's got, you could buy this whole place."

"That's not the point," Carol said icily. The notion of using her husband's resources for her own research was not a new prospect, but it never lost its insulting connotation. She had come to expect that from her detractors, but Freeland's remark was too similar to Garner's chide from the previous day. "Do you guys compare notes on this stuff?"

"I'm only saying we don't need their consent," Freeland said. "Guys like Bouchard and your pop are like outhouses. They're full of shit and virtually obsolete thanks to more useful modern conveniences. So are you gonna go at them with a shovel, or go inside where it's warm and you've got a magazine rack and maybe one of those fuzzy pink covers on the lid?"

"Very colorful, Saunders," Carol said. "Thank you for comparing my father to an outhouse."

"I wouldn't be the first one," Freeland said with a wave of his hand. "I figure it's an insult to most outhouses."

"We'll start at the cave and work our way outward, sampling at quarter-mile intervals along the current," Garner said.

"With what?" Carol asked. "We're not equipped to do any kind of nearshore plankton sampling. Even if we knew where to look, the station's hardly got any suitable nets. Besides, the boats we've got would be smashed against the rocks before we got the gear over the side."

"She's right," Garner agreed. "Looking for this bug with nets and bottles alone is like hunting butterflies with a shotgun. We've got the bodies ready to go looking for this thing, but we're going to need a better set of eyes."

"Something like your Medusa," Carol agreed.

"Yes, but she'll be out on the *Exeter* for another week. Besides, she needs a ship that size to work, and a ship that size can't work close to shore."

"Is there anything else around here we can use? Something smaller?" Ellie asked.

"Funny you should ask, my dear," Freeland said quietly. As they watched, he began shrugging into his oilskin coat.

A heavy rain was falling and fog had shrouded the area as they left the station and followed the bobbing of Freeland's light down the path toward the shore. Freeland trudged ahead of Garner, Carol, and Ellie, water coursing in rivulets off his long coat and the wrinkled brim of his military-style boonie cap. After a hundred yards they came to the diving officer's shed, which doubled as a storage facility for the life jackets and other equipment for the station's modest fleet of boats. A single security light hung from the corner of the building, reminding Garner of countless nights when he had used that light as the sole point of reference to find his way back to the station after nightfall.

They followed Freeland up a rickety staircase bolted to the side of the building. At the top, he paused and fished a tangle of keys out of his pocket and unlocked one of the few locked doors on the entire campus. Entering the loft, they were greeted by the smell of sawdust and aged neoprene. As Freeland snapped on the light, they could see several rows of overladen shelves built in among the rafters, and forgotten equipment of every description hung down from the ceiling.

"I never knew this place was here," Carol said.

"We take storage space wherever we can get it," Freeland said. "And wherever we get it, we never get around to cleaning it out."

"I see what you mean," Carol said. "This takes pack-ratting to a new level."

Freeland seemed mildly offended. "Pack-ratting, you say? I say welcome to the station's maritime museum. Yessir, our own private little Louvre, right here in the boathouse."

Pulling back the corner of a large burlap tarpaulin along the rear wall of the loft, Freeland exposed a large PVC float about the size of a small barrel. Its interior had been packed with electronics, and a single, high-resolution camera lens protruded from one end. The significance of the device was lost on Ellie, but to Carol and Garner it was a familiar companion.

"I'll be damned." Garner stepped forward and ran a hand lovingly along the battered blue casing of the instrument. "If Garg could see this, he'd wet his pants laughing. I built this thing for five hundred bucks."

"It would have been more than that if we hadn't 'borrowed' most of the parts," Freeland said.

"Permanently borrowed. For no money and without anyone's consent," Carol said, smiling in spite of her disapproval.

"What is it?" Ellie asked.

"The beginning of the end for my father and his microscope," Carol said.

Freeland cackled. "Good riddance, if you ask me. Step aside for the folks who deserve it."

Ellie remained nonplussed as Freeland grinned at her, evidently revering this particular piece of memorabilia. "He's too modest to tell you, but you're looking at the ingenious little gadget that first took plankton research out of the Dark Ages and put Mr. Garner into the history books."

13

They began loading the station's aluminum skiff an hour before dawn. Though ungainly to maneuver in rough water, the boat provided ample deck space and good access to the water from its low gunwales and twin dive platforms. Ellie helped Carol retrieve Mark's field gear from the lab, then they brought over some of Carol's equipment from the cabin of the *Albatross*. Once the gear had been secured, they attached the *Albatross*'s dinghy to the skiff with a towrope. The smaller boat would come in handy for navigating the waters immediately off the unforgiving shores of Diana Island.

Garner and Freeland carried the relic plankton sampler down from the loft, patched it into Carol's laptop computer to check its operation, then carefully stowed both in the skiff. The device was not nearly as temperamental as its successor, but it had far more fragile and unprotected pieces. The rubber gaskets and moving parts hadn't been properly looked at in more than five years, and Garner found himself wondering if it would collect anything besides sloughed-off rust.

With the boat loaded, they clambered back up the dock ramp to the dive shed, where they donned drysuits complete with boots, gloves, and hoods. Even before sunrise, the sealed neoprene suits were stiflingly hot. Adding the full-face diving masks Freeland had scrounged for each of them produced a nearly suffocating effect inside the full ensemble.

"Wouldn't the CDC's emergency response team like to see these get-ups," Ellie said. "I'd say this puts *The Hot Zone* back a few steps."

"It'll keep the water away from you," Freeland said. "Assuming we still need to do that."

"Assuming we ever did," Garner said. "Saunders, you're a miracle worker, finding this gear on such short notice."

"It ain't pretty, but it'll help if we find something."

"And if we don't, we'll just evaporate into a pile of salt from heat exhaustion," Carol said.

"We have to find something in the next couple of days," Garner said, surveying the small mountain of equipment they had assembled. "If we don't, we might as well pack up and go home."

"I'm sure some folks'd like to see that," Freeland said, nodding his head up the hill toward Bouchard's office on the station's top floor.

"Charles, too," Carol grumbled. "Nothing like a tragedy to really bring a family together."

Freeland's comment renewed the group's determination as they returned to the skiff, bringing with them half a dozen high-capacity scuba tanks. They loaded the tanks into racks along the skiff's gunwales, leaving plenty of space along the railing. Among the last things Freeland brought aboard was a small pile of zippered sheaths molded from thick black vinyl.

"Body bags," Ellie said with professional recognition. "I hope those are only for any sea lions we find."

"Where did you get them?" Garner asked. "Or do we really want to know?"

"You'd be surprised what a feller can dig up around here," Freeland said. "In the way of field supplies, I mean."

Freeland made the two-mile crossing to Diana Island with the skiff's dual outboard motors at full throttle. Garner, Ellie, and Carol hung on to the railing as the aluminum hull slapped loudly against the incoming chop. As the sun began to climb above the horizon, all were grateful for the momentary refreshment of the breeze and the comparatively cool water splashing up around them. The size of the waves measurably increased as they rounded the northwestern fringe of the island. Freeland reduced their speed, following Carol's directions as she pointed out the approach to the surge channel.

"The wind is going to keep us out a ways," Freeland shouted to them over the engines. "Not that we could get this thing much closer, even on a calm day."

"This'll be fine," Garner said. "We can bring anything we find with the dinghy back here, then use the skiff to do a couple of tows with Betty."

"Betty?" Ellie asked.

Carol nudged the plankton sampler with her foot. "This is Betty. Betty Bloop."

"Cute."

"Maybe. Then he called the next one Veronica, until Sergei and I re named it Medusa." She winked at Freeland. "A better name for 'the history books,' right?"

"Still an' all, I wouldn't mind a little insurance to take in there with us," Freeland said, meaning the cave.

"Like a canary in a coal mine?" Carol asked.

"Dr. Harmon, you surprise me with your cavalier disregard for life," Freeland said. "I was thinking of sending Ray Bouchard in ahead—still, in a really tiny cage."

"What are the chances one of the local residents accidentally stumbled onto the same thing Mark found in there?" Ellie asked.

"Unlikely," Carol said.

"I've been hearing that a lot lately," Ellie said. "But people keep turning up dead."

"The island is uninhabited," Freeland said. "The only people who come out here are the occasional researcher and maybe a charter boat." He nodded to the west, where two small vessels were already making their way out over the drop-off to deeper water. There they had come to expect fish to congregate in a narrow zone where nutrients and zooplankton were upwelled to the surface from the colder bottom water.

"Except for the cave, there's nothing but a cul-de-sac at the end of the inlet," Carol continued. "The cliffs go up from the beach at least eighty feet. Nice and private," she added, her thoughts drifting back to her own adolescence, then later, to her years with Garner.

They drew lots, leaving Freeland to mind the skiff while the three others climbed into the dinghy. As they moved closer to the shore, Garner trained a pair of high-powered binoculars on the rocks at the mouth of the channel. The sun, just then cresting the trees, illuminated a large brownish object near the fringe of the small gravel beach. He passed the binoculars to Carol for a second opinion.

"It could be a *Zalophus* carcass," she said. "Then again, it could be a log or a piece of driftwood. So much for an expert opinion."

As they closed to within fifty yards of the channel, the radio at their feet crackled to life. "All right, you three," Freeland's voice called out. "Get those damn masks on. You could be running out of fresh air."

The trio quickly complied, pulling on the scuba gear and fitting the full facemasks over any skin left exposed by the drysuit's hood. Carol began to sweat immediately, her breath coming in thin rasps, rapid and shallow, through the second-stage regulator. The mildly claustrophobic sensation reminded her why she had chosen to study whales—to study sea life without spending too much time trapped in a rubberized cocoon such as this. Whales, in fact, spent only five to ten percent of their time at the surface, but they were too large and dove too deep to follow appreciably with scuba gear. Carol liked the arrangement she had made of tracking them with her microphones from a sunny, stable boat deck. *If you possibly can,* one of her senior-year biology professors had advised, *specialize in something found only in the tropics, something that's utterly beautiful on film, or something that's damn good to eat.*

In contrast, Ellie looked like a natural in the ungainly equipment, which Carol noted with some resentment. For a petite woman, she seemed to have a good deal of physical strength to complement her emotional resolve. In the brief time she had known her, Carol couldn't imagine Ellie Bridges sweating for any reason.

Garner brought the boat into the channel, then cut the outboard motor and tilted it up, away from the rocks. Gliding toward the end of the tiny inlet, they discovered the remains of two large sea lions and what looked to be part of a third. Inspecting the animals more closely, they could even discern the clean, angular cuts of a scalpel blade where Junckers—or someone—had taken tissue samples.

Garner and Carol began their survey by making a series of shallow dives. Beneath the surface of the turbid water, they found the remains of several more sea lions, the flesh and viscera stripped almost entirely from their reduced skeletons. Witnessing the sheer magnitude of the devastation, Carol could imagine how overwhelmed Mark must have been at this sight. As unbelievable as the scene now appeared, it was likely that the carnage Mark had first seen was much worse. In the way that nature cleanses her wounds, many of the most decayed carcasses had slipped beneath the surface and been trapped there.

Ellie assisted them in bringing the specimens to the surface, sampling the tissue and blood wherever possible, and towing the larger remains back to the skiff. Garner returned to the bottom several times, gathering samples of water as well as the thick mud that was perennially trapped in the shallow inlet.

As they worked, a small mink crept down the cliff face, stopping to watch them with some interest before being startled back into the underbrush by a raven that swooped down to the tide line. "That's encouraging," Garner said, his voice rasping noisily through his exposed respirator. "If anything nasty came through here, it looks like it's moved on."

"Should we try to breathe out here?" Ellie asked. "It looks normal enough, and frankly, I'm starting to feel a little ridiculous."

"We're all running low on air," Garner said. "We either risk it or we go back to the station for refills."

In her suit, Carol was beginning to feel faint from heat exhaustion. "Our little friend might be able to wear a fur coat in August, but I've had enough." She put a hand on her facemask and poised to remove it.

"Carol . . ." Ellie began.

"Be careful, Carol," Garner cautioned. "From what we know of this thing, I'm inclined to believe you, but—"

"Call it field science," Carol said. "The woodland critters seem to be fine, and if I have to wear this full-body condom another minute, I'm going to have a conniption." With that she pulled off her mask and hood as if it were a painful Band-Aid.

"Told ya," she said, her smugness tempered with genuine relief to be breathing unassisted once again.

Then, gazing upward, she suddenly frowned. "Oh shit."

Garner and Ellie waded back to the boat. "What is it?"

Carol followed the mink's escape route up the side of the inlet and pointed. "Look at the trees," she said.

Garner and Ellie craned their necks upward to view the tree line high above them. Several of the old-growth conifers had shed the needles from the lower third of their branches. Others showed a brownish discoloration nearly to the top.

"The damage appears to be pretty localized," Garner observed. "See? The cliff below them has eroded, exposing the root systems."

"Maybe they just dried out," Ellie offered. "It has been a warm couple of months."

"Dried out?" Carol said, challenging her. "I've seen Marine Corps defoliant that didn't work that well."

"Defoliant," Ellie repeated, not entirely comfortable with Carol's choice of words. As a medical student, then as a doctor, Ellie was well familiar with death on a microscopic level, from bacteria to earthworms to human cadavers. Yet something about the lethality of this menace—or collection of menaces—and the disparate collection of symptoms seemed too complete, too widespread to be entirely natural. "What about that? Is it possible that this agent is some kind of new biological weapon?" Ellie said aloud.

"There's no such thing as a new biological weapon," Garner said. "Just new combinations of the same tried-and-true building blocks."

Garner waded to the base of the cliffs, placing a handful of the fallen burnished needles in a plastic bag. "Dead, but not dying," he announced, examining them.

"So am I going to be the only canary around here?" Carol finally asked.

Garner and Ellie each removed their facemasks, only after radioing their intent to Freeland. Once again, it appeared as though the mysterious killer left no residual influence in the areas it had touched.

Finally, they trekked over the weathered bedrock to what had been informally christened "Mark's Cave." The three of them stood in the cool shade of the atrium. "I didn't expect to find anything in here," Garner said, offering an ad hoc eulogy. "I just thought we should thank the Junkman for being so damn predictable."

After a moment alone with their own thoughts, the three left the cave in silence.

Before leaving the shore for their final return to the skiff, Garner and Carol made certain that all of the larger samples were properly fixed with a dilute solution of formaldehyde. "This fixative is probably the most deadly thing in this inlet now," Garner remarked. He had often considered it most ironic that the principal duty of a field biologist was to collect all manner of fantastic organisms, kill them with any number of lethal, often carcinogenic chemicals, then study the corpse in order to better appreciate the organism should another example ever be found.

Their small collection of promising information now gathered, Garner steadied himself in the small boat against the rising swash. "The tide's coming back in," he said. "We should get out of here while we still can. Let's see what Betty can tell us."

They towed the two nearly intact sea-lion carcasses back to the skiff, where Freeland helped to make them fast against the gunwales. The three members of the landing party climbed aboard minutes later, finding room amid the accumulated pile of filled body bags. While Garner prepared his antiquated plankton sampler for use, Carol steered the skiff out toward the drop-off of the island's fringe, where they could better deploy it.

Apparently bored by a slow day of fishing, the occupants of the two nearby charter boats took immediate notice of the skiff. "What'cha got there?" asked one of the fishermen. Carol recognized him as one of the silent majority at the hearing.

"Just trolling for a little plankton," Garner said. "We'll keep our distance."

"Don't matter today," the fisherman hollered back.

"A goddamn wheatfield would have more fish in it," one of the fisherman's charges complained.

"We told you so," Ellie called back.

"Lady, if you knew fishin' at all, you'd know there's gonna be slow days," the fisherman said. Evidently, his customers knew nothing of the public hearing, and he wanted to keep it that way. "Everything's just dandy out here."

Angered, Carol grabbed a paddle and splashed the water next to the recovered sea-lion carcasses. "What do you call this, then?" she shouted. "A pretty slow day for these fellas? It looks like they've been swimming in battery acid."

The fisherman laughed and let out a slow belch, placating his customers. "Shit, lady, they ain't my fish. They's my *competition.*"

"Not for long," Carol retorted, raising her middle finger to the man's turned back.

"So much for charming the natives," Garner muttered as they set back to work.

Garner and Freeland made last-minute checks of Betty and slid the device overboard. Neutrally buoyant at a depth of six feet, the sampler obediently sank to the end of its tether and went to work. As Carol moved the skiff slowly forward, a stream of numbers began spooling across the screen of Carol's computer.

"Medusa could learn a thing or two from her elders," Garner said with admiration.

"Couldn't you all," Freeland grumbled.

They towed Betty slowly along the west coast of the island, first perpendicular then parallel to the shore in even tracks of varying depth. Replacing the sampler's collecting bottles as each rank was filled, they made a longer tow north, passing close to Mark's former field sites. The rookeries were practically in the shadow of the outlook where Charles Harmon had built his imposing wooden retirement home, and Garner wondered if the old man had ever bothered to look out the window to watch his stepson work. Garner saw Carol's gaze drift from the ream of incoming data to the darkened windows of her father's house. After a long moment, she wiped a tear from her eye with the heel of her palm, unaware she was being watched.

Two hours later, as Freeland brought the skiff through the mouth of Bamfield Inlet, they could see the familiar shape of the mail boat from Port Alberni moored at the government dock.

"The *Lady Rose* is in," Freeland said. "We should get your pathology specimens on board, packed in dry ice."

After the experience of that day, Ellie's enthusiasm was measured. "What if all these samples come up blank?" she asked, addressing no one in particular. She placed a tender hand on one of the sea lions being towed alongside the skiff. "Where do we look next?"

"North," Garner said. "Assuming there was a bloom on the west side of Diana and it's somehow moved on. Depending on the species, plankton blooms will move in one of two ways. Either the bloom occurs offshore and the wind pushes it against the coast, or it originates in a shallow coastal area and is moved out to sea. Either way, the surface currents here at this time of year should push it north."

"And if there's nothing to the north, either?"

On the top floor of the marine station they could see Charles Harmon and Raymond Bouchard gazing down at them. Garner flashed them a toothy smile and produced a friendly, overhead wave.

"Then we owe those two bastards a nice bottle of scotch," he said.

This time, at least it wouldn't cost Garner $12 million to admit he was wrong.

Ellie continued to be impressed with the research facilities on hand at the marine station. While some of the tissue samples had to be sent to a pathology lab in Victoria for a complete workup, Saunders Freeland had ensured that there was very little a marine researcher couldn't do from the station's third-floor lab. After calling the local Fisheries and Wildlife office to report the dead sea lions and have the remains collected, Carol helped Ellie prepare and mount the remaining *Zalophus* tissue samples for inspection under the BMS lab's electron microscope and high-powered dissecting scopes. Viral infection would have to be tested for elsewhere; Carol suggested a marine-mammal research facility in San Diego and sent them the details by e-mail.

As Freeland carefully removed the water samples from Betty's plastic underbelly, Garner downloaded the data from her onboard computers and gave it a cursory inspection. While the population numbers were significantly diminished, there was certainly nothing like what he and Zubov had seen out at Papa. In any event, there was a month's worth of number crunching to be done from Betty's half day of work. Most of it could wait until they had properly examined the contents of the bottle samplers.

"Some of the more decomposed samples are loaded with bacteria, which you'd expect," Garner said. "Nontoxic gram negative. Healthy. A few of the diatoms and dinoflagellate species I'd expect here in late summer, but nothing remarkable." He was still looking in the fluoroscope. "There's an amazing variety of forms here, too. I'll have to send some samples down to the NEPCC for identification."

"The NEPCC?" Ellie asked.

"North East Pacific Culture Collection," Garner explained. "One of the best collections of marine phytoplankton and microbes on the planet. It's operated out of the University of British Columbia in Vancouver."

"Sort of a house of horrors of oceanic microorganisms," Carol said. "But an invaluable resource. Daddy probably gave them the source material for half of their collection. I think he has it on his speed dial; I know the curator there loses a few more hairs whenever he gives her a call."

"Identifying bacteria—and even some dinoflagellates—is nearly impossible in the field," Garner explained. "Often you get only a few individuals, so to increase the amount of workable material, you have to culture them."

"And none of you is worried about any kind of quarantine situation?" Ellie asked.

"Yer still breathin', aren't you?" Freeland said.

"So was Mark," Ellie said. "For a few hours, at least."

"It's still a long shot," Garner said, "but assuming that whatever got to Mark also got to the *Sato Maru,* or even originated with the *Maru,* it seems to vanish completely. There have been no adverse effects from any of us who boarded the *Maru,* and you saw how the inlet has already recovered."

"It kills and moves on, leaving no trace."

"Apparently, at least from the samples we've looked at so far," Garner said. "The trick is to figure out *why* it's moved on and use that to anticipate where it's going."

"Once we find it."

"We'll find it," Freeland said. When they returned from their collecting trip, Bouchard had called him into his office for a lengthy closed-door discussion. Garner couldn't imagine Freeland knuckling under to the station director any more than he could imagine Bouchard firing a staff member as valuable as Freeland. However, it did appear that the two had reached an animated resolution on the most appropriate use of the station's equipment, and such criteria did not include a repeat of that day's events. From now on, Garner would have to work from the *Albatross* or the *Pinniped,* however impractical the sailboats were for ocean sampling.

The four of them looked at the processed samples until midnight, finding virtually no evidence of known toxic diatoms or dinoflagellates. Garner noticed Freeland's posture beginning to stiffen—the elder man's arthritic back was evidently bothering him after the long day—and told him to call it a night. Even with his painful limitations, Freeland's sinewy body was as tough as an iron bar. He didn't punch a time clock and would think nothing of working through the night if need be. However, it was beginning to look as though such dedication was hardly necessary.

Carol rinsed out the last of her specimen dishes, stretched, and said she would be retiring as well. Garner couldn't tell if she was relieved or disappointed at their lack of tangible results. It seemed as though she had resigned herself to the possibility of repeating the exercise in another locale the next day. She wandered across the lab to the large windows. The lights of the Coast Guard station across the inlet illuminated a small helicopter pad in the adjacent clearing. Seeing this, Garner thought of his recent trip in the Nolan Group's helicopter with Darryl Sweeny, Nolan's overly rigid personal assistant.

Where the hell is Nolan during all of this? Garner thought, recalling the tears in Carol's eyes, alone and frightened as she gazed up at Harmon's cabin that afternoon. *Where is her husband's support at a time like this?*

"Are you going to call Bob? Tell him the latest?" Garner asked.

Carol glanced at her watch. "No. He'll either be asleep or still at the office. He's been coordinating a case against the Hanford nuclear plant in Washington. It's kept him pretty busy. I asked him to come up, to take a look, but . . ." Her voice grew quiet, drifting off. "I guess there's not much point in calling him until we find something. He didn't sound too interested on the phone."

"I'm sorry to hear that," Garner said.

Carol looked at him evenly, not certain whether Garner was referring to her absent husband or his own missing financier. "He's a busy man, Brock. There's nothing for him here."

"I'm beginning to agree with you," Ellie said, looking up from her scope and rubbing her eyes. Then she looked at Garner. "But let's keep at it. I'm game to keep working if you are."

"Of course," Carol said, giving Ellie a flat smile. Not only was the good doctor apparently indefatigable, but she had settled in well as Garner's eager assistant. The twinge of guilt Carol felt was not because she felt her ex-husband was undeserving of such support, but because she herself had rarely found the time to give Garner the same rapt attention while they were married. "I'll get some sleep and relieve you in the morning," she finished.

They said their good nights, Carol retiring to her cabin and Freeland going home to his. Ellie suggested to Garner that they check on the sleeping pair every few hours to see if they developed any delayed symptoms. They *appeared* fine, but anything was possible.

"Sounds like you miss doing your rounds at the hospital," Garner said.

"Don't remind me. I'm going to run out of leave time at the hospital without our finding anything, much less anything conclusive."

Left alone with Ellie, Garner picked up the last of the biopsy samples from the body of Alan Peters. He placed a few drops on a slide and slipped it under his microscope, increased the magnification a thousand-fold, and began his slow scanning motion for seemingly the hundredth time that night. Ellie busied herself by packing up some of the samples she had already examined and reviewing the copies of the pathologist's report from Victoria.

As Ellie moved around him, freshly showered since dinner and wearing a change of borrowed clothes, Garner couldn't help but notice the fresh, soapy scent of her skin wafting delicately above the otherwise dusty and mildly acrid odor of the lab. The scent caught him unawares, playing on his fatigue, distracting him with visions of Ellie's curly brown hair, her innate joie de vivre, and those blue eyes that never seemed to lose their brightness. . . .

Something on the slide suddenly grabbed his attention. "Got something," he said, refocusing the scope. Despite Ellie's continued inquiries, he examined the specimen for another five minutes without uttering another word. Charles Harmon's book had been open on the lab bench all week, and now Garner flipped through the identification key with practiced ease. Finally convinced this was no mirage, no possible mistake, he pulled back from the scope. "Bingo. Take a look at that."

Ellie peered through the twin eyepieces, focusing on the structures Garner had positioned at the end of the stage pointer. She saw several ranks of small, leathery spheres no larger than a single cell. Each had the beginnings of a minute, fibrous groove in the silicon armor around its equator.

"Ever seen that in the lungs of a dead man?" Garner asked.

"Never. What are they?" Ellie asked.

"*Pfiesteria* cysts. The same genus anyway, but a species I've never seen before," Garner said. "Using the older identification keys, it could also be a species of *Gymnodinium,* but in this case I think I trust Harmon's accuracy." He inspected the sample again, referring to the texts spread out before him. "Most dinos can be identified by shape at this degree of magnification. *Pfiesteria* is tricky; it radically changes its shape over its development, morphing from cysts to amoeboid to motile cells of different sizes." He looked a moment longer, as if not wanting to confirm the worst of all possible candidates they could be facing. The much higher magnification afforded by the electron microscope would provide the ultimate details and confirmation, but . . . "It's *Pfiesteria*. I'm sure of it," he said aloud.

Pfiesteria. At the sound of the killer's name, Ellie's ears tingled and goose bumps prickled on her arms. At once they had both confirmation of its identity and a reminder that an organism that could kill in such horrifying ways was resting just beyond their fingertips.

"I can't imagine how the medical examiner missed it," she said.

"I can't imagine he'd even be looking for something like that or would know what the cells looked like if he was."

Ellie took another long, careful look, committing the appearance of the cysts to memory. "They don't look so bad," she said, steadying herself.

"The cysts are dormant. From there, *Pfiesteria* grows through twenty-three more life stages as it matures. As far as anyone has determined, each phase develops a more advanced morphology, a different feeding strategy, and more lethal chemical defenses. This bug has got one of the most complicated life cycles ever described."

"So what starts it—their life cycle?"

"Your guess is as good as anyone's," Garner said. "But while it's in a dormant state, at least we have the time to guess." He moved to the phone and dialed the home number of the NEPCC's director. While he had a positive identification of the genus, there were some aspects to the dinoflagellate's structure he had never encountered, notably the jelly-like mucus that seemed to encase the cells.

His next call was to Charles Harmon. The time had come for the old man to lose a little sleep with the rest of them. Garner was also willing to admit they needed some help. If his fears proved correct, not a single community within fifty miles was safe.

"Looks like you might need to book a little more time off," Garner said, returning to Ellie's side.

To Ellie, the foreboding threat and implications of her malpractice suit suddenly seemed a distant memory. This single discovery might offer hope for her vindication, but it was also an indication that they had only begun to grasp the horror of the situation at hand. How many more people—how many more Caitlin Fultons and Mark Junckerses and unsuspecting divers—would be exposed to this killer before they could find it? How many victims were out there in all those hundreds of square miles of unforgiving ocean?

Then, rising once again from the depths of Ellie's imagined fears, came the thought that this killer was too complete to be a random creation of nature. This killer was designed to survive, to destroy its adversaries, and to reproduce at any cost.

Her throat went very dry. She looked again at the innocuous tissue sample with its foreboding accretion of dormant cysts.

Thousands of them.

14

The young actress crossed her legs and pretended not to notice how the gesture transfixed the seventeen-year-old mate of the charter boat *Serenity*. And if the starlet didn't mind the ogling, her companion, television-producer-turned-entertainment-mogul Howard Belkin, minded even less. Candace was only a handful of weeks over twenty, and Belkin enjoyed being noticed whenever he had her on his arm. He imagined younger, handsomer men and women wondering how he could retain such an attractive series of shapely concubines. The answer, of course, was power.

Liam Cole, the captain of the *Serenity,* had never heard of Howard Belkin or his girlfriend and welcomed the odd-looking couple onto his boat with measured contempt. Cole kept reminding himself that he had bills to pay, a first mate to employ, and a belly to fill. He had survived good times and bad in the local economy of Neah Bay, often cutting his rates to the bone if it meant the possibility of a repeat customer at a higher rate. He generally liked his charges, liked showing them how to fish, helping them to stave off seasickness, and sending them home with a cooler full of the day's catch limit. But seeing the arrogant actress and her trembling, aged "husband" step awkwardly onto his deck that morning made him think he had found a new species of primordial ooze on the bottom of the charter-fishing client pool. After an hour—a single hour—Cole was ready to refund their money and deliver them over to one of his many competitors. After two hours he was ready to use them as bait—the one with the nice legs could go second.

Howard Belkin ignored Cole's obvious animosity. He was on vacation and enjoyed his every need being served. Born in Brooklyn before World War II, Howard Belkin was the only child of a vaudevillian father and radio-jingle-singing mother. It was his parents' reputation for good work that opened many doors for him in Hollywood and his own physical shortcomings that seemed to close them just as fast. A childhood bout with polio and a severe case of teenage acne left him too pallid and frail to be taken seriously in a lead role. He lacked the creative vision of a director, but he had a manic drive and an innate sense for the kind of shows people would pay to see and so eventually became a producer.

Belkin's first hit came in the mid-1970s with a prime-time television series about a trio of crime-fighting flight attendants, or stewardesses as they were known back then. *Bluebirds* was at the top of the ratings for four seasons and made national celebrities of its three costars—two former cosmetics models and a would-be news anchorwoman. It wasn't long before Belkin Entertainment was a major player in Hollywood, diversifying into feature films and video. A few of his riskier ventures drove him to the brink of financial ruin, but he always came back. In a town known for its ephemeral nature, he had kept enough contacts to remain a survivor. To hang around the spotlight, if not illuminate himself.

Then, two years ago, he had released a thinly veiled soft-porn vehicle about roommates in a trendy college coed dormitory. Now he had fashion designers, record companies, and fragrance makers lining up to get product shots on the show. He met two hundred girls a week just like Candace, each more willing than the last to do whatever was necessary for even a bit part. He knew he had a hit on his hands once again when

CNN reported the story of a sophomore at Georgia Tech who had died from alcohol poisoning after playing a drinking game like the one she'd seen on *Hampton House.*

"If you gotta go, that's the way you oughta go," Belkin remarked to one of his development lieutenants, slapping the boy on the knee. "Go out with a party scripted by H. L. Belkin."

Now, at the age of seventy-eight, Howard Belkin no longer sought the spotlight for himself. He had the requisite palatial home in Malibu. He had enough money, from his residuals alone, to buy people's attention and rent all the drop-in pussy he could handle. His name was now enough to get the most preposterous of ideas off the drawing board and into production, perhaps the truest measure of success in his business.

"We've got a place in Seattle, but we've been looking at property in the San Juan Islands," Belkin said, lighting a Cuban cigar. He used the same leaf supplier as Schwarzenegger and was proud of that, too. "We're thinking of moving up here full time."

"Why?" Cole said. It was more of an appeal than an inquiry.

"L.A.'s a shithole," Belkin said. "That smog's a fuckin' killer. They've been saying that for thirty years, but I'm beginning to believe it. At least my lungs are, and I thought my stogies would've petrified them long ago." He punctuated his point by slipping into a series of phlegm-laden coughs. "Besides, Candy's got a problem with the water there, all the lead in it and crap like that."

"*How*-ard," Candace whined in a tone engineered to irritate. "You know I hate being called *Candy*. It's *Candace*. How is anyone going to cast me as a serious actress if you keep calling me *Candy?*" Candace's twinkling, almost aligned eyes forever suggested vacuous incomprehension, no matter how upset she tried to be.

"Don't worry, sweetheart," Belkin said. "You'll get roles just as long as we keep the *can* in there." He bellowed at his own joke, cutting his laughter short as he saw her begin to pout. "Don't worry, sweetheart," he repeated, patting her knee reassuringly. "I've got you all lined up for a great role in a project early next year. In fact, if *you* don't take it, they'll probably offer it to Julia Roberts."

"That's what you said about the *last* role," she said.

"Some things take time. You know that," he patted her again, letting his hand linger on her tanned thigh.

Candace uncoiled her long legs and leaned forward to pat Belkin's sallow crotch. "Yes, *sweetie,* I certainly do." She lit a low-tar cigarette off of Belkin's Cuban and climbed up to the cockpit to smoke it.

"Now, ain't that a piece of grade-A ass?" Belkin said to the crew. The tip of his cigar glowed red as he flashed a yellowed smile. "Yes, sir, grade-fuckin'-A."

Cole said nothing, keeping his mind on the bait.

At ten o'clock that morning they had their first strike of the day. The starboard-side line stiffened momentarily, then just as quickly slackened. Cole's first thought was that Toby, the mate, had inadvertently backed them over the line and keelhauled it, but the line had been drifting well away from the gunwale when it went limp.

What the hell could break five-hundred-test line?

Cole climbed up to the cockpit and looked in the direction of the line. A large gray silhouette appeared just below the surface, followed moments later by a robust dorsal fin as the fish rolled itself over.

"Jesus H. Christ," Belkin said, pointing excitedly. "That's a great white! That's a goddamn great white shark!"

Sunning herself on the foredeck, Candace looked up from her *Glamour* magazine.

"I doubt that, Mr. Belkin," Cole said. "Whites are pretty rare around here."

"It's probably a big salmon shark, maybe a seven-gill," Toby agreed. "They come up closer to the surface in the summer."

Candace smirked and went back to her magazine.

"Like hell it is," Belkin shot back, leaving his seat and scrambling to the rail with surprising agility. "I produced three documentaries on white sharks for the Explorer Channel. I know a white when I see one, and I've seen more than the two of you put together."

That much was probably true, if one were counting photographs or film footage. Cole had been fishing Juan de Fuca for seventeen years and had seen only one white shark; Toby had never seen one. While *Carcharodon carcharias* was one of about a dozen shark species known to inhabit these waters, only a few had ever been reliably identified. Most had been found washed ashore, long dead and probably starved, lost, or simply deranged. Cole could have relayed this information, but instead decided to preserve his client's enthusiasm.

"You're the boss," Cole said. If it was a white, the captain felt a fraternal sympathy for it. If it had strayed this far north, the two of them were probably not too far different. Both were only just surviving, preying on any incidental bottom feeders that might cross their paths. For the money Belkin was paying, Cole would swear on the Bible that they'd just caught Moby Dick.

If it was a white shark, it was a small one. Cole guessed it to be a ten-footer, but he couldn't yet see the tail. The fish was obscured in some kind of murky cloud, possibly blood, which led Cole to his next conclusion: the fish was probably injured. Its struggling was too weak, and it didn't appear to be swimming right.

"It ain't dead," Cole said. "Sharks don't have an air bladder and they're heavy. If she was dead, she'd sink straight to the bottom."

"How do you know it's a 'she'?" Candace called from her chaise.

"If it was a male, he'd have claspers under the tail," Cole said.

"Right," Belkin said. "They come together to form the penis." He demonstrated, touching his elbows together and drawing his forearms together until his hands touched. "Well-hung, those bastards, too."

"If it's the penis, why are they called claspers?" Candace asked.

"Aristotle thought they were too big to be reproductive organs," Cole said. "So he thought they were used to clasp on to the female during mating."

"Aristotle Onassis studied sharks?" Belkin said. "You're full of shit."

"No, Aristotle *Aristotle*—"

Just then the fish started thrashing, corkscrewing its body and throwing the water into a violent tumult. As its conical head thrashed back and forth, the shark snagged a second and third line from the *Serenity*'s aft poles. These lines did not break from the shark's teeth; instead, they were wrapped around its gleaming body.

The strain on the quarterdeck was immediate and intense. Two cleats broke free as the lines attached to them were ripped overboard. The *Serenity* was immediately pulled over to starboard, its hull groaning under the sudden load. Candace screamed as she was thrown to the deck. Toby grabbed for a fish billy and tried to club the shark on its massive head, to no avail. The teeth of the struggling fish rose from the water and snapped at him.

"Cut the lines!" Cole shouted, disappearing down the hatchway.

Toby retrieved a machete-sized knife from the tool locker and slammed it down on the first line, snapping it with a loud *thwack!* The sudden release of tension made the boat yaw left, sending Candace sliding toward the opposite rail, still screaming.

"What are you doing!" Belkin yelled at Toby. "This is my *catch*! I *want* this fish."

"An' he wants us," Toby said, preparing to part the next line.

A large split appeared in the fiberglass coating of the deck. From below, Cole cursed loudly and started the bilge pumps.

"No!" Belkin said, stepping forward to grapple with the much younger and stronger man. "Don't you dare, you little punk."

Cole returned from below with a .44 pistol. "Stop it right now!" he shouted, lifting the gun in Belkin's direction.

Belkin glimpsed the gun and backed away, his hands raised as he tried to steady himself on the rolling deck. "Whoa there, Skipper. I didn't mean it. I was just telling Gilligan here not to fuck with my trophy."

Cole lowered the gun, pointing it aft. "Get out of the way," he said, then unloaded four shots into the shark's head. The fish bucked once, twice more, then finally went limp.

The *Serenity* stopped audibly complaining but retained her starboard list. For a moment there was no sound except that of bilge pumps and the three men panting, catching their breath. Even the water swirling around the fractured hull was utterly silent.

"To the hunt," Belkin said, raising an imaginary glass in toast. Cole ignored him.

Toby leaned over the transom and hooked the shark with a gaff, pulling it closer. "This has got to be a seven hunnert pounder if she's an ounce."

The side of the shark's head was a bloody, pulpy mass from where the bullets had penetrated the eye and lodged in the thick skull. "Look what you did to it," Belkin shouted at Cole. "You ruined my trophy."

"It's not a goddamn moose," Cole said. "We'll get you the jaws. Those alone will pay for your trip today. You don't want the whole thing. The skull is made of cartilage and the meat is full of ammonia. It reeks once it begins to rot."

Toby gagged from his head-down position over the side. "I think it's started already. Smells like piss." The more the blood rushed to his head, the more he could feel a prickling sensation through his outstretched arms and face. "It's making my eyes water."

The boy continued to tug at the carcass, trying to attach a line to the head and haul it up high enough to flay out the jaws. From the cockpit, Candace watched his struggles with some appreciation of his muscular back and tight buttocks. "Is it dead?"

Toby grunted an affirmative, rolling the shark over with the gaff. "Whatever killed it got here long before we did." The fish's tail—in fact, the entire body posterior to the first dorsal fin—was almost completely eaten away in strange, semi-circular pieces. Given the simple skeleton of the shark, the remains resembled little more than a half specimen, trailing tattered, half-eaten vertebrae. "I reckon the thing was already dead when it took our hook, just too stupid to know it."

"Aw, I wanted to see the clappers," Candace whined.

"Claspers," Cole said. "Sorry to disappoint you."

"What do you think could have done that?" Belkin asked. "A killer squid?"

Sure, it was a three-hundred-foot killer squid with eyes as big as a house and clappers like a Cadillac, you dumb ass, Cole ruminated. "Could have been another shark, or a killer whale," he said aloud. "Jesus, what a mess. Not much of a trophy here, even without the bullets. I guess you'd like a picture of it hung up with you standing beside it, but for one thing we're not equipped for towing or hoisting something this big. For another, there isn't anything left to hang."

"I want the jaws," Belkin said firmly. "If you want to get paid, you'll get me those jaws."

"You're the boss," Cole repeated, his sympathy for the once-striking animal increasing. He knew commercial fishermen who harvested sharks by the hundreds, capturing them on long lines of hooks stretched for miles along the sea bottom. Many also practiced "finning"—the incalculably wasteful process of removing the jaws, fins, and other marketable pieces of the shark, then throwing the rest of the animal back, often still alive but unable to swim. Looking at the tremendous, impressive ranks of triangular teeth, it seemed an equally unjust fate to see such majesty, such perfection of design, come to an end on the bookshelf of someone like Howard Belkin.

"See? I told you we'd catch something." Belkin was grinning up at Candace. "How's it feel to be sleeping with a Master of the Universe?" He turned to the shark. "How does it feel to *you*, you fucking piece of dog food? How does it feel to fuck with a *real* survivor? A *real* fucking predator."

"I thought dead sharks attracted other sharks—they're cannibals, right?" Candace said, unimpressed and mildly disgusted. "So . . . where are the others?"

Cole was about to begin to explain the rarity of any kind of sharks in the strait, when he realized the merits of the question. A fish this size, injured or sick, should have attracted any number of opportunistic scavengers. But even now there was an eerie lack of other marine life. No fish darted in and out of the cloud of blood escaping the shark. No birds settled on the surface to feed. And Toby was right about the rotting smell, like ammonia but too strong for this one fish. . . .

With a gasp, Toby suddenly flipped over the side of the boat and belly-flopped into the water. A single running shoe fell off and landed on the deck as the boy began to shriek at the shocking coldness of the water. Cole, Belkin, and Candace looked at the single shoe, then at each other, before bursting out in laughter.

"I can see I hired no one but the best," Belkin laughed. With the exertion, he suddenly found it more difficult to catch his breath. There was a burning sensation in his nose and chest that didn't taste like tobacco. Or cocaine.

Cole, too, was laughing at the comical sight, even though he knew he had only minutes, if not seconds, to retrieve his mate from the water. He grabbed a life preserver on a lifeline and brought it to the rail.

"Help me!" Toby screamed.

Cole realized that the boy's screams came from more than the cold. For a panicked moment he wondered if the shark had come to life yet again, seizing Toby in its powerful jaws. Leaning over the side, he could see that Toby was now several feet from the fish, thrashing madly in the water.

"Help meee!" Toby screamed again, his words drowned by a fountain of blood erupting from his throat.

Cole threw the life preserver out to the boy and frantically dragged him back to the boat. "Grab my hand!" he shouted at Toby, who seemed oblivious to either his captain's voice or his own proximity to the boat. The color had drained from his face, and his neck began to swell as his body convulsed.

In his extended position, Cole now felt strangely light-headed and numbed. As the water and blood splashed onto him, he felt a burning on his face and hands. The smell of the fetid water made his eyes tear.

Cole grabbed Toby's hand and pulled upward. To his horror, the boy's arm came away in his hand, torn away completely from the shoulder. Cole shook the arm free from his grasp. The limb thudded heavily to the deck, landing directly between Candace and Belkin.

It was then that Cole could see the incredible damage to Toby's body. The flesh seemed stripped away from the boy's torso, all of his ribs now exposed. He couldn't still be alive, he couldn't possibly still be screaming, Cole thought to himself, his mind going black. The realization that the screams were no longer coming from Toby but from Candace on deck was the last memory Cole had before he toppled into the searing water. He vanished without a trace.

Howard and Candace were suddenly alone on the boat. There was no sound from the water except wavelets lapping against the hull. The severed limb and the single shoe were all that remained of the *Serenity*'s crew. They had no idea where they were, no idea how to pilot the boat, and there was not another vessel in sight.

Shivering uncontrollably, Candace stumbled backward and collapsed in the doorway to the main cabin. She couldn't catch her breath. Her crystalline eyes, terrified and unblinking, stared pleadingly at Belkin. "Howard, do something. *Do something!*" she screamed.

Kismet. Out of the calm blue sky, at the age of seventy-eight, Howard Belkin had finally been given his chance to play the hero. In the real world, it would be Howard Belkin—not Eastwood, or Gibson, or Costner—who in the final reel would rescue the desperate young starlet and sail away with her into a perfectly framed, sepia-toned PanaFlex sunset.

A part of him had been waiting his entire life for this role. Howard Belkin had his dream shot. The crew, the cast, and the audience were watching, hanging on his every word. *Quiet on the set, please, people. Okay, actors to your marks. Lights, please. Kill sound . . , camera . . . and—ACTION!*

Howard Belkin wet his pants.

15

Following the first glimpse of the killer, Garner had decided to divide the efforts of their investigative team. Carol accompanied Ellie to the city of Victoria, where they again autopsied the bodies of the two divers and the Salish Indian boy. Carol telephoned the station later that day, excitedly relaying the news that they might have found several *Pfiesteria* life stages trapped in the tissues of the divers; once they had instructed the coroner what they were looking for, finding more cells of the dinoflagellate came easily. They agreed to take whatever specimens they could from the hospital and return to Bamfield the next morning, where Garner or Harmon could complete the identification.

Garner and Freeland were equally busy but ended up with far less to show for it. In the morning they deployed Betty from the skiff and headed north across the sound, the first of three separate trips that day. Although they would need more time to look at the plankton samples, the data from Betty's infrared cameras showed nothing unusual about the properties of the water column. In the afternoon, they once again pleaded their case to Ray Bouchard. With the finding of *Pfiesteria* cysts in the laboratory sample, the station director was ready to concede his support to a partial closure of the nonreservation campgrounds and fishing areas north of Nitinat River. Reservation land was beyond the official jurisdiction of the Fisheries and Wildlife Department, but the community elders there agreed to curtail their fishing activity in the area until a proper site survey could be performed.

For his part, Charles Harmon spent the rest of that day hunched at the lab's electron microscope, examining the *Pfiesteria* sample. While Harmon reserved opinion on the gravity of the matter, he concurred with Garner's identification and even lauded his observational skills and persistence. From there it seemed to be his own fascination with the organism—so innocent-looking yet so potentially vile and so far from home, isolated in its state of semi-hibernation—that focused his attention. Watching him work, handling the settling chambers and microforceps with such expertise, Garner felt his own sense of appreciation return for the old man. He was privileged to be watching the methods that had defined their field; in his waning years, Harmon had obviously not lost any of his dexterity, nor his sense of wonder at the subject matter.

"Why don't you come with us?" Garner offered. "If you're up to the trip, we could use you down in Nitinat."

Harmon chuckled in the way he always did when faced with perceived frivolity. "I haven't been 'in the field' for twenty-five years," he said. Suddenly uncharacteristically modest in the face of Garner's invitation, Harmon fiddled nervously with the placement and volume of his hearing aid. "As it is, I consider it a good day when I can navigate a passage to my bathroom. Out there"—he tipped his cane in the direction of the open Pacific—"out there is for younger men."

Garner was inwardly amazed at the sudden warming of Harmon's demeanor. It was as if, in finding the slightest trace of the organism against formidable odds, using an abomination such as Betty to find this needle in a haystack, Harmon was finally ready to pass the torch to his successors. Garner found himself wishing that he had a witness to this exchange and, most of all, that it would be Carol.

Thanks to the combined efforts of Garner and Harmon, they had determined the cysts to be from a new, if incompletely described, species of *Pfiesteria*. The killer had a face, and now it had a name. Although final confirmation of the request would have to come from the International Council of Taxonomic Nomenclature, Garner and Freeland derived what they considered to be a fitting moniker, and Harmon concurred with surprisingly little resistance.

Until further notice, the new species would be known as *Pfiesteria junckersii.*

That evening, Charles Harmon asked one of the station's technicians to return him to his island, and he climbed slowly up the narrow path from his private dock, clutching the small portfolio of sketches he had made. As twilight faded into darkness, Harmon's home seemed strangely empty and without warmth. He lit a fire and shuffled around the utterly silent structure, realizing that he felt lonely for one of the few times in his entire adult life.

He padded into his library, a glass of single-malt whiskey in his hand, and settled into the chair behind his desk. It would surprise many people—Carol and Mark foremost among them—that Harmon kept several pictures of his children and his former wife among the trinkets on his impressive collection of bookshelves. He had gazed upon those images so often they were committed to memory, as were the contents of the newspaper articles about them and the research papers written by them, which Harmon hoarded in his desk drawer.

Then there was the set of twenty-year-old sketches he had recently retrieved from a musty folder in the attic. Sketches of an organism that bore a remarkable resemblance to the "new" species he had been drawing all day and that he and Garner had just christened *Pfiesteria junckersii.* The last time Harmon had worked with this bug—molded it with his own hands—he had called it, simply but sufficiently, Batch 9.

The sketches had been retrieved only hours after he learned of his stepson's death, yet the implications of the hearsay evidence about what Mark had found were far too chilling for Harmon to consider seriously.

So the faded drawing had occupied the corner of his desk, respectfully undisturbed, like a sleeping rattlesnake. Until today.

What Harmon had drawn those many years ago was the outcome of one of the first attempts at applied biological weaponry. He could still clearly recall the faces of the Department of Defense operatives who first met with him while he was a professor at the University of Washington. They were well-read about his life's work to that time and intensely interested in neurological afflictions such as amnesic and paralytic shellfish poisoning. They wanted to discuss the possibility of isolating these compounds from toxic dinoflagellates to use as offensive weapons and were willing to invest in the research, using a substantial amount of black project funding courtesy of the U.S. government.

Anthrax, cryptococcosis, pneumonic plague, Rocky Mountain spotted fever, ricin, sarin, psittacosis, and other "A-list" biological weapon threats were amply available and cheap to produce, but many of them were inefficient, hit-or-miss killers. Many (anthrax certainly excepted) simply fell apart when exposed to boiling water, ultraviolet light, or the stresses of aerosolization. What better carrier, then, than a hearty marine organism that could produce the toxic agent itself? Dinoflagellates provided interesting candidates for this, but most dino species favored tropical water, while most (suggested) foreign threats to the United States had coastlines in temperate waters. Within this conflicting set of parameters, Harmon began the search to find, or create, a hypertoxic dinoflagellate tolerant of cooler water, ocean turbulence, and elevated levels of pollutants.

Three years of research and development led them to the same conclusions that Harmon had openly hypothesized at their initial meeting: that toxic plankton agents although potent, were inherently difficult to isolate, much less synthesize, making their wide-scale production impractical when compared to the arsenal of chemical weapons the military had already developed. His employers—the Army Chemical and Biological Weapons Corps and the Navy's Biological Defense Program were the foot soldiers, but it was the U.S. Department of Defense that administered the programs and dreamed up where to apply these forces—also wanted something that was fast-acting and virtually undetectable, conditions that were generally considered to be mutually exclusive when discussing marine pathogens. It would take an oil drum of the unrefined toxin to stop an attacker in his tracks, and in such a case the drum itself would likely be more effective as a weapon.

Then a man by the name of Adam Lockwood, representing a top-secret branch of naval intelligence, had signed the paperwork authorizing Harmon to continue his work. Deferred from the formulation of a direct-action weapon, Harmon had been instructed to develop an indirect agent. This involved the genetic engineering of a particularly lethal dinoflagellate that could be used to deplete foreign fish stocks or gradually increase the incidence of debilitating nervous disorders in populations deemed hostile to the U.S. national interest. Eventually, their search had led them to *Pfiesteria piscicida,* a dino highly toxic to fish and found in the Gulf Stream off the mid-Atlantic United States. That species was then crossed with a more resilient species, *Pfiesteria pacifica,* an extremely rare but aggressively reproducing congener that Harmon himself had first described in the semi-tropical waters off Baja, California.

Their experiments ultimately failed, at least from a military perspective. While the new hybrid organism—Batch 9—was much more stable and produced a more potent toxin, it was essentially sterile and unable to procreate except under unreasonably high incubation temperatures. Harmon's work was discontinued, and soon after, he retired to his home in Barkley Sound to write, away from the meandering of academe and the meddling of Big Brother. At least that was the excuse he most often used. In truth, he was utterly terrified by the implications of what might have happened, had he succeeded. What had once been a top-secret investigation into weapons development had, twenty years later, indirectly become the Army's Chemical and Biological Defense Command—or CBDCOM—centered at Maryland's Aberdeen Proving Grounds. The lessons learned from the research of Harmon and others had helped to develop the military's preeminent installation for chemical and biological warfare-threat response.

Sometimes, though not often, Harmon would wonder what had ever been done with his *Pfiesteria* work. He had always assumed he would take the secret of his research to the grave. Conversely, Batch 9, that most remarkable hybrid, didn't seem to *have* a grave. Its dormant cysts could ostensibly survive for years without any apparently essential nutrient. Harmon thought of the scores of courses he had taught where students poured all manner of biological wastes and chemicals directly down the drain of the laboratory sink. This was in the days before such materials were considered hazardous to the environment and were regulated accordingly, but even now the practice was continued out of laziness—why take the time to record, isolate, package, and incinerate what you could quickly sweep under the rug? Given the trailing-edge technology of the military facilities he had worked in, it was entirely likely that the same fate had befallen the deadly cultures they had created. Some dim-witted ensign or private had probably been ordered to simply dump them out into the waste stream of Elliott Bay. Now, two decades later, there had somehow been a natural outbreak of what they had once produced only briefly in the laboratory. There was no way of knowing for certain how the two *Pfiesteria* species could have come into contact—though the explosion of global trade routes was one possibility—or how nature had produced a viable population from such a hybrid.

The sound of an approaching boat engine drew him from his reverie. He extinguished the light and moved to the large picture window. Overlooking the sound, he could see the small expedition from the marine station returning from another tow of Garner's (yes, it was remarkable) automated contraption. He watched the running lights of the skiff course smoothly through the darkness until it rounded the point to the east, with Freeland steady at the wheel. Now, looking north, Harmon could just see the dark silhouette of Tzartus Island, where Mark was buried.

Harmon shifted his gaze to the amber liquid that rolled around the bottom of his glass. He admired the persistence and resolve of his children and, more reluctantly, even that of Garner. It didn't seem that long ago that Harmon himself would have been leading the charge to investigate some mysterious new microorganism, instead of standing on the shore with all the utility and relevance of a dusty old textbook. Except, in this case, he believed he might truly hold all the answers and could only pray that he would be proved wrong. *Pfiesteria junckersii* indeed.

A cool liquid dripped onto his cheek and he realized that he was crying.

Harmon turned away from the window. His radiophone sat on a small metal table on the other side of the study, and he looked at it for a long moment. Perhaps it was time to give a call to his old friend Admiral Lockwood.

Freeland and Garner agreed to leave the next day, once Carol and Ellie had returned from the hospital. Discussing this plan to take Betty sampling along the outer coast, Freeland advised against taking (literally, stealing, given Bouchard's locked-down attitude about the expedition) the skiff, which was open to the elements and not equipped for an extended trip. Instead, they would take the *Albatross* and the *Pinniped,* either towing Betty from one of the vessels or stringing the sampler between them in a kind of bos'n's swing.

The sudden reversal of official policy regarding the beach closures was met with mixed opinion. While the offshore fishermen in Bamfield breathed a sigh of relief that their livelihood was, for the moment, preserved, a decidedly different mood descended over the town as word of the Nitinat samples was passed around. That night, when Garner and Freeland retreated to the usually collegial sanctuary of the town's pub, they could feel the eyes of everyone in the room shift in their direction.

"Folks don't know whether to thank you or string you up," Freeland said as they occupied a table near the fireplace. "Kinda puts the *turd* in martyred, don't it?"

"I'm getting used to it," Garner grumbled. "I'm willing to take my chances either way."

Freeland nodded at the row of small portholes looking out onto the pub's parking lot. "Do you remember where all those brass fittings come from?" he asked.

"The *Van Lane*," Garner said. "That Japanese car transport that hung a left onto Cooper Island."

"Exactly," Freeland said. "The captain was listening to the advice of his navigator in a dense fog, and the navigator, on his best estimate, thought they were fifty miles south of here, at the mouth of Juan de Fuca Strait." He took a long draw on his beer. "That was some kinda bad advice, based on somebody's idea of knowledge."

"What's your point?"

"My point is, folks around here made the most of a bad situation. Once that fat-ass boat run aground, they were all over it, taking anything that wasn't bolted down. It's years later, the ship is long gone, but we're still looking out her windows and patching our boats with engine parts from her cargo that went 'missing' before her owners could get up here to investigate and salvage her proper. My point is, folks around here are good at tightening their belts. They're used to that. They're also used to making the most of the breaks they get.

"My point is, don't do what's right for this place. You get the truth, and worry about the rest of these sorry bastards after that."

Garner downed the rest of his beer and went to the bar to get two more. On the next stool was Stu Templeton, the head of the fishermen's union. As Garner walked up, Templeton wheeled on his seat and pointed Garner out to another man. "Here's the guy you should be telling," Templeton said, his finger waggling in front of Garner's chest like an arthritic cobra. "This guy'll find a mermaid in a bathtub for ya, if the money's right."

"Tell me what?" Garner asked, dismissing Templeton's drunken assertion and looking at the man.

"I was just telling Stu here about a charter boat they found off Cape Flattery, down in Washington State," the man said. "Liam Cole's boat. Only Liam is missing, his crewman is missing, and there's a sleazeball Hollywood producer and his big-titted girlfriend dead in the hold. The hull is fractured all fer shit, and tied to the stern is a twelve-foot white shark with about six foot of it chewed off."

"Chewed off?"

"*Eaten.* Guy I know down in Neah Bay said it looked like someone dipped it in acid."

"When was this?"

"Yesterday. Last anybody saw of Cole was the day before."

"What about the passengers?"

"Don't know. I heard somebody say they suffocated."

"Fuck off," Templeton said.

"I said that's what I *heard,* asshole."

"How does someone suffocate to death in the middle of the goddamn strait?"

"The old bastard probably got his head stuck 'tween her titties," someone else piped up, sending a smattering of laughter around the bar.

Garner got as much information as he could from the men, including the name and phone number of the supposed witness. He returned to the table and, as he relayed the story to Freeland, quickly swept aside the ashtray and the basket of condiment packets. Laminated into the tabletop was a nautical chart of the southwest coast of Vancouver Island.

"How far do you figure Cape Flattery is from here?"

"As the crow flies, about forty, fifty miles," Freeland said. "Why?"

Garner tore the corner off a napkin and wrote on it the date of Caitlin Fulton's apparent exposure to tainted shellfish. He did the same for the estimated dates of exposure for Mark Junckers, Peters and Burgess, and Liam Cole's boat, then placed the chits on Diana Island, Nitinat River, and Cape Flattery, respectively.

"Real pretty, Will," Freeland said. "Care to impress me with some origami now?"

Garner took out a pen and began scribbling some calculations on the remainder of the napkin, comparing the dates on the chits he had made with the distance scale indicated on the chart. "This is impossible," he said, using a bent drinking straw as a makeshift set of distance calipers. "I don't know how I could have missed it. Well, no, I missed it because it's impossible." He looked up at Freeland. "That's the second time this month I've said that; I've never said that."

"What are you babbling about?" Freeland asked.

"Based on what we *have* found in the Nitinat samples and *not* found in the Diana samples, I've been assuming that any bloom would be traveling north."

"Right. Carried along with the surface currents."

"Passively, planktonic, right," Garner said. "But look at the dates," he said, indicating the chits marking the map. "Mark made his discovery five days *before* the divers were killed and three days *after* the Fulton girl was brought in. Now this boat turns up off of Flattery five days *after* the divers and forty miles to the south."

"Meaning what? Multiple blooms?"

"Possibly, but unlikely."

"What, then?"

"There's no longer anything in the water at Diana, and I'd be willing to bet we won't find anything left at Nitinat either," Garner said. "If you look at these points and divide the distance between them by the time between exposures—between victims—you get an almost constant rate of three knots and a steady progression from north to south. A single bloom moving at three knots against the current." Garner would have liked to add the *Sato Maru* to the start of this timeline. He wanted to believe this bloom was somehow linked to the "abiotic stasis" they had found and wanted at least some evidence that it originated in the waters somewhere east of Papa. However, he didn't know the freighter's position when it purged its ballast, nor to what degree the passing storm might have accelerated the slick's course to shore; a calculation of the bloom's progress across the open sea needed more information.

Freeland stared dumbly at him. "*Against* the current? But how?"

"I don't know; like I said, it should be impossible. And we'd better hope it is." He reached across the table and cleared the area in the southernmost portion of the chart. "Because if it keeps moving at this rate, on this course, it's gonna go right up the Strait of Juan de Fuca. To here."

Garner's fingertip slid along the map, coming to rest at a point midway between the cities of Vancouver and Seattle. "From here it can ride the surface currents either north or south."

"Which way?" Freeland said.

"Take your pick," Garner said. "A million people to the north, two million to the south. With nowhere else for it to go."

16

Carol and Ellie returned from Victoria early the next morning. All were anxious to get their new expedition under way, but equally intriguing were the samples they had managed to acquire from the medical examiner's office. Garner divided the various cells into culture dishes, eventually separating out what looked to be some eleven different life stages of the same bizarre new species, *Pfiesteria junckersii.*

"Show these to Charles," Garner suggested. "He'll have a monograph on this bug published by noon."

On closer inspection of the more mature life stages, the microbe seemed designed for calamity. Like its relatives in the genus *Pfiesteria,* this species possessed an unusually large peduncle, a funnel-shaped feeding tube that could be inserted into the cells of its host. Tiny organelles on the tip of the peduncle could transfer a corrosive fluid into the host, dissolving its cells. Like most dinoflagellates, it possessed a pair of flagella, whip-like appendages used for swimming and propulsion. Significantly, the organism's single-celled body also contained large vacuoles, storage spaces for consumed food and manufacturing sites for its battery of nox-

ious defenses. It appeared to possess a statocyst, an organelle to help determine its position and orientation—much like the inner ear of humans—which was extremely rare among plankton. Nearly every sample
they examined also contained trace amounts of a clear, mucoid substance
that apparently served as a binding agent between cells. It reminded
Garner of a gelatinous spider's web, possibly used for collecting prey and
connecting individual cells into a colony of sorts. The electrolytic content
of the substance might even permit a primitive kind of intercellular communication.

"Hitler couldn't have imagined a bug this nasty," Garner said. "It's
similar to the other *Pfiesteria* species I've seen, but it's a more advanced
predator. The slightest changes of morphology here and there; the tiniest
of mutations. And in a colonial form, the whole could be a lot more
deadly than just the sum of its parts."

Like the cysts they had discovered, all the mature *Pfiesteria* cells returned from Victoria appeared to be dead, or dormant. Taking a small
rank of cells, they tried oxygenating the support medium, agitating it,
even coursing a mild electrical current through it. Nothing seemed to en
liven the monster.

Then they applied a mild heat source. The cysts endured water temperatures of 40 degrees Fahrenheit, then 50, then 60. At 70 degrees, the
dormant cysts began to show signs of resurrection. At 80, then 90 degrees, the water in the culture dish began to roil with the activity of the
enlivened cells. As the scientists watched, the cells' tiny armored shells
split open along their hexagonal plates, or theca. Feeding on the culture
media with increased vigor as the temperature continued to rise, the cells
developed hair-like cilia and grew into an amoeboid form a hundred
times larger than the vegetative cyst.

Ninety-eight degrees. Human body temperature.

The twin hulls of the *Albatross,* piloted by Garner and Ellie, and the *Pinniped,* piloted by Carol and Freeland, left Bamfield and sailed down the
outer coast of Vancouver Island, stopping to deploy Betty for one out of
every five nautical miles. They found nothing unusual on the first leg of

their journey, up to and including Nitinat Inlet, where the abalone divers had met their demise. The two crews moored overnight at this location, comparing notes between the field samples and the forensic reports. In the morning, Garner and Freeland donned their gear and performed a series of shallow dives, collecting water and sediment samples. Though laden with nutrients from the river's runoff, there was nothing unusual about the material they collected, as Garner had hypothesized. If *Pfiesteria* had visited this place, it had now moved on.

They continued south toward Cape Flattery using the same on-again, off-again technique with the plankton sampler. Irregularly at first, but with increasing frequency, the data coming from Betty would suddenly drop off. All indication of particulate or dissolved organic matter fell to almost zero. Freeland suggested that the well-worn equipment was finally beginning to show its age or had possibly developed a short circuit. However, reviewing their track, Garner once again noted a pattern to the dropouts, which became more apparent when he marked the locations on the chart. There appeared then an irregular, funnel-shaped area with almost no life in it—another theoretically impossible "abiotic stasis." With Ellie and Freeland glancing through the samples nearly as quickly as Betty retrieved them, there was still no sign of *Pfiesteria* in any of its disparate life stages.

Garner decided to follow the abiotic stasis south, turning ninety degrees into the current each time the data coming from Betty returned to normal levels. In this way the two boats were able to track the wake of the slick, following it by "smell" in the same manner that a bacterium finds food or a shark follows the scent of blood.

"If we really are sailing through the wake of the bloom, without sealed containment suits," Ellie said, "then why aren't we feeling the same effects as the others?"

"I think it depends on the degree of the exposure and the concentration of the dino cells themselves," Garner said. "The mate on the *Sato Maru* kept his distance from the colony as it was incubating in the ship's hold, but the others weren't so lucky. He also had a much larger body mass, which is probably what also saved the one diver, at least for a while."

"Then by the time the cells reached Liam Cole, their toxins had reached a much more lethal concentration," Ellie said.

"Right, but the thing to remember is, this isn't a virus that permanently contaminates everything it touches," Garner said. "It's a moving, predatory mass of toxic cells with temporary local effects. The closer we get to it, or it gets to us, the more deadly the symptoms will be."

"Then what are these 'holes' in the ocean?"

"The slick's calling card. The residue of the colony's feeding, which collapses after a few days. The hole at Papa eventually closed, as did the one at Diana Island and Nitinat River. Right now we're only chasing its shadow, but it's better than nothing."

As if responding to Garner's comment, the *Albatross's* radio crackled. Carol was calling them from the *Pinniped*. She told Garner to look ahead, port side.

With the binoculars, Garner could see the *Pinniped* and, beyond, the area to which Carol was frantically pointing. Garner spotted a low, rounded shape in the water. Another, then another, followed it. He counted eight objects in all, though there could have been more submerged lower in the water.

It was a pod of killer whales, *Orcinus orca,* floating limp and unmoving in the water.

Seeing the spectacle, Garner ordered Carol and Freeland to protect themselves with the drysuits, as he and Ellie did the same. Moments later they were back in their drysuits, their breath hissing through the second-stage regulators in the full facemasks. By then the sailboats had entered the downstream wash of blood coming from the whales, which briefly defiled the pristine white hulls of the boats before being carried away.

"This one still has a heartbeat!" Carol shouted, and immediately deployed her microphone array. She hoped to register some of the low-frequency sounds still rumbling through the animal's vocal chords, and moments later she was rewarded for her efforts. It was unrealistic to expect any kind of communication with the animal, but perhaps the recording would lend itself to some later interpretation.

Twenty minutes later, the whale's heart stopped beating, and all audible vibrations were lost.

Using Betty, they quickly determined that whatever cells had been in the area had moved on but that the depletion in the ambient nutrient and plankton levels was still pronounced. Sea birds were the first marine life to return to the area, then a few fish, but all remained conspicuously away from the dead whales.

This time Garner was the first to remove his facemask and test the air. He radioed the news of their discovery to the Coast Guard, who said they would send a cutter to the site and notify the state wildlife department. The others were too tired to move. They stripped off their protective suits and sat in a small group on the deck of the *Pinniped,* trying to swallow from small cups of warm tea and contemplating the wholesale killing in the water around them.

Ellie looked at the water, where scavengers had begun to move in. "I thought it was only lethal to mammals—humans and sea lions, now whales—but you said it also killed sharks, which are fish."

"Pathogens can sometimes jump from one type of animal to another," Freeland said. "It's diversifying its diet by feeding on fish as well as mammals. Maybe it needs to—the bigger it gets, the hungrier it gets."

"But the fish here, now, seem to be unaffected."

"These fish are cold-blooded," Garner said. "A white shark is, too, but it also has the ability to retain some of its metabolic heat, keeping its body temperature a few degrees above its environment. On a microscopic level, the dinoflagellate probably does kill indiscriminately, but anything with fins and a brain will get the hell out of its way if it can. As a colony, I think the slick seeks out sources of warm blood. That would explain both the feeding response we saw in the lab and the reason why the colony moves on."

Carol shivered despite the sun's warmth. The two boats stopped searching momentarily and weighed anchor, moored to an island of flesh floating in the middle of a hole in the ocean.

Boat and shipping traffic through this portion of the strait was sparse and infrequent; if anyone noticed the two boats clustered around the injured whales, no one bothered to approach. The relative isolation of the *Pinniped* and the *Albatross* made the sudden and direct approach of a large white vessel all the more intimidating. At first Ellie thought it was the Coast Guard cutter, but it was too large and lacked the trademark red slash along the side of the hull. Garner recognized the vessel as a converted minesweeper—at roughly two hundred feet in length and maybe eight hundred tons it was comparable to the *Exeter*—then noted the familiar color scheme of the sleek helicopter tied to the pad on its afterdeck.

"It's the *Kaiku*," Carol said excitedly. "Bob's flagship. After the sinking of Greenpeace's *Rainbow Warrior,* the *Kaiku* became the most recognized vessel in the fight against commercial whaling."

"You must be very proud," Freeland said flatly.

Garner had mixed feelings as he watched the massive *Kaiku* approach. Bob Nolan was evidently ready to make known his personal support for their expedition. However, Nolan wasn't known for his anonymity in such gestures, and Garner began preparing himself for the public spectacle that would certainly follow.

Bob Nolan himself stepped out onto the *Kaiku*'s foredeck and moved toward the bow. His smile radiated confidence, and his arms were extended high above his head in an exaggerated, long-distance embrace.

"Nice work, folks," Nolan shouted as soon as the ship approached close enough. He flashed them a sporty, almost insulting thumbs-up. "Thanks for holding down the fort until the cavalry could arrive."

"It sounds like he actually believes that," Ellie remarked to Garner.

"You can bet he does," Garner said. "But George Custer was the cavalry, too."

"Problem solved, I guess." Freeland shrugged. "Break out the champagne and I'll start arranging the ticker-tape parade."

"Hello!" Carol, shouting back to the *Kaiku,* was too excited by the ship's arrival or too accustomed to her husband's personality to notice his self-promotion. She waved back vigorously, returning Nolan's megawatt smile. "Just in the nick of time."

"Tell that to these whales," Ellie muttered.

Hearing the comment, Carol whirled around and glared at her. "Don't start." Then she regarded Garner and Freeland as well. "Isn't this what we've been waiting for? Some help?"

"It's not the help, it's the pomp—" Freeland began.

"Then let's put some Nolan Group muscle behind this mess and see what we can accomplish," Carol finished.

"It couldn't hurt," Garner conceded, then looked again at the huge, garish hull of the *Kaiku* and added, "much."

Nolan helped them clamber aboard his ship and gave Carol, Garner, Ellie, and Freeland a tour of the ship while they briefed him on the situation. Though dated in its design, the *Kaiku* was impressively equipped. In addition to the helipad (which, like the hull, had NOLAN painted across it in fifteen-foot gold letters) and a small armada of shore launches, the vessel was also equipped with winches to deploy anything from water bottles to submersibles. Garner noted the ports that had been cut into the formidable hull below the waterline, allowing continuous underwater viewing. In short, the *Kaiku* was the perfect vessel for tracking the *Pfiesteria* slick; it was the perfect vessel for almost anything, improving radically on the Cousteau Society's *Calypso,* the vessel after which it was modeled.

The ship's ample mess had been converted to what Nolan proudly described as a "war room" for this particular expedition. Racks held a full complement of charts for all areas from Clayoquot Sound to Puget Sound. GPS, Landsat, and a battery of radiophone and radiofax equipment established ship-to-shore communication. Nolan had even purchased several racks of specimens from the NEPCC, which were now securely housed in newly installed walk-in coolers.

Carol stopped to admire a rack of two dozen Racal containment suits, complete with hoods, boots, gloves, and self-contained respiration and communication rigs. The suits themselves were intended to be disposable, and in the event they ran out of them, Nolan had also packed several cases of Tyvek bodysuits and thick rubber gas masks. "We could have used these on Diana Island," Carol said. "Darling, you really do think of everything."

"Not everything," Freeland said. "Where's the beer fridge?"

Nolan stepped over to a stainless-steel refrigerated locker on the opposite wall, opening it to reveal an ample supply and variety of beer.

"I thought booze was illegal on U.S. research ships," Freeland said.

"*Government* research ships," Nolan corrected him. "This is a privately held vessel."

"Well, then, I'd like to privately hold a beer," Freeland admitted.

"I know a guy on the *Exeter* who would love this assignment," Garner said as Nolan continued his immodest tour. On the decks below them, a small army of laboratory technicians—most of them looking no older than college sophomores—were already preparing to examine the whales. Carol and Ellie quickly went down to the water level to oversee them.

"Welcome to the world's newest floating biocontainment facility," Nolan bragged. "I've set up the ship's entire ventilation system with HEPA filters," he said. HEPA—high-efficiency particle absorbing—filters were routinely used in biohazard facilities to screen out even the smallest virus particles. "Portholes on the first three decks have been sealed and the interior of the ship raised to a positive air pressure to keep the good air in and the bad air out. I've also draped some polyethylene sheets over the main hatchways and hooked them up with UV lighting and enough bleach to clean a white sale. If we need to decontaminate anyone, it won't be as effective as a formaldehyde or a ChemWash shower, but on short notice, beggars can't be choosy." Nolan winked at Freeland, as if knowing he had just rewritten Freeland's record book for jury-rigging and that that fact would be especially annoying to Freeland. "We've still met Biosafety Level Three containment standards."

"I must admit, I'm impressed," Garner said.

"When I heard about what was going on out here, I couldn't refuse," Nolan said.

"But Carol said you did," Freeland challenged. "A couple of times. What changed your mind?"

"I was retained by David Fulton, the Seattle architect. He came to me with the story of his little girl, and it nearly broke my heart." Garner was amazed at the ease with which Nolan switched gears from gracious host to dramatic sincerity.

"An architect had the money for all this?"

"I said *retained*," Nolan said. "Not hired. We work on a contingency basis, like a personal-injury lawyer. We represent victims' rights." Now he was Bob Nolan the class-action attorney. "At least one child was dead, and then Howard Belkin—a fine man, a fine producer, ever see his work?—was possibly killed by the same thing. Apparently, Mr. Belkin's inheritors and insurers are already getting rabid, and executors of his will are willing to compensate us well for clarifying the nature of his tragic demise."

"Ah, there's the hook," Freeland said.

Nolan returned to dramatizing. "The only hook we have here is the investigation of a pathogen that preys indiscriminately on the young and the old."

"We don't know any of that yet," Garner warned.

"Of course we don't, Garner," Nolan admitted. "But that's the spin I'm going to put on it for the news reporters."

"News reporters?" Freeland asked.

"Of course. Belkin Entertainment wants a production out of this, and I said I'd deliver it. They've even assigned a documentary film crew to follow us around, and the *Kaiku* is carrying more cameras than a tour bus. The film crew would be here already, but I had my PR people set up a news conference with David Fulton and two of Howard Belkin's widows. Then my people will bring anyone who's interested out here on a Nolan launch, for lunch." He laughed at his own wordplay.

"Are you sure it's wise to go public with this? I don't see the rationale in generating hysteria until we can identify the threat more completely," Garner said.

"Hysteria paid for this ship! It paid for that beer in your hand," Nolan said, returning to the trademark smile, too perfect to be natural. "What you *don't* see, Garner, is that nobody *cares* if a couple of fishermen got killed up in Canada. And if a few tourists died up there, too, well, that's a shame. Blame it on the water and settle it in court. But as soon as that bug floated itself across the forty-ninth parallel, it entered U.S. waters. Now it's a bona fide territorial threat. It's killing children and the elderly. It's killing our warm and fuzzy friends, the marine mammals.

And that makes it more than just a shame. That makes it a media event, or else my name ain't Bob Nolan, friend."

"The good news is, we didn't screw up." Garner was talking to Zubov on the *Exeter,* using the radio aboard the *Kaiku.* "I checked my math, and assuming you didn't drop her or beat her into submission, Medusa is probably working fine. In fact, she's the only reliable source of data we've got."

"So how do you account for this big row of zeros on her organic data plot?" Zubov asked.

"I still don't know for certain, but we're getting the same thing— these abiotic stases—here, too. They hold up for a day or two, then eventually collapse."

"What is it? Anoxia? Low oxygen from the nutrient load?"

"Negative. The source of them appears to be a carbon-based mucus produced by a species of dinoflagellate no one has ever seen before—including us, so far."

"What do you mean?"

"We're still groping in the dark, trying to get a handle on the size and location of the slick. So far it's been hit-or-miss, and of course it's possible that the dino itself is produced from excessive nutrients. We've been using Betty to find the dead spots in its wake, but her resolution isn't nearly as good as Medusa's."

"So what's the bad news?" Zubov said, the connection crackling. "I hate to ask."

"The bad news is, this thing is big and it's very nasty. We've got a massive, toxic slick out here that appears capable of withstanding significant wave action. For as much as we've been able to track it, it seems to be heading directly into Juan de Fuca Strait. We think it likes the warmer water temperatures in the shallows. And the taste of warm blood."

"Christ. Where did it come from?"

"Believe it or not, I think it started in the hold of the *Maru* and floresced when it reached land, Barkley Sound."

"You mean it contaminated *us*?"

"No, that's where this mucoid substance seems to help us. I think it binds the cells of the bloom into a kind of colony. When the slick moves, it *all* moves, which may be partially responsible for its ability to move against the currents at such an unbelievable rate."

"But you think the freighter was the incubator? Down in the hold, where I was?"

Garner considered this. "If it was, the freighter crew saved the mate's life when they chained him outside; the ventilation was probably enough to keep him alive. The rest of the crew slowly succumbed to the toxins concentrated inside until it was purged from the bilge."

"The bilge!" Zubov said. "I was down there, too."

"Serg, I think it was long gone by the time we got there, if it ever was there to begin with."

"Are you sure?" The big man's voice suddenly sounded shakier.

"Believe me, if you had been exposed to this thing, there wouldn't be any question about it," Garner said. "It kills unbelievably fast, attacking the bloodstream and the nervous system and turning them to jelly. It makes Ebola look like spring fever. It also seems enamored of blubber."

"You're not reassuring me, man," Zubov said.

"Then tell Robertson we've got a critical situation and I need Medusa brought here. I could use the *Exeter,* too, but if I can't recruit you guys, I'll have to use the *Kaiku.*"

"The what?"

"Nolan's ship. I told you the circus here is getting larger. But we do have plenty of beer."

Garner waited as Zubov conferred with Captain Robertson on the *Exeter.* He then relayed word that there was a massive storm front moving in on them from the southwest.

"The good news is," Zubov said, "with this storm blowing up our ass, we'll be coming home early."

"And the bad news?" Garner asked cautiously. He d̶ to hear anything more about storm activity. If his hypothesis correct, it was another storm that had been responsible for the *Sato Maru*'s inexperienced crew purging her ballast and releasing the *Pfiesteria* from its incubator. The same storm then helped to bring the slick to shore, where it was discovered by Caitlin Fulton, then the Junkman.

"The bad news is, if this storm is really as big as it looks on radar, that slick of yours is going to end up in downtown Seattle in half the time."

17

They were like astronauts exploring a bloodied alien landscape.

Carol assembled a small landing party of technicians and took a Zodiac into the middle of the pod of slaughtered killer whales. There were at least a dozen bodies on the surface, and each was carefully inspected in turn by the team of scientists dressed in the orange containment suits from the *Kaiku*. The suit helmets had radio headsets to communicate with the *Kaiku,* though it was easily possible for the team members to communicate directly with each other through their Plexiglas face shields. Surprisingly lightweight, the suits were nonetheless ungainly, and leaning out over the pontoons of the Zodiac to perform dissections was not a simple operation.

Carol was now well familiar with the kind of damage the *Pfiesteria* colony could bring, but her assistants were not, and they could not mask their horror at the sight of the once majestic animals drifting in a bloody slick. Carol had worked with some of the Nolan Group's technicians before, mostly graduate students in their mid-twenties, who might have been employed for oil-spill cleanups or even widespread fish kills. But this was clearly more than any of them could have imagined, and they were tentative in their approach to collecting the necessary blood and tissue samples. Carol found herself several times having to call them out of their ghastly trance, back to the task at hand. Several of them looked almost childlike inside their oversized suits; their nervousness was clearly audible in the irregular hissing coming from their respirators.

"Keep it together, folks," Carol coached them. "I know it's messy. It's a huge job. But it isn't any worse than those fin whales we cut out of that Russian driftnet in the Aleutians." This was an overstated comparison, but one she hoped would keep the troops focused. The whales in the Aleutians had been strangled in a derelict spool of driftnet more than six miles long. It had entangled the whales and sliced deeply into their flesh, bound them until they eventually suffocated, but it had not *liquefied* them. The whales they now faced had been practically turned inside out by their killer, and there were many more victims.

Although the microscopic data would take several hours to collect, Carol's superficial examination of the carcasses showed that the whales had almost identical wounds. Except for some scarring around the mouth and blowhole, the heads of the animals were intact, at least externally. Behind the pectoral fins, however, their digestive tracts had been ruptured by some highly corrosive substance—the fat-soluble toxins of the mutated *Pfiesteria*. The lungs, stomach, and intestines could no longer be identified, and huge chunks of blubber had been sloughed completely from the skeleton. Past the dorsal fin, little more than the vertebral column and the tail fluke remained. The water itself was laden with blackish gray tendrils of ambergris. It was believed the ambergris protected the whale's gut from the claws, spines, beaks, or other hard parts of the prey it consumed. Large prey, that is—squid, sharks, tuna, or sea birds. The microscopic dinoflagellate had been ingested as a predator, not prey, taken in through the whale's mouth and swallowed before the host even detected its presence.

With its taste for warm blood, this species of *Pfiesteria* would flourish in the gut of the whales. Carol recalled how the organism had reacted in the laboratory to the application of mammalian body temperatures, how its various life history stages vigorously uncoiled and extended their long peduncles to feed insatiably on any available surface. She could imagine hundreds of millions of those cells in the belly of a warm-blooded whale, eating their way outward through the body wall. The skeleton, including the spines and fins, would be more resistant to such an attack, being comparatively stronger tissues and less heavily supplied by blood.

Garner was right. The clues left by the fresh wounds on these animals painted a clear picture. *Pfiesteria junckersii* thirsted for warm blood. Marine mammals and humans were the most plentiful source of that. The small, semi-circular wounds Mark had found on Diana Island were ugly enough. What this latest group of victims had encountered was infinitely more destructive. As the killer moved, its cells were either becoming more lethal or more plentiful. Or both.

The team had to work fast. Not because scavengers might disturb the forensic evidence—as with the sea lions, there was a conspicuous lack of marine life around the carcasses—but because the bodies were so thoroughly shredded that they would become waterlogged and sink to the bottom within a few hours unless properly secured. The coming storm front was now threatening to blow anything in the strait directly inland. Carol tried not to think of the repercussions if the *Pfiesteria* neurotoxins, present in such obviously high concentrations, became airborne and were dispersed over a human population. The researchers had to locate the slick before the storm hit, or the colony might be splintered and spread over tens of miles and dozens of potential landfall targets.

Carol's partner grasped her firmly around the waist as she reached over the side of the Zodiac, using a large, scythe-like dissecting knife to slice away a piece of the last whale. As she pulled at the runny tissue, the whale's body pitched and rolled in the waves, threatening to drag her overboard. Several times she glanced down at the greasy, bloodied slick lapping only inches below her outstretched torso. Was the colony still down there? Were it not for the thin containment suit, would she be inhaling the *Pfiesteria*'s chemical defenses? The whales might have encountered the slick fifty miles from this spot, or the team might be floating atop a thriving, breeding, feeding colony at this very moment.

———

Aboard the *Kaiku,* Garner, Freeland, and Nolan gathered on the bridge and tried to pinpoint the slick's most likely position within the strait. Ellie stood nearby and watched them mark a series of bearings on the chart.

Zubov's latest weather report had been less than reassuring. Garner plotted the *Exeter*'s last coordinates on the chart and estimated her arrival time. The ship should be entering the strait within twenty-four hours, with the storm front arriving less than twelve hours after that.

"We believe the slick moved down the coastline at a steady three knots against the current," Garner said. "Betty confirmed that by tracking its shadow, but we lost the track once we entered open water. Finding the whales out here helped us, but we don't know which way the slick went next. Once it reached the mouth of the strait, it should have been pushed inland by the tidal current." He indicated the direction, eastward toward the end of Juan de Fuca Strait where it bifurcated north, to the Strait of Georgia, and south, into Puget Sound.

"Wouldn't that also bring it into fresher water?" Nolan asked. He knew the tremendous effect the Fraser River outflow had on the local oceanography. The estuarine conditions it created could extend for miles into Juan de Fuca Strait and often affected the course and behavior of local fisheries. "I thought most dinos couldn't tolerate a large drop in salinity."

"That's true," Garner said. "But most dinos don't like the turbulence of open coastlines, and they can't swim actively against the current. From what we know of it, this bug is tough enough to swallow anything the conditions out here can throw at it."

"The fishermen are still fairly indifferent to all of this," Ellie said, "because it's not affecting their fish stocks. So if this thing is so destructive, why isn't it killing more fish? Why the apparent change in diet?"

"The slick may have learned to swim," Garner said, "but as far as we know it's still confined to the surface. Mammals and humans are, too, in the sense that we need air to breathe and we use the surface. Fish have the option of swimming beneath it, where the cells may not be as concentrated."

"It seems to behave a lot like an oil spill," Nolan said. "Marine mammals and birds are the hardest hit because they live at or on the surface. Next comes the phytoplankton, which die when the light is blocked out, and the bottom dwellers wherever the slick hits land. Unless it's a really dilute hydrocarbon, fish can escape the worst effects."

"If the slick made it this far, we know it got across the mouth of the strait." Garner traced a line along the southern edge of Juan de Fuca Strait, the northern coastline of the Olympic Peninsula. "According to the tracking data from Betty, I'd say it's going along the shore next. The water is comparatively shallow, so it'll be warmer and more stable. There are also a lot of little fishing towns along there, and I think we should tell them to close their marinas until further notice. We'll also have to alert the shipping traffic to the possibility of taking in some of the slick with their ballast."

"Hold on," Nolan said. "Let's not go hassling the port authority for no reason. We just sailed through that area, and we didn't see a thing."

"How did you know what to look for?" Ellie asked.

"We didn't," Nolan admitted. "But we ran a sidescan sonar profile the entire way."

"What's that?" Ellie asked.

"It's a kind of sonar that sends out a cone-shaped pulse from the ship in either direction of the cruise track," Nolan said, obviously pleased that the *Kaiku* could afford to be fitted with the expensive apparatus. "The reflected pulses give us a picture of the ocean floor in little slices. A computer then pieces the slices together to build a map of the bottom."

"But the slick isn't crawling along the bottom," Ellie challenged.

"True, but wherever it is, it will have some density to it. The sidescan routinely reflects images of schools of fish, zooplankton, even internal ocean waves and thermoclines. Anything that shows a change in density in the water column."

Garner wasn't convinced. "We don't have a clue how big this slick really is, but I'm willing to bet it still gets most of its energy from the sun. Don't forget it's part plant."

"Meaning what?" Ellie asked.

"Meaning that not only is it on the surface, but it's probably spread itself as flat as possible. It's trying to maximize its size so that its cells can respire, and a large surface area will give it greater stability against wave action. For all we know, it could be concentrated in the top six inches of the water column and dispersed over several square miles. If that's true, even the best sonar couldn't differentiate it from the surface itself."

"I still say we would have seen something," Nolan said defiantly. "We were running surface-scan radar for most of the trip as well."

"There's a lot of water out there, Bob. Maybe too much to try cornering a ghost. I don't think even Medusa and Betty sampling in parallel could give us the data in time. It takes too long to deploy and redeploy the equipment."

"So where do we begin looking?" Ellie asked.

"My model says to survey the southern shore first," Garner said.

"Your models have been wrong before," Nolan said. "I think they've outlasted their welcome in these parts."

Garner looked at him evenly. "I hope I *am* wrong, Bob," he said. "I hope this thing had a nice big feed here and just kept on going out to sea. But if we've got less than twenty-four hours to set up some preventive measures, I think we should check out the most densely populated areas first. If I'm wrong, we start moving north. You can set up the search pattern any way you like, just as long as we don't lose the slick over the sill."

"The sill?" Ellie asked.

"This coastline is almost entirely a flooded fjord system. Deep, V-shaped valleys carved out by glaciers thousands of years ago, then flooded by the sea. That's why the beaches in this area have so little sand; there's nothing for it to rest on." Garner tapped the chart between Victoria on Vancouver Island and Sequim Bay in Washington State. "Right here is the foot of the fjord that marks the end of Puget Sound. The sill."

"Why is the sill so important?" she asked.

"The sill prevents the deeper water from mixing in and out of the fjord. Anything that gets trapped inside the sill eventually settles out. Only the surface water is exchanged with the outside ocean," Garner said.

"Ideally, we need to hem this thing in before it reaches the sill. Otherwise it'll get trapped in the inner strait," Nolan added. "The bottom gets increasingly complicated there. It's a real labyrinth, and there's no telling where the currents might move the slick."

"Or where it might move itself?" Ellie asked.

"The worst-case scenario is if it gets over the sill and finds a backwater," Garner said. "The currents don't move it at all in that case. The cells will settle out, forming seed beds on the bottom."

"Isn't its dormancy a good thing?" Ellie asked.

"Not if we're trying to stop it for good," Garner said. "The cysts of some dino species can remain dormant for ten or twenty years. There's no telling when they'll come back."

Ellie shook her head, dismayed. "So where do we start? If the slick is invisible to sonar, how do we look for it?"

From the console behind them, Freeland began to whistle. They all recognized the tune as "Glow, Little Glow Worm."

"Of course!" Ellie exclaimed. "Bioluminescence! Dinoflagellates glow when waves move over them. Cold light produced by their metabolism. I remember my father explaining it to me when I first saw it as a kid."

"The only problem is, *Pfiesteria* isn't known to bioluminesce," Garner said.

"And Saran Wrap isn't known to be opaque," Freeland said. "Unless you have enough layers of it. If the slick is as big as we think it is, we should be able to track it by the way it changes the color of the water."

"So we need an airplane? A helicopter?" Ellie asked.

"We've got the copter," Nolan said. "The next flood tide is just before daybreak tomorrow. If there's anything to see, that would be the best time to look." He noticed Garner's expression. "Oh, that's right," he said. "You don't like to fly, do you, Brock?"

"A satellite image would give us the best view," Garner said, ignoring the chide. "But with these overcast conditions, we'd need something with infrared cloud penetration." He looked at Nolan. "How are your connections with NASA?" he asked, only half-serious.

"Funny you should mention that," Nolan said, motioning Garner and the rest of the group aft down the passageway.

They stepped through a hatchway to the former officers' mess, which had been converted into a seagoing telecommunications studio. A large bank of monitors showed several different broadcasts, from CNN to the

Weather Channel. Another showed the operations going on outside, the team working on the whale carcasses.

"Impressive, but do you get HBO?" Freeland asked.

"No," Nolan said as if he were working on adding it to the list. He flipped several toggles, adjusting the weather maps shown on the screen. "And it looks like our weather satellite feed is out, too."

Ellie was having trouble placing the camera angle as it tracked Carol's group in the water. It didn't seem to originate from the *Kaiku*.

"Direct video feed from the documentary crew," Nolan explained. "Belkin's studio has given me exclusive broadcast rights for any footage we bring back."

Garner was impressed by the speed with which Nolan and the *Kaiku* had positioned themselves on center stage for the investigation. He had clearly done his homework, or had someone do it for him. Nolan gave the outward impression of a man in control, at least in terms of the arrangement of his toys. The danger, as Garner knew, was that Nolan couldn't know nearly as much as they did about the nature of the *Pfiesteria* slick and had, so far, foiled their tutelage more often than accepted it.

Yet another monitor showed Darryl Sweeny clipping a lavalier microphone to his lapel and squinting in the harsh lighting of a camera rig. The younger man still appeared fraught with nervousness, but he was evidently much more at home in front of the media than ferrying researchers in from the North Pacific Ocean. Sweeny appeared to be preparing to speak to a gaggle of reporters gathered dockside somewhere, but Garner could not place the location.

"Where is this?"

"Neah Bay," Nolan said, nodding toward the shore.

Just then the camera panned to show the shark from the ill-fated charter boat. Its tattered remains had been slung up on a pulley like some grotesque trophy, or as if the fish itself were somehow responsible for the current situation.

"This is our closed-circuit feed," Nolan said. "We'll be linking to them by phone once the press conference gets going."

"So you were serious about going public with this."

"Garner, it's already gone public. Belkin's backers had a shit fit when they got the news. They want answers. If they can't get answers, they want ratings. And David Fulton is ready to sue half of British Columbia, including Dr. Bridges here."

The scene on the television switched to David Fulton at the podium. "Turn it up," Garner said to the engineer.

David Fulton looked worn and pallid, every bit the image of a father who had spent two weeks mourning the loss of his child to inexplicable causes. Darryl Sweeny stood near his elbow, part nursemaid, part legal counsel, part image consultant.

"I am not here as an expert. I am not a scientist," Fulton read from his prepared statement. "I am here as a foot soldier. A messenger. My daughter Caitlin was an early casualty in a bizarre ecological nightmare that I fear we are only now beginning to realize." He gestured toward the shark carcass. "This is an indication of what this latest threat can do to one of the most ferocious animals in the world. This is what is happening in our oceans—from pollution, from obscene mismanagement, from God-knows-what. I am told my daughter was killed by toxic shellfish poison. I am told this is the result of a toxic dinoflagellate, a species known as *Pfiesteria*. . . ."

Garner leaned forward. "For a non-scientist, he's sure up on his terminology," he said, glaring at Nolan. "You've been coaching him."

Nolan maintained a maudlin expression. "He's the father of a victim, Garner. He needs answers to provide closure on his grief. I only relayed to him what Carol told me about your own diagnosis."

"But we don't know—"

"That's right," Nolan silenced him. "We don't know. We've got this big, amorphous, *uncaptured* boogeyman out here somewhere. A big question mark—more defined than it was, but still a question mark. But if we want this story to sell, if we want those cameras to notice it, we need to illustrate the bad guy. We need a microscopic Darth Vader for them to make up their fancy graphics and consult experts like you and Carol and give a face to this fucking vampire so we can hold on to the spotlight. Without that we might as well be peddling little green men."

On the monitor, Darryl Sweeny had returned to the podium, fielding questions from the reporters.

"Are you saying that there's a freighter somewhere out there carrying the same organism? The source of this *Pfiesteria* bloom?" a reporter asked.

"Not at all," Sweeny assured him. "The Nolan Group has sent an investigative team to the freighter we believe was point zero of the outbreak. We've agreed not to disclose the ship's name or the name of the shipping company, but it does check out fine now."

That much was true, thought Garner. Zubov and the *Exeter*'s technicians had confirmed that the *Sato Maru* contained nothing even remotely similar to the dinoflagellate. That inspection had come before they had positively identified the microbe, but Nolan's own team had faxed them a preliminary report of all major organisms found in the bilge water of the freighter. Other than elevated bacteria, copper, and hydrocarbon levels, there was no sign of anything unusual.

". . . As soon as we have a definite fix on the slick's location, the Nolan Group will be coordinating the front lines to round it up for good," Sweeny finished.

"Christ," Freeland said. "What do you think this is? Hunting season for the Loch Ness Monster? Now every bastard with a rowboat is going to go out looking for this thing."

"The more the merrier," Nolan chirped. "The more eyes looking, the more exposure for us."

"The more people potentially at risk to die," Garner said sternly.

"And the more essential our disaster management team will look during the crisis," Nolan said.

Garner backed off, tried another tack. "Sweeny said we were going to 'round it up' once we find it. How do 'we' plan to do that?"

"Spillage booms," Nolan said. "I've got four dozen oil spill containment floats on the way right now."

"You're planning to deploy booms in front of a storm system?" Freeland scoffed. *More money than brains,* his look at Garner said. *You're just figuring that out?* came Garner's wordless reply.

"Saunders is right," Garner said. "Booms are good for collecting a surface pollutant, but only under calm conditions."

"We're using Mason booms," Nolan said. "Built and tested in the North Sea. The same kind we used for our job in Prince William Sound."

Nolan was referring to his group's contribution to the cleanup of 11 million gallons of crude oil after the grounding of the *Exxon Valdez* in 1989. Nolan had used the exposure to springboard his company's participation to a global scale, in the end marketing it as though it had been "their job" and not the concerted effort of some two dozen companies and contractors from six countries. Unlike several of those other contractors, who were accused of foot-dragging, the Nolan Group had deposited its checks and quickly moved on to its next marketing opportunity. As the current spectacle grew around them, Garner realized that Nolan probably intended a similar ploy for this "job."

The broadcast now showed a still photo of Carol, tagged with a strip of computer-generated text identifying her. The image was of her somewhere off the coast of Hawaii, her darkly tanned face wearing a huge grin, her beloved humpback whales in the background.

"Of course we are very concerned with the deceased animals found out here," Carol's voice-over said, even and polished in its presentation. "In the past decade, incidents of viral infections in marine mammals have increased significantly. In 1988, more than eighteen thousand harbor seals were killed by a virus in the Baltic Sea. A similar strain of virus—a *morbillivirus,* similar to the viruses that cause distemper or measles—has been responsible for the deaths of hundreds of dolphins. Tumors are being found with increased frequency in turtle populations, and blooms of toxic microbes such as *Pfiesteria* are occurring with frightening regularity. Many of these outbreaks can be correlated with increased levels of nutrients and pollutants pumped directly into our coastal waters. The ultimate economic cost may be incalculable. But the cumulative damage is increasing each year . . ."

"She might mention the same health effects in fishermen, surfers, and children," Ellie said.

"No ratings in that," Freeland said sarcastically. "Surfers aren't as cute as harbor seals."

"Speak for yourself," Ellie murmured.

"This isn't even live," Garner said, nodding at the monitor. "Carol is still outside with the technicians."

Nolan nodded. "We recorded that this morning, just in case there were any questions from the marine mammal contingent."

"The 'marine mammal contingent'?" Garner asked. "Is there anyone who isn't a demographic with you?"

The *Kaiku*'s engineer spun around on his chair, lifting his headphones off his ears. "Ready for you in five seconds, Bob. Four . . . three . . . two . . ." He nodded his head, indicating a small table microphone on the console. Nolan toggled the talk button with practiced ease.

"Mr. Fulton, this is Bob Nolan, live from Juan de Fuca Strait aboard the *Kaiku,* my research flagship. My sincerest sympathies go out to you, your wife, and family. You have suffered a tremendous loss, but it will not be in vain. We are currently tracking what we believe to be a transitory bloom of the dinoflagellate *Pfiesteria,* the first of its kind in the Pacific Northwest. As the first line of defense in this tragedy, we have some of the finest experts in the world to help us out, and I assure you we will close the lid on this potential ecological disaster. . . ."

As Nolan spoke, his voice was broadcast over a second still photo, an obviously staged publicity shot of himself smiling confidently from the deck of a Nolan Group vessel.

"As recently as yesterday," Nolan continued, "I was in contact with Governor Denning. He has pledged his government's support to resolving this issue and fully compensating anyone suffering a loss as a result of this unfortunate natural phenomenon. We are assembling a system for containment of this hazard and certain contingencies are in place as a backup arrangement. Governor Denning and I will also be appealing to the President for his support, if necessary."

"Amazing," Freeland muttered under his breath. "An absolutely, one hundred percent content-free statement."

Garner and Ellie could only watch as, on the engineer's cue, the broadcast showed a montage of Bob Nolan meeting with Denning as well as archival footage of other heads of state and several Hollywood celebrities renowned for their outspoken support of the environment. The clip was set to music at a low background level, and Garner recognized the tune from the current pop charts. The montage ended with a picture of Nolan and Carol at a black-tie function, his arm wrapped confidently around her waist.

Watching the Nolan Group's impressive on-the-fly television production of their situation, Garner couldn't help but be reminded of his own futile efforts in '91. Nolan was effortlessly surpassing Garner at his own game while single-handedly proving one of Freeland's favorite credos: *left to the masses, bullshit beats brains any day of the week.*

"Rest assured," Nolan said, winding up his sermon. "The Nolan Group is on the case now. There's a new kind of killer out here, and we're gonna catch it before it does any more harm. As you now know, my own wife lost her brother to this menace. Despite our tremendous grief at this time—or perhaps because of it—we are tracking this killer with unprecedented vigor. So, for the Fultons. For the fine widows of Howard Belkin. For your family and mine. My friends, I give you all my personal guarantee."

18

As they waited for dawn to come, Garner and Freeland transferred all of their essential gear to the *Kaiku*. Ellie, too restless to sleep, found some food in the galley and paced the length of the research vessel on nearly every deck, stopping and chatting with any crew members she found on the post-midnight watch. One of the mates offered her a tour of the hull's underwater observation pod for a closer look at the whales, but Ellie had already seen too much of the bloody carcasses corralled against the side of the ship. She had seen enough death, period.

From the bridge she could look out over the strait, tinged in bluish light from the moon, now muted by high clouds. It looked too still and serene to imagine that the slick was anywhere in their immediate vicinity. Another Nolan research vessel had joined them that day, bringing Darryl Sweeny. Later still, boatloads of field investigators from the Coast Guard and the Department of the Interior had come to examine the whale carcasses. Curiously, there had been no further support from the military. Working closely with Carol, the reconnaissance teams could find no further trace of the active *Pfiesteria* slick, and the all-clear had been given for them to take off their exposure suits. The phantom had vanished once again.

Farther out, past their own disparate, free-floating marina, Ellie could see the lights of the large freighters making their way into and out of the ports of Puget Sound and the Strait of Georgia. The hulking ships dwarfed the pleasure craft and fishing boats that shared the waterway, each respectfully deferring the right-of-way to larger vessels. During this, the marine equivalent of rush hour, the boats found their way past each other with a camaraderie that would have made their landlocked counterparts envious. Ellie wondered if any of them had heard the news of the *Pfiesteria* threat or even cared about it, given their resolute, money-making schedules. Then she remembered Garner's account of the *Sato Maru* and the charter boat with its dead passengers and missing crew and wondered if any of those distant lights could be another ghost ship. Shivering at the thought, she returned inside.

In the television control room, various weather images were now featured on many of the monitors. The storm front, with its swirling arms of white cloud cover, looked ominously close to their current position. So far they had experienced only an increase in the wind and irregular rain showers, and Ellie knew the worst was yet to come.

"My God," she said to the engineer. "It looks like a hurricane."

"Right now it is, based on wind speed. Sixty-five knots," the engineer said. "But NOAA expects it'll lose some strength over the next few hours."

"I thought the water was too cold to have a hurricane coming this far north," Ellie said. "I mean, I've never heard of it."

"And I'm sure that the storm has never heard of your little dinoflagellate," the engineer said. "But it looks like Mother Nature's gonna dump us all together in the next twelve hours."

Ellie was concerned by the young engineer's cavalier attitude. "Have you ever seen what one of these storms can do? Firsthand?" She could predict his answer.

"No, ma'am," he said. "And I'm not looking forward to finding out this time. Not firsthand."

Ellie walked down the narrow corridors between the cabins of resting technicians and crew, wondering how any of them could find the calm to sleep, given the urgency of locating the slick. She stepped through a hatchway into the main research laboratory, which was as capably equipped as the rest of the vessel. Carol Harmon had set up her equipment over one of the lab benches, securing the smaller pieces with strips of duct tape. Her hair was pulled back into a ponytail, and a set of lightweight headphones rested on her ears. As Ellie drew closer, she could see Carol manipulating a waveform on the monitor. She was listening to her whales.

Carol jumped as she sensed Ellie's approach, then laughed nervously.

"Sorry to interrupt," Ellie said, not completely in earnest. She needed someone to talk to.

"I'm listening to the recording I made of the one surviving orca," Carol said. She unplugged the headphones and played the recording through the computer's external speakers. The vocalizations sounded weak, distorted. "I can't define the vocalizations that easily," she said. "The throat was probably severely damaged, and her lungs were filled with fluid. She was literally drowning in her own blood."

Ellie could see, vaguely, what Carol meant. Compared to the other waveforms, the recording of the injured whale looked blurred and ill-defined, like a poor photocopy. "Can you tell what she was saying?" Ellie asked.

"It's difficult," Carol admitted. "Even on a healthy specimen, it's hard not to put your own perspective on what they might be communicating. That's one of the main reasons this research hasn't gotten more acceptance. It's a constant temptation to over-interpret obscure segments with human nature. Even the word *communicating* connotes that they care a whit about explaining themselves to us."

"As if she's saying she's hurt or describing her pain," Ellie offered.

"Exactly, but that's nonsense. The best I can determine so far is that she was calling to her young, comforting them and trying to lead them out of the slick."

Ellie could feel the tears welling in her eyes. "I might expect that, too," she said. "And it isn't just a projection of your own maternal instincts?"

"Those portions of the waveform match almost exactly with other killer whales I've recorded during predator attacks. It's not an infallible guess, but it's a scientific one. At least I can reference a ninety-eight percent match over all frequencies."

"Now that you've identified it, what will you do with it?" Ellie asked.

"It's too soon to tell." Carol shrugged. "But if it's a warning or some kind of direction to avoid danger, maybe we can send it out in advance of the slick."

"You mean, a deterrent to other whales or seals that might swim through the area?"

"Right. Assuming we can get an underwater speaker set up to broadcast it."

"And assuming we can find the slick," Ellie said. "It's a noble gesture. Too bad there aren't more people around here worried about issuing warnings."

Ellie was referring to Bob Nolan's lackadaisical attitude about warning the local coastal community, and Carol knew it. "Bob's walking a bit of a tightrope right now," she said. "That's exactly where he likes to be. He wants to keep maximum interest in the story, play up the element of danger, then show the world how he can step in to save the day. For his usual fee."

"*Can* he save the day?" Ellie asked. "Does he even know what he's up against?"

"Do any of us?" Carol said.

"I think some of us know more than they're telling," Ellie said. "I still can't believe that a naturally occurring organism could do this. Could look like this, breed like this, or kill like this."

"I took you as being too sensible to be a conspiracy theorist, Ellie," Carol said.

"Not a conspiracy," Ellie corrected. "Just malevolent human intervention. Someone with a background like Charles's could easily try to culture an organism like this. Maybe even manage to turn it into an incredibly destructive weapon."

Carol's expression only dismissed Ellie. The notion that dinoflagellates could be designed as a weapon or that Charles Harmon would know something about it seemed equally ridiculous to her.

To Ellie, Carol's forced ignorance on the subject was not quite as unnerving as the rookie crewmen on the boat or their egotistical leader, but it came close. "At the very least, where is Charles's 'fatherly advice' when we could use it the most?"

"You don't know my father," Carol said with a patient grimace. "Wherever this thing came from, Bob's in charge now," she said. "I don't expect everyone to agree with his methods, but Bob is a brilliant man. He took some convincing, but now that he's got his resources committed to this, I'm sure he's the best man to clean up this mess."

"You can cut the PR crap with me," Ellie said. "You weren't there today when he systematically vetoed Brock and Saunders's suggestions, then went on TV to tell everyone to sit back and relax. 'No problems here, folks. Hell, bring up the kiddies for a front-row seat.' "

Carol's hard edge had returned. "If I recall, you wanted more public awareness about all this. At least that's what you said at the hearing."

"Awareness of what? Bob's not telling them what we know, or what we think we know. He's not preparing them for a worst-case scenario. This is all a harmless ghost story he can use to get ratings, and while he's controlling the shots, the real experts can't do their job. He's taking bits and pieces of someone else's expertise—Brock's in this case—and peddling it out there to serve his own purposes, regardless of the consequences."

An acidic smile curled on Carol's lip. She was obviously annoyed by Ellie's attraction to Garner. The message was clear and she only needed to add, "Brock is a grown-up, Ellie. He can call his own shots. If he felt constrained by someone else's rules, he'd take off and write his own. I know—I've seen him do it."

The rotors of the helicopter were already turning by the time Garner arrived on deck. Nolan himself was in the pilot's seat, with Freeland and Darryl Sweeny strapped into the back on either side of several equipment cases. Like Garner, all were wearing orange Racal containment suits. Until they located something, there was no need to don and pressurize the hood of the suits, which would only waste the battery on their self-contained forced-air respirators.

As Garner approached the helipad, Ellie stepped out of the shadows. The wind from the rotors whipped her hair around her face. Garner couldn't help but notice how tired and drawn she looked.

"I wanted to wish you good luck," she said.

"I take it you haven't slept," Garner said.

"Has anyone?" she said with a weary smile. "Occupational hazard, I guess. I'm used to it."

She suddenly looked fragile, vulnerable. Garner wrapped his arms around her and gave her a hug. "The *Exeter* should be here in another two hours. The *real* cavalry is on its way. Maybe even with some field technicians who know more than how to look good on camera." He gestured toward Sweeny and Nolan. "We'll be back just after sunrise, I hope."

"Brock . . ." she began.

"Don't worry," he said, gazing directly into her eyes and losing himself for a moment in their warmth. "We'll have a line on this thing before noon."

"Promise?"

"Yeah. Promise." He smiled.

I hope so, her expression said. She watched Garner turn, stoop low, and climb into the helicopter. Almost immediately, it lifted off the deck, rising into the predawn blackness above and quickly vanishing except for its running lights.

Ellie turned and looked out over the water. Sometime during the night, yet another Nolan vessel—this one flat-topped and resembling a barge—had drawn alongside the *Kaiku*. Stacked on its deck were several large containers, similar to grain hoppers in their design. The containers looked utterly foreign to the rest of the equipment she had seen, yet also somehow familiar. Where had she seen this type of container before?

Water traps. The containers were huge locking buckets, like the kind carried by aircraft dispatched to put out forest fires. What on earth could Nolan have in mind for those?

"For a minute I thought you might have chickened out on us," Nolan chided Garner after they had taken off. "Don't worry, I'll keep her steady for you." The helicopter was much smaller than the one that had retrieved him from the deck of the *Maru,* with a much shorter range. Even with most of the cargo compartment empty and all the unnecessary adornments stripped away, there was barely enough room for the four men.

"Keep both doors open back there," Nolan instructed Sweeny. "Wide open. If there's any chance we're gonna run into some aerosols or bad air, I don't want them accumulating inside the cabin. We've got the suits, but I figure fresh air is still our best defense."

Almost immediately, the too-familiar ball of cold steel settled into Garner's gut. From the moment the thin skids of the helicopter left the pad, an uneasiness crept through his entire nervous system. He was grateful that the pitch blackness beyond the windows would lessen the sensation of flight, at least for a while, but the noise and swirling air washing through the open cabin doors provided a constant reminder of where they were. The small size of the craft and the lack of a horizon on which to focus only increased the likelihood of his becoming disoriented.

Nolan's undue concern for Garner's acrophobia was clearly intended to unnerve him. For whatever reason, Nolan was trying to keep Garner off balance enough so that he could continue to run the show himself. But Garner knew that as soon as they found the slick and determined the extent of its threat, common sense would have to override Nolan's show-manship, quickly and decisively. When that happened, he only hoped that it wouldn't be too late.

Far below, the small congregation of study boats could be seen falling away from them. The pod of whales was now cast in an icy white light, and several of the vessels were coming alive as the morning watch took over. After sunrise, they could expect the gallery of pleasure boats and news helicopters to return, perhaps tempting fate by inching even closer. Of course, Nolan's film crew would be there to capture every gruesome moment.

At its largest dimensions, Juan de Fuca Strait was 100 miles long and 25 miles wide, with an average depth of over 200 feet. There was simply too much water to adequately sample with Betty, Medusa, or any other single-source device. Without a proper radar image of the area, there was little they could do except look for anomalies on the sea surface.

"What are we looking for again?" Sweeny said. "Phosphorescence in the water?"

"Bioluminescence," Garner said.

"What's the difference?"

"Phosphorescence comes from the absorption of heat. Bioluminescence comes from a chemical reaction within the organism. It doesn't require or produce heat, so it's called 'cold light.' "

"Whatever," Sweeny said, unimpressed.

"Just look for little flashes of light on the water, on wave fronts, or in ships' wakes," Freeland said.

"How little?"

"About a tenth of a second." Freeland grinned as Sweeny rolled his eyes at the challenge. "Don't blink."

They made three complete traverses of the strait before the sun began to rise through the broken overcast to the east, and they saw nothing. The flickering light should have been produced as the incoming tide moved over the bloom, but either these cells did not naturally floresce or the helicopter had yet to fly over the slick at the proper angle. As the sun rose higher, they would begin looking for a discoloration of the surface or a flattening of the wind-generated waves where the slick changed the ocean's surface tension.

As they turned back toward the north, Sweeny pointed out two large vessels steaming toward the *Kaiku,* a long string of bright orange spillage booms in tow behind each one. "The rest will be arriving this afternoon," Sweeny said. "We've got up to ten miles of them, if necessary."

The equipment cases in back contained several data-transmitting current meters—modified transponders—that could be activated and dropped into the middle of the slick. They had also brought several canisters of fluorescent green dye, similar to the compound naval aviators used to mark their location in the water after a crash landing. The transponders, in conjunction with the dye, would keep the slick at least partially visible until the crew could contain it with the spillage booms. Even in the relatively calm conditions, the booms seemed ludicrously insufficient. Waves washed over them easily, and the joints between float sections looked fragile. Their first and only line of defense was little more than that—a line.

As dawn broke, they could see the *Kaiku* and her escorts far off in the distance. Despite their formidable size and construction, the vessels looked like vulnerable toys placed before the expanse of the Pacific Ocean to the west. A thick black wall of storm clouds crept ominously toward shore.

"You mentioned 'certain contingencies' in the broadcast yesterday," Garner said into his headset, looking over at Nolan. "What do you have in mind?"

"If spillage booms are his first idea, I hate to think what's at the bottom of the barrel," Freeland said from the back. He and Sweeny were now looking out either side of the helicopter with powerful field glasses.

"You said the cells are attracted to warm blood. I'm guessing they're equally attracted to warm water, perhaps even a concentrated source of heat like a water-treatment outflow."

"Or a whale."

"Exactly. But either way, the colony is seeking heat conducted through the water. So on the way up to Neah Bay, we placed a series of fixed CTDs." The CTDs—or conductivity, temperature, and depth meters—were used to define water conditions in a given area. Both Medusa and Betty were fitted with similar devices, but carried them along with them as they sampled. Fixed CTDs recorded ocean conditions at a given spot. "We've recalculated the warmest thermoclines in the strait in the past twenty-four hours. That's where we expect the slick to move."

"And?" Freeland coaxed.

"And our data agree with the model Brock suggested," Nolan admitted. "So our first contingency is to try and steer the slick away from the inhabited areas using a submersible hot deck—an artificial thermocline."

Garner was only vaguely familiar with hot deck technology. Large, submerged platforms up to fifty feet long that could be towed behind a ship, hot decks were designed to heat the hull plating of icebreakers and other vessels trapped by ice floes. They could rapidly heat the water surrounding the hull in order to keep metal components from becoming too brittle and sampling rigs from freezing. In application the still-experimental devices were rarely used, since the extremely high heat capacity of water meant that the hot decks required too much power to be practical for extended use. The heat was also devastating to both plant and animal life, boiling them in seconds. It seemed that Nolan had learned little from the fiasco that was Prince William Sound after the *Valdez* accident. There, the Nolan Group had pioneered a method of scouring the affected shoreline with hot-water jets from high-pressure hoses. What they had touted as a quick and effective cleanup system had ultimately killed many more organisms than the spilled oil.

The helicopter passed over another vessel cruising toward the *Kaiku*. Its open deck was filled to capacity with what looked like purple crystals. It was hard to see the material, covered as it was by thick polyethylene sheeting.

"Contingency number two," Nolan said. "Industrial-grade potassium permanganate."

"What the hell for?" Freeland asked.

"The temperature profile of the ocean only tells us where the slick is going. But if it's warm, why does it go anywhere? It doesn't seek heat to *feed,* it seeks heat to *reproduce.* It could stay in place and filter food from the passing water. Another thing in common with all the places it's been found is a high copper content in the water."

Garner agreed. Zubov had mentioned that the bilge water of the *Sato Maru* was polluted with trace metals, and they had found elevated copper levels at Nitinat Inlet and Diana Island. Ordinarily, any significant increase in biologically-available copper would likely have killed off an ordinary dino as well, but this bug continued to defy convenient description.

"That's right. The water below us is exceedingly high in copper, too, from a combination of factors. Call me an old softie, but I don't think this bug wants to be feeding on whales, or human beings for that matter. Its feeding becomes too inefficient that way. It can feed on plant material. It can feed on sunlight. So why doesn't it?"

Garner's mind was racing, stepping ahead of Nolan's convoluted logic. "Ordinarily, the *Pfiesteria* would feed on lower plant material. Phytoplankton, bacteria, and cryptomonads."

"But if the copper content of the water is too high . . ."

"Its natural food source is probably depleted."

". . . Leaving it to acquire more exotic tastes, or die."

"The copper would also deplete the levels of a dino's natural predators: rotifers and ciliates," Garner said. Without the influence of predation, the dinoflagellate population would be left essentially unchecked.

"But if we can dump some potassium permanganate into the water around the slick," Nolan said, "the permanganate will bind the excess copper, and the lower food sources will return. The ciliates and rotifers will rebound, too. We've already tested it in the lab."

"I can't believe you're contemplating this," Garner said. "The strait isn't a goddamn petri dish. Do you even know what effect a large-scale dump of potassium permanganate will have out there? Have you thought about the effects of dilution? What about a lethal increase in pH? What you're proposing could upend the entire ecosystem."

"You'll never get the state to go for it," Freeland agreed. "It's too risky."

"I don't need the state's approval," Nolan said smugly. "As of this morning it's gone over their head. I had a conference call this morning with the White House. Based on my briefing, the President himself authorized the dumping, if necessary." Nolan turned in his seat and fixed his eyes on Freeland. "Get that? *The President himself.*"

"I didn't realize the Commander in Chief moved the Nolan Group around in his war room, too," Freeland said.

"He does now," Nolan said. "He's part of *our* war room now, and he knows it."

Garner was still evaluating Nolan's plan. "Even if dumping the permanganate works on the slick, how long do you think it'll take for the ciliate population to return? The system responds on a scale of months, not minutes. By that time we could have a whole new set of problems on our hands."

Nolan held up his hand. "I've considered the possible costs," he said. "I've also considered the potential expenses if we do nothing. The argument ends right there. I say so, the President says so, and we'd all be just as pleased as punch if you said so, too, Mr. Garner."

Garner chose to say nothing.

"And imagine how it's gonna *look* on TV," Nolan continued, fully enjoying this moment. "A fleet of Bell Hueys dropping clouds of purple cough syrup on this most uncommon cold. *Apocalypse* fucking *Now* on psychedelics and codeine. Beautiful."

"You wanted to know what was at the bottom of the idea barrel," Garner said to Freeland.

"I'm sorry I asked," Freeland said.

"Extreme measures for extreme times," Nolan said. "First we have to find it and corral it. And if we find it, we're going to make sure we don't lose it again."

"There," Freeland said. The certainty in his voice made the rest of them turn around, craning their necks to the place he was pointing.

Now they could all see it, a quarter mile off, extending nearly a mile from shore: a sudden change in the sea's surface. The small wind-generated wavelets—cat's paws, as sailors sometimes called them—abruptly ceased, leaving only a flattened, greasy texture. The discontinuity extended for miles, though miraculously none of the local shipping traffic lay anywhere near it. Moving closer, they could see that the slick *was* bioluminescing, a faint glittering generated by the waves stimulating each cell. Then they saw the fine, silk-like mucus floating just below the surface, the binding agent that gave the slick its definition and strength. It was as though a huge, wafer-thin cloud had been stretched beneath the surface. Much easier to see were the sporadic outcrops of trees, which had been branded a sickly brown color, just like the forests on Diana Island. There was clearly still a concentrated aerosol component to the *Pfiesteria*'s toxins.

"Video, Darryl, video!" Nolan yelled. "Are you getting this?" Sweeny already had a heavy, professional-quality newscam raised to his shoulder.

"Suits on," Garner said. He, Freeland, and Sweeny sealed their exposure suits and turned on their respirators. Nolan's hands remained on the controls, his helmet peeled back behind him.

"Get your helmet, Bob?" Garner asked.

"In a minute," Nolan said. "Darryl, get a shot of this over my shoulder. Make sure you can see it's me piloting."

Nolan brought the helicopter down to two hundred feet. As Sweeny followed Nolan's directions, Freeland pulled the side door fully open, slipped out of his seat, and began sorting through the equipment.

"Strap yourselves in," Garner said. "Safety lines." Freeland turned his harness around and motioned to Sweeny, who tied himself to the airframe, then did the same for Freeland.

They worked quickly, with Garner kneeling between the pilots' seats while loading the dye canisters and passing them to the men on either side. Leaning out on the helicopter's skids, Freeland and Sweeny activated the canisters, then let them fall into the slick below.

Garner watched the first few canisters hit the surface and break open, revealing the fluorescent green contents. Ordinarily, the dye would float passively away from the point of impact, marking the spot at the head of a long, willowy tail. These, however, were immediately consumed by the slick. The dye compound was taken up by the cells—invisible from this height—and passed from one to another through the mucoid film. Within minutes, the contents of each canister had been dispersed over a quarter mile or more.

"Christ," said Garner, shaking off his vertigo as he looked down over the side. "It's grown into one gigantic organism. A single colonial lifeform." All along, he had been expecting a huge morass of cells, individual cells, each tumbled and dispersed on its own independent tack by the combined effect of the waves and wind. What he now saw was a single, gigantic creature, a carpet-like monster stretched over several square miles. What now lay below them rewrote all the rules about life in the sea, about the capacities of life on earth. And, in its horrifying implications, the capacity of death as well.

"The water here is too shallow for big ships," Nolan commented, clearly oblivious to the causes of the dry-mouthed terror Garner was now feeling. "That's why we missed sensing it, but not by much."

Garner focused on the growing fluorescent slick washing along the coastline below. It was within five miles of the closest towns on the Olympic Peninsula. If the slick was still moving eastward, they had less than two hours to capture it.

As Nolan maneuvered the helicopter over the center of the slick, the other men continued to load and jettison the harmless dye. The green coloration spread and spread below them, independent of any wind or wave action.

"I don't like the looks of this, Bob," Garner said. "We're right over it. Put your hood on, at least until we know how extensive the aerosol is." Once again, Nolan ignored him.

Sweeny had taken up the newscam again. "This is amazing. Absolutely awesome."

"Back to work, Darryl!" Freeland yelled. "You'll have plenty of time to take pictures later."

Sweeny set down the camera and climbed forward, pulling out a knife and flaying open the packing straps on the transponders. In his exaggerated haste, a protest to Freeland's reprimand, the blade came back too quickly and sliced into Freeland's exposure suit, splitting open its forearm. Unlike their hoods, the exposure suits they wore were not pressurized. The surrounding air could quickly seep into the tear.

Freeland cursed Sweeny's stupidity and quickly located some duct tape. Garner helped him patch the suit, but the damage concerned both of them. The repair could provide only a temporary seal, and they had no other suits.

Garner got to his feet and moved aft to assist Freeland. Suddenly, the helicopter bucked in midair, scattering the passengers and equipment.

The first of the transponders clanged against the door frame and fell overboard, yet to be activated.

"Watch it!" Garner yelled at Nolan as the helicopter bucked again.

"It's not me," Nolan said. The fear in his voice confirmed that the helicopter's sudden movements were beyond his control. He coughed several times, and his own movements seemed slower, jerky. Tears were welling up in his irritated eyes, and seeing this, Garner grabbed Nolan's hood himself and clamped it down over Nolan's collar. He thumbed the blower unit and felt the whoosh of purified air fill the hood.

Nolan's hands were still gripping the controls. The helicopter seemed to stabilize, then they could hear the pitch of the engine change, struggling under the increased force of the strained fuselage. A metallic-sounding automated voice came from the dash. *"Stall . . . stall . . . stall . . ."*

"Nolan, quit screwing around!" Garner shouted. If Nolan was trying to induce his acrophobia, it was working. Garner felt his guts rise up against his ribs, a dull ache thudding in his head, throbbing louder than even the rotors whirring noisily above his head. Garner could see Freeland just ahead of him, bracing himself against the doorjamb as he activated, loaded, and jettisoned the next transponder. Behind him, Sweeny was still fumbling with the video camera, trying to keep his balance in the sudden turbulence.

"Stall . . . stall . . . stall . . ."

Nolan's eyes scanned the array of warning lights that suddenly lit up the helicopter's control panel. One in particular caught his attention: LOW OX.

"The air pressure's too low," he shouted back to the rest of them. "The engine is suffocating. Drop what you can; we have to get out now!"

If Nolan increased the throttle, he risked stalling the engine completely. As he tried to maneuver laterally, the tail rotors threw the rear end of the helicopter into a wild spin. The men in the back were tossed back and forth. The harder Nolan tried to grip the control stick, the more the helicopter seemed to resist.

In the rear, Freeland and Garner activated the last of the transponders. Garner fought a growing fog, vertigo threatening to steal away the last of his visual acuity as the helicopter pitched and spun.

The helicopter rocked again, throwing Garner and Sweeny hard to the floor and knocking Freeland out the open door. Through the savage vibration, Garner saw Freeland's safety line snap taut, then begin to unravel. *Sweeny didn't fasten it properly!* Garner's thoughts screamed through his growing blindness. Garner threw himself across the cabin, one arm grappling for Freeland's, the other trying to grasp the end of the safety line. Six feet below the floor of the helicopter, Freeland swung wildly on the safety line, trying to find a handhold.

The safety line released from its ring just as Garner's hand closed around it. The full weight of Freeland's body slammed through his shoulders. "Hang on, William!" Freeland bellowed.

"Help me!" Garner yelled at Sweeny.

Sweeny was being tossed around as well. He dropped the newscam, then toppled over the scattered equipment cases, reaching for Garner.

The helicopter angled sharply upward. *He's climbing. Nolan's trying to climb out of the aerosol to get the engine to catch,* Garner thought. He wondered how much altitude they had lost and braced for the impending crash.

Then he saw it. The tape over the gash in Freeland's suit had come open. The skin of his forearm was clearly visible, and as Freeland twisted and turned on the line, the tear opened even wider. Garner could see the panic in his friend's eyes as they both noticed the opening. The panic turned to terror as the exposed skin began blistering and peeling as a result of the toxic aerosol all around them.

The helicopter spun back in the other direction, and Sweeny landed heavily on top of Garner. Both men seized the safety line and began pulling Freeland up. Then another jolt, and the bulky newscam bounced past Garner's field of view. It toppled out of the helicopter and slammed into the face shield on Freeland's suit, cracking the Plexiglas wide open before falling into the slick below.

For a moment it felt as though the helicopter had stabilized. Nolan's attempt to climb out of the aerosol seemed to be working. Then the blistering that Garner had seen on Freeland's arm spread with impossible speed across his friend's face, turning it an angry red color and mixing with the blood pouring from his smashed nose. Freeland began to scream and clutch at the peeling skin, in his agony frantically pulling away from Garner's grasp.

"I've got him! I've got him!" Garner could hear Sweeny yelling. Garner could see Sweeny's hand grasp Freeland's for a sickeningly brief moment. Garner locked eyes with Freeland, willing his friend to hold on for a few more seconds. Then Freeland's grasp slipped from the line as the muscles of his hand and arm were dissolved away and split apart inside the leaking suit. The rest of his body pitched backward, falling three hundred feet into the slick below, his screaming lost in the howling of the engine.

The colony quickly closed over the spot where Freeland entered the water. His body, or whatever remained of it, never returned to the surface.

19

Retreating to the periphery of the noxious aerosol cloud, the Nolan Group helicopter circled for another twenty minutes as the men looked for any sign of Freeland. Garner's tenable acrophobia was quickly replaced by sickened, anxious fear for his friend, and he grew increasingly frustrated as he studied the surface of the slick. The fluorescent green dye and free-floating transponders rolled and shifted in the water but remained contained within the mucoid boundaries of the slick. They found nothing, not even a scrap of Freeland's orange Racal suit. Finally, running dangerously low on fuel, Nolan turned reluctantly back to the *Kaiku*.

On the return trip, Sweeny's face was sallow and pale, eyes drifting and unfocused, hands absently gripping at his seat. He looked like a scolded child on a miserable family vacation. Nolan continued to cough inside his hood, and his face looked flushed. His uncharacteristic silence concerned Garner much more. He wondered if the loss of Freeland and the near ditching of the helicopter had delivered a much-needed message to Nolan. They had finally glimpsed the size and latent ferocity of the slick firsthand. They had seen the burned and brindled trees along the unsuspecting shoreline. What they had witnessed still seemed impossible to comprehend.

Then there were the slick's human victims. Twenty-four people so far, dozens of marine mammals. How many more were yet to be discovered in the slick's wake, and how many now waited, utterly unsuspecting, in its path? This was not going to be a routine cleanup operation, and a harmless resolution seemed highly unlikely. Despite his public persona, Nolan was not the type to make decisions based on emotion. Garner wondered if behind Nolan's bravado there was a "contingency" to retreat while the mission was still profitable, as he had done in Prince William Sound. And Kuwait. And the Gulf of Mexico.

As they approached the ship, Garner could see the silhouette of the *Exeter* entering the strait off Cape Flattery. Its familiarity was reassuring, but after the events of that morning, Garner found himself wondering if even they could truly accomplish anything. Now all he could think about was getting Medusa into the water. He could now put his trust in Robertson, McRee, and Zubov to deal with the task at hand. Whatever their recourse, it meant placing more lives—the lives of more friends—at the mercy of the slick.

Over the headset, Garner was patched through to McRee on the *Exeter*'s bridge, and he quickly summarized the situation. There would be no time for a full debriefing or a proper welcome home. Nolan confirmed his sponsorship of the *Exeter* as part of the containment operation, and Garner immediately began coordinating the deployment of Medusa.

"She's primed and ready to fly, boss," Zubov reported. The cheerfulness of his tone told Garner that the strain in his own voice was becoming evident.

"Not before we get the *Exeter* protected," Garner said. "We'll ferry you some exposure suits." In order to deploy Medusa properly, the surface ship would have to pass very close to the slick, if not directly through it. "I don't want anyone near that thing without protection—biohazard suits and HEPA filters," Garner continued. "Send all nonessential crew over to the *Kaiku*. At the least, they can help Nolan's technicians clean up the mess behind us. From there, we can use the launches to get them back to shore."

"Where's the goddamn Navy?" Zubov said, reflecting Garner's own concerns. "They've got to be better equipped for something like this."

"In the eyes of the military, this thing is still a natural phenomenon, not a disaster or offensive threat," Garner admitted. "CBDCOM or USAMRIID should be here, too. And the CDC. But until an hour ago, we couldn't even confirm the existence of a natural agent. We've got a doctor with us, and Nolan's staff have been on the phone to the Navy, the CDC, and CBDCOM since this thing began. Now it looks like we've got White House approval to call in anyone we need."

"Screw 'em," Zubov said. "By the time they get mobilized, this thing will be all over, anyway. At least, it'd better be."

Garner shrugged out of his seat belt, pulled off his helmet, and swung down from the helicopter before it was fully on the *Kaiku*'s deck. He peeled back the top of his exposure suit, the fresh air cool and bracing on his sweat-soaked body. Behind him, Darryl Sweeny broke out of his trance and leaned out of the rear door of the helicopter. "Hey, Garner—" he called out. "Garner, come back."

Garner spun on his heel and started to reply. Then he saw Freeland's defunct safety line still clutched in Sweeny's hand and his rage boiled over. Garner lunged at Sweeny, yanking the smaller man easily to the deck.

"What the hell did you think you were doing out there?" Garner yelled, his knee coming down hard on Sweeny's chest, pinning him. "A man's life was at stake and you were taking pictures of it, you little shit!"

Sweeny struggled and tried to respond, his wire-rimmed glasses fogging up. "I—was just doing what Bob said—"

"That's your first mistake," Garner said. "Listening to him is going to get a lot more people killed."

Nolan moved quickly to restrain Garner. "He's right, Brock. I told him to take the video," Nolan said. "If you want to blame anyone, blame me."

Garner dropped his hold on Sweeny and turned on Nolan. Garner's right hook was solid and fast. His fist smacked into Nolan's eye, spinning him around and dropping him to the deck with a thick moan.

"Consider yourself blamed," Garner said. He left the two men supine on the helipad and stormed off in the direction of the *Kaiku*'s war room.

Standing at the foot of the afterdeck stairs was the director from Nolan's documentary film crew, a thin, nervous-looking man who had been severely seasick since arriving the previous evening. The man scratched at his beard, gaping at the drama he had just witnessed.

"Wow," the director said.

"Too bad you didn't get that on film," Garner hissed, shouldering past him.

As the morning progressed, the film crew and a few reporters shuffled up from their cabins and wandered the *Kaiku*, shooting sound bites and B-roll footage of the operation. Now and then Nolan would specify a shot he wanted and provide a few words of expository narration. The documentary director complained that Nolan's new shiner would create continuity problems in post-production. The eye had begun to blacken and swell noticeably, then, equally obvious, had been covered up with theatrical makeup.

Nolan assigned Sweeny to communicate their finding to the news media and issue an advisory bulletin through the Coast Guard. As the word went out, the *Kaiku*'s radio room was deluged with calls demanding more-specific information. Sweeny fielded most of these with competence, spieling long winded but purposely nonspecific answers to the rest. News helicopters from two local stations and a third from CNN provided a nearly constant din in the air above. For now, the whales remained the center of attention, if only because Nolan and Garner alone knew the precise location of the slick. Once Nolan's media machine was fully on-line, the next responsibility—providing the facts necessary to act on the posted warnings—would revert to Garner.

As soon as the film crew had gone back down to water level to interview Carol, Nolan steered Garner into an alcove.

"Nice makeup, Bob," Garner said. "It really brings out your cheeks."

"I want you off my ship, Garner," Nolan said icily. "Go back to the *Exeter* and run your operation from there."

"Why? So it'll be easier for you to pull up stakes on this little circus tent and disappear while your retainer is still in the black?"

"If you come near me or my staff again, I'll slap assault charges on you."

Looking at Nolan this close, Garner saw that he expressed a slight facial tic when he was upset. Garner had never noticed it before.

"Really? What about Sweeny?" Garner said. "Saunders is dead because of him. I could just as easily charge you with attempted murder for the way you handled that helicopter."

Nolan pulled back the front of his storm jacket, revealing a handgun in a thick leather holster. "Don't you fucking tempt me," Nolan hissed. He turned and stalked off down the corridor.

"Your director's got you playing Dirty Harry now, huh, Bob?" Garner called after him.

Nolan turned back. "Don't push it, Garner. I mean it. You can spend my money, but stay the hell out of my way."

The *Exeter*'s entry into the operation was implemented smoothly. A dozen personnel—including Zubov, McRee, and Robertson—remained on board, while the rest of her crew and science team were shuttled to the *Kaiku*. Ellie joined Garner on the launch delivering the biohazard suits.

"Are you ready?" Garner asked her.

"Ready for what?" she asked.

"You've got to brief these guys on what to expect," Garner said. "You're our Chief Medical Officer now."

Ellie blanched. "You've got to be kidding. I'm not an expert on this. All I know about *Pfiesteria* is in those books you gave me."

"Not true," Garner said. "You've seen it in the lab, too."

"What about the CDC? What about USAMRIID? They're the ones with expert credentials."

"You've got the same credentials as the rest of us: you're *here,*" Garner said. "Secondly, you've seen what this bug can do up close, which is something no one at USAMRIID or the CDC can say. And thirdly, these guys are my friends. They deserve the best."

As the crew of the *Exeter* gathered in the officers' mess, their intuition was to give Brock Garner and Ellie Bridges their undivided attention. Ellie had never been less prepared to give an impromptu public-health seminar, but she managed to quell her nervousness and follow Garner's lead. Their audience looked as though they still needed some convincing as to why the present problem was more important than simply ignoring it and traveling a few miles farther to home port.

"Less than two miles from here is a massive toxic plankton bloom," Garner began. "We believe the species or species complex involved is from the genus *Pfiesteria*. It's a tough, nasty bug usually found in stagnant estuaries. How it got here is still anybody's guess, but it's just become our problem. I took a look at it this morning. It's approximately eight square miles in size, held together by some kind of durable mucoid suspension. It's been tagged with fluorescent green compound and transponders, so it'll be easier to track, at least until nightfall. It also has a toxic aerosol associated with it. The aerosol *isn't* marked, so anytime you get near the slick, you will be required to put on biohazard suits. If you find yourself in the water with it, pray that your containment suit is completely sealed. Otherwise, it isn't contagious and it doesn't infect nonliving surfaces. If you think you're getting too close to it, you probably are. Pull back and regroup."

"Like an oilrig fire," one of the winch operators offered.

"Exactly," Garner said. "Only this one is still out of control and growing. It's on the move, and it's heading for Puget Sound. The containment suits are our only protection when working inside or downwind of the slick, so wear them and report any symptoms to Dr. Bridges." Garner had, in fact, told Ellie about the neurological symptoms he had seen in Nolan. Ellie had asked to examine Nolan but was waved off. Nolan clearly wanted no evidence of his carelessness in the helicopter to be revealed. "It goes without saying that the operation is somewhat at the mercy of the elements," Garner concluded. "We're at the mercy of the wind and the waves and this gale coming through tonight."

Ellie then gave the crew a recap of what she had seen in the ER and the health effects of the slick as they understood them so far. "In all likelihood, the slick was 'born' in the bilge of the derelict freighter you discovered. How it got there in the first place we don't know, but the conditions were apparently suitable enough to act as an incubator for the *Pfiesteria*. The crewmen probably died of respiratory arrest or trace amounts of the dinoflagellate's toxin in their food supply. Severe paralytic shellfish or finfish poisoning."

This jibed with what Garner, Zubov, and McRee had observed. The lone survivor avoided the food and kept his cabin well-ventilated.

"The slick was purged into the ocean and pushed ashore by a storm front, probably gaining strength and size," Garner added. "Exposure to the aerosol likely killed Caitlin Fulton, Mark Junckers, and a few acres of coastal forest, but the slick itself had moved on by the time we found the dead sea lions or the whales."

"The poachers at Nitinat weren't so lucky," Ellie said. "They probably swam right through the bloom and were killed almost instantly. The little boy succumbed to the aerosol, but his grandfather was apparently exposed to a much smaller dose. Perhaps none at all, if the slick had already moved."

"And it moves all on its own," Garner added. "This thing is no longer planktonic. The jelly that holds it together has given it the ability to move seemingly at will."

"Are you saying this thing can *think*?" Robertson asked.

"In a way, yes," Garner speculated. "But I'm still banking on our ability to think better."

"There are at least four ways to become exposed to the toxins," Ellie said. "Direct contact with the skin, ingestion, inhalation, or incidental transmission through open wounds."

"What are the symptoms?" McRee asked Ellie.

"At first, a burning of the eyes and lungs," Ellie said. "Runny nose, nausea, paralysis, violent mood swings, headaches, increased blood pressure, and possibly a loss of short-term memory. That's the aerosol neurotoxin going to work."

"Sounds like McRee going to work," Zubov said, and the crew around him chuckled.

"And I'll assume none of you big, strapping gentlemen are lactating," Ellie said, "so I won't waste any time talking about possible contamination of mothers' milk. Anyone with hepatitis, kidney disease, diabetes, HIV, liver disease, or a weakened immune system should probably also step back from the front lines. We can't take any additional health risks."

"Liver disease?" McRee laughed. "You just eliminated ninety percent of these sots."

"We don't know the exact properties of the toxin because we haven't been able to collect and isolate it," Garner said. "Precedent is obviously no help to us, and the toxins produced by the *Pfiesteria* cells will adopt different properties based on the water temperature, the amount of sunlight, cell concentration, and food supply."

"Exposure to the cells themselves is, as far as we know, absolutely lethal," Ellie said. "The cells feast on warm blood and dissolve the skin with a potent, fat-soluble toxin that's as effective as battery acid. From the tissues we've examined, it can dissolve an entire whale within a few days."

"My God," McRee said. "It could eat through Sergei in less than a *month*!" Again, more laughter. The crew was hearing every word; the humor was welcome to keep everyone's nerves at ease. The debriefing had given them all they needed: a target. After a brief orientation on using the Racal and Tyvek containment suits, the crew dispersed back to their stations, ready for another day at the office.

"See? You did fine," Garner said to Ellie.

She chewed her lip. "The next time you deputize me for something, I'd like to at least know about it in advance."

Garner brushed back Ellie's hair, took her face in his hands, and kissed her.

"Ellie, I've just deputized you."

With Garner's touch, the tension within Ellie ebbed. "Thanks for sharing," she breathed.

———————

Garner's next destination was the *Exeter*'s bridge. The crew patched into the transponders dispersed that morning and allowed the GPS to begin transmitting its data stream on the slick's position. Two of the devices had misfired—including the one that fell out of the helicopter before activation—but the remaining five appeared to be working. Although the devices were reporting their location accurately, there was not yet any way of determining whether they had remained within the cell mass.

The next step was to prepare to tow Medusa through the slick. The *Exeter* would have to approach the slick as closely as possible from the upwind direction, letting Medusa trail out to the side of the cruise track. Once the sampler was activated, they could begin collecting data on the conditions within the slick itself. Adding Medusa's findings to the water circulation data from the current meters and atmospheric data from the Doppler, they could then construct a predictive profile of the slick.

"I want dummy floats dropped into it, too," Garner said. "If that mucus is as thick as it looks, the more flotsam we can add, the better we'll be able to see it."

"What about the dye?" Robertson asked.

"I'm worried about dilution," Garner said. "We didn't add nearly enough to clearly mark the slick, and what we did drop was spread out immediately. Once the color begins to weather, we'll lose our best view of it."

"We could use the permanganate," Zubov said, nodding toward the Nolan barges a quarter mile away.

"I hate to try, but we might not have any other choice," Garner admitted. "The permanganate will mark the area and, if Nolan's right, maybe even act as a chemical deterrent on the slick's behavior." He radioed the *Kaiku* and confirmed these arrangements. The water buckets were filled with the crystallized potassium permanganate, and two Coast Guard S-61N helicopters were placed on alert to assist with the dispersal. Like the *Exeter,* the helicopters would have to approach the slick from an upwind direction. Alternating runs, the helicopters would bomb the slick with the powder, much like water bombing a forest fire. The permanganate solution would hopefully bind enough copper in the water to slow the slick's progress and stop its feeding. Any increase in pH, slight or profound, would affect the *Pfiesteria* cells first.

Garner mentally ran through the remaining list of equipment available to them. The hot deck was impractical. They would have to tow the device through the slick, and its heat—from what they knew of the colony—would not only attract the cells but promote the hatching of any dormant cysts. The crew's ability to do any sampling of the slick on the surface was limited to the winch capabilities of the *Exeter* and the *Kaiku*. Hovering above the slick, any helicopter drawing too close to the aerosol might be suffocated, as Nolan's helicopter had been. Although aircraft were rarely useful on station, a low-level radar map would be helpful to the operation. Unfortunately, all of NOAA's local resources were monitoring the storm. Using the *Kaiku*'s underwater observation pod would be utilitarian but might expose too many crew members to the slick. The *Exeter* was now the expedition's working vessel, and Garner's team would need all the biohazard suits available. Garner cursed again at the limited vision of Bob Nolan's containment plan. Equipment and materials for some kind of quick-fix ecosystem management plan, but comparatively little consideration given to saving human lives.

"Where's the storm front?" Garner asked the *Exeter*'s weather officer.

"Fifty miles and closing," the woman said. "It's still coming in on a wire."

"Slowing?"

"Nope, but it's a steady tack. We've got twelve hours to batten down the hatches."

Another twelve hours would have them under nightfall again.

"Lights," Garner said. "If we have to baby-sit this thing in the dark, I want it lit up like Wrigley Field. Let's see if these TV crews can make themselves useful."

Zubov let out a sarcastic chuckle. "It must be nice to have pockets deeper than one's conscience."

"Oh sure," Garner said. "Haven't you heard? Nolan and I are fast friends now." He winked. "It's for the children."

"Just as long as you include the children of Ma and Pa McRee among them," McRee said.

Nolan reconnoitered with the camera crew and loaded them onto a launch for some wide-angle shots of the operation. Over the next hour, Carol supervised as the whale carcasses were untethered from the *Kaiku* and the ship was put on a heading to intercept the slick.

As they got under way, Nolan returned to his stateroom, arriving just as Carol stepped out of the shower.

"I managed to fight off the allure of the bed and settled for a bracing shower instead. God, I'm exhausted," she said, rubbing a towel through her hair.

"It'll be worth it," Nolan assured her. "We've got enough press out of the past twenty-four hours to generate new contracts for the next five years."

"And it's far from over," Carol said. At her husband's silence, she stopped and looked at him. "Bob? We're not done, right?"

"I don't know," Nolan said. "The *Exeter* is here; two Navy LSDs are on their way up from Everett as an escort. It could be time for the bank-rolling of this little adventure to revert back to the public sector."

"What do you mean, *back* to the public sector?"

"It doesn't matter, Carol."

"Bob, please tell me. I've been too busy to talk to you about this, but it does seem a little odd, even for you, to take up the case of David Fulton pro bono. Howard Belkin, too. I'm glad you're here, but I want to know *why* you're here. Who's really paying for this?"

"It *doesn't matter*," Nolan repeated. "Their money is the same color. Same number of pennies to the dollar."

"Bob, people could still *die*," Carol said incredulously. "A *lot* of people." As she took his hands in hers, she noticed that her husband's fingers were trembling.

"Then maybe I'd rather let someone like Garner take the blame for it. He can afford it more than I can."

"This isn't about money, or reputation. It's about duty."

"Is it?" Nolan said. "Is duty what your father had in mind when he built this thing?"

Carol shook her head. "What are you talking about? What 'thing'?"

"The mutated *Pfiesteria*. The colony. Do you think Charles was thinking about the wildlife of Puget Sound when he agreed to breed it? Don't you think he knows this would come off better as a military exercise?"

Carol was stunned, uncomprehending.

"Why do you think the Navy is taking such a stand-back approach to this?" Nolan said. "They know what they're up against, because they financed it. Charles was the man they asked to create it, and the money from it built his cabin. It probably also paid for your college fund."

"It killed my brother—" Carol began, then stopped. If Charles had known about this *Pfiesteria* all along, had engineered it himself, wouldn't that explain his vehement denial of its existence? Would he stand up in public and spread outlandish lies about Mark to cover up his own research? The notion that she could even suspect it of her own father left a cold lump in the pit of her stomach.

The truth was, she might never know the truth. She slowly sank to the bed, her mind numb. At the top of her building rage was the thought—the remotest shred of possibility—that Ellie's naive assertions about Charles's hidden "expertise" could be correct while his own daughter had remained utterly blind. What had given an upstart like the young MD such license in human nature?

And why, at this very moment, did Carol even care what Ellie thought?

"If they cultured this organism as some kind of weapon, why are they using it *here*?" she asked. "Or was this an accident?"

"It wouldn't be the first time."

"But surely they know how to stop it," she said, unable to look at her husband, her mind racing with unspoken possibilities. "An antidote or some kind of counteragent?"

"That's what the permanganate is for," Nolan said. "And the hot deck. How else do you think I got them up here on such short notice?"

"So they'll work?"

Nolan studied his wife's face. "Until this morning, I'd hoped so. Now I'd have to say Garner himself is the only serious counteragent we've got."

"If they don't know what will work, then why aren't they trying something else? Why is Brock out there on his own?" That any agency would let a manufactured threat go unchecked in order to deny involvement was not improbable, but that made the idea no less reprehensible. That her husband could only now confide such information to her was mortifying.

"If you knew about this, how could you just let it happen?" she asked her husband incredulously. The man who stared back at her had become a complete stranger.

On the *Exeter,* Garner and Robertson coordinated the positioning of the containment booms with the captains of Nolan's ships. The barges would wait for the arrival of the *Exeter* and the *Kaiku,* and each ship would take up a train of the booms, drawing them together around the leeward edge of the slick. They then had to stabilize the floating morass against the storm.

"Do you have a location in mind?" McRee asked. "Where do we rendezvous with them?"

Garner checked the latest list of current data. "We've got less than three hours before the slick reaches Juniper Bay," he said. "We're going to have to intercept the slick west of there, before it hits any areas of human habitation." Garner confirmed this with the ships towing the booms. "They'll be in range in twenty minutes. Nolan made sure they have their own biohazard suits."

Robertson gave the course and speed to the *Exeter*'s navigator. "Three hours doesn't give us much time," Robertson said. "Especially if we have to deploy that rat's nest of yours first, then reset the A-frame to take the booms."

Garner thought for a moment. The data Medusa would provide about the *Pfiesteria* colony would be instrumental to any eventual plan to defuse its threat. "Let the *Kaiku* take the first train of booms, slowing the slick while we sample with Medusa. When we've got what we need, the *Exeter* can switch over to take the second train and close the containment."

McRee scratched his head. "Dammit, Brock, this isn't *Swan Lake*. You know how much deck space the Medusa rig takes up. You know it'd be tight switching one for the other on the winch in that amount of time even if nothing goes wrong."

"Nothing's going to go wrong."

"Something *always* goes wrong with that bitch," McRee said.

"Not today," Garner said. "We had our designated fuck-up this morning." He thought of Sweeny's incompetence, the last glimpse he had of Freeland, falling away from the helicopter. "We can't afford any more."

Behind them, Zubov was studying the data coming in from the slick. "Where are we planning to catch this thing?" he asked.

"West of Juniper Bay," Garner repeated.

"No, *where* are we going to catch it," Zubov said. "Against the shore, in the shallows where you found it?"

"Neither ship can maneuver in that shallow depth," Robertson said. "We'd have to drag the booms around the offshore fringe, using them to hold the slick against the shore, like a beach seine."

"Holding it in place is going to lead to a lot of shore damage," Garner said. "Not to mention the possibility of the aerosol drifting inland."

"And if the slick was in deeper water?" Zubov said.

"That would be safer, sure," Garner conceded.

"Not for us," Robertson said. "If we do this in open water, we leave ourselves fully exposed to the storm. If we drop the booms and run, that slick'll be tossed around like a cork out there."

"It's a moot point," Garner said. "There's no way we can arrange to tow the slick offshore in the time we have. That would take a massive coastline containment effort."

"That's why I asked," Zubov said, tapping the monitor. "Look at this."

The four men looked at the numbers flicking across the computer-generated map. According to the data recorders, the colony was moving into deeper water entirely on its own.

"Can that be right?" McRee asked.

"If it is, we just got our first break," Garner said.

20

On August 26, death came to the town of Juniper Bay, Washington. Among those who rose early—which was most of the fishing-based population—few heard or noticed the Nolan Group helicopter flying low over the coast, then traversing the strait several times, slowly progressing in their direction. None of them saw the occupants drop their sampling instruments into the water, the near crash, or the loss of Saunders Freeland.

To the ragtag assemblage of local gillnetters and seiners who made their way home from the fishing grounds around 4:00 A.M., the weather-beaten marina looked no different than it did most mornings. The fleet fishermen returned in time for breakfast, tied off their boats, and ambled up the rocky footpaths toward home. After a hot shower, a plate of eggs, and some conversation with their families, they would fall into bed and lapse into a sweaty sleep through the worst of the day's heat. A long but unremarkable night.

Conversely, the heat this year was remarkable. The air temperature rose quickly after sunrise and stayed uncomfortably high all day.

Though the continued brilliant sunshine was welcome on the usually rain-soaked coast, not even the relief of a sea breeze could be counted upon to break the late-summer heat. Encouragingly, the TV weathermen promised some temporary relief with the coming storm. In response, the men had worked longer and harder than any night in recent memory to get their catch in. If the storm was going to be as severe as the forecast predicted, the heavy rains and wind would stir up the bottom, scattering the fish stocks or sending them deep, cutting the catch for as long as a week. Then it would be the long weekend, when several of the men would acquiesce to the wishes of their loved ones and stay home, doing family activities, working around the house, or preparing their nets for the fall season.

To any fishermen still awake late that morning, the brief news item about potential red-tide conditions was unremarkable. Toxic plankton blooms could have a drastic effect on shellfish catchments, but most Juniper Bay fishermen relied on finfish for their livelihood. Like the heat itself, such warnings were inevitable and didn't last long. Those who knew anything about plankton blooms assumed that the storm would break the stable water conditions along the coast and that the threat would subside. It was all part of the natural ebb and flow of nature. They went back to work, or slept, or—remembering the weathermen's piss-poor track record for forecasting—thought about where they would fish the following night.

That was how it happened that, on the morning of August 26, the denizens of Juniper Bay's subsidiary economies felt the first symptoms of the slick's approach. Its invisible aerosol slipped silently into town on a gentle but persistent summer wind from the north.

Among the first affected were the children playing in the small park overlooking the shallow inlet. As they climbed and swung on aged gym equipment blistered and rusted by years of bracing sea air, several children began to experience red, irritated eyes and runny noses. Their mothers attributed these symptoms to summer allergies or the thick scrub brush that grew in abundance around the park. While a few would venture to Foster's Pharmacy for some advice and supplies, the majority simply gave out Kleenex and hugs. They took their children home for lunch and suggested some indoor activities like coloring books or Nintendo, then turned their attention to the daily household chores or perhaps the afternoon soap operas. They could have no way of knowing how sick their children would be by dinnertime. The parents of Juniper Bay would soon be as ill-prepared as David and Karen Fulton had been to learn that their children would not live through the next twenty-four hours.

To the elderly at the Miromar retirement home, August 26 began as just another summer day, sticky and uncomfortable, but at least another day. Sitting outside in whatever shade they could find, many of the residents developed irritated eyes and sinus pain and blamed it on the heat. Working in the Miromar's modest garden, some attributed their sudden difficulty in breathing to simple overexertion. Others developed stomach irritation and discomfort in their bowels that rapidly escalated into violent nausea and vomiting. As the understaffed facility was suddenly hit by a pandemic of strange, seemingly unrelated illnesses, several of its pledges began to die. Whatever it was, the nurses and support staff were ultimately no more immune to the same symptoms. The town's closest approximation to medical assistance was quickly overrun by an assortment of skin irritations and respiratory problems, blurred vision, and uncontrollable tremors.

Along Main Street, nearly everyone seemed to have contracted the same flu-like symptoms overnight. Some blamed pollen. Others, feeling sick to their stomach as well, thought it might be a kind of dysentery or bacteria in the town's water supply from a lack of fresh water replenishment. By mid-afternoon, Foster's had run out of diarrhea and stomach medication, and half the town's retail workers had gone home sick.

On Euclid Street, a Pac Bell lineman was discovered hanging from a telephone pole. He had apparently suffered a stroke and fallen from where he was repairing a transformer. A length of cut line wrapped around one leg hung the lineman upside down and dangling eighteen feet above the roof of his utility truck.

On Mercer Road, a pregnant woman fainted behind the wheel of her car. The vehicle rolled downhill for four blocks before crashing into a stone retaining wall. The woman remained pressed against the steering wheel for several minutes before anyone took notice, the continued wail of the car's horn drifting mournfully through the town like an air-raid siren. Her immediate concerns for her unborn baby's health were quickly replaced by deep-seated panic over her own condition. Headaches and chills would take her life within two days.

At the local high school, a Red Cross blood drive sponsored by the local Girl Scout troop was marred by the suddenly violent reaction of one of the donors. The elderly man began shaking uncontrollably on his cot, blood and saliva dribbling from his nose and mouth. The attending nurses were able to restrain the man's thrashing until it subsided. The man died before the ambulance arrived.

The worst affected were those who had spent the day around the town's waterfront. Within minutes of exposure to the inlet water, several dockworkers had developed painful welts and sores on their skin. By noon, most had begun to cough up phlegm as their lungs filled with fluid, blood, and pus. On the water, outboard motors inexplicably stalled, leaving several charter boats drifting in the shallow coastal water, which had taken on a strange greenish color and a bitter, cloying smell. Some of these boats felt the strange conditions ebb as they moved farther into the strait. Others would be found drifting or would be blown ashore in the hours after the storm, their passengers and crew suffocated by the acidic air.

Within six hours of exposure, eighty percent of the town's population would be experiencing symptoms akin to nerve gas contact. The trees and shrubbery would begin dropping their leaves in an unseasonable and dramatic parody of autumn. In countless kitchens and on serving counters around town, milk would curdle in its container and food would be permanently tainted for anyone left to consume it.

Within twelve hours, half the town would be dead or airlifted to hospitals. Some would die in their sleep, oblivious to the threat that had taken their lives. Others would watch in horror as their ulcerated flesh began to rot on their bones, their struggles growing increasingly weak as the toxin paralyzed their respiratory systems. Most would die with their eyes still open, blank expressions somehow pleading for an answer to the question: What caused this?

Within eighteen hours, every single person remaining in Juniper Bay would keep themselves within arm's length of a radio. They would hang on every word of the latest reports about the weather and the containment operations in the strait.

In the narrow shallows along the southern edge of Juan de Fuca Strait, the colony had exhausted its food supply. The morning flood tide had helped to carry it here, but the bottom was hard and broken. The paucity of flora and fauna provided little sustenance. The victims claimed by the slick's toxic aerosol could not feed it. The sludge and garbage around the marina held some promise, but the smell of hydrocarbons and tin-based nautical paint was cloying and unpalatable. Worst of all, the water was turbid and thick with mud, depleting the amount of available sunlight. The concentration of dissolved oxygen in the water was too low for its cells to properly respire. As the colony had grown in size, so had its energy demands and its hunger. Electrical impulses emulating complaint flickered back and forth across the thin neural network provided by the colony's mucus envelope.

The tide was beginning its first ebb of the day's cycle, and the colony used this momentum to pull itself away from shore. It floated passively on the surface as the water level slowly fell, then stretched itself toward deeper water. First it allowed the renewed supply of oxygen to percolate throughout its formidable mass. Then it began to strain ocean plankton from the sunlit layers of the open channel.

Within hours, the colony's decay had stopped. Its cysts began hatching once again and its growing cycle was reactivated.

In the storage vacuoles and statocysts of each of its cells, the colony could sense that the barometric pressure was dropping quickly. The onshore wind from the west was increasing, as was the cloud cover. The light levels were changing, and the increased chop of the waves tugged urgently, threatening to disperse the colony. Flotsam that the slick had encountered bobbed and rolled within it, irritating its cells and creating resistance against movement through the water. The debris smelled of warm blood, however, and that was reason enough to feed. The colony concentrated its digestion on the impediments, much as a trapped animal gnaws at its restraints.

Soon the resistance to its movement would be gone.

21

With the news cameras about to roll tape, Bob Nolan was no longer smiling. In fact, silently and surprisingly, he had begun to come unglued. Beads of sweat reflected the glare of the lights, and the tension in his face caused a venous bulge to appear on his tanned forehead. He blinked his eyes and the slight facial tic had become almost constant. The first bulletin from the CBDCOM quarantine of Juniper Bay had been in his hand for less than ten minutes; it already felt as though a month had passed. Fortunately, the confusion and frantic preparations aboard the *Kaiku* made him a less attractive target.

"How did this happen?" he barked at Garner over the radio. "Why didn't we post a proper warning?"

"You know as well as I do," Garner said. "We've only got a handful of markers in the slick and about as much dye, both probably concentrated in its densest region. We still don't have any way of knowing how thin the colony has spread itself."

"Dammit, you said we had two hours!"

"I did, but we have no way of accounting for the movement of the aerosol," Garner said. "It's far more diffuse and not measured at all by the transponders or CTDs. This isn't just an oceanographic problem we're dealing with."

"No shit, Sherlock!"

"Bob, we're doing the best we can."

"Then do it faster!"

"Just keep the wolves entertained while we go to work. *Exeter* out."

Nolan cursed again and read the CBDCOM bulletin for the dozenth time in as many minutes. Fully three-quarters of the town's population had been exposed to "some kind of nerve agent." Half of those exposed were already in critical condition, with no apparent culprit. Three dozen people and ten animals were confirmed dead. While the symptoms suggested biological activity, whatever had caused the sudden illness could no longer be detected in the vicinity of Juniper Bay. Having claimed leadership in the containment operation, Nolan now had to provide an explanation for the horribly unexpected sequence of events. If his team was in such tight control of the situation, then how did this happen?

"Two minutes, Bob," one of the broadcast engineers said.

Nolan looked up from the bulletin, panic clearly visible on his face. Across the war room, only Carol registered the expression, and hers was far from sympathetic. "I've been trying to radio Daddy for the past hour," she said. "There's no answer. Bob, what's going on?"

"Don't worry," Nolan said. "It's under control."

"What's under control? Are you going to tell me that what happened at Juniper Bay was all in someone's grand design? Is the Navy just sitting out there, waiting to see what happens to us so they can go dump this mess on China or North Korea next?"

"What happened at Juniper Bay is nobody's fault but Garner's. It's his model."

"And your stupid secrets that kept him from using it."

"We were too late!" Nolan hissed, then faltered. "An hour too late."

"I gave you a *week* to come out here," Carol said coolly. "But you had to hold out for more money. More *drama*. Congratulations, you got it."

"One minute, Bob," came the engineer's prompt. A woman stepped in to daub the perspiration from Nolan's face and apply some more makeup to his swollen eye.

"We're going to stick to Garner's plan," Nolan said. "That's all there is to it. We don't have any choice. But if this thing fails, it's his fault, not mine. Understood?"

Carol stood her ground, staring at her husband.

"Ma'am? You're in my shot," the cameraman complained.

"You coward," Carol said to Nolan.

"I've been called worse." He gave her a reptilian grin. "So have you."

"Ten seconds, Bob . . ."

"Honey? The shot?" Nolan shooed her back with his hand.

Carol turned on her heel and stormed away.

"Dammit! If you knew about this, why didn't you say something earlier?" Carol nearly screamed in the confines of the *Kaiku*'s radio room, inspiring the radio operator to step out for coffee now that Charles Harmon had been reached by his daughter.

"I don't know any more about it than you do, dear," Harmon said in a measured tone. "Garner made the identification, and his appraisal seems sufficient." His daughter's persistence might have forced him to stop "screening" his calls, but he was clearly in no mood to be goaded into discussing specifics. At least, not over the radio.

"Why don't I believe that?" Carol sputtered. "Why am I inclined to believe Bob over the word of my own father?" She relayed the inferences that Nolan had made about Harmon's work and demanded to know if they were true. "I'd say it's because you've been such a callous, insensitive bastard since Mark's death, but you'd probably correct me on that, too."

"Please don't dwell on Mark," Harmon replied quietly.

The mention of Mark seemed, for the first time, to have a softening effect on Harmon. Her father was not being stubborn, Carol realized; he really *didn't* know what to say. That didn't exclude the possibility he knew something about this organism, only that he didn't know how to say it.

"I didn't know you had any sort of positive identification beyond what we saw in the lab," Harmon continued. "They said on the news—"

"Forget about the 'positive identification,' " Carol said, exasperated. "Do you or don't you know where this dino came from?"

"No, I don't," Harmon said. He was telling the truth about that.

"Then why would Bob lie about it?" Carol said. "Why would he suggest this *Pfiesteria* is some kind of weapon that you—"

"Carol," Harmon said abruptly. "Unless you are on a secure military band, I don't think you want to be talking about accusations and hearsay."

The oddness of Harmon's comment forced Carol to stop her attack and listen for the message between his words. *Unless you are on a secure military band.* Why would Harmon suggest that, unless he knew the military was somehow involved? The media was carrying no word of a Nolan/military collaboration on this, so why would her father suggest as much? Regardless, the suggestion that somebody might be monitoring the *Kaiku*'s radio transmissions was a definite warning.

Carol took a deep breath and started again. "Daddy, is this species like anything you've ever seen?"

"Yes, it is," Harmon said. "It looks like several species I've worked with. Especially *Pfiesteria.*"

More code. *He* had been working with *Pfiesteria.* He had seen *"Pfiesteria junckersii"* before but had lied to them about it. She thought again about the public hearing and how the more forcefully the case had been made for an exotic bloom of *Pfiesteria,* the more her father had sputtered and all but condemned the notion as preposterous. Harmon and Bouchard had each been covering their asses, but for markedly different reasons.

Carol was silent for a long moment, absorbing the magnitude of her father's deception, yet admiring his courage to—if only in double-speak—admit it to her at this point.

"Daddy, what can we do about this?" she asked. "What can we possibly do to stop it?"

Harmon's reply came a long moment later. "I don't know," he said. This she knew was the truth, unaltered and direct. Her father, knower of all things known, demigod of the entire field of marine pathogens, admitted he *did not know*.

Then Carol heard even more unexpected words from her father. Words that revealed to her exactly how much danger they were now in and rekindled her sense of unbridled fear once again.

"I love you, Carol," Harmon said, his voice barely audible. "I am very proud of what you and Brock are trying to do out there."

"I love you, too, Daddy," she said, slightly amazed at how easily and naturally the words came, even after all this time.

"Do what you can," Harmon said. "But if that isn't enough, then please . . . just come home safely."

In his home on Helby Island, Charles Harmon hung up the radiophone and immediately felt the dank chill of the room soak into his bones.

He was lonely again.

He was out of scotch again.

He was out of answers for the first time.

He shuffled through the cabin and considered radioing the marine station for a water taxi. Bouchard had scotch, and if Bouchard wasn't in, the library was always open. Harmon was halfway back to the radio before he admitted he didn't really want to go anywhere. His daughter was in a great deal of danger, fighting to right a wrong from twenty years ago. Fighting to stop a once-nonviable monster that would, it seemed, haunt the Harmon family to its last proud member.

Harmon moved to his living room and located the remote for his television set. There was no need to search the dizzying array of satellite channels to find CNN—it was already there. The channel hadn't wavered since Carol, Garner, Ellie, and Freeland left Bamfield. Now there were updates on the situation to the south at least once every hour. Bob Nolan was conducting his usual circus with uncommon effectiveness, and twenty million Americans sat transfixed, watching the spectacle and wondering what in hell was really going on out there, prodded every few minutes by the doom-laden voice of James Earl Jones.

Harmon alone knew exactly what they were watching, but he had no answers for them, either. The monster had a name, but it did not have a solution.

He settled back into his recliner and focused his weakened eyes on the television. Within minutes, CNN's live coverage of the events at Juniper Bay returned to the screen. James Earl Jones excepted, Harmon could barely hear what was being said and adjusted the volume on his hearing aid. As usual, the confounded device amplified not only the volume of the television but also the ticking of the pendulum clock in his study and the sound of the waves on the beach below.

The magnified cacophony was enough to drive a sane man crazy.

Hell, it could drive almost anything to the brink of self-destruction. . . .

Taking the lead in the containment operation, the *Kaiku* was the first vessel to intercept the trains of spillage booms. While the service tug held the lead end of the train, the *Kaiku* took up the trailing end, carrying a five-mile line of floats north, then west in a wide arc around the shoreward side of the slick. It began to rain, and as the wind increased, so did the chop across the surface of the water. Were it not for the viscosity of the slick—the cells' attraction to themselves—portions of the slick would easily have slopped over the barrier as the sea conditions worsened.

On the *Exeter,* Garner and Zubov prepared Medusa for deployment. The *Exeter* was now less than one nautical mile away from the last recorded position of the slick. The onshore winds and flood current were ideal for their next task: to let out enough line to allow Medusa to fly through the slick, downstream of the *Exeter.*

As the two men worked quickly on the ship's afterdeck, a single news helicopter circled around and came down for a closer look. Garner glared up at it and waved the newsmen away with his arms. The pilot of the helicopter waved back, but maintained his position.

"Stupid bastard," Garner said. "Tell the radio room to order him back." The memory of Freeland's loss from the suffocated helicopter kept gnawing at his concentration, fueling his anger. Now, on top of that, Juniper Bay had been compromised because they were too late in locating the slick. How many more lives would be lost because they were moving *too damn slow*?

"Move, move, move!" Garner barked at the winch operator.

"Ready," Zubov confirmed. "All circuits are working."

Minutes later, Garner's sampler was lowered from the A-frame into the water, then let out a quarter mile. Slowly, the wire angle slid to starboard as the sphere entered the slick.

Garner ran back to the main lab and began checking Medusa's data reports. His eyes registered and interpreted the numbers on the computer monitor nearly as fast as they were produced. He wasn't merely skimming them. He mentally recalculated every figure as it was read.

It was a good hair day. Within minutes, information about the density and composition of the slick began to enter the databanks on the *Exeter*. A series of monitors set up in the lab showed real-time snapshots of the plankton composition of the colony. Garner could already identify several *Pfiesteria* life history stages; Medusa's computers would compare these images to digitized micrographs and begin to calculate the age structure of the colony. As soon as that process was complete, Garner would download all the data and interpolate it with the atmospheric and hydrographic information provided by NOAA. The model would be complete. His crystal ball would be fully formed, but weeks' worth of data analysis and software engineering were needed to make it practicable.

The storm would be on them in less than two hours. They didn't have *time* for this. They had to focus all their available resources on containment at this point. On the other hand, if Nolan's containment booms failed, they might not ever get another chance to sample the colony and find its weaknesses.

The intercom on the lab bench buzzed. "Brock, you better get out here," Zubov said. "You won't believe this."

Garner ran back to the afterdeck and found Zubov at the rail, looking forward. Following his friend's gaze, Garner saw the source of Zubov's latest displeasure. A small contingent of fishing boats was bobbing its way directly toward the *Exeter*. Like the *Sato Maru* before them, they appeared completely oblivious to the *Exeter*'s tack and the array of sampling gear she had deployed.

Garner grabbed Zubov's radio and called the bridge. "McRee? Who the hell is that?"

"Buncha fishermen from Dungeness and Juniper Bay, they say," McRee said. "They're calling themselves the Saviors of the Shore."

"What do they want?" Garner asked.

"They said they want to talk to the man in charge."

"God's busy, and I'm not taking His messages," Garner said.

"They said that they want to talk to you," Zubov said. "And that they have a present for you."

Garner climbed down to the drop-down platform at water level to meet with the lead boat, a small seiner registered in Dungeness. The man who spoke to Garner over the gunwale was not the boat's captain, but a man identifying himself as John Jakes. Jakes had a tough, spade-shaped face that was deeply tanned and topped by a severe crew cut peppered with gray. Like the rest of the boat's crew, Jakes was wearing hip waders, a heavy oilskin coat, and a military-issue gas mask as a makeshift biohazard suit.

"These men lost family and friends at Juniper Bay this morning," Jakes quickly explained. "This goes beyond the health of their fishing grounds, Garner. They've heard the Coast Guard warnings, and they are volunteering to stay out here and help. These men want revenge."

Garner shook his head. "No way. We can't have a bunch of vigilantes out here. Foolishness has cost us enough lives already."

"Don't tell me you couldn't use a few more lines and nets to secure these booms," Jakes said. "These men are up to the task, if you tell them how."

Garner considered Jakes's offer for a moment. "All right. But you have your men follow my orders to the letter, got that?"

"Clear as crystal," Jakes said. "And in exchange for your consideration, I wanted to give you this." He opened a small metal case and took out a laptop computer. As Jakes handed the computer over, Garner noticed that the man wore no gloves. The palms of his hands looked uncut, the nails trimmed. Whoever Jakes was, he wasn't a fisherman. Glancing around at the other boats, Garner saw that the others were more like Jakes than anyone local to this part of the strait. A few of them even wore military-style CBW suits.

Covert operations? Military personnel hiding from the news copters by blending with the fishermen? But why?

"What's this?" Garner asked, eyeing Jakes with new suspicion.

"You're familiar with Polygon?" Jakes asked.

Garner was. Polygon was a military software program designed to interpret the behavior of chemical agents following dispersal. With the software, field units could use ambient weather data to estimate the area potentially exposed to a chemical or biological weapons attack. Garner had used an early version of it at Newport to predict the behavior of oil slicks and had adapted some of its basic subroutines for Betty.

"The latest version," Jakes said. "Loaded with the latest NOAA figures on this storm front, population data, and the readings from your transponders. Depending on what your sampler sees inside the slick, we should have an accurate determination of possible exposure."

"Who's *we*?" Garner asked. "Who do you work for, Jakes?"

Jakes tapped his watch. "Time's a-wasting, Commander Garner. You have all the pieces you need to stop this ugliness from getting any uglier." He nodded at the collection of fishing boats stretched out behind him. "These men are counting on you. We all are. We'll be awaiting your instructions."

The fact that Jakes had addressed him as "Commander"—his rank (actually Lieutenant Commander) when he retired from Naval Intelligence—unnerved Garner. Virtually no one in his academic circles paid heed to his service record, and Nolan would not have divulged such information to anyone from the media without Garner's consent. Nolan was working overtime to promote this operation as a private venture; falling back on military resources and personnel would be anathema. The fact that Jakes knew Garner's experience with the Polygon program—and had access to it—was itself enough to link him with military intelligence, but which branch?

Garner set Jakes's laptop in the *Exeter*'s lab and patched the data feed from Medusa into the plotter. He located Ellie in the ship's infirmary and showed her the main features of the software program.

"If you get any data on cell concentration in the victims, if anyone gets sick from exposure, tap someone to enter the information here." Using the keypad, Garner drilled down into the software's data processors. "With each data point, the software will run an analysis, comparing the toxins we encounter to all the ones in its database."

Proprietary data, thought Garner as the model began working. *Whatever passes through this machine can now be considered government property. But to whose intelligence and to what end?*

"Tell Nolan to sit still long enough for me to use a tongue depressor on him, and I can get started," Ellie said.

"You think he got exposed in the helicopter?" Garner asked.

"In the helicopter, and on the launches, and every time he pulls off his hood with the slick as a backdrop for his precious 'live shots,' " Ellie said.

"Has Carol talked to him?" Garner asked. Carol would be the only one among them to whom Nolan might listen.

"She has, but he's still doing his Little General schtick," Ellie said. "Talk about 'violent mood swings.' I'm noting his symptoms and hoping to hell that if it was a significant exposure, he wouldn't still be walking around."

For the moment, the benefits of running Polygon outweighed the costs. As the NOAA atmospheric data, slick recorders, and Medusa's samplers were compiled, the slick's profile was rendered on the laptop's screen. It appeared as a three-dimensional entity suspended in a grid-based representation of the ocean, morphing as the numbers defining the colony continually changed. Data on the slick's estimated mass, dimensions, and growth began spooling down the data frame on the screen.

Garner stopped the program and began running forecasts through the data compiler. Jakes had included census data for Puget Sound, and using this information, Garner could begin estimating human exposure.

17,000 EXPOSED; 3,400 FATALITIES, read the estimate, given the current conditions and an unprotected population. Those numbers were cut by nearly 80 percent assuming an even moderately successful evacuation.

Then Garner changed the variables to reflect his worst-case scenario—the escape of the slick over the sill into Puget Sound and full dispersal of the colony by the coming storm into an unprepared population. He then corrected for rainfall and dilution effects, as well as the weathering of the slick itself.

562,000 EXPOSED; 332,200 FATALITIES, read the program's estimate.

"Oh my God," Ellie said quietly.

"There you go," Garner said. "It's our job to get that number down to zero." He reset the program to provide real-time predictions based on current data and returned to the main deck.

But how, thought Ellie, alone once again.

The rain had begun in earnest. The first of the stadium-sized lighting panels offset the coming overcast and nightfall, but the team would clearly need more illumination. To the east, the Coast Guard helicopters and USMC Hueys had begun their bombing runs with the crystallized permanganate, dropping the loaded buckets onto the exposed fringes of the slick. As the purple compound mixed with the green dye, the shape and extent of the slick became more pronounced. Garner had tried to factor in the effect of the solution on the slick's behavior but had run out of time. For all of Jakes's generosity, he should have provided a computer programmer to adapt the software on the fly.

Garner found Ellie standing with Zubov, who was barking orders into a bullhorn, directing the smaller boats around the *Exeter* as the A-frame was refitted to take up the second train of containment booms.

"I want you back on the *Kaiku,*" Garner said to Ellie. "If anything happens out here, that's going to be the safest place."

"Why can't we *all* be in the safest place?" Ellie said. "Brock, I can handle this. Let me stay here."

"The *Kaiku* will be our field hospital, and they need a doctor," Garner said. "I want you near the medical supplies if things get any worse. We'll stay here to make sure they don't. And don't forget to transmit any data you get for the Polygon plotter. We'll come get you when this is over."

Ellie heard the shopping list of duties Garner relayed, but focused on the man. She studied his sharp gray eyes, the small whitish scar on one brow, for a long moment. She committed that face to memory and believed in the truth it held. If Garner believed anything other than what he said, it didn't show.

"Good luck," she said.

"There's a first time for everything, I suppose."

Ellie hesitated a moment, then quickly pressed her mouth to his in a warm, urgent kiss. "Please be careful," she whispered as she pulled away and stepped into the launch.

Garner kept his eyes on Ellie as she slipped away into the driving rain. *I'll come get you when this is over,* he repeated to himself. *I swear I will.*

As he climbed back to the bridge, the *Exeter*'s radio operator intercepted him. "Fax for you, sir."

"Hold on to it," Garner said. "We haven't got time for any more reporters' questions right now. They can find out what the hell is going on at the same time as the rest of us."

"It's from Dr. Charles Harmon," the operator said. "Your eyes only."

Garner took the fax from the operator. The first two pages were a series of Harmon's sketches. The resolution had been compromised by the radio transmission, but they clearly depicted cells of *Pfiesteria junckersii.* Most of the drawings seemed to highlight the structure and position of the cells' balance-seeking statocysts, but there were no legends or comment. On the last page was a tacit and curiously pedestrian message in Harmon's shaky script, wishing them well with the expedition. The note then provided a series of radio instructions for contacting Admiral Lockwood of the U.S. Navy.

YOU'LL KNOW WHEN AND HOW TO USE THIS, the message ended.

"Well, thank you all to hell, Obi-Wan Kenobi," Garner muttered. "I'll work on your riddles after we survive this storm." He folded the paper and stuffed it in his pocket.

22

Ellie stood outside the *Kaiku*'s wheelhouse, her hands around a warm cup of coffee, and admitted to herself that she had never felt farther removed from her intended element. She looked out toward the storm clouds building behind them, then focused beyond the deserted helicopter pad to the scattering of vessels in the water around them.

The *Kaiku* currently held one end of the spillage booms that had been assembled to capture the slick. For the moment, the train of booms had been drawn around in a deep crescent, open to the west. The bright orange forms floated well above the surface of the water, and Ellie had seen the workers deploy a weighted curtain from each boom that restrained the slick up to fifteen feet below the surface. The *Baxter* had taken up the other end of the booms. In a few minutes, the ships would begin drawing the two ends of the booms together, cinching the menace in a huge, thick-walled pouch that would encircle nearly eight square miles.

Would that be enough? Nolan assured everyone that the spillage booms were the best ever made, but the solution they had ultimately come upon to stop the slick now seemed, at least to Ellie, hopelessly inadequate and naive. Carol, and Freeland before her, had said that such booms were best reserved for sheltered, coastal areas, and Garner had pointed out that shallow water was exactly the place *not* to lead the slick. Then came the word of the approaching storm, and any thoughts of killing the slick turned to discussions of how to, if only temporarily, retain it in the snare they had set.

Dispersed along the outside of the booms between the *Kaiku* and *Exeter* sat nearly every gillnetter, tugboat, and seiner from the marinas and dockyards of Juniper Bay and Dungeness. No one had asked the fishermen to come—in fact, the Coast Guard had vehemently advised against it—but still they came. The small, weathered crews donned the flashy biohazard suits from the Nolan Group's lockers or scavenged their own most durable protection, took logistic direction from Garner, then set to work securing the booms. They wanted only to protect their fishing grounds, their livelihood, and the sight of Honest Bob Nolan's gaudy lariat was enough to spur them into action.

The massive, floating structure with the lines and guide wires crisscrossing its surface now looked like something out of *Gulliver's Travels*. But this giant had no firmness, no finite form. This giant was a ghost. As the booms closed in on the slick, compressing its surface area, it would surely only collapse upon itself, extending deeper to compensate. Even under ideal conditions, the booms could not hold indefinitely in open water. For all their expertise and bravado at containment, no one wanted to claim responsibility for the actual cleanup. No one yet had an answer as to how they might manage to "slurp" such a large volume of water off the surface, or into what containment they could filter the surface water. It would take an oil tanker to hold the slick, and even if the thick, viscous accretion of cells didn't simply clog the filters, then where could they ever purge the tanker?

In the meantime, they had somehow managed to contain a massive biological reactor in the middle of the open sea. Now, before anyone could try to defuse it, they had to hang on for their lives to see if, where, and when the storm would hit.

The driving rain ahead of the front was at least helping to keep down the levels of noxious aerosol. Flying beneath the low overcast, Nolan's

air-strike force continued to dump their loads of potassium permanganate across the ever-decreasing opening in the booms. Even from this
distance, Ellie could see that the slick had stopped moving—had ceased
creeping and flowing across the waves toward the mainland like some
kind of evil cloud—and for that she was genuinely relieved.

For the briefest of moments, Ellie regained her Hippocratic passion
and felt her ire begin to rise. Why did every argument to protect the environment fail so completely in the face of profits or simple human negligence? Why did human convenience unequivocally cast the deciding
vote in matters of responsible conservation? She thought of the public
hearing back in Bamfield and of Bouchard's salesman-like, Woodsy Owl
homilies—*Remember: The Solution to Pollution Is Dilution*—and
clenched her teeth. Tell that to the people in Prince William Sound, or
the Jersey shore, or the Gulf of Mexico. Tell the surfers in Northern California that the painful rashes they bring with them from the water are a
suitable "solution" to pollution.

And did any of that really matter anymore? Wasn't her idealistic con-
servationist resistance equally unsuitable here? Whether the threat was
natural or imposed by humans, Ellie could not imagine something more
destructive than the slick before them. Admitting that, how long before
the bombers ran out of their magic purple deterrent? How long before
the wind changed direction or increased enough to scatter those fragile-
looking booms in a hundred different directions? What then?

The scale of the scene alone was enough to frighten her. The consequences of anyone's foolish judgment were utterly terrifying.

I'm needed here, she assured herself. It was the fallback, self-inflating
delusion of any doctor, irrespective of evidence or circumstance to the
contrary. If she had been needed at all here, it was only to provide superficial care to various members of the containment crew or to give an
ad-hoc debriefing on the effects of *Pfiesteria* exposure. There were some
minor respiratory problems and skin irritations among fishermen who
had drifted too close to the containment. A broken finger on a deckhand
who had dropped a counterbalance weight. Assorted bumps and bruises
to the Nolan Group flatlanders unaccustomed to moving around on
ocean swells. With the news from Juniper Bay, she had asked to be trans-

ferred immediately to the mainland, but by then a USAMRIID emergency response team had already locked down the area. For all her "experience" with this killer and its effects, her emotional proximity to its victims, to the military she was nothing more than another small-town doctor. One without a security clearance and, therefore, only a nuisance. Considering the carnage for which she had prepared herself, the reality had been less trying on her than her slowest shift in the ER. So instead she began alternating between the equally ridiculous alternatives of fear and duty. *I want to get away from here. I should be back at the hospital fighting to keep my license. The hospital doesn't need me; they said so in so many words. I'm needed on the* Kaiku.

Several launches from the *Kaiku* and the *Exeter* raced around and among the fishing vessels. Ellie saw a Hurricane inflatable hull skip through the swash off the *Kaiku*'s bow. Someone was standing in the bow, barking instructions through a bullhorn. Garner. The reluctant field marshal, commanding his troops against the most devastating natural disaster this area had ever seen.

Ellie couldn't help but notice that, while many of the others looked ludicrous, even comical, in their ungainly space suits, Garner remained handsome and somehow austere. In control of this surreal situation without even trying. He was not at all swept away by the scale of this horror; for that reason alone, the others seemed to gravitate to his leadership. Ellie herself couldn't help but admire him. No, it wasn't only admiration. Looking at him now, Ellie might even admit the possibility of falling in love.

So that's *what men are for.* She smiled.

As if hearing her thoughts, Garner suddenly looked up from the water below. Seeing her standing out in the open air, he waved her back inside. "We're not out of this yet," came his mild reprimand over the bullhorn. Ellie nodded and complied, continuing to watch from inside the bridge.

Ahead of them, no more than fifty miles distant, was Garner's current home base—Friday Harbor and the San Juan Islands. Seeing the rugged, windswept cliffs of the semi-exposed shoreline reminded her of the west coast of Ireland, which she had visited on a post-graduation vacation.

The memories of that trip—like the hospital, her decrepit flat, the Honda, and so much of her life before the past weeks—now seemed to belong to someone else.

Ellie knew these islands had been the site of one of the last remarkable skirmishes between the United States and Britain. In 1859, American and British soldiers had gone to battle over the accidental murder of a pig that had, in its porcine belligerence, failed to recognize the established territorial lines. The San Juan Conflict, or "the Pig War" as history had remembered it, trampled the scenic but militarily irrelevant landscape of San Juan Island for nearly twelve years. If it were not for the fact that monuments of the event had been built and stood to this day, the entire battle might have been written off as an absurd joke.

Perhaps it was only her Canadian perspective on things, but it seemed as though history—the Pig War and the War of 1812 rolled into one—was repeating itself on this same body of water. This time the fishermen in their tiny boats took on the role of the revolutionaries, fighting to preserve their land claim. This time the tyrannical invader was Mother Nature herself, and Bob Nolan might be considered the troublemaking pig. This time the American military, for all its showing of strength, remained aloof and distant. The two large Navy vessels maintained their position five miles from the booms. Watching. Silent. Waiting for the rest of them, the freedom fighters, to struggle and fail. If what Garner had postulated about the military's interest in the slick as some kind of biological weapon was true, then they were all part of a deadly human experiment, while the national news media got it all on tape.

Trench warfare, thought Ellie, as she gazed down on the small fleet of boats moving around the floating barrier. *They look like soldiers digging in on a toxic battlefield.*

Ellie's hand reached out and came to rest on the clammy surface of the window. Behind her, she heard the *Kaiku*'s radio operator relay the latest weather warning and wondered how accurate such forecasts could ever possibly be.

Darkness was coming too soon.

———

The containment of the slick continued at a feverish pace during the next hour. Working in tandem on separate launches, Garner and Zubov continuously circled the slick, shouting orders to the fishing boats and Nolan Group vessels clustered around the outside edge of the containment booms.

Garner's plan was to get the slick as secure as possible, with the lines and supports for the booms attached primarily to the *Kaiku* and the *Exeter*. The largest ships would anchor on either side of the containment pen, facing directly into the wind. Once the slick was secured in this way, the smaller boats could be let go to head for shelter. By late afternoon, the waves had already grown dangerously large for the smallest boats, the Zodiacs and dinghies, and soon the heavy launches would have to be tethered to their parent vessels. A blatant disregard for safety was only part of the reason for Garner's annoyance when he saw Nolan loading his documentary crew into one of the *Kaiku*'s launches and heading out into the steepening chop around the booms. Unless they were going to help with the lines, their presence on the water was more of a liability than an asset.

Garner hailed Nolan's boat and asked him what they intended to do. Nolan made some offhand remark about needing close-up footage of the slick as the storm approached and that none of the film crew was comfortable enough around boats to do it themselves.

Garner shook his head. "It's too dangerous. Take them back inside."

"What's the matter?" Nolan scoffed. "Don't you trust my driving anymore?"

"As a matter of fact, I don't. And I'm not going to get these fishermen out of here anytime soon if they see you coming out for a photo shoot."

"They'll be fine," Nolan said. "Besides, I've got liability waivers from all of them."

"The film crew or the fishermen?" Garner asked.

"*All* of them. They're all private citizens."

"Glad you've got your priorities in order," Garner said sarcastically.

Garner had called the *Kaiku* earlier to ask Nolan about John Jakes. Nolan denied knowing anything about Jakes and called Garner's observations about the suspicious-looking crewmen assigned to each of the boats "paranoid."

"People up here are tough," Nolan said. "Remember how they picked up after Mount St. Helens?"

"If this slick gets dispersed by this storm, St. Helens is going to look like a pimple on prom night," Garner said.

"These men are out here with nothing to lose," Nolan said. "I can't imagine a more dedicated team to work with."

Or a more dangerous one, Garner thought bitterly.

Though they were all expecting the worst, the arrival of the storm was no less intimidating. The wind and rain continued to increase throughout the day, backed by an ominous black wall of clouds moving in from the west. The upper atmosphere rumbled almost constantly with thunder, split open intermittently with flashes of lightning. The forecasts were accurate: the storm was blowing directly up Juan de Fuca Strait and threatening to take the entire containment operation with it.

Several of the "Saviors' " boats remained in place, rolling in the high seas between the larger vessels, tending to the booms, and avoiding the fallout of the slick as it roiled and tumbled inside the booms. Many of the lighting grids shorted out soon after the conditions worsened, casting the entire area in an eerie, half-shadowed glare.

Garner and Zubov returned their launches to the *Exeter,* the waves slamming them against the larger hull several times before the boats were fully secured. Drenched and breathing hard, Garner clapped a hand on Zubov's shoulder as they rocked on the launch platform.

"Nice work," he said.

"I hate rain," Zubov said, his face red and slathered in mist. "Doesn't it seem like we always have to work in the rain?"

"It's out of our hands now. At least until this passes."

"You think this is gonna pass?" Zubov asked. "I was gonna start gathering animals two by two. If this wind gets any stronger, your ass is gonna get blown all the way back to Iowa."

"Right now I'd welcome a cornfield."

The two men turned to go inside the *Exeter,* but something caught Garner's eye. A single launch, rolling and tumbling in the waves behind the *Kaiku.*

Nolan and his film crew. Nolan, again, without his Racal helmet on. As close to the edge of the slick as he was, the driving wind and rain were the only things keeping him alive.

In the howling wind, there was no way to know if the boat was having engine troubles, but it was definitely foundering, losing its struggle against the wind. The low hull would steer one way, then the other, each as ineffectual as the other in bringing the smaller boat closer to its destination. The lights of the small boat vanished behind a rolling wall of water, then reappeared, only to vanish again in the next wave trough.

A savage gust of wind swept between the two boats, twisting the containment pen on its restraints. Nolan's launch was spun away from the *Kaiku* and tossed against the train of containment booms. Through the driving downpour, Garner saw a single figure topple out the closed boat. Two of the other passengers reached after their companion.

"Man overboard!" Garner yelled, spurring Zubov into action. They quickly untethered one of the launches and rolled away from the *Exeter.*

Crossing the worst of the wave front, the launch slammed up and down as it moved toward the *Kaiku.* Garner could see that the figures remaining in the boat were wearing their hoods, meaning that Nolan was the one who had fallen in. It also meant that those remaining in the boat were the least experienced at bringing him back aboard.

"This is crazy!" Zubov shouted. "Let the stupid bastard go under." As the launch was tipped nearly end-over by the next wave, they knew they could all be overboard soon.

It took them an eternity to cross the open water to the *Kaiku,* then circle around the larger vessel to reach the launch. Three figures on the other launch were still trying to throw a line to the fourth, who bobbed in the water, rising and falling with sickening velocity in the tumult. The line wrapped around one of the figures in the boat, then suddenly he—or she—was also in the water. Garner peered through the Plexiglas face shield of the second figure's hood and recognized him as the film crew's director. Seconds later, the launch rode up and over his head and he disappeared into the maelstrom.

Drawing closer still, Garner could see Nolan's hands flailing in the water, reaching for the line Garner offered him. In their collective concentration on Nolan, no one was steering the second launch, and it quickly slid backward, slamming against the containment booms. With the next wave, the launch rolled over, tossing its remaining two passengers over the booms and into the slick.

Garner flung a life ring into the water, setting it perfectly, just behind Nolan, with the rope trailing between his flailing arms. As he reeled Nolan in, Garner could see ocean water pouring in over the open collar of Nolan's biohazard suit. The suit was filling with water, which was partially responsible for Nolan's inability to swim or maneuver. Panic accounted for the rest.

The next wave brought the launch toward Nolan, and for a sickening moment Garner thought they would lose him under the boat's keel. The two launches were now dangerously close together and at any moment could slam together, crushing Nolan in between.

"Hold on!" Garner shouted, reaching over the gunwale. The boat rolled, nearly pitching Garner into the water, but Zubov held him back.

If Serg is holding me, who's steering *us?* thought Garner. It would take only a strong wave to dump them over the boom and into the colony. Then again, considering Nolan's open suit—*Will there be anything left of him to save?*

With the passing of the next wave, the launch went down as Nolan's form was tossed up. The discrepancy was enough to leverage Nolan's waterlogged bulk, and they heaved him into the bottom of the boat.

"We'll never make it back to the *Exeter,*" Garner shouted to Zubov. "Take us to the *Kaiku.*"

The next massive wave struck the launch bow-on, throwing it high in the air. Garner lost his footing and fell back into something hard and metallic, striking his head.

Then there was only blackness. . . .

23

The P-3 Orion left the main runway of the Whidbey Island Naval Air Station and turned west, flying directly into the approaching storm front. Powered by four Allison turboprop engines supported by a triple-reinforced airframe, the aircraft coursed with brutish determination into the task at hand.

The flying weather station was on the second of three nearly around-the-clock watches dispatched from Whidbey to monitor the severe storm approaching land across the Northeast Pacific. The job of the nine crewmen and four meteorologists aboard was to take atmospheric readings from within the storm for up to ten hours from altitudes as low as 200 feet. The data they collected would be transmitted immediately to NOAA computers in Washington, D.C. The computers would then run the data through a series of forecast and hindcast numerical models in order to determine not only the storm's most likely site of landfall, but also its potential for destruction.

The recent warming of the surface waters of the Pacific Northwest had redefined the "expected" oceanic weather patterns. The most power-

ful of ocean storms occurred over warmer water—usually 70 degrees
Fahrenheit or more—where a tremendous amount of moisture and energy could be drawn aloft into the upper atmosphere. The worst of such
storms might dump a foot of rain in a single day, raise the surf break
twenty feet, or carry ninety-mile-per-hour winds. An hour into the
flight, the scientific crew already considered the current storm among the
worst of the worst.

The plane's only civilian passenger, a reporter from the *Seattle Post-
Intelligencer,* unbuckled himself from his seat and moved cautiously forward. Large metal racks of scientific equipment groaned and protested
on either side of the narrow corridor as he made his way forward to the
aircraft's weather station. As a boy growing up in Texas, he had learned
to fear severe weather, then gradually, to accept it. He had long ago forgotten the childhood experience of huddling in his aunt's root cellar
when the tornadoes hit; the past two hours with the storm trackers had
returned this fear with a long-overdue vengeance.

Crouched between two massive banks of computers, two of the science crew pored over a large satellite map spread over a low worktable.
Unlike the information provided by a satellite, flying through the storm
rendered a three-dimensional animation of the storm clouds, giving the
front form. The barometric instruments—housed in a red-and-white
striped antenna that projected from the nose of the Orion like a nar-
whal's tusk—sensed the ferocious breath of the storm. The electronic
dropsondes deployed through a hole in the floor of the airplane moni-
tored the storm's erratic mood swings and reported them with clinical
objectivity. In quantifying the storm in this way—describing its proportions, suggesting a personality profile—the scientists animated the satellite's snapshots into a living monster.

Between readings, the meteorologists explained the airplane's
weather-tracking system to the journalist. On the monitors, they showed
him the data being generated by the Orion and where the data were being downloaded and compared with mobile Doppler radar systems on
shore, attached to weather balloons, and on research vessels like the *Exeter.* Working together, the components of the system would be used to
calculate a best-guess forecast for the next twelve hours. The first of these

forecasts would be on the morning news before the Orion even returned to Whidbey.

"How large an area are we scanning with the instruments?" the reporter asked, nodding at the radar swatch.

"At the moment, eight hundred square miles, but we could go wider," one of the scientists remarked.

"And how much of that is covered by the storm?"

"All of it." The scientists saw the reporter's reaction and grinned at each other. "That'll take you from Houston to El Paso without even touching the outlying storms we haven't got time to worry about."

"There's only so much of a storm's behavior we can try to predict," the second meteorologist said. "We follow the primary momentum—we usually have to focus on the main storm front and leave the rest to chance."

"Where is the main system going? Where will it hit?"

"Storms normally come out of the southeast this time of year and lose strength when they move north, over cooler water. Sometimes you'll get one out of the northwest that'll soak Vancouver Island, but those still lose most of their bite before they get to the mainland. I said *normally*—this year has almost been a crapshoot."

"Nobody said we get paid for accuracy," the second meteorologist said with a chuckle.

"Well, I do," the reporter said. "So what about this storm?"

"Right now the storm front is at Storm Force—ten out of twelve on the Beaufort scale, or a Whole Gale in seamen's terms. That means winds of sixty miles an hour. Not even a Category One hurricane on the Saffir-Simpson scale, but close enough. She'll slow down a bit as she begins to feel her way onto shore, but don't you worry, she'll still be nasty enough when she hits."

"And *where's* that gonna be?" the reporter asked again, trying to jot down the information about the Beaufort scale as the plane bounced and rocked around him.

"This one is heading straight up Juan de Fuca. We've put out boating advisories already. Anything smaller than an aircraft carrier better take cover."

Head for the root cellar, the reporter was reminded, a child once again. *Find a sturdy hiding place and keep your head down.*

The Orion pitched and bucked against the strong headwind. Stepping forward farther, his knees trembling as the shaking of the airframe translated through his body, the reporter ducked his head through the cockpit hatchway. He tightened his belly against the bitter residue of the coffee he had consumed during the preflight briefing, the effects of motion sickness amplified by his standing position. It would be effortless for him to vomit right here, all over the cockpit floor. But the Navy crew already regarded him with enough of the polite disdain they reserved for visitors, and besides, Texas boys didn't sick-up in public.

"How's it lookin'?" he asked the pilot, shouting to be heard above the ambient noise.

"Wet," the pilot hollered back.

"We wouldn't have to be up in this shit at all if Congress made good on its promise to cut their funding to NOAA," the copilot grumbled.

"An' if they had, we'd be out of a job, flying an airbus charter into Reno twice a week," the pilot remarked.

" 'It's not a job, it's an adventure,' right?" the reporter asked.

"If this is adventure, I'd rather be flying the goddamn airbus," the copilot said. He was beginning to look a little peaked as well.

"Don't let him fool you," the pilot said. "Frank here is no different than the rest of us. You know what they say: everyone talks about the weather, but—"

"—But the smart ones stay in bed and get their info from the Weather Channel," the copilot finished. He jerked his thumb toward the back of the plane. "Look at the eggheads back there. Every one of them's got a Ph.D. in some goddamn thing. Me? I've got a two-year college degree and a military pilot's license. Larry here, too. The rest of the crew barely has a high-school equivalency. Yet here we all are, nice and cozy on the same rickety roller coaster. Go figure. If we all go down together out here, what'd all that education get them?"

"I think they said the same thing about the *Titanic*," the reporter offered. "Only their class society was based on income."

"Good analogy." The copilot nodded. "But don't worry. No one's calling this thing 'unsinkable.' " He banged the sidewall of the cockpit with the heel of his fist. "Nope—we *know* she'd sink like a fuckin' brick!"

"Fall like shit off a shovel," the pilot agreed.

The Orion was hit again by another severe gust. Something heavy toppled over in the rear, and they could hear one of the scientists curse. On the instrument panel, the radar console glowed almost entirely green, silently revealing a two-hundred-mile-wide swath of torrential rain driven by a tongue of wind measured at sixty knots—Violent Storm Force on the Beaufort wind scale. The blip representing the Orion had only just begun to breach the first arms of the front, yet around them the fuselage wailed as if it were about to burst apart into so much aluminum foil. The reporter had seen a small battalion of mechanics swarm over the aircraft's fuselage and wings before take-off, checking the tightness of the exposed bolts and rivets. After this single flight, the joints would need to be checked again before the Orion was allowed to fly again.

"The guys in back said this was just a strong gale," the reporter offered.

"Is that all?" the pilot said. "Then how 'bout you drive for a while?" The reporter declined the offer.

"Don't worry," the pilot said to the reporter, wrestling the controls. "It'll get worse before it gets better, but it *will* get better. Always does." As the Orion shuddered once more, the pilot suddenly looked less certain of his prediction.

The intercom buzzed, followed by instructions to turn farther into the eye of the storm. This time the pilots didn't need to protest: the Orion's aging frame did it for them.

"These things must be built to last," the reporter said.

"Forty years, under normal conditions," the pilot said.

"You call these normal conditions?"

"Nope. And because of the amount of stress these planes take," the pilot said, "the manufacturer recommends decommissioning them after every three thousand storm hours or so. So the first one we bought was retired at three thousand. They held the second one together for five thousand, then a wing strut broke. This is our third, but there's no money to replace it."

"On how many hours?"

"Ten thousand. Practically a virgin—the other two Orions are over twelve." The pilot winked at the copilot. "That's what budget cuts get you. Put that in your article."

The Orion bucked again. The reporter lost his balance, banging his head as he gripped the edge of the hatchway. He tried to ignore the statistics just relayed by the pilot. "Have you guys ever seen anything like this? It looks like a real bitch."

The pilot gripped the shuddering yoke more tightly. His eyes flicked to the radarscope, finding it increasingly difficult to conceal his growing disbelief.

"No, mister, the CO who ordered my ass up here looks like a real bitch," he said. "This storm looks like the end of the fucking world."

24

A ship's bunk. Dry. Aboard the *Kaiku*.
Ellie's touch.

Garner's world slowly came back into focus. "What happened?" he
mumbled. The words alone were enough to spread pain through his
skull. He could hear the storm still raging outside, but it appeared to be
subsiding.

"You took a pretty bad knock," Ellie said, still holding a cold com-
press to his head. "Hit your head on an anchor. You've been out for about
twenty minutes."

To Garner, it felt as though hours had passed. Then he noted that his
hair was still wet from the rain and the chill was still in his bones. His exposure suit had been stripped away, and he smelled noticeably of bleach.

"The documentary crew is lost," Ellie told him. "All three of them
vanished into the slick, and we haven't seen them since."

"What happened to Nolan?"

"Bob's in the next cabin," Ellie said. "Carol's with him. His skin is badly scarred, but it's not spreading. The rain and the seawater helped to dilute the toxin, and we've stabilized him with a mild bicarbonate solution. You saved his life, Brock."

"Another case of poetic injustice. Three innocent people dead, but smilin' Bob Nolan comes out okay."

"Shh. He's far from okay. But he's our first survivor."

"That's because you do good work, Doctor," Garner said.

"Getting better all the time," she said, a tight grin creasing her lips. Unlike too many of her other patients, Garner had lived through his exposure to the colony. His eyes had opened, and he was able to give her another smile. There was a reason for that.

"And Serg?"

"He's on the bridge with the others. He single-handedly carried you, Bob, and the boat back on board. Cursing the whole way, of course."

"He knew you had beer on board. Did the booms hold?" Garner asked. He began to sit up. He thought of the wind pushing the slick farther inshore, the rain—*the rain!*—diluting the surface waters. If this species was anything like estuarine *Pfiesteria,* it would *thrive* in brackish water.

"I don't know. Sit still," Ellie instructed. "You need to rest."

"Later."

"No, *now.*"

They heard something large tear loose on deck, banging heavily against the *Kaiku*'s superstructure. "Later," Garner mumbled again. He rolled off his bunk and began climbing toward the bridge, Ellie following him. There was another bang, and the ship lost electrical power.

Garner looked at Ellie in the darkness, listening. Outside they could still hear the wind, but the chatter of rain seemed to have lessened. The storm had passed; now they had to get topside to assess the damage left in its wake.

The lights on the bridge of the *Kaiku* flickered once, twice, then came fully on as the ship's generators restored power. From the appearance of the deck below, it was evident that not all of the ship's lighting was back on-line. Despite her tonnage, the large vessel still rocked, skittish and uncomfortable in the storm's wake.

Garner, Zubov, and Sweeny, gathered on the bridge, held on to anything solid they could find and looked to each other for a solution.

Zubov cracked the top on a can of beer, breaking the strained silence.

"The booms are broken," Garner confirmed, scanning the area with his night glasses. "And whatever we'd caught inside them is long gone."

"You mean it's *loose?*" Sweeny jabbered, regaining his nervous pale. "What do we do now? If it's loose again, it could be anywhere. Anywhere! It could have spread for *miles*. We've got to get out of here!"

"*Here* is the one place we know it *isn't,*" Zubov said coolly.

"Damage control first," Garner said. "Let's deal with the victims we can see." He picked up the radio and sent the word out to the Saviors of the Shore, offering the *Kaiku*'s medical supplies to anyone who needed them. Most of the captains deferred the offer of assistance, preferring to continue the search for anyone lost overboard.

"The Coast Guard can get them," Sweeny said. "Why are we wasting time on this?"

"The Coast Guard ships don't have enough room," Garner replied patiently. "They'll have to come here until we can airlift them to the mainland."

"Oh no, you don't," Sweeny said. "Anyone still alive out there was just washed right through the slick. We're not bringing anyone aboard the *Kaiku* who poses a risk of contamination. Send them to the *Exeter*."

"The *Exeter* doesn't have adequate medical facilities—"

"If that slick hit them, they're dead anyway," Sweeny continued. "They just don't know it yet."

Zubov started to reply, then fell silent. He knew that Nolan's arrogant little stooge was probably right.

"They should come here," Carol said from the hatchway. Everyone turned to look at her as she came up from the infirmary. Her face was ashen, but her eyes smoldered with contempt at Sweeny's conduct. "It's only right that they should come here. We owe it to them."

"Carol," Sweeny began, his confidence returning. "We appreciate the gesture, but—"

"Who's *we,* you little fucker?" Carol screamed at him. "This is Bob's boat, and if he isn't able to give the orders, then I sure as hell will!"

Sweeny adjusted his glasses and stared back at her smugly. "Actually, Carol, if anything happens to Bob—as it unfortunately has—*I'm* the one who has the veto power for resource allocation. If you don't like it, you can file a complaint with the Group's Board of Directors. Right now I'm in command of the *Kaiku,* and if this situation gets any further out of hand, I won't hesitate to recall her to Everett."

"Then we'll use the *Exeter,*" Carol said defiantly.

"Actually, the Nolan Group's authority includes the *Exeter,* since we are currently covering her operating expenses," Sweeny said.

Carol stood and glared at Sweeny, too angry for words. Zubov tried to reach out a comforting hand to her, but Carol only shrugged it away.

Garner looked out through the rain-streaked glass. Scattered in the water between them and the *Exeter,* a half-dozen gillnetters could be seen, their batteries struggling to maintain power as the boats foundered and struggled against the fractured booms. He could see men moving about on two of the boats; several more were being hauled out of the water or climbing out themselves. If the rain obscured Garner's view, it had probably also helped to preserve the men's lives; while most of them wore gloves and gas masks, few had more than Tyvek bodysuits and ponchos for protection.

Barely discernible in the distance were the running lights of the two Navy ships.

"Get me a secure channel," Garner said to the *Kaiku*'s radio operator.

"Mister, I'm not sure we've even got an antenna left after that—"

"Get me a channel *now*!" Garner spat out. The mate looked nervously at Sweeny, who seemed to have measurably increased his physical size in the past few minutes.

Sweeny waved him on, and the mate patched the bridge through to the *Kaiku*'s radio room. "The last thing I need to add to this situation is a mutiny," Sweeny muttered, and turned back to the chart table.

Garner took the headset offered him and gave the operator the radio-phone number of Whidbey Island NAS from memory. A moment after that, the call was relayed once again, through Everett, then to a DARPANet trunk line. Garner took Charles Harmon's fax from his pocket and read the numbers from the bottom of it to a second operator. The headset clinked as the connection was made and the receiver picked up on the other end.

"Lockwood." The voice that answered was quiet but firm. Despite the lateness of the hour, there was no indication of interrupted sleep. The call had been anticipated.

"Admiral, this is Brock Garner."

There was a pause on the line. It was not surprise or uncertainty, but a measured hesitation to precisely determine the next course of action.

"Commander Garner," the Admiral finally said. "If you're calling this number, I suspect we're all in a great deal of trouble."

25

"I must assume our little problem is on the loose again." Adam Lockwood's grim, matter-of-fact tone was nearly as annoying as Sweeny's cowardly histrionics. To Garner, most disconcerting of all was Charles Harmon's apparent knowledge that this contact would eventually have to be made.

"Admiral, what the hell is going on out here?" Garner said, his tone measured. "What do you mean, '*our* little problem'? If you're aware of the situation we're facing, then where's *our* military support?"

"You've already got it, Commander Garner," Lockwood said. "Commander Jakes has contacted you."

"Yes, but why the thinly veiled covert op?"

"We didn't have any choice, Garner. This has been an unfortunate incident, and one for which we cannot justify overt involvement. But Jakes is a valuable asset out there. He's a top-level adviser to CBDCOM, and he's been our point man for a number of joint military exercises in domestic BW preparedness. I assume you're familiar with those."

Garner was. During the 1950s and '60s, coinciding with the height of

Cold War hysteria, the U.S. Army had performed more than 230 "domestic exercises" to chart the potential of biological-warfare agents in American cities. Using relatively harmless bacteria such as *Bacillus subtilis* and *Serratia marcescens,* the military conducted systematic inoculations of subways and taxicabs in New York and Washington, D.C., then tracked the bacteria's dispersal through the resident population. State highways, public beaches, airports, and bus stations in Virginia, Florida, Pennsylvania, California, and Hawaii were also used for such dispersal tests. In more dramatic operations, Navy minesweepers sprayed San Francisco with *Bacillus globigii,* U.S. bombers sprayed the unsuspecting city of Winnipeg, Canada, and the Army Chemical Corps inoculated the air-conditioning system of the Pentagon.

"I assume you're trying to encourage me," Garner said, recalling some of his own military assignments ordered against enemies that no longer appeared on any map. "But Jakes is too young to have that kind of experience," Garner said. "He couldn't have been more than a child in the sixties."

"Who said anything about the sixties?" Lockwood said. His tone was noncommittal, offering only a complete unwillingness to elaborate.

"So why are you getting involved now?" Garner asked.

"Because it seems we no longer have a choice."

"If Jakes is your idea of a 'valuable asset,' I guess I'd expect something more from him than a laptop computer," Garner said.

"You've got it. Anything you need."

"Admiral, what *does* the military know about this thing?"

"At this time, a helluva lot less than you do," Lockwood said. "That's why Charles Harmon nominated you to call the shots. So far, I'm inclined to believe him."

Garner picked up the fax once more and studied the sketches of *Pfiesteria* and the details of the cells' sensory organelles. "Harmon sent me a fax, but he isn't known for his directness." *How do these two know each other?* Garner wondered. Harmon had no military service record, and the military had no interest in plankton blooms. Unless . . .

"Are you going to tell me this is some kind of biological weapon?"

Garner asked. "An experiment? Is it a natural phenomenon or a foreign threat?"

"None of the above," Lockwood said. "It's no experiment, and it isn't natural. It's not foreign either, but it sounds pretty damn threatening to the rest of us."

"It isn't natural?" Garner asked. "You mean this species of *Pfiesteria* was *engineered*? How come we didn't know anything about it?"

"There are a lot of things you don't know anything about until now," Lockwood said. "You should know that as well as anyone."

"That's not the assurance I was hoping for."

"Assurances don't change the predicament we're in," Lockwood said. "What's your latest Polygon projection?"

"Insufficient data," Garner said. It was becoming his stock answer. In truth, he hadn't looked at the plotter since the storm, but he knew that whatever it said was temporarily limited in its applicability. "That storm could have scattered the slick along a dozen different vectors and probably tossed half our transponders out of the water. We need updated meteorological data, too."

"You're flying blind, in other words," Lockwood said.

"In other words," Garner agreed. "Can we get some NOAA planes in the air?"

"Consider it done," Lockwood said. "I'll get an Orion from Whidbey NAS assigned to your operation and have the data relayed to any coordinates you'd like."

"The sooner the better," Garner said. "Aircraft imaging will be the quickest way to relocate the slick."

"Agreed," Lockwood said. "We'll also get some boys in the water to help collect those spillage booms for you. That'll free up all your manpower to keep chasing this thing. What did Harmon suggest?"

"Nothing. Just a series of morphological sketches, without any explanation." *Cryptic* did not begin to address the shortcomings of Harmon's message. Like Jakes's assumptions about the Polygon program, the sketches suggested that Garner knew enough of the background to properly interpret them.

Then the logic of Harmon's missive suddenly dawned on him.

"Bioacoustics," Garner said. "Harmon must think the statocysts—the balance-sensing organelles—in this *Pfiesteria* are its Achilles' heel. He thinks we can kill it, or stun it, by bombarding it with sound waves. We've tried high-frequency sounds to destroy problem shellfish stocks like the Zebra mussels in the Great Lakes. The animals can be killed, but the method still leaves the shells behind. Then we found out we could use *low*-frequency pulses to affect organism behavior."

"Something like an ATOC transmitter?" Lockwood asked.

"Exactly," Garner said.

Administered by the University of California and the U.S. Department of Defense, the $40 million ATOC—or Acoustic Thermography of Ocean Climate—project used low-frequency active sonar to determine specific water properties. Since sound was conducted proportionately faster in warmer water, the LFA transmitters could provide, among other data, very accurate temperature readings between the sound source and a series of listening stations.

From his own background in naval intelligence, Garner knew that most of the world's oceans had been wired with sophisticated hydrophones since the earliest days of the Cold War and the $16 billion SOSUS—Sound Surveillance System—program. With strategic military installations at Bangor, Bainbridge Island, and Whidbey Island, Puget Sound and Juan de Fuca Strait were a vital part of this network. Hydrophones once used to listen for Soviet submarines were now routinely utilized in scientific research, including listening for undersea earthquakes and whale vocalizations. Researchers were often informed of such natural phenomena while they were still occurring, vastly enhancing the scientists' response time and consequently the useful data derived from being present at ground zero. For their current purposes, the ATOC unit wouldn't even need a listening array—simply a transmitter generating a frequency attractive, repulsive, or somehow disorienting to the *Pfiesteria* colony.

"If ATOC is the solution," Garner said, "where can we track down a transponder array?" Garner had been involved in some early ATOC development while stationed in Newport. The only ATOC operations he knew of were based in Hawaii and Baja, California. "How soon can we get it here?"

"About ten minutes," Lockwood said. "Look out your front window."

In the distance, the two Navy LSDs had broken anchorage and were now on course toward them.

The scarring on Nolan's face, torso, and lower body was intense. His space suit had been unzipped when he fell from the launch and had quickly filled with seawater and minor concentrations of *Pfiesteria* cells. Painful red welts were raised wherever the mucus had touched Nolan's flesh as the skin reacted to the toxin. After only seconds of exposure, the cells had burned large, weeping lesions in several places on his body, bringing blood to the surface in angry bruises and marbling the ragged edges of skin around them. The capillaries of his eyes and nostrils had burst, causing bright, oxygenated blood to pool there, just below the surface. Nolan was conscious, recumbent, and taking water, but only sporadically. Intermittently, his speech would slur or lapse into stuttering as he relayed to Carol and Ellie what had happened out in the storm.

To a casual observer, the change in Bob Nolan's healthy, lean appearance would be nothing less than mortifying. But for those in the makeshift infirmary aboard the *Kaiku,* Nolan represented the first survivor of direct exposure to the slick. That in itself was cause for reserved celebration. Ellie speculated that the heavy rain and the dilution of the seawater lessened the effects of the fat-soluble toxins. The worst of the damage was limited to the upper dermal layers. Except for the memory of the three filmmakers he had lost to the colony, Nolan would probably recover completely.

Ellie and Carol thoroughly washed Nolan's injuries, then treated them with a medicated salve. As Ellie moved on to examine the others injured in the storm, Carol studied her husband's face, which had taken on a pallid cast, waxy and translucent in the muted light coming through the porthole.

"I'm sorry," she said. "I'm so sorry."

"For what?" He patted her hand, his voice hoarse, his words slightly slurred.

"This whole thing has cost you too much. It's cost all of us too much. I'm beginning to think you were right to want to leave this mess for the Navy. This strain of *Pfiesteria* was probably their mess to begin with."

"No, it was the DoD's idea," Nolan said. "Or the State Department. Either way, it's a little late to take the money and run."

"I'd settle for getting us out of here alive. All of us." She settled her head against his shoulder. "I can't believe I nearly lost you."

"How bad is it?" Nolan asked, indicating his scarred face. He tried to sit up, reaching for a mirror on the bedside cabinet.

"Not yet," Carol said, gently trying to hold him back.

Nolan picked up the mirror and saw his new reflection for the first time. Wetness welled up in his eyes, but only for a moment. His tears were gone with the next blink, replaced with a determination Carol had rarely seen in her husband. The expression was angry and emotional—dangerous.

Nolan rolled over, wincing in pain as his exposed flesh brushed against the bedding. He reached for his clothes, then paused. "Where's my gun?" he said.

"In the drawer," Carol said, trying to soothe him. "Safe. You don't need to be packing it around."

"Yes, I do," Nolan said. He struggled to his feet and began dressing.

John Jakes escorted Garner and Zubov over to the LSD *Albany* in a Navy launch. The ATOC transmitters were neatly assembled on the deck, covered in a thick protective plastic.

Zubov let out a low whistle. "Oh man. Carol's gonna *love* you for this." Seeing Jakes's puzzled look, he added, "She likes whales. These transmitters don't."

"She's going to need some convincing that this is our only solution," Garner agreed.

Even locked in their housings, the portable ATOC LFA transmitters looked ominous. Each one was nearly four feet on a side, constructed inside a reinforced cage painted with antireflective paint. Designed to be towed from a surface ship, the transmitters were completely waterproof and carried their own power source. At full operation, the sonar cone could produce a pulse of 220 decibels, louder in sound intensity than a jet engine at close range. While the engine noise from even a modest-sized freighter could carry for up to fifty miles in the dense underwater environment, ATOC transmissions could be heard across entire oceans. In application, the project technology could be used for purposes ranging from modeling ocean circulation to transoceanic communication systems. It had not been overlooked by the military that ATOC technology could also help to develop ultra-sophisticated devices for detecting quiet submarines or to disorient aggressive vessels—"deafening" their electronics while leaving encrypted allied communications unaffected.

Environmentalists—Carol Harmon vocal among them—bristled at such speculation and at the potential harm to marine mammals. One branch of the program's research specifically intended to test directly the effect of sound bombardment on whales. Some whales could emit pulsed or "stun" vocalizations—sonic pops of 200 decibels or more—to disorient their prey, but the effect of massive sound bombardment on the whales themselves was not clearly understood. Among conservationists, the alarm was raised for all whale species. Public interest groups were outraged, arguing that ATOC transmissions might deafen or even kill some species. At the least, whale communication and migration could be adversely affected. The ATOC program was lobbied heavily to provide detailed environmental impact statements before proceeding with the controversial research.

"I'm still open to alternative suggestions," Jakes said.

"Not on this watch," Garner said. "The storm blew away our only chance to sit on this thing and think about how to neutralize it from a safe distance."

Through the Coast Guard, the Navy continued posting small-craft warnings under the guise of a weather bulletin. This, they hoped, would reduce the amount of shipping traffic on the west side of Admiralty Inlet. Then Sweeny called another press conference for later that day to discuss the "management strategy" for the slick. These pedestrian disinformation efforts were largely negated by the brilliant sunshine that broke following the passing of the storm and the scores of boaters taking to the water to enjoy the last weekend of the summer.

Within half an hour, data were already coming in from the NOAA Orion. The slick was located five miles northwest of Port Townsend, meaning that at least parts of it had passed over the sill into the inner strait and that the rest would soon follow. Admiralty Inlet provided a natural path for the slick to flow into Puget Sound. Though the coastline was broken and irregular the entire way, there remained no further obstacles for the colony as it approached Bremerton and Seattle.

From the Doppler radar images sent back to the *Albany,* Garner could see that the torrential rain had significantly dispersed the slick and weathered the dye, but the colony had thankfully remained intact. The permanganate solution, if it had ever been effective, served now as little more than a secondary marker for the location of the *Pfiesteria* cells.

The slick also looked much larger than it had when contained inside the booms. Was this dispersion simply dilution, or was the colony continuing to grow? Without more data on the colony's cells, Garner had no way of knowing for sure. Ironically, until they could be certain what was going on inside the organism, they would have to keep the slick alive. They could not afford to have the slick disperse further or begin to die and deposit dormant cells into the sediment of the inner strait. Their only recourse would be to use the ATOC array to steer the slick into an isolated embayment. Once the colony had been contained and stabilized, they could determine the best way to kill it.

Somehow.

A second Polygon system on the LSD had begun to reassemble the data model estimating the slick's potential for dispersal. The revised plot included the latest oceanographic and atmospheric data, as well as a two-dimensional rendering of the slick. Garner gave a series of scenario parameters to the Polygon technician and watched as she quickly entered the speculation into the system.

??? EXPOSED; ??? FATALITIES [VARIABLE UNVERIFIED], came the response.

Garner issued another series of parameters, then another, with the same result.

INSUFFICIENT DATA ON CONTAMINANT [VARIABLE UNVERIFIED].

"What do we do now?" Zubov asked. "Get Medusa wet?"

"Yes," Garner said. "And get Betty deployed from the *Kaiku*. Use the two collection sources to get as much data as we can on cell concentration and response." Zubov was on the radio to the *Exeter* almost before Garner had finished issuing the order.

Garner turned to Jakes. "Can you have one ATOC transmitter ready for deployment on each LSD?" Jakes relayed the order to the helmsmen on both Navy ships. "We'll cruise around the outside of the *Exeter* and the *Kaiku* and try a couple of test runs. We need to find a frequency we can use to stop the progress of the colony, or at least adjust its path."

"Do you want to use the containment booms again?" Jakes asked.

"We can use any that weren't wrecked by the storm," Garner said. "I'd just as soon push the slick into a sheltered area somewhere and take our chances."

"That's a lot of pushing," Jakes said.

"Then let's have two more LFA transmitters ready to go, just in case."

"In case?" Jakes asked.

"In case this idea actually works."

Jakes sent the orders to the two LSD crews as Garner turned back to the chart table. His mind raced, working ahead of the Polygon plot and the two-dimensional maps set out before him. He visualized the basin the slick had entered, its contours and potential dead ends, the way an alpine skier anticipates a downhill run. If the ATOC array could indeed be used to steer the slick   and he was yet to be convinced of that— where was the best place to intercept it?

Garner had to dismiss any guesses about the colony's behavior, its ability to swim or change its course, until his samplers could provide a closer look. Falling back on the known variables, the colony had to be regarded as an inorganic contaminant that had passed over the sill and into Admiralty Inlet—a risky assumption but a necessary one under the present conditions. Garner double-checked the latest CTD data and current and wind conditions, then compared these to the bathymetric contours he had constructed in his mind.

Rounding Dungeness and Kulakala Point, the first inlet was Sequim Bay, which was nearly closed off from the strait by Kiapot Spit. Discovery Bay was the next large inlet along the shore, but the shallows of Dallas Bank blocked a direct entrance to it and might even deflect the colony to the east. That meant the slick would most likely be carried around Quimper Peninsula and Port Townsend. Kilisut Harbor provided another catchment location, but the area was too heavily populated; Admiralty Bay was right in the middle of the Navy's operating area off Whidbey Island. So the slick would have to be turned south, into Admiralty Inlet, which would guide it into Puget Sound and a near straight-line path into Seattle.

Following only the wind, currents, and its own momentum, the "mindless" colony could not have chosen a more populated route.

A moment later Garner had calculated their best, and last, position to intercept and divert the slick along this troubling but highly probable route. He tracked this position back to the chart and located it with his finger, smiling grimly at the result.

The intercept point would be approximately 48 degrees North Latitude, 125 degrees 35 minutes West Longitude, off Mutiny Bay on the west coast of Whidbey Island.

The nearest town would be across the island, on Holmes Harbor:

Freeland, Washington.

The *Exeter* and the *Kaiku* were quickly freed of their attachment to the containment booms. To the chagrin of the *Kaiku*'s boatswain, a man by the name of Byrnes, Zubov supervised both arrangements from the after-deck of the *Exeter,* barking orders into his headset microphone. Soon the vessels broke their storm moorings and headed east.

Garner returned to the *Kaiku,* where he debriefed Nolan, Carol, and Ellie on his conversation with Admiral Lockwood as they made way to

Port Townsend. Nolan was uncharacteristically quiet as he listened, obsessively rubbing salve into his exposed skin.

"Are you *insane?*" Carol said. "You know I spent four years lobbying against ATOC use in Hawaii. It's too dangerous."

"More dangerous than this slick?" Garner asked. "More dangerous than dumping trainloads of permanganate into an open ecosystem?"

"That doesn't make it right," Carol said.

"We've run out of options!" Garner said, his exasperation showing. "Charles figures we can influence this thing using sound pulses, and I guess he ought to know."

"And what do *you* know about his work?" Carol asked. She was still reeling from Nolan's revelation.

"Nothing," Garner said. "But you just confirmed my suspicions that he was involved in engineering this thing. I also know that if he knew how to stop it, he'd tell us directly, not slip us a treasure map to interpret."

"Then let's focus on what we do know," Ellie said.

"Garner is right, Carol," Nolan admitted. "Any whales still alive out here are just going to end up like the others unless we try this."

Carol gritted her teeth. "But don't you *see?* This slick is destructive enough without making the situation ten times worse with these overblown solutions. At two hundred decibels—"

"*Up to* two hundred decibels," Garner said. "We won't be dealing in superlatives. I was going to start with fifty, changing frequency on the fly until we see some response."

"Brock, what do these sonar pulses sound like?" Ellie asked.

"Sound like?" Garner asked. "Anything you want." He shrugged. "The frequency is the key element. Any sound at all can be modulated to it. . . ."

Ellie looked at Carol. "Do you see where I'm going with this? Your waveforms."

Carol considered the suggestion. "You mean, transmit the waveform of the injured whale to warn off others?"

"If the frequency matches, why not?"

"The frequency won't match," Carol considered, "but that won't affect the content of the vocalizations."

"It won't have to," Garner said. "The sound itself should be a damn good air-raid siren."

"But if we can use anything as the sound source . . ." Ellie said.

"I'm willing to try it," Carol said. "Brock?"

Garner was looking at the latest Polygon plot. "It's as good a place as any to start," he said.

"It's still a one-way effort," Nolan said. "We'll be pushing the slick in one direction by repelling it from other directions."

"That's what Jakes said, too," Garner agreed. "We've potentially got a lot of repellent, but I'd feel much better if there was something *attracting* the slick on the other side."

"What do you propose to use as bait?" Carol asked.

"A whale," Garner said. "I think we should build a whale."

26

On the whiteboard in the *Kaiku*'s war room, Garner wrote the words HOW TO BUILD A WHALE. Below this he scrawled a large question mark, then began to diagram what he had in mind to Zubov and Sweeny.

"The thermocline we plotted was broken by the storm," Garner began. "Whatever thermal layering there was is gone, so if the colony is still seeking heat, it may be temporarily disoriented."

"The ATOC transmitters could be used to provide an updated temperature profile," Zubov said.

"True, as could the CTDs if we had time to redeploy them. But the hydrophones would need to be calibrated for receiving. Even if Jakes could do that, there won't be a significant temperature gradient yet, and we still have no way of knowing which *way* the slick might follow the heat, especially if it's been agitated," Garner said. "I'd rather give them something irresistible that doesn't leave the direction to chance."

"The hot deck?" Sweeny offered.

"As a start." Garner nodded. "We tow the hot deck—literally, the size and temperature of a whale—through the colony, slowly, and use it to attract and concentrate the cells. If it's hot enough, maybe we can excyst all the cells, reducing the chance they'll settle out into seed beds. Next, we deploy a forward ATOC transmitter and broadcast Carol's waveform from it. The vocalization might work as an attractant for the cells and, hopefully, a deterrent for any other whales in the slick's path. Then, as the cells converge on this signal, we take fine-scale pictures of them using Betty and Medusa. If nothing else, we can use the data we get to correct the model."

"How the hell are you going to deploy all this stuff at once?" Zubov asked.

"Six ships," Garner said. "The *Kaiku* takes the lead with the hot deck and the transmitter. We follow her with a pair of submersibles carrying Betty and taking ambient readings. Medusa can be let out from the *Exeter,* since she's already set up there. The Navy LSDs bring up the rear with a repelling ATOC array."

"Like herding sheep," Zubov suggested, the concept dawning on him. "Billions and billions of little tiny sheep."

"Serg, you've been at sea *way* too long," Garner said. "But I hope we can lead the slick into shore using this method, adjusting as we go. Then, once we run out of draft, we jettison the hot deck and pull back the *Kaiku.* Hopefully, the slick will have enough momentum to keep rolling inshore."

"Landing on some secluded area, I assume," Sweeny said.

Garner referred them to the chart. "Here. Port Gamble."

Zubov laughed. "Hoo, baby. Good name."

"It's a small, closed inlet," Garner said. "And probably our last chance before the slick enters Puget Sound."

Zubov studied the chart, unconvinced. "Christ, the entrance is hardly a straight shot, is it? It'll be like driving a Cadillac through a phone booth."

"If anyone can do it, you can," Garner assured him. "And pluck a quarter from the coin slot along the way."

"There's Indian reserve land in there," Sweeny noted.

"True, but that means it's also less populated and it's away from the mainland," Garner countered. "A perfect catcher's mitt."

"With the city of Seattle as the backstop," said Zubov.

"What about the media and these Keepers of the Coast, or whatever they're calling themselves?" Sweeny asked.

"You can get on the radio and tell them all thanks but no thanks," Garner said. "Tell them to get the hell back, and have Jakes fire on them if they don't listen." Garner watched as Sweeny began scribbling in his notebook. "Darryl, I was just kidding about firing on them," Garner added.

"What about the aerosol?" Zubov asked.

"The forecast says we've got more rain showers coming in tonight," Garner said. "If the weatherman lets us down, we'll douse the bay with buckets of water, just like we did with the permanganate."

"Simple, yet elegant," Zubov said sarcastically, his arms folded across his chest.

"Think so?" asked Garner.

Zubov scoffed. "Not bloody likely. Sure, it's elegant. It might even work. But what you're proposing is pretty fucking *complex,* Brock. You'd need all the arms of Vishnu working the winches."

"That's you," Garner said. "You can coordinate the deployment topside while we go below."

"In two submersibles, by your plan," Zubov said. "Where do you plan to get them? The Navy doesn't have any small subs out here with them."

"Nolan's got them down in the hold," Garner said.

"You have *two* minisubs?" Zubov asked Sweeny.

"The *Cyprid* and the *Zoea.*" Sweeny nodded. "Identically outfitted and specially built for the *Kaiku* by Nautile in France."

"Yeah, those domestic, off-the-rack subs can be a real pain in the ass," Zubov said, shaking his head. "This thing's got two of everything. It's like Noah's Ark without the smell."

Garner contacted Jakes aboard the *Albany* and relayed their plans for deploying the gear to corral the slick. They began with the hot deck, moving it into place on one of Nolan's barges directly behind the *Kaiku*. Once the *Kaiku*'s main winch had deployed the submersibles, the hot deck would be attached to it and the neutrally buoyant heating structure would be rolled into the water. Jakes arranged for a Navy helicopter to deliver an ATOC transmitter from the LSD *Columbus,* and they quickly attached it to the *Kaiku*'s starboard winch amidships. The device was set off the side of the ship on a drop-down platform known to mariners as "the chains," and its electronics were patched through the *Kaiku*'s telecommunications studio, where any variety of controlled signals could be selected for transmission.

Jakes would control the operation of all ATOC units from the *Albany,* ensuring that his ship and the *Columbus* were kept in position north of the slick. Beginning with a preprogrammed range of frequencies, the ATOC units would begin probing the slick at two-minute intervals. Zubov agreed to catch a ride back to the *Exeter* in the Navy helicopter to oversee the deployment of Medusa, but only after he helped get both the *Kaiku*'s submersibles in the water, quickly and in series, from the ship's single A-frame.

Sweeny had the main hold opened to the *Kaiku*'s aft deck. He, Garner, and Zubov climbed down into the stern of the *Kaiku* for a look at the submersibles. Zubov ran an affectionate hand along the smooth hull of the *Cyprid*. "Ceramic," he said, admiring the obvious craftsmanship. "Sweet. Even stronger than most titanium hulls developed by the Navy, if you can afford them."

"Bob insists on the best," Sweeny said, "and a spare of the best to keep in reserve." He indicated the *Zoea* in the adjacent hangar.

"You need a second pilot," Zubov said. "None of the kids on this tug are gonna know how to fly one of these."

"They know less about surface support," Garner said. "I need you up here, calling the shots from the *Exeter*."

"Then what are you gonna do?" Zubov said. "Clone someone who's competent?"

Freeland, Garner thought. *This whole scheme could have come straight out of Freeland's head, and Saunders Freeland is* exactly *who we need right now.*

"I'll do it," came Nolan's voice from the catwalk. They turned and looked up at Nolan, his face still horribly scarred from his exposure to the colony. Once again he had come topside with the hood of his bio-hazard suit pulled back jauntily, his gloves stuffed in his knee pockets, but Garner supposed they were still too far from the periphery of the slick for that to matter. The trembling in Nolan's exposed hands had become quite noticeable; Garner was about to scold Nolan for the tenth time about his casual attention to his own safety but decided they didn't have time for more head banging.

Carol stood at Nolan's side, obviously uneasy with this confrontation, not to mention the fact that her husband was out of bed at all.

"Carol and I will take the *Zoea*," Nolan continued. "Garner, you and Darryl can take the *Cyprid*."

"I don't think I need Darryl as—" Garner began.

"A chaperone?" Nolan said.

"—Ballast, I was going to say."

"This is Nolan Group equipment," Nolan said. "I want someone I can trust on each sub. It's still my reputation and my money that's at stake here." He caught the last few syllables of this order as his words began, slightly but perceptibly, to slur.

"Look at yourself," Garner said. "Your skin is practically *dripping*. You can barely stand up. Aren't you at least a little concerned about infection?"

"Carol can help me," Nolan said. "And you know you don't have any other pilots you can use. End of story." His hand slid over his gun holster, offering a reminder if not a direct threat.

"Aye aye, Captain Bligh," Zubov said. "It's still your sandbox. Just let me help get these babies in the water without a scratch."

Garner saw the same determined set to Nolan's eyes that Carol had seen. Bob Nolan the commandant had returned. *He's in over his head and he knows it,* Garner thought. *He's fighting to regain some kind of control of this uncontrollable situation, and he's gonna get more of us killed in the process.*

The mismatched convoy of vessels had passed Dungeness spit by mid-afternoon. As planned, the *Kaiku* led the way, with its ATOC transmitter, and the twin submersibles at the ready and the Nolan barge with the hot deck close behind. Next came the *Exeter* with Medusa set on its main winch. The *Albany* and the *Columbus* brought up the rear, their own ATOC devices at the ready.

As Garner noted their position on the chart, he saw that the slick had passed completely over the sill into the fjord system. However they were going to isolate and destroy the colony, there could be no pieces left over. If it sank into the depths of Puget Sound as dormant or semi-dormant cysts, the colony would remain a potential threat to the area for years, if not decades.

Following the latest images sent to them by the Orion, they soon made visual contact with the slick. The dye had continued to weather, leaving the slick's shape vague and ill-defined but still discernible against the rolling waves. Nolan conducted the semi-evacuation of the *Kaiku,* sending all nonessential crew and personnel to the Navy LSDs or to the mainland and leaving a skeleton crew of sailors and deck hands to manage the deployment of the gear. McRee did the same aboard the *Exeter,* where Ellie was dispatched to supervise the dispensing of biohazard suits and respirators.

Within minutes the deck of the *Kaiku* had become a clearinghouse for cables, power cords, and sampling equipment. Zubov supervised the movement of the gear on and off the A-frame, barking commands from the railing or swinging down to water level on a makeshift bos'n's chair and looking—to Garner's way of thinking—every bit like Santa Claus shuttling up and down an invisible chimney.

First over the side was the *Kaiku*'s ATOC transmitter, lowered from the chains to a depth of ten meters, or one atmosphere. An umbilical to the *Zoea* would give Carol some direct control of the transmitter's output from her laptop, but this same umbilical would limit the *Zoea*'s maneuverability. Jakes would retain final firing command on the ATOC ping.

Next, the *Cyprid* was lowered from the *Kaiku*'s stern. Bobbing in the swells behind the ship, Garner stretched from the *Cyprid*'s open hatch as

Zubov hung suspended from the bos'n's chair, quickly slinging Betty between the two submersibles and activating her samplers and camera array. Like Carol's line to the ATOC unit, Betty's output was connected to Garner in the *Cyprid*.

"You work pretty fast for a man hanging in midair." Garner grinned, ratcheting the last of the locking bolts into place.

"Guess I'm used to having my ass in a sling," Zubov grumbled.

As Garner slipped back through the *Cyprid*'s hatch to join Sweeny, Zubov stopped him. "Good luck down there," he said.

"From here on, luck has nothing to do with it," Garner said, and flashed Zubov the traditional thumbs-up before Zubov slammed the submersible's hatch shut.

Above, the *Zoea* was already being swung into position on the *Kaiku*'s A-frame. Carol confirmed a good connection with the ATOC unit, then Nolan followed Garner's lead as the submersibles glided out of the stern's shadow. The hot deck was brought into position, attached to the *Kaiku*'s main winch, then slowly rolled into the water. Having worked on several icebreakers in the Canadian Arctic, the *Kaiku*'s boatswain, Byrnes, was well experienced with controlling the device and soon had it heating a thin envelope of water to 90 degrees Fahrenheit.

After ensuring that everyone left on board was fully outfitted in exposure suits, the *Kaiku*'s minimal bridge crew set a course directly through the slick. After one last check of the deployment protocol, Zubov climbed aboard the Navy helicopter. As he settled back in the small seat, exhaustion weighed heavily on him. He needed a bunk, a beer, and a brunette, and was too tired to be particular about the order. From the air he could see the parcel of heated water around the hot deck and the two submersibles following dutifully behind, flying on either side of Betty.

In less than two hours, Garner's mechanized "whale" had become a reality.

Damn your overeducated ass, Garner, this might actually work, Zubov said to himself. As the *Exeter* quickly approached, his thoughts returned to more familiar territory: the complex sequence of events soon to be expected in deploying Medusa.

———

"What's the depth here?" Sweeny asked, as Garner brought the *Cyprid* around in a wide turn on the end of Betty's guide lines. The rocking of the ingress and the splash of surface waves against the hull had subsided. Now only the gurgling whine of the sub's impellers gave any sensation of movement in the tiny ship.

"One ninety, two hundred feet," Garner said. "We're inside the sill, in kind of a No Man's Land, but we'll run out of bottom soon enough."

Sweeny had been in a submersible only once before, and that had been in an amusement park. The confines of the *Cyprid*'s cockpit were uncomfortable and clammy, and the air tasted bottled and stale. He looked out one of the sub's small portholes and peered into the gloom far below. The sunlight was truncated less than fifty feet below them, but Sweeny still glimpsed rows of low, flat-topped seamounts. Far off to their right, the bottom tilted sharply upward to form the sill. Sweeny could now see what Garner meant about things becoming trapped in the drowned fjord system and was uncomfortable with the notion that the *Cyprid* had just joined the list of potential candidates.

"Have you ever driven one of these things?" Sweeny asked.

"Flown," Garner said. "We're flying. And I have, once or twice." To Sweeny, it now seemed to be a question with an obvious answer. Not only was Garner operating the sub with skill, but a palpable look of serenity had come over his face. Unlike his jaunts in the helicopter, Garner seemed utterly at ease underwater.

"Remind me to thank Bob when we get back." Sweeny stared at the curved wall of the cockpit and took comfort from Zubov's comment on the strength of the ceramic hull.

"*Cyprid,* this is *Zoea,*" Nolan's voice came over the headset. "Setting course on one-niner-zero."

"Roger, *Zoea,* will follow," Garner said into his microphone, then added with a wry smile to Sweeny, "*Niner?* Gosh, he's professional."

Sweeny's eyes suddenly widened, and he pointed to a rivulet of water trickling down the cockpit wall. "Oh shit! We're leaking!"

"Condensation," Garner said. He registered Sweeny's doubtful look. "It's not a leak; it's our own respiration. Taste it. It'll be fresh water, not saltwater."

"How can you be sure?" Sweeny asked. "I mean, once we get inside the slick, who's to say it won't start dissolving the sealant or something?"

"Because 'Bob insists on the best,' remember?" Garner said.

"So how do we stop it—the condensation?"

"Stop breathing," Garner said with a laugh. "If we spring a leak, you'll know. At depth—five hundred meters, say—that trickle would be a jet strong enough to cut you in two."

"Seriously?" Sweeny said.

"Darryl, *relax,*" Garner said. "We're not going deep enough to experience any pressure effects. The surface is eight feet above your head."

"It's the bottom I'm worried about."

"Suit yourself. I'm going to take a minute and remind myself why I'm a biologist," Garner said, and nodded toward the pilot's window. "We're entering the slick."

Gazing through the *Cyprid*'s main porthole, Garner got his first close-up look at the living colony. The cells coalesced in the wake of the *Kaiku,* luminescing slightly as they glanced off the glass. The thick, mucoid secretion Garner had discovered in the lab now dominated his field of view: alive, swirling around individuals too small to be seen, yet providing an astounding intercellular communication system. Garner had devoted half his life to the study of the sea—most of the past six years exclusively to plankton—and this was still utterly unlike anything he had ever seen.

No described dinoflagellate, including *Pfiesteria,* was known to produce such an abundant secretion, much less enhance its propulsion and communicate intelligence with it. Despite what the creature creators of B-movies would have their audiences believe, fluid secretions, slime, and mucus were costly for an organism to produce. Even in saltwater, the loss of so much moisture from the intracellular fluid would produce a metabolic drain too great for any amount of feeding to recoup. The copper levels this species tolerated, the durability of its cells, its exponential re-

production, and amplification within the ecosystem were also nearly beyond belief for any naturally occurring species.

Yet here it was, tightly wrapped around the *Cyprid,* the *Zoea,* and the
Kaiku, funneling itself directly into Puget Sound and challenging the
collective disbelief of these human "experts" along the way. If there ever
existed an organism that could be used off-the-shelf as a biological
weapon of mass destruction or to provide the foundation to build one,
this was it. Surely this killer had *begun* as a relative or species of *Pfiesteria;*
the similarities were too pronounced to dismiss that. It might itself have
been a naturally occurring organism, once, but some bizarre departure in
its design—whether engineered or occurring by chance—had produced
this elegant colonial nightmare. Whatever it had become, the slick was as
close to an alien organism, an alien *intelligence,* as Garner had ever encountered. Eye-to-eyes with it, he now had to admit it was—

"Beautiful," Garner said, entranced. "Absolutely beautiful."

Flotsam and assorted nekton enveloped by the slick on its travels
were now recirculated in the mucus as a series of perpetually recycling
convection cells. Cysts, dead cells, and inorganic debris were all processed within the slick as it moved, feeding, growing, and regenerating
itself as it swam against the tide. Garner could almost imagine the sound
of the cells trickling over the hull—countless trillions of hard, cellulose-
based capsules moving together as a single organism. Existing only to
feed, to breed, to survive. Several times Garner had felt awe at the design
of nature, but to imagine that humans had had a hand in engineering a
creature such as this was all the more remarkable. He raised his hand
and settled his fingers against the cold glass of the porthole. The colony,
so deadly yet so beautiful, swirled and flowed less than an inch away.

Zubov's voice over the headset broke Garner's reverie. "How's it
lookin' down there, troops?"

"I hate to admit it," Garner said, "but this is a gorgeous thing to
watch up close."

"We're ready to try the first pulse with the forward transmitter,"
Carol said from the *Zoea.* Jakes confirmed that the *Albany* and the *Columbus* were ready with the follow-up arrays. "Setting first waveform at

fifty decibels, zero-point-nine-five kilohertz," Carol said. "Pinging now."

"Do we plug our ears or anything?" Sweeny asked Garner.

"No," Garner said. He couldn't help but add: "Nice chaperoning."

Inside the *Cyprid*, Garner and Sweeny could hear the pulse as a thin *criiick*ing sound. Although they knew it was originating from the direction of the *Kaiku*, any sense of orientation was lost. A moment later, the response ping came from the LSDs.

Criiick-criiick.

"Serg?" Garner said into his microphone. "Anything?"

"Negative," Zubov said. "Cameras show no change in orientation. Keep trying."

Using a series of transmissions in a systematic progression, Carol and Jakes's crew began moving quickly through series after series of frequencies. Carol adjusted the frequency on her waveform, then passed it through the forward ATOC transmitter using a cascading array of frequencies, while Jakes and Zubov experimented with the decibel level. At 0.5 kilohertz, Zubov told Carol to hold the frequency steady and told Jakes to increase the decibel level.

"I think we've got something," Zubov said. "Medusa's showing movement toward the forward LFA in two, no, in four cameras." Jakes stepped up the volume on Carol's waveform again. "Yes! I think we've got the little bastards' attention. Hold it right there!"

In the *Cyprid*, Garner and Sweeny could hear Carol shout out in delight and begin chattering with Nolan, or rather, *at* Nolan. Nolan's responses were muffled over the headsets and too indistinct to decipher.

"Bob?" Garner said. "You okay?" Nolan mumbled something in reply. "What's that?" Garner asked again, listening, frowning.

"I said I'm *fine*, you prick," Nolan's voice suddenly bellowed over the headset. "Man your post and *shut* the *fuck* up." The verbal assault seemed unduly harsh, even for Nolan.

"Easy now, Bob," Garner said. "The bug isn't the only thing down here with sensitive ears."

"Can you believe that?" he heard Zubov say to someone on the *Exeter*, though loud enough for everyone on the comm channel to hear. "They censor gangsta rap on the radio, but not trash talk like that. Where's the FCC when you need 'em?"

After another twenty minutes of cycling through the frequency and decibel parameters, Zubov's voice broke into the conversation once again. "Whoa! Try that last one again."

"The attractive or the repulsive?" Jakes asked for clarification.

"Repulsive," Zubov said. The *Albany* and the *Columbus* complied. "Yes! That's got 'em."

"What is it, Serg?" Garner asked.

"The cells in Medusa's flow-through just jumped like you wouldn't believe," Zubov said. "Reminds me of a school of squid, or fish startled by a flash of light. They all jerked away at once."

"Then we've got their attention the other way, too," Garner said. "John, try it again, louder."

A moment later, the ATOC array produced the same sound, audibly louder inside the *Cyprid*. Garner called out the last set of readings from Betty, and Zubov compared it with the same parameters from Medusa.

"Definite repulsive movement," Zubov confirmed.

"You ought to know about repulsion. I've seen you on a date," Garner said.

"I resent that remark," Zubov muttered back. "There it is again. Repulsive movement on all cameras."

Over the headset, Garner could hear someone on the ATOC crew let out a whoop of celebration. The pushing force of the ATOC system had been found. Garner told the LSD crews to repeat the repulsive ping on a higher frequency, reporting any deviation in the slick's response. "Push," Garner said. "Push this damn thing for all you're worth and keep pulling it with Carol's waveform on the forward transmitter."

"All right, folks," said Zubov. "We are now nineteen nautical miles north, northwest of Port Gamble, depth one-three-zero feet and rising." McRee cut in to pass a set of course corrections to the *Kaiku*'s bridge crew, then Zubov continued: "Carol, keep the frequency on the attractive ping as it is. I've got a pod of whales on the sonar, and whatever you're doing stopped them from moving any closer. Bob, move in a little closer to the hot deck and prepare to surface. Let's get everyone out of there before we run out of draft—no pun intended."

"We need more time," Garner said. "Betty's not as fast as Medusa, or as accurate. If we can't synch the data sources from within the slick, the Polygon plot will be biased and we'll lose our estimate of the colony's structure."

"English, Brock," Zubov said.

"The model will be off," Garner said.

"Screw the *model*. If we hit Port Gamble on the money, you won't need it."

"And if we miss, the model will provide our only evacuation plan for half the population of Seattle," Garner said.

"Unless you put the reins on this little wagon train, you'll be able to warn them as we're cruising down Pike Street," Zubov said.

"Bob? What do you think?" Jakes interjected. His voice was momentarily lost in a barrage of static. "Dammit!" he said to someone on the *Albany*. "I told you to get those goddamn news copters *back* and *off* our main comm channel."

"Bob?" Zubov said. "Yo, Bob?"

There was no response from the *Zoea*. In fact, there had been no transmission since Nolan's sudden outburst. Garner strained to listen, the hiss of white noise suddenly cold and forbidding in his ears.

"Carol?" he said. "Bob? Come in, *Zoea,* do you copy?"

Suddenly, the *Cyprid* shuddered violently, rocking Garner in his seat and banging Sweeny's head into the bulkhead. "What the hell—" Garner began. The submersible suddenly spun 180 degrees, winding Betty's tether around its tail wing.

"What's going on?" Zubov said.

"We're hung up on Betty's rigging," Garner said, fighting the controls.

"Where's Nolan's ship?" Jakes demanded.

"It was just here," Garner said, finally bringing the craft under control. He craned to look out the window, where the shape of the *Zoea* had been only seconds before.

Then he saw it. The lines that had snagged the *Cyprid*'s diving planes were in fact the portion of the rigging that was supposed to be attached to the *Zoea*. Where the other submersible had been, there was now only empty space.

From below him in the capsule, Sweeny suddenly shouted, "There they are!"

Garner scrambled down from his seat to look, seeing only the faintest outline of the *Zoea* below them, belly up, and tumbling into the deep.

"Sub down! Sub down!" Garner shouted into the radio. "They've broken all umbilicals and are sinking directly below us."

"Can you assist?" Jakes said.

Garner was already back at the controls, working the impellers back and forth to loosen the hold of the broken lines. "Negative," he said. "We're tied onto the rig." Garner cursed and worked the controls, quickly moving through several maneuvers intended to find an escape route from the tangled rigging.

"All stop!" Zubov shouted to the *Kaiku*'s bridge crew. Another shudder rocked the *Cyprid* as the rigging protested its change in momentum.

"*Albany* to *Zoea,* do you copy?" Jakes said.

There was no reply from the other submersible, which had now vanished from sight as well.

Sweeny's voice came on the line for the first time, sounding reedy and frightened, asking for details on the situation. Zubov cut him off and told him to shut up. All listened again, straining.

Only silence.

"*Zoea,* this is *Exeter,*" Zubov said again. "*Zoea,* come in, please." Inside Garner's cockpit, his friend's voice sounded distant and metallic. Carol and Nolan had vanished from sight, falling into the deep blue void below.

"*Zoea,* this is *Exeter*. Do you copy. . . ?"

27

Ninety feet below the surface, Carol struggled to stay conscious as the *Zoea* tumbled toward the bottom without power or control. Instinctually, she replayed the events of the past few minutes to try and make sense of what had happened.

At first, the flight had gone well. Bob certainly knew how to handle the *Zoea*—he had had the craft built to his own specifications, in fact. He held the *Zoea* straight and true between the *Kaiku* and the *Cyprid,* suspended securely on the rigging Garner had engineered. While Carol worked to establish the attractive ping on the ATOC unit, Bob kept the ship even with the other submersible, holding Betty's sampling ports perpendicular to the flow as the craft moved forward through the slick. Carol had been vaguely aware of the chatter on the headset, of her husband's complaint that the colony's mucus might clog the impellers and overheat them, but for the most part her attention had been focused on the computer screen in front of her.

Carol had heard Zubov identifying the repulsive ping and Jakes telling them to wait. The *Zoea* had fallen quiet as they listened to the exchange between the *Cyprid,* the *Exeter,* and the *Albany.*

Then, without any warning, something had gone terribly wrong. One moment Carol was looking at the computer, checking her last frequency modulation, and the next the sub was spinning out of control. Hearing Bob shout out in shocked surprise, she had turned to look at him, had seen his hands moving quickly, frantically over the controls and his face growing ashen. For a split second she thought he was having some kind of seizure—more subtle neurological decay—as a result of his low-level exposure to the *Pfiesteria* cells. Except that he looked like he was trying to back away from something.

Then she saw what her husband had seen.

Floating outside the main window, snagged on one of the submersible's articulating arms, was what Carol knew must be the body of Saunders Freeland.

Freeland's orange containment suit had been shredded. After three days enveloped by the slick, whatever flesh had not been stripped completely from his bones was bloated and hemorrhaged. Sliced and ripped tissue drifted silently in the current, sprouting from every opening in the tattered space suit like an obscene underwater scarecrow.

Nolan screamed again and moved his hands rapidly over the controls, trying to back the sub away from the specter outside. His movements were forced, wasteful, grinding the twin control sticks back and forth on their rubber skirts. To Carol, her husband appeared to be fighting to control his own limbs as much as the sub itself. His face and neck twitched with muscular spasms, and his eyes blinked rapidly to clear the sweat that was trickling down his forehead.

The sound of the impellers changed their pitch, suddenly slowing and struggling.

"This goddamn slime!" Nolan said. "The shit's overheating the impellers." Whether this was true, Carol could not know. Garner had reported no problems with the *Cyprid*'s controls, but then again, he most likely wasn't having a tantrum in the cockpit.

"Bob, *settle down,*" Carol said. She pushed the talk button on her headset, trying to raise Jakes or Garner. The unit appeared to be dead.

Then she saw the problem: in his thrashing, Bob's foot had kicked the phono plug for her headset out of its jack.

She curled herself forward in the spinning sub, reaching for the disconnected wire between Nolan's feet. She nearly had it in her grasp when Nolan drew his gun.

"Stay there!" Nolan screamed at her. His voice boomed in the confines of the capsule. His entire upper body had begun to quake with frantic nervous decay. *"Just stay there. Everything is under control, understand?"*

"Bob, I'm trying to *help* you," Carol said. "You have to settle down—"

"Shut up shut up shut up!" Nolan screamed, banging the handle of the gun savagely against the pilot's window. Tears welled up in his eyes as his tantrum intensified. The lesions on his face had begun to drip. The throttle of the right-side impeller, temporarily forgotten, was pushed wide open, sending the *Zoea* into a tight spin. The rigging stretching from the hull protested loudly on its cleats, sending the craft spinning back in the opposite direction. *"Just shut up. I know what I'm doing. . . ."*

"Stop it, Bob!" Carol screamed, struggling to keep her balance. "Stop it right now!"

At the sound of Carol's voice, Nolan stopped hammering the glass and turned to look at her. His eyes were glowering and angrier than Carol could ever have imagined. Then Nolan raised the gun and pointed it at her, its barrel wavering in the tight confines of the capsule only a few feet from her face.

"Can't you see we're all going to die out here?" Nolan screamed at her. *"We're going to die and it's* your *fucking fault!"* Even in his rage, his voice was slurred and warbling.

Fighting its restraints, the submersible continued its uncontrolled spin, throwing Carol and the loose equipment to the floor. In frightening contrast, the barrel of the gun remained steady.

Still trembling, *looking* at Carol but not *seeing* her, Nolan cocked the trigger.

Carol crawled back against the far side of the capsule. Nolan was perched in front of the capsule's only exit; past him was the certain death of the slick. For a long moment she was aware of nothing but the gun and the sudden, unfathomable rage she had just seen. She couldn't even bring herself to look at her husband.

"Get away!" she heard him say. *"Just get the fuck away from me!"* Then she realized that he was screaming not at her but at Freeland's corpse, or the colony, or both.

She heard the sound of metal slamming against the hull several times, then the most terrifying sound yet: the pilot's window shattering, a sharp, pressurized *bang!* as the Lexan-bonded glass fractured and split from its steel frame.

Then water. Lots of it. Pouring into the capsule all around her.

Carol looked up and saw the ocean coming in through the fractured porthole. A massive shaft of pig iron—part of the main bridle attaching them to Betty—had been driven through the main window of the out-of-control sub.

Carol fought to register what she was seeing. The sub had hit the bridle end-on, pushing the massive iron frame through the porthole. The shaft continued forward, driven by the sub's momentum, and pierced her husband's chest. Nolan was run through by the shaft, pinned to the pilot's seat as his legs reflexively lashed out in defense. He started to scream, but the sound was cut by the acidic water that poured over him, devouring his flesh.

Carol's motionless shock turned to panic. Her husband was dead, the hull had been compromised, and the *Zoea* was flooding.

Carol caught a whiff of something caustic in the air. She first thought it was the toxic aerosol of the *Pfiesteria* cells, but then realized it was the *Zoea*'s batteries. The electronics of the submersible were burning, and the control panel quickly shorted out, leaving her in near blackness. She fumbled around her neck for the hood of her watertight containment suit and quickly pulled it on, watching in disbelief and terror through the thin faceplate as the capsule filled with water. As the sub's suspended weight increased, the iron was wrenched downward. With a loud, metallic scrape, the bridle relinquished its hold on the broken porthole, and the sub fell away from the rest of the rigging. Nolan was left with a gigantic bloody pulp where his rib cage had been as his body floated free of the pilot's seat.

The sub continued to fill with water around Carol. *How much weight can the umbilical take?* she wondered. *Will they still be able to haul us out?* Then she realized that the *Zoea* was sinking. It had come loose from the rigging and guide lines and was tumbling, end over end, toward the bottom.

Pressed to the floor of the blacked-out submersible, Carol fought to remember its design, locating its main internal features by touch. She knew that both of the *Kaiku*'s submersibles were equipped with emergency air cylinders and life jackets with tracking units. She recalled how ridiculously small the air cylinders were—tinier than a child's thermos bottle—and wondered how such devices could ever be expected to assist survival. The *Zoea* was built to dive to depths of over 3,000 meters, hardly practical for life jackets, but she knew—didn't she?—that the sub couldn't yet be more than a hundred feet from the surface. The ship continued to sink, slipping deeper and deeper with each second she delayed.

Get out of here! Carol commanded herself, pulling open the small storage lockers one after another and groping inside until she found what she was looking for. She screwed the bottle onto the auxiliary respirator port on her helmet and opened the bleed valve, regulating her breathing until she had regained some of her composure. The clean, bottled air she now inhaled did not need to be passed through the HEPA filters on the blower pack, but it would not last long.

Emergency ascent. Forced exhalation. Move it!

Carol grabbed the two remaining cylinders and hooked them into the belt of her suit. Then she pulled up the pilot's seat and withdrew a life jacket from the storage locker there. She struggled to slip the life jacket over her containment suit, eventually tying the straps around her arms and chest with absolutely no idea whether it was properly positioned. What she really needed was the small tracking device stitched into the jacket's shoulder, which would be activated as soon as she reached the surface.

She moved to the hatch at the top of the hull. As the sub had completely filled with water, the pressure had equalized on both sides of the hatch, and it should swing open easily. As she unscrewed the locking bolts, something large brushed against her from behind.

Her husband's lifeless body.

Carol remembered the look of deranged terror on his face just before the power went out. The anger of his expression, the scarred skin on his face slowly decaying. She would carry that dreadful image of her husband with her for the rest of her life.

Take him. You have to take him with you. No one deserves to be left down here.

She considered turning back for one last look at him, one last attempt to pull him from the *Zoea,* but knew she would only be compromising her own chance for survival. She had to leave.

She placed her hands on either side of the open hatch and moved forward. Something grabbed her, holding her back. A scream lodged in Carol's throat. *He's grabbing me,* she thought. *Bob is still alive and he's trying to drown me!* She kicked out frantically, spinning around in the tight confines of the *Zoea's* surface tower. Then she realized that it was only the respirator pack on her back, hooked on the edge of the portal, that was restraining her.

Through the porthole, she could see Freeland's shredded Racal suit still clinging to the outside of the sub. The slick was a floating graveyard, probably carrying with it the undigested remains of all its victims, Carol thought. And it was out there, now waiting for her. Escaping the prison cell of the submersible, she would have two directions to choose from—a continued free fall to the bottom or a controlled sprint for the surface, possibly surfacing into the slick itself.

Go! Go! Go! Her body screamed in protest as the *Zoea* rolled over once again in its downward tumble.

With a final thrust, she threw herself through the open hatch. As her legs cleared the portal she was suddenly alone in the pitch-black water, disoriented, and still dizzy from the tumbling submersible. Freed from the confines of the capsule, the containment suit was awkward and ungainly, impeding her movements but at least providing a thin barrier of protection from her surroundings. Her suit was sealed against the water, but it was not insulated or pressurized. Cold water pressed flat the small envelope of warmed air against her skin, and she quickly began to freeze.

She had minutes before hypothermia would threaten to paralyze her completely.

How deep am I? she wondered, then, with dawning panic, *Oh my God, which way is up?* Her mind fought to stay conscious as she began to swim, finding her sense of direction. *Keep swimming, keep swimming,* she repeated to herself in an angry mantra. The air in the reserve tank was already beginning to thin, and she adjusted the flow. The deeper she was, the more the air would be compressed and the more quickly it would run out. She sipped at her meager supply, conserving it despite the protest of her aching muscles and joints.

As she approached the surface, she would have the opposite problem. The air in the cylinder, in her life jacket, and in her own body would expand, providing increased buoyancy but potentially rupturing the vessels containing it, including her blood, stomach, lungs, and throat. She didn't think she had been at depth long enough to worry about the bends—the release of nitrogen bubbles in the bloodstream that would come with a reduction in pressure—but she would need to exhale continuously to expel the increased volume of air and counteract its expansion in her lungs.

Forced exhalation. Slow and steady. Don't hold your breath. . . .

As Carol's eyes adjusted to the gloom and her head cleared, the faint glow of sunlight from the surface came into perspective. How far up? Was the colony still above her? How far would she need to swim laterally?

And did it really matter? The surface could be her only possible destination.

Carol switched to a fresh cylinder, bleeding the compressed air underwater like a scuba regulator. Then she located the tracking device on her life jacket and continued swimming for the surface.

Garner purged the *Cyprid*'s ballast and brought the small ship to the surface. As he pulled on his containment suit and opened the hatch, the *Kaiku*'s deck crew threw him a temporary mooring line. For the moment, the submersible was stranded on the surface. The A-frame still carried the hot deck, and Betty's broken rigging had become wrapped around the *Cyprid*'s tail fins and landing rails.

Climbing out onto the *Cyprid*'s surge-washed deck, Garner now saw that the A-frame itself didn't look right. One side of the boom appeared twisted and bent. The *Kaiku*'s boatswain quickly confirmed this while Garner and Sweeny climbed up to the afterdeck.

"When that rigging snapped, all hell broke loose up here," Byrnes said, breathing heavily inside his Racal hood. "The winch jammed and three cables locked up."

"Anyone hurt?" Garner asked.

"Damn right there was," Byrnes said, trembling. "One of the cables snapped and decapitated one of my men."

The news struck Garner like a slap. What had gone wrong so suddenly? Had the winch crew's inexperience or panic cost Carol and Nolan their lives? Garner got on the radio to the *Exeter* and asked Zubov to fly back to the *Kaiku* to assist them.

"I can handle my own ship," Byrnes said indignantly. He was still slightly annoyed at Zubov's commandeering of the ship's resources earlier.

"I can tell," Garner said sarcastically. "But I need someone who can handle the rest of this mess."

Looking at the *Kaiku*'s deck, "mess" was an understatement. The A-frame was hopelessly damaged, bent down toward the water at a cockeyed angle. The *Cyprid* was stranded in the water, the *Zoea* was lost, and there was no way to disengage the hot deck. Along the gunwale, a spattering of blood was all that remained of the decapitated crewman. More chilling to Garner was the utter transparency all their lives had acquired. Beginning with the men aboard the *Sato Maru,* in Barkley Sound and now Juan de Fuca Strait, death continued to fall around him like a silent cloak. Another anonymous body did little to change their predicament one way or another.

Garner headed to the main lab and checked the latest Polygon projection. The leading edge of the slick was now a quarter mile behind the *Kaiku,* following the hot deck and recoiling from the ATOC units on the LSDs. Port Gamble Bay was still more than three miles away, and they had lost the forward ping from the *Kaiku*. From here in, any number of variables could move the slick away from the ATOCs' prodding. Garner typed in the hypothetical scenario that the slick would miss Gamble Point, factoring in Medusa's latest data on the colony.

335,000 EXPOSED; 178,230 FATALITIES, estimated the Polygon.

Garner scowled and closed the screen on the laptop.

"Is the software working?" asked one of the *Kaiku*'s technicians.

"I hope not," Garner said, heading quickly back to the afterdeck.

Zubov arrived on the *Exeter*'s launch minutes later. "Any word on the *Zoea*?" he asked.

"Nothing," Garner said. "Jakes is trying to assemble a team of SEALs to dive for them. Assuming we've just lost surface contact with them, they should have another six hours of power and oxygen."

"I don't see how they could have *any* oxygen left," Sweeny said.

"What do you mean?" Garner asked.

"I saw a helluva lot of bubbles coming out of the *Zoea* as she was going down," Sweeny explained. "It looked like they lost all their air, all at once."

"You mean an implosion?"

Before Garner could react to the news, one of the omnipresent news helicopters passed low over the *Kaiku*. Garner could see a cameraman inside, his newscam pointed at them.

"I thought Jakes ordered the media to get back," Garner said.

"Like *that's* gonna work anymore," Zubov said. "Nolan got his wish. This thing is headline news now."

"Until their engines suffocate, like Nolan's did," Garner said bitterly.

"Right now they've got the best point of view on this. Maybe we can use the extra eyes to track the slick," Zubov offered.

"Then get them doing something useful," Garner said. "But I want them at least a hundred yards outside the aerosol zone and four hundred feet up. We can't give them any more specific directions until we know this thing's concentration and how it behaves. God only knows how they've survived this long."

Overhearing this exchange, Sweeny left off his inspection of the damage to the *Kaiku*'s deck. "This operation is over, Garner," he said, the tremolo not quite hidden in his voice. "Assuming we can ever find my boss, I can assure you there will be a full retraction of Nolan Group participation in this operation. That includes the *Kaiku and* the *Exeter*—"

Garner turned to face Sweeny. His expression alone was enough to make Sweeny flinch. "Not now, Darryl," Garner said. "Not now."

"We're picking up a jacket tracking signal from the *Zoea,*" Zubov called out.

Garner spun around. "How many?" he said.

"Just one," Zubov said.

"That's better than none," Garner said. "Let's get to it."

Zubov studied his friend's face. "Brock, it's only a tracking signal; it doesn't mean there are any survivors."

"We're overdue for a survivor, so let's put the porch light on."

Warmth.

As the water continued to lighten around her, Carol began to feel strangely warm. She realized that the sensation was not the sunlight penetrating the surface but the result of an unusually distinct thermocline. Then she remembered the hot deck and knew she was close to salvation.

She had no idea where she was, whether the *Kaiku* was miles away or whether she would surface in the middle of the colony, only to die as soon as she tried to take a breath. Her limbs ached from exertion, and her mind was numbed. She felt like a jellyfish, lucid and thin, gliding along in the ocean's currents, utterly powerless to control her own direction. Except up. Up to the light, to the surface . . .

Her arms, then her head, broke into the sunlight, already angling to the west. As she rose and sank in the waves, she glimpsed portions of the shoreline and then a nearby ship, which she did not recognize. Her lopsided life jacket left her bobbing at an awkward angle. As she adjusted its fit, the tracking device began its automated chirp.

Exhausted, Carol floated in the water and fought to avoid unconsciousness. The water around her looked clear of mucus, and she surmised she had surfaced upwind of the slick. Soon she could see a Navy launch coming toward her between the swells. Safe for the moment, but her exhaustion alone felt like enough to drag her back to the bottom if she stopped treading water for even a second. The air cylinder attached to her regulator tasted stale and cold. It had probably been used up long ago; she was now only rebreathing the air trapped inside her helmet.

Floating, floating . . . a single cell trapped at the top of an ocean of water and the bottom of an ocean of air.

A powerful pair of arms wrapped themselves around her chest—*Oh my God, Bob!*—and hauled her from the water. She was set down on the landing platform of a smaller boat, the Navy launch she had seen. She was aware of several muffled voices moving around her and frantic hands working on the fasteners of her containment suit.

Then her small cocoon was pulled open, and the warm August air rushed in to greet her chilled flesh. A man's mouth closed over her own, filling her with warmth. His breath entered her, expanding her lungs and returning sensation to her numbed extremities. As she teetered on the edge of consciousness once again, she realized that she recognized the smell of the man's skin.

Brock. Once again, he had somehow been there to catch her.

28

In the middle of the Sunday dinner hour, the mayor of Seattle interrupted all local television and radio programming, including the broadcast of the Mariners–White Sox baseball game. In the wake of the season's worst storm—a massive disturbance that the Weather Channel had downgraded from a Gale to a Near Gale even as it dumped four inches of rain in two hours, then barreled east into the Cascades—the real emergency for her city was just beginning to take shape.

The news, first from Juniper Bay and then from Port Townsend, clearly affected the mayor as she read prepared statements from the U.S. Coast Guard and the local field director of USAMRIID. According to these statements, now verified by the U.S. Navy and a spokesperson from the Nolan Group, the toxic plankton bloom they had been closely monitoring was dangerously close to the city, potentially endangering the shores of Puget Sound and Elliott Bay. There was the possibility that within hours a neurotoxin as deadly as any chemical warfare agent would be blown into the city's waterfront.

The mayor then read the list of possible symptoms to be expected from exposure to the slick's aerosol contaminants: runny nose, tearing, or excessive salivation, burning of the nose, mouth, or eyes, severe headaches, fainting, nausea, diarrhea or intestinal cramps, blistering or sloughing of the skin, blindness, trembling, or other neurological disorders. *My God, what's left?* the mayor thought as she put down the bulletin and presented the city's disaster management plan. The plan, such as it was, was based on a list of public health advisories produced nearly a decade previously by William Garner, the same scientist at the center of the current safety operation. What had been scorned and laughed at by the public as a waste of state funds in 1991 and 1992 (the mayor herself had made a campaign issue out of it as an example of government paranoia and gullibility) now provided the only resource even hinting at how to treat the sick and injured. Unfortunately, the guidelines he had drafted then were intended to address a slow, almost undetectable contamination of the region's shellfish and the treatment of potential victims. Nothing could prepare them for the toxic cyclone now bearing down on them and the large-scale destruction it threatened to bring with it.

The Emergency Broadcast System would relay updated NOAA wind and tide information every ten minutes. All nonessential shipping traffic would be curtailed for the next twenty-four hours, with the state retaining the option to suspend all traffic until the threat had been fully contained. The dockyards and the downtown core were ordered evacuated within ten blocks of the waterfront, a precaution that was later revised to at least twenty blocks. Residents from Edmonds to Vashon Island were encouraged to stay indoors with windows and ventilation systems shut, to conserve water (retaining an ample supply for drinking and flushing exposed flesh), to cover or contain all foodstuffs, and to monitor the EBS for further updates.

As the mayor finished speaking, the questions came spilling forth from the press gallery. Most of these were tactfully deferred to her chief of police or the city's disaster management coordinator. For the remaining questions, the mayor managed to reclaim the confident public face that had served her well in the past two civic elections, but inside she felt as though she were crumbling. In truth, she didn't know what her city could expect from this pending disaster, and she had no idea if they would be properly prepared, even in the unlikely event they were given sufficient warning.

How does the current Pfiesteria *threat compare to, say, anthrax or dioxin?*

Is there any evidence of local industry contributing to the problem?

How will this affect the fish stocks in the strait?

Is there any truth to the claim that the aerosol affects children and the elderly most severely?

What contingencies are in place if the slick reaches the port of Seattle and becomes trapped there?

The questions numbed the mayor, turned her perfect smile to wood. She could feel a groundswell of panic rising on her city's streets, and she had absolutely no way to assuage their fears. There wasn't a mayor in the country who had dealt with anything like this, and she was terrified of becoming the first. She thought of the small convoy of ships now shown constantly on the local and national newscasts and prayed that the brave souls out there—Garner somewhere among them—knew what to do.

With nearly every eye in the Pacific Northwest fixed on their television sets, the competition for breaking coverage of the slick's progress was intense. Three networks dispatched news helicopters to cover the scene, while scores of reporters clad in still-pressed Army CBW suits and military-issue gas masks descended on Port Townsend. Aerial views of the *Kaiku* and the *Exeter* filled the broadcasts, interspersed with speculation about Bob Nolan's loss at sea and live shots from several points overlooking Juan de Fuca Strait and Admiralty Inlet. The Navy had set up an unofficial quarantine of the area, but with their attention now drawn to locating the *Zoea* and keeping the slick corralled on Garner's orders, strict barricades to the public were largely nonexistent.

In the *Kaiku*'s telecommunications studio, Garner watched the broadcasts with the sound turned off. Wholly uninterested in the reporters' speculative jabbering, he instead studied the footage for glimpses of the slick. As far as he could determine, the ATOC units were keeping the slick in a true line toward Port Gamble, and the hot deck was still drawing the colony forward along its artificial thermocline.

Sweeny slipped into the studio behind him. "This is unbelievable," he said to Garner. "You can't *buy* PR exposure like this. Screw the official quarantine. Let's let them get it all on tape."

The view from one helicopter in particular was much closer than the others. As they watched, the camera was brought in low over the water, south of the *Kaiku*. Garner could hear the thudding of its rotors approaching and stepped out onto the superstructure to watch. Zubov was already there, shielding his eyes against the sun. A Bell Jetranger with CHANNEL 4 NEWS stenciled on its side turned sideways to permit its camera operator a better view of the *Kaiku* out its open cabin door.

"Where the hell is Jakes during all of this?" Zubov said. "He's our official sheriff out here."

"He's coordinating the search for the *Zoea*," Garner said. "For now, it's probably best that we keep the attention of the cameras on us."

"How do we compete against *this*?" Zubov asked. "Show them some cleavage?"

A second news helicopter, this one a Channel 7 McDonnell Douglas 500 with its unmistakable teardrop-shaped fuselage, moved in to join the Jetranger, apparently encouraged by its competitor's unchecked progress below the four-hundred-foot limit. For the next few minutes, both news crews jockeyed for the best shots of the damaged winch and the *Cyprid* bobbing in the *Kaiku*'s wake.

Behind them, a bulky Sikorsky S-61N helicopter was dispatched between the *Albany* and the *Exeter*. A team of five SEALs was dropped from the rear cabin of the thick-bodied military helicopter directly above the last known position of the *Zoea*. Almost in unison, the two news helicopters left the *Kaiku* and moved to a vantage point directly over the spot where the Sikorsky was working.

"It's getting crowded up there," Garner said.

"They're too close," Zubov said.

"I know. Tell Jakes to give them a little more discouragement. *Now.* We don't need them flying into the aerosol."

"No, I mean they're too close *to each other*—" Zubov began.

Almost before the words were out of Zubov's mouth, the first of the news helicopters, the Jetranger, suddenly dipped and spun in the air. Either its pilot had succumbed to the aerosol or, like Nolan's helicopter, its engine had suffocated.

As the second news helicopter quickly pulled back, the Jetranger went into a flat spin, dropping nearly a hundred feet directly onto the main rotor of the Sikorsky. The two helicopters exploded in a fireball that threw shrapnel, rotor blades, and other wreckage across the surface of the slick. The largest chunk of wreckage fell into the water exactly where the Navy divers had been deposited, and a pool of flaming fuel spilled out across the top of the slick before being quickly extinguished in the waves.

The Channel 7 news helicopter reacted to the collision as if suspended on an elastic cord. One moment it was pulling away from the devastating collision; the next it was moving in for a closer look at the sudden spectacle. Wreckage from the collision continued to rain down over the area, including a single rotor blade severed from the Sikorsky. The broken rotor spun through the air, slicing cleanly into the cockpit of the remaining third helicopter. The crippled MD 500 hovered a moment longer before it, too, exploded and plummeted into the sea.

The radio was instantly alive with communication between the *Albany,* the *Columbus,* and the *Exeter,* as a rescue team was hastily assembled and sent out to look for survivors among the scattering of greasy, burning debris.

Aboard the *Kaiku* there was only stunned silence.

In the *Kaiku's* pressurized, clean air infirmary, Ellie listened to Carol's account of what had happened on board the *Zoea,* then gave her a complete medical examination, accompanied by a Navy doctor with a specialty in decompression sickness. It was already dark by the time the physicians cleared Carol to leave the *Kaiku's* infirmary, provided she went directly to her bunk.

Ellie filled a thermos with coffee, donned a fresh containment suit, and went looking for Garner, making her way away from the gathering of military, NOAA, and Nolan Group personnel in the war room and toward the point of the bow. She opened a small hatch and climbed down a ladder four decks to the *Kaiku*'s underwater observation pod.

Garner was there, looking out the large view ports at the slick. Hearing her approach, he looked up and gave Ellie a weak smile. "Sssh," he said. "I'm trying to hide."

"Carol said I might find you here," Ellie said. "Some people around here know you better than you'd like to admit."

"And the rest?"

"The rest of us just might be in love with you, if you weren't such a show-off." She wrapped her arms around Garner and gave him a kiss. Then another. "Besides, I missed you," she said.

She took a seat beside him and poured two cups of coffee. "Here, I figured you could use this." The positive air-pressure cell of the ship extended to the observation pod, so she could safely remove her helmet and gloves. Ellie unzipped her bodysuit, peeling it off to the waist. The conditioned air felt cool and soothing against the sleeveless T-shirt she wore underneath.

Garner accepted the hot drink and turned his attention back to the view ports. Over the past hour, the *Kaiku* had regained its position inside the slick and had lured the cells to within four miles of Port Gamble Bay. Foulweather Bluff now loomed large before them, presenting the possibility of deflecting the slick east, into Puget Sound, rather than south, into the north end of Hood Canal. Once inside Hood Canal, the nautical charts warned of a local magnetic disturbance that might deflect compass bearings as much as two degrees as they tried to wrangle the slick into the shallows of Port Gamble Bay. The same disturbance could, theoretically, also distract the colony from its attraction to the ATOC.

From the observation pod, Garner and Ellie had a nearly unobstructed view of the bottom and the ship's keel. The *Kaiku*'s underwater lights were cast across the rising bottom, revealing a series of low gravel bars and rock debris. Amidships, the ATOC transmitter could be seen dangling from the chains, still audibly emitting the last waveform Carol had been able to input from her computer. Off the stern, the hot deck was suspended in mid-water, turned at an awkward angle by the damaged winch but still attracting a high concentration of cells. Above them, the colony extended across the surface as far as they could see in every direction. As the shallow undulation of the ebb tide rolled along the surface, waves of bioluminescence radiated through the colony like miniature lightning.

"I remember my first visit to one of these observation pods," Garner said. "It was on the *Calypso,* Cousteau's ship. He had the captain chase a pod of dolphins across the open ocean at ten or fifteen knots, and we watched them porpoising in the ship's bow wave from this very spot. Until now, I couldn't imagine a more beautiful sight."

"That certainly would've impressed *me,*" Ellie admitted, wrapping her arms around him again. "This whole operation just keeps getting more and more impressive." As Garner held her, Ellie began to weep, partly out of fear and partly from this temporary sense of peace and security. She recalled the feelings that had overcome her on her last shift at the hospital and silently wished them away.

No more. Please, no more death. Just let me enjoy this moment a little bit longer.

"Tell me this is all there is," Ellie said, nodding toward the window. "Tell me that no one will see anything like this ever again."

He couldn't. Outside, the colony caressed and teased the glass, circulating between warmer and cooler water in its self-generated thermal cells, individual capsules ceaselessly changing from one delicate but deadly life stage to another. The ATOC pings had been unpleasant to the cells but did not kill them. Based on the latest camera shots and cohort analysis from Medusa, Garner knew they had cultured a population consisting almost entirely of adults. The hot deck had catalyzed the *Pfiesteria* cells' reproduction enough to hatch nearly all of the dormant cysts. To continue slow heating would only accelerate this process, and slow cooling would yield more cysts.

"When Charles Harmon created this species," Garner said, "he was only tinkering with a design that's been on earth for millennia. There's a passage in the book of Exodus—the plague of blood—where the Lord says, *'With the staff that is in my hand I will strike the water of the Nile and it will be changed into blood. The fish in the Nile will die and the river will stink; the Egyptians will not be able to drink its water.'* Who's to say that wasn't a firsthand account of a red tide? And *Pfiesteria* has probably inhabited the Gulf Stream for ages. It's only lately that it's made headlines, and even now it may be too late. Around the world, toxic plankton blooms have increased to the point where people have no choice but to take preventative action."

"You really know how to put a girl at ease," Ellie said.

"Job security," Garner said. "I was just thinking about your little spiel about saving the planet—a human-sustaining planet—and whether we were meant to be its landlords in the first place."

"After the stupidity I've seen in the past few days, I'm almost inclined to let microbes take it all back," Ellie said. "There's no sensible accounting for human nature."

"Harmon just accelerated the potential in nature when he built his biological weapon," Garner said. "One that's easy to breed, cheap to produce and reproduce, with the capacity to destroy the entire economy of a seafood-dependent nation. But he missed the mark."

"It sounds like you think this thing isn't lethal enough," Ellie said

"Oh, it's lethal enough—now," Garner said. "It kills faster and more effectively than any venom or chemical weapon I've ever seen. The beautiful growth on the other side of those windows has the ability to kill more people than a nuclear bomb, with the strategic advantage that it leaves all inorganic structures intact. It kills, then moves on. Can you imagine if someone could harness its power as a weapon? Create a famine. Put some in a fascist dictator's toothpaste. Spray the aerosol over a major city. Inject it into the air-conditioning system at a football game and kill sixty thousand people without spilling the nachos. A nearly perfect biological weapon. But that's only half its potential."

"What's the rest?" Ellie asked.

"I think Charles knew he would fail," Garner said. "These days, the recipes to make a biological weapon can be found in any public library. The materials can be bought mail-order by anyone on a university campus. So why would the military invest in toxic dinoflagellates? Charles would have known that the cell concentration needed to produce such a lethal neurotoxin was impossible to generate in the open ocean. I think he was just trying to make ends meet for himself and his family. He used the military's research funds for as long as his conscience could take it. I'm guessing he failed, happily, then used the money to support his own intellectual pursuits in peace."

"The cysts have probably been out here for decades," Ellie said. "Waiting for just the right combination of conditions."

"In any event, we know this *Pfiesteria* wasn't engineered to kill marine mammals. But it does prey on their warmth. The cells don't hear vocalizations, they hear *heat*. Their statocysts are sensitive enough to acoustically track temperature. Harmon started out engineering a cell that could produce a super-potent toxin and inadvertently developed the biological equivalent of ATOC."

"Do you mean these cells can act like tiny hydrophones?"

"Yes, but they're infinitely more sensitive to low frequencies," Garner said. "Medusa's cameras showed that. Believe me, if Lockwood knew what Serg and I saw in the data, he wouldn't be in such a rush to kill this thing. With a little more R and D, they'd have a listening and communication network that regenerates itself and is virtually impenetrable to attack. I think Charles knows that, too, and he wants to hide it from the wrong ears, so to speak. He wants us to make this nasty experiment go gently into the night once and for all."

"So what are we going to do?" Ellie said.

"The only thing we *can* do," Garner said. "Annihilate the colony before anyone else dies. Before someone else puts two and two together and tries to actually use the slick as 'applied technology.' "

"It's still the same question," Ellie said. "How do we kill it?"

Garner's silence unnerved Ellie. His eyes steeled, studying the colony only inches away. He refused to make any placating remark to set her at ease; his truthfulness was complete.

She loved that about him.

Ellie ran her fingers over Garner's face, drinking in his features. Along Garner's angular jaw, slowly coursing them around his semistraight nose, then finally over the small, whitish scar on his brow that looked something like a lazy-*S*.

"So where did you get this?" she said, indicating the scar. "I've been meaning to ask you."

"A souvenir from my Navy days," Garner said.

"An old war wound?" she said, half-seriously invoking her most tender bedside manner. "Battle scars from the high seas?"

"Shore leave," Garner said. "Ho Chi Minh City. A drunken Australian sailor clipped me with a broken beer bottle. He was going for my eye, but I ducked."

"Okay, who started it, Commander Garner?" Ellie asked sternly.

"Neither of us. Or both of us," Garner said. "As I recall, I stepped in to defend the virtue of a reluctant young woman, and the Aussie didn't agree."

"But you did it anyway and saved the damsel in distress, right?" she asked, moving closer, looking at Garner.

"I did," Garner said.

"Because it was the right thing to do, right?"

"It was."

"And did she ever thank you, this damsel?"

"She did," Garner said with a wry smile. "And as it turned out, she wasn't that virtuous after all."

"Oh, really," Ellie whispered, her mouth now very close to his. "And what would constitute a lack of virtue, after all?" She kissed him full on the mouth. "Something like that?"

Garner moved his body against hers and returned her kiss. "No, it was really more like this," he breathed, kissing her again. "And like this. And this." His demonstration continued.

"Ohh, that trollop," Ellie said.

"The worst kind," Garner agreed, now exploring the full extent of Ellie's exposed skin. "Can't believe I took a bottle for her." He pulled Ellie's T-shirt away, caressing her naked torso with his hungry lips. "Now, *you*, Dr. Bridges, would be worth at least a six-pack."

In the confines of the observation pod, Ellie stepped out of her suit and peeled Garner's off his broad shoulders. They found each other, exchanging their warmth, releasing the tension they both felt.

Moving against each other, consolidating their fears.

Sharing this one moment in time.

To completion.

They lay together in the quiet seclusion of the observation pod. Garner wrapped his arm around Ellie and drew her close, exhaustion closing his eyes even as he tried to rouse himself and return to the main deck.

Ellie pressed her body against his, feeling his warmth, languishing in the feeling of their closeness and how the confines of the pod no longer seemed confined at all. She reached up and lightly traced her fingernail over the scar on Garner's forehead, still finding it incredible how, after all the worldly and dramatic adventures this man had no doubt experienced, he had survived them all with just this one scratch—and that from the most absurd encounter of all. The muted crease of whitish tissue was no longer than half an inch. It looked no different from the scar tissue of moles, warts, and seborrheic keratoses she had removed with cryotherapy while she was working as an intern in Doc Melnyk's dermatology clinic. That was perhaps why the blemish had even caught her eye; she had seen hundreds just like it. After applying liquid nitrogen with a swab or a spray gun, the growths of dense tissue would just drop off, frozen off at the epidermis and eventually leaving nothing but a flat white scar—

Ellie gave a sudden start, jolted out of her reverie. Beside her, Garner sat up.

"I know, I know," he said. "It was nice while it lasted, but we still have to save the world."

Ellie could hardly contain herself. The words burst from her lips: "What about cryolysis?" she asked. "What if we fractured the cells with liquid nitrogen?"

You're starting to sound like Nolan, Garner began to say, then he was struck with the significance of Ellie's words.

"We can't boil the entire inlet," Ellie reasoned. "And even if we could, gradually, using the hot deck, it would only cause the cells to multiply. They *like* heat."

"The aerosol would expand, too," Garner said. "But if we were to freeze the cells with the liquid nitrogen . . ." His mind raced, putting the pieces in place. "Severe cooling followed by explosive heating. And I do mean explosive."

Garner took Ellie in his arms and kissed her again. "Dr. Bridges, I like the way your mind works," he said, getting dressed again.

"Job security," she replied, pulling her suit on and following him quickly back up the ladder.

When he reached the main lab, Garner nearly ran into Zubov coming in the opposite direction.

"Eight dead," Zubov said. "Two in the Sikorsky and three more in each of the news choppers."

"What about the SEALs?" Garner asked.

"It's a miracle, but none of them was injured," Zubov said. "The good news is, Jakes now has a fix on the *Zoea*. They should have the sub back on the surface within an hour."

"Excellent," Garner said. "If there's any chance—any chance at all—that the *Zoea* was filled with water from the slick when it went down behind the sill, we can't leave it at depth, where the *Pfiesteria* cysts can be redistributed by the bottom currents."

"What do you want them to do with it?" Zubov asked.

"Put it in tow behind the *Kaiku* for now," Garner said.

"This ship's starting to look like a friggin' charm bracelet," Zubov said, then noticed Garner's eyebrow rise in questioning amusement. "What? I know what a charm bracelet is. My kid sister wore 'em."

"Until we find something that works, we need to keep all the pieces of this thing together," Garner said.

Garner found Sweeny in the *Kaiku*'s war room, looking wistfully at the latest Polygon projection.

"Where did Nolan get all that permanganate?" Garner asked him.

"Olympic Scientific Supply in Bremerton," Sweeny said. "Why?"

"Contact them and see if we can get some liquid nitrogen," Garner said.

"How much is 'some'?" Sweeny asked.

Garner typed some estimates into the Polygon plotter. Liquid nitro-

gen had an extremely low heat capacity; that of seawater was comparatively high. Fortunately, they wouldn't need more than enough to cover
the slick with a thin veneer.

"In round numbers, ten thousand gallons should do it," he said.

Sweeny blanched. "We'll never get a barge loaded and up here in
time," he said.

"Probably not," Garner said. "And even if we could, we probably
couldn't maneuver it inside the inlet." He got on the radio to the *Albany*
and relayed his request to Jakes, adding to his wish list enough helicopter
support to ferry the liquid nitrogen directly to the deck of the *Kaiku*.

"You don't ask for much, do you, Garner?" Jakes grumbled.

"You offered to get me anything," Garner said.

"I did. But the cupboard is getting bare," Jakes said. "Anything else?"

"Yes," Garner said. "We'll need something to sink the *Kaiku*."

"Now *that* we've got," Jakes said.

In a tidy bungalow north of Bangor, Washington, the jangle of a telephone broke the post-midnight silence. Donald Porter groaned, rolled
over in bed, and lifted the receiver from its cradle. He mumbled hello
and listened to the voice on the other end of the line.

"It's for you," he said, nudging his wife and handing over the phone.
Midnight calls were not infrequent in their home—in fact, they were entirely too frequent—but on the first night of three scheduled for R&R,
the intrusion was particularly annoying.

Margaret Porter listened to the instructions provided by the caller,
frowned, and asked to have them repeated. In twelve years of marriage,
Donald Porter had never heard his wife ask for a repeat of instructions of
any kind, and this alone was enough to make him sit up, concerned. He
switched on the bedside light and waited intently for his wife to complete
the call.

"What is it, baby?" he asked as she handed the phone back to him.
"Who are you going to war against today?"

"You wouldn't believe me if I told you," she said.

"Try me."

She repeated as much of the conversation as she could and watched her husband's reaction. "Told you," she said, as she crawled out of bed and stepped into the shower.

Thirty minutes later, Captain Margaret Porter arrived at the main gate of the facilities housing the U.S. Navy Submarine Group (SUB-GRU) 9. Her familiar blue Suburban was saluted through the main gate and she parked in her assigned spot at the foot of the third pier inside the gate. A plank at the far end of the dock led her to the deck of SSN-638, one of about two dozen Sturgeon-class nuclear attack submarines in the U.S. Navy fleet. Over the past five years, Porter, the Navy's first female and African-American submarine commander, had come to know and admire every square inch of the 292-foot, 4,250-ton boat with its bulbous pressure hull and tall, jaunty tail fin set slightly forward.

Her company car.

Victor Bennett, Porter's executive officer for the past four years, met her at the foot of the conning tower, flashed her a salute, and handed her a hard copy of the same orders Porter had received over the phone. Bennett seemed no less assured by the orders than Porter's husband had been.

"Is this for real?" Bennett asked Porter as she took the orders from him, barely adjusting her stride as she passed.

"Seems simple enough to me," Porter said. "Sail out into the sound, torpedo and sink a stranded civilian vessel, and ignite a toxic slick of unknown origin."

Bennett shook his head. "And the reason for this?"

"Don't you watch the news?" Porter seemed surprised.

"Yes," Bennett said. "But why *us*? Surely the Army's got better weapons to deal with this," Bennett pressed. "Fuel bombs, napalm . . ." He began reciting a deadly arsenal of ordnance versus those housed in the SSN-638. "Hell, from this distance we could lob a couple Tomahawks at the target without leaving the dock."

"*Stealth,*" Porter said. "Perhaps they would like us to employ stealth as only an attack submarine can."

"Stealth," Bennett repeated.

"Ours is not to question why, but only to ask, 'Why *not?*' " Porter quipped. "Maybe whoever called this little get-together wants something a little lower profile than napalming domestic soil or the rockets' red glare," she suggested. "Something a little quieter and more precise." She flashed Bennett a wink. "Or maybe they just know how much I love to blow things up."

She started up the tower. "Come on," she said with a tired grin. "Let's go do the deed and get back in time for a stack of waffles at IHOP."

SSN-638 made way less than an hour later, cruising on the surface at a steady ten knots. Though nearly as long as a football field, the submarine boasted a draft of less than thirty feet. The bathymetry she would face offered little hazard to navigation, which could not be said for the larger Los Angeles–class submarines. The sea was calm as she made her way almost silently out the north end of Hood Canal, then northeast, past Point Hannon to the designated location at the south end of Admiralty Inlet.

Even without coordinates, the crew could have located their destination simply by following the underwater cacophony of ATOC transmissions being produced by the *Albany* and the *Columbus*. Amused at the blatant acoustical indiscretion, the submarine's sonar operators piped the sounds over the PA system for the entire crew to hear.

"Can you believe that?" Bennett asked Porter.

"And I thought country music was an awful racket. . . ." the captain mumbled.

Once they were within the prescribed range, Porter contacted the *Albany* and its temporary commander, John Jakes. Jakes quickly apprised her of the situation, then patched her through to Brock Garner on the *Kaiku,* her assigned target.

"Good morning, Commander Garner," Porter said. "This is Captain Margaret Porter of the SSN-638."

Over the radio, she could hear Garner chuckle. "I see somebody's still got a good sense of humor about all of this," he said.

"Did I miss something funny?" Porter said. In her groundbreaking—rather, ceiling-breaking—thirty-year career, she had weathered her share of chuckles.

"It's just been a very long night for us," Garner said. "So I find it kind of reassuring that they'd send us the 638."

Only later would Porter appreciate the irony of her vessel's selection for the task at hand. As Garner knew, pennant number SSN-638 was named the *Whale*.

29

"**W**hat's your status?" Jakes asked Garner from the *Albany*. Porter listened in from the *Whale,* as did Robertson and McRee on the *Exeter* and the captain of the *Columbus.*

Garner relayed the information as he understood it from the *Kaiku*'s captain and boatswain. "The A-frame is buggered and can't be used," he began. "The hot deck is still attached—it's working, but it's beginning to drain our power, and we'll need to shut it down completely within the next hour. Some of Betty's loose rigging is tangled over the rudder. That'll cost us some maneuverability, but we can't put a work crew down there while we're still in the slick."

"What about the *Cyprid*?" Jakes asked.

"We'll jettison it as soon as possible," Garner said. "One of your ships can temporarily adopt it. I'd like to wait as long as possible to pull up the ATOC transmitter. The same goes for Betty. There's still a chance we can use that equipment to target the colony once the hot deck goes offline."

"So our main workhorse is crippled, or at least badly gimped," Jakes confirmed. "What do you propose?"

"Once the nitrogen gets here, we'll put the canisters directly on the back of the *Kaiku*. Then we'll have to wire them for detonation to release as much of the liquid at once as possible."

"We'll never find dewar canisters we can fit with quick-release ports," Jakes said. Given the physical and thermal properties of liquid nitrogen, it was typically stored in specially designed dewar canisters having a thermos-like vacuum bottle and a tapered top that vented through a specially designed cap.

"We don't need them," Garner said. "Just something that will split the dewars open and that Serg and I can rig easily. Once that's set, I'd like to run the *Kaiku* straight into the bay and dump the nitrogen overboard. All at once, if possible—the quicker the better."

"You'll never get the *Kaiku* back out," Jakes said. "Not in that depth, with half a rudder and all that crap hanging off her platforms. Have you told Sweeny yet?" So far, only Jakes and Zubov had been apprised of Garner's plan to martyr the *Kaiku* for the sake of capturing the slick.

"What he doesn't know can't hurt us," Garner said. "I think if we run the *Kaiku* aground as far as possible into the inlet, the shoreline will provide a natural containment for the slick. The hot deck will continue to draw the colony in around the hull in the shallows while the water bombers keep the trees doused and contain the aerosol."

"I've already ordered an evacuation of the north end of the island, Port Gamble, Point Julia, Little Boston, Lofall, Kingston, and the reserve lands," Jakes said. "There were the expected complaints and some holdouts, but within the next hour we should have a two-mile buffer zone cleared for you."

"Once the slick is contained and concentrated around the *Kaiku*," Porter interjected, "that's when you'll dump the nitrogen tanks?"

"Right," Garner said. "The liquid nitrogen will bind the cells of the colony and freeze them solid. Once that's done, the *Whale* will be free to fire on the *Kaiku*. The explosion will hopefully ignite the colony, fracturing or incinerating the cells before they can form cysts."

"You've seen too many movies, Garner," Porter said. "You can torpedo the *Kaiku,* but she isn't a munitions ship. She's a converted minesweeper with one thick-assed hull."

"I take it you've never seen liquid nitrogen boil under evaporation," Garner said.

"That's thermal expansion," Porter corrected him, "not the incendiary force you'll need."

"What do you suggest?" Garner asked.

"More fuel," Porter said. "If you want enough of an explosion to ignite that inlet, we'll have to add some more fuel to the *Kaiku*."

"That deck is already pretty crowded," Robertson said from the *Exeter*. "If you plan to detonate the nitrogen tanks first, isn't there the chance of a fuel explosion at the same time?"

"Put the fuel in the aft hold," Jakes said. "That way there's less risk of an explosion when you run aground. Not much less, mind you, but at least you won't be leading with your chin."

"Good idea," Garner agreed. "We can put the extra fuel in the submersibles' hangar, then close the hold and set the nitrogen on the afterdeck."

"A floating bomb," Porter mused. "Who gets to fly this kamikaze mission?"

"We'll go with a skeleton crew," Garner said.

"So to speak," Zubov quipped.

"Serg and I will coordinate things on the deck, and we'll take a bridge crew of three—captain, mate, helmsman," Garner continued. "Once we're aground, the crew can be airlifted out and the water bombers can begin their run. Serg and I will be the last ones off, just before we blow the tanks."

"You've got guts, Garner, I'll give you that," Porter said.

"You've also got all of us depending on one hell of a big roll of the dice," Jakes said. "Don't fuck it up."

"Thanks for the vote of confidence," Garner said.

As he signed off, Garner caught Zubov's sidelong glance. *He's right—don't fuck it up.*

"Good plan, Brock," Zubov said aloud. "Simple, yet elegant."

"Absolutely not," Sweeny blurted, his upper lip trembling. "You guys are out of your freaking minds." His scalp was perspiring as he ran his fingers through his thin scrub of reddish hair.

Carol and Sweeny had joined Garner, Zubov, and the *Kaiku*'s designated bridge crew in the war room. Although Sweeny sputtered at the very notion of using the ship for target practice, Carol was surprisingly supportive. Garner suspected that her ordeal on the *Zoea* had been enough to change her perspective on the use of her husband's former belongings.

"Brock's right," Carol said. "Whatever is left of our 'whale' has all but ruined the deck hardware. The *Kaiku* is no good to us now—we can't use her properly and we can't move her without losing the use of key equipment like Betty and the hot deck."

"Do you have any idea what this vessel is *worth*?" Sweeny said.

"Compared to how many more human lives?" Carol said. "Bob gave his life following Brock's plan. I think we owe it to him to see this thing through to the end."

She's lying, Garner thought, studying Carol's expression. *She's playing the role of the erstwhile widow for Sweeny's sake, but inside she wants to sink everything Nolan stood for, starting with his flagship.*

Sweeny turned to the *Kaiku*'s crewmen. "What do you guys think?" he asked them.

"You're in charge," the captain said. "Give us the coordinates you want and we'll put her there—on a sandbar out there or back in her slip in Everett."

"Even if it puts you out of a job?" Sweeny challenged. The helmsman and the first mate looked at their shoes, not answering.

"Nolan's got plenty of other ships," the captain said. "I figure I could still find a home on one of those, especially since whatever I do in the next two hours, I'm just following orders."

"It's a write-off anyway," Garner said. "We'll get Jakes's men over here to rip up anything that isn't bolted down and stow it on the *Columbus* or the *Exeter*. Don't tell me the insurance won't pay for it. Hell, you might even turn a profit for your board of directors."

Sweeny said nothing, chewing at his lip and shifting his gaze from Garner to Carol to Zubov. "I hate this," he said. "I hate being pressured."

"Then make a goddamn decision!" Zubov exploded, taking a threatening step toward Sweeny. "We haven't got time for this bullshit."

"Okay," Sweeny said. "Do it. But I'm coming along to monitor your actions."

"We wouldn't dream of going without our chaperone," Garner said.

Zubov followed Sweeny out of the war room to begin identifying the equipment and other materials to be salvaged from the ship. The captain of the *Kaiku* radioed the *Exeter* and the *Albany* to coordinate the ships' position. Once the *Kaiku* had been loaded with the extra fuel and the nitrogen canisters, Garner, Zubov, Sweeny, and the bridge crew would take the *Kaiku* into shore, and the *Exeter* would deploy Medusa into the slick to verify that the cells were reacting as anticipated. When—if—the liquid nitrogen fixed the colony, the *Whale* would be cleared to fire on the *Kaiku*.

Garner followed the exchange of radio contact with manic attention, snapping corrections to one party or another as he adjusted the plan of attack. When everything appeared to be mobilizing in the right direction, he drew a deep breath, running his fingers through his hair. He turned to leave the war room and saw that only Carol remained, watching him quietly from a seat near the Polygon plotter.

"This projection is seriously flawed," she said, indicating the computer. "It doesn't calculate the effect of using Commander William Garner to avert the disaster."

"That's because it's designed to be very precise," Garner said. "I'm just making this up as we go along."

"Well, then, Walt Disney should have had your imagination," she said.

"Walt Disney is dead," Garner said. "The rest is just Mickey Mouse."

"Your father would be proud of you," she said. "Hell, *my* father would be proud of you."

"We're not out of the woods yet," Garner said. "Or into them, as the case may be. I want you to take a launch over to the *Columbus,* or at least the *Exeter.* Wait there until all this is over."

There was no bravado, real or sentimental, left in Carol. She studied Garner's face for a moment, silently conveying that message to him. She could not stay aboard the *Kaiku* any longer. "Good luck," she said.

"Yeah," Garner said with a weary smile. "I've been getting that a lot lately."

The first of an entire squadron of Bell UH-1 Huey helicopters carrying the liquid nitrogen appeared just before 3:00 A.M. Within the hour, the full complement of one hundred 100-gallon dewar canisters had been lowered to the *Kaiku*'s stern and carefully guided by Zubov into two equally weighted piles, one on either side of the keel. The weight of the canisters, in addition to the barrels of fuel loaded into the aft hold, pushed the *Kaiku*'s stern very low in the water. The hull groaned in protest, then gradually found its new equilibrium.

"Will the change in draft affect our beaching?" Garner asked the captain.

"Nah," he said. "Draft's only ten feet at the bow, and there's a pretty constant depth of four or five fathoms. We should be able to park it almost on top of that log boom at the foot of the inlet. That'll leave almost a quarter mile of shoreline around us with nothing but trees."

"What's our top speed?" Garner asked.

"As she is, maybe nine knots," the captain estimated.

"Your runway will be a mile and a half," Garner said. "Can you make it?"

"Yeah," the captain said. "We'll get her up to speed. It's gonna be one hell of a wreck."

"These things come with airbags, don't they?" Garner joked, then headed aft to join Zubov.

As each Huey deposited its load of dewar canisters on the *Kaiku,* it re-treated to the Nolan barge to collect the water buckets. The buckets were dragged in the strait, filling them with seawater to the helicopters' 3,800-pound payload limit, then ferried to the inlet. The helicopters rose high over the tree line and released their respective loads in series, laying down a massive wall of water to dilute and suppress the slick's aerosol. The Hueys were reliable workhorses in the military's arsenal but as water bombers were not as effective as the hulking Martin Mars "flying boats" employed by logging companies. Water bombers could drop up to 7,200 gallons of water in a single pass—twenty times more than the buckets Nolan had provided—but were far less maneuverable than the helicopters. Moreover, any Marses within range of Puget Sound were battling the late-summer forest fires in the Cascade Range mountains.

As the fifth deluge of water in fifteen minutes smashed into the water just off the *Kaiku*'s rail, Zubov looked up from where he was now wiring the canisters to detonate.

"Why do we always have to work in the rain?" he complained, seeing Garner. "I *hate* rain. I really do."

Garner watched Zubov crimping the wire contacts together, attaching each canister to a small explosive device Jakes had sent over from the *Albany.* Once again, the Navy had assumed that the *Exeter*'s crew could use their equipment with little or no instruction. "Are you sure you know what you're doing?" Garner asked. "No offense, but I've come across your wiring jobs before, and they could use some work."

"Piece of cake," Zubov said. "Just like a big ol' string of Christmas lights. Jakes said his four-year-old daughter could wire this thing."

As soon as Zubov finished rigging the canisters, Garner gave the all-clear for the *Kaiku* to proceed into shore. Above, the helicopters contin-ued to dump seawater on the north end of the bay while the ATOC transmitters on the *Albany* and the *Columbus* began pushing the slick with renewed intensity. From the *Exeter,* McRee confirmed that the indi-vidual cells of the colony were still recoiling from the LFA signal, mov-ing directly for the inlet.

The captain of the *Kaiku* had his ship to maximum speed in less than a mile. Meanwhile, the ship's helmsman wrestled the rudder and the array of equipment hanging off the ship to keep them on course.

"What do you want me to do?" Sweeny asked the ship's mate.

"Look at that thing and call out the numbers you see," the mate said, showing him the ship's depth sounder. "Use the intercom so they can hear you out back."

"Niner-five feet . . . niner-three . . ." Sweeny began, following the sounder's readout. "Like that?"

"You don't have to say *niner,*" the mate said. "This isn't *The Bridge on the River Kwai.*"

"Nine-one . . . nine-zero . . . eight-eight feet . . ." Sweeny said.

"Good," the mate said. "You can stop counting when it gets to zero."

On the afterdeck, Garner and Zubov found a secure position against the superstructure and held themselves in place with a coil of inch-thick line, a makeshift seat belt.

"Brock, we don't really *know* what's gonna happen to this thing when it hits bottom, do we?" Zubov said. The shoreline slipped past them, punctuated by the heavy sound of the *Kaiku*'s diesel engines straining at full throttle and the persistent metallic shuddering of the twin mountains of nitrogen canisters.

"No, we don't," Garner admitted. "The hull is packed as tight as we could get it, but beyond that, we're pretty much a highly flammable battering ram."

"I thought so," Zubov said.

"Six-two . . . five-five feet . . . five-two . . ." came Sweeny's anxious, reedy voice from the bridge.

The *Kaiku* surged through the bottleneck of shoreline forming the inlet to Port Gamble Bay, threading the eye of a needle barely three hundred yards wide and twenty feet deep.

"Zero-five-five miles to impact," the ship's mate added.

"But the odds of you guessing wrong are pretty small . . . right?" Zubov said.

"If I didn't know you better, I'd say you were getting nervous," Garner said.

"Nervous? Nah," Zubov said.

"Scared shitless?" Garner asked.

"Yeah, that's it," Zubov said. "I was just thinking about a saying my grandmother had about heaven and hell. She said if you ever get to choose between them, take heaven for the view and hell for the company."

"Forty feet . . . three-eight . . ." said Sweeny.

"So which would you take?" Garner said.

"Thirty . . ."

"Cutting engines. Brace for impact," the captain's voice came over the ship's intercom.

"Serg?"

The noise of the ship's engines fell away, and suddenly there was only the forceful splashing of the water around the hull.

"I say: fuck the view," Zubov said.

The night air was split by the sound of tearing metal as the hull crashed into the foundation of the island's bedrock. The *Kaiku* slammed into the rock reef exactly on her mark. The men could hear equipment, abandoned glassware, and pieces of bulkhead tear loose from their positions on the decks below and slam forward, sending reverberations through the entire ship. The *Kaiku* angled bow up, twisted on her exposed keel, then slid backward again, coming to rest with her stern angled sharply down into the inlet and her observation pod completely out of the water, pointing toward the tree line. As her momentum came to a jarring stop, the loose pieces down below crashed back toward the stern in a rain of debris that lasted for several seconds.

Then silence again.

Zubov let out his breath in a loud whoosh. "I lied. I'd go for the view."

"It isn't over yet," Garner said. "Here comes the hot deck. Brace yourself."

Seconds later the hot deck, which had been pulled along by the broken A-frame, slammed into the stern of the *Kaiku* like a gigantic, out-of-control surfboard. The front of the hot deck peeled back with the force of the impact, driving its leading edge up and out of the water. The hot deck seemed to hesitate on end for a moment, then rolled over and crashed into the water beside the ship.

Before the *Kaiku*'s wake had fully washed past them, the first of two Coast Guard Sikorsky helicopters arrived to collect the men from the ship. They listened as the *Exeter* confirmed Medusa's data that the slick had been drawn fully into the inlet.

"Let's get out of here," Garner confirmed. "Prepare to dump the tanks."

The detonator Jakes had issued them was radio-controlled, designed to activate the charges on the canister from a remote switch box. The bridge crew cut the power to the main engines and the hot deck, then Garner told them to climb aboard the Sikorsky. "You, too," he said to Sweeny.

"I'm afraid not," Sweeny said. "I don't leave this ship until you do."

"Oh for chrissakes," Zubov said. "What are we gonna do? Steal an ashtray?"

"Check the detonators for any loose connections," Garner said, and Zubov complied. Garner and Sweeny took one more quick trip through the entire hull, then rejoined Zubov on the stern. The second Coast Guard helicopter was brought into position, and it lowered a body harness to the ship. Zubov and Sweeny clipped themselves in and shared the next trip up on the winch; Garner followed them, last to leave the deck.

"All right!" Zubov shouted as Garner stepped into the helicopter's cabin. "Let's put this goddamn nuisance to sleep once and for all."

On Garner's command, Zubov held up the detonator for the canister charges. With a devilish, satisfied grin, he pressed the master button.

Nothing happened.

"*Shit!*" Zubov cursed, and punched the button several more times. He and Garner looked out the door of the helicopter. The canisters remained neatly stacked on the deck.

"Maybe we should call Jakes's four-year-old," Garner said, glaring at Zubov.

"We have to go back down," Sweeny said to the pilot.

"No time," Garner said. "We can't run the risk of a delayed explosion." He pulled on the wire coming off the Sikorsky's winch, still clipped to his safety harness. "Send me down," he said to the crewman.

"It's too dangerous," Zubov said. "Those canisters might blow at any second."

"Or they might not," Garner said. "And once the hot deck cools off, there'll be nothing to hold the slick in place." Garner moved out onto the step platform. The helicopter rocked with the shift in its weight, and Garner felt the pit of his stomach. "It's okay," he said to Zubov through a tight grin. "I really *love* this kind of stuff."

The helicopter's crewman started the winch, releasing Garner quickly downward to the *Kaiku*'s afterdeck. From nearly two hundred feet in the air, Zubov thought his friend looked impossibly small compared to the ship and the twin piles of canisters. Garner dangled on the end of the line like a graceless spider, spinning slowly as the wire unwound, suspending him tantalizingly close to his objective.

Twenty feet above the deck, the winch suddenly stopped. Panicked, Zubov whirled around to find the wire at the end of its spool.

"This is all you've got?" Zubov asked the crewman.

"It's been spliced," the crewman said. "No one said we'd need more wire."

"You *always* need more wire!" Zubov fumed. "Lower!" he called to the pilot, motioning his hand downward. "We need to get him lower."

The pilot complied, moving the Sikorsky down and slightly to the right. As a growing crosswind buffeted the helicopter, the compensation turned out to be much more than was required. For one heart-stopping moment, Zubov watched as Garner glanced off the *Kaiku*'s superstructure, then was swung precariously out over the slick itself. On the return swing, Garner lunged out with his hands and gripped the slanted edge of the ship's helicopter pad.

"Hold it steady," Zubov said to the pilot, his eyes fixed on Garner.

"I'm trying, sir," the pilot said. The helicopter rocked again, pulling back savagely on Garner's harness as he tried to hold on to the ship.

"Try a little harder," Zubov shouted. "You're going to rip him in two. Give him some more slack."

"Any more slack and we'll be putting this thing down on his head," the pilot said.

The pilot lowered the helicopter again, this time enough to drop Garner fully onto the deck. Garner skidded across the sloping surface toward the pile of canisters and began checking the connections for the detonator, twisting open several dewars as he did so.

"We're running out of time, sir," the crewman said to Zubov.

Come on, come on, Zubov pushed Garner with his will. As Garner progressed, a smoldering stream of liquid nitrogen began flowing out onto the deck. At minus 320 degrees Fahrenheit, the liquefied nitrogen gas was already boiling by the time it struck the deck plates and trickled toward the water.

Suddenly, a green light showed on the switch box Zubov held in his hand. Garner had found the short in the circuit and activated the detonator. Before Zubov could fully register this fact, he saw the first rank of dewars explode. The force of the detonation was enough to set off a partial chain reaction.

"Run!" Zubov screamed down at Garner, though he knew it was a futile effort. Even if Garner could hear him over the sound of the helicopter and the frothing nitrogen, there was nowhere for him to run.

On the deck below, Garner whirled around and raced away from the small mountain of canisters as it released a flood of the roiling clear liquid. As the first detonation ripped the pile apart, Garner had no choice but to fling himself overboard, his body tumbling into empty space and plunging toward the surface of the colony . . .

. . . then swinging up and away from the *Kaiku* as the wire attached to his harness snapped taut.

Zubov was about to give the order to pull Garner away from the ship when Garner motioned to be lowered again, back onto the deck. The pilot reluctantly complied.

"What the hell is he doing?" the crewman asked.

"He's trying to climb back into the ship's lab," Zubov said. As the thick fog of condensation below them cleared, he could see the reason why. "The detonation only blew half the canisters."

Garner scrambled back up the *Kaiku*'s slanted deck, climbing inside the door of the main lab. As the weight from the port-side nitrogen canisters was released into the water, the *Kaiku* rolled to starboard on its grounded keel. The hatchway came down on Garner's suspension wire, rocking the helicopter and making the gears of the winch scream in protest. On the opposite side of the cabin, Sweeny slammed into the open doorway and was thrown out into space. As Zubov and the crewman whirled around, Sweeny disappeared from view, his scream lost to the roar of the rotors as he fell from the helicopter. As they watched, Sweeny's flailing body hit the transom of the *Kaiku* and hung there for a moment before pitching over into the water.

"Dammit," the pilot cursed, trying to keep the craft under control. "What's going on back there?"

Garner reappeared a moment later, carrying something in his hand. Zubov recognized it as an improvised Molotov cocktail.

Garner waved up at the helicopter, asking to be lifted back up. The crewman moved to the winch and hit the switch to retract the wire. It reeled in through several rotations of its spool, then suddenly jammed. Though much of the slack had been taken up, Garner remained on the deck of the *Kaiku*.

"The winch is out," Zubov yelled. "Get us up and out of here now!"

As the helicopter lifted, Garner's harness slammed into his chest, pulling him up and backward, away from the ship. Zubov saw Garner reach out and throw the Molotov cocktail at the base of the remaining canisters. As Garner cleared the *Kaiku*'s superstructure, the handmade grenade exploded, rocking Garner on the end of the wire. Garner covered his head and turned himself away from the sudden tongue of flame that erupted around him and his flame-proof suit. As the helicopter pulled up, its occupants looked down with amazement on the spectacle below.

A second avalanche of liquid nitrogen was expelled as the starboard canisters poured out into the water, releasing a dense fog of boiling evaporate. As the searing cold of the nitrogen struck the surface of the colony, the *Pfiesteria* cells dispersed it through their mucoid network, drawing it by capillary action through the entire colony as they had done with the dye markers. Within seconds, the entire surface of the inlet was frozen over with a ghostly white sheet that extended from the shore around the *Kaiku,* past the hot deck, and along the length of the inlet. The coloration abruptly ceased at the seaward edge of the slick.

"It worked!" Zubov said. "Merry fucking Christmas!" he shouted at the crewman. Moving quickly, using the last of his strength, Zubov pulled in the last hundred feet of winch wire hand over hand, finally dragging Garner into the helicopter.

"I hate flying," Garner said and collapsed on the floor of the cabin, gasping.

In his prone position, Garner suddenly felt the helicopter twist and buckle in the same way it had when Nolan was piloting. Garner shook his head, trying to clear his vertigo. "The air below us is contracting," he began. "We're gonna—"

"*Stall!*" the pilot said as the helicopter began to spin. "Hold on back there."

"Climb out of it!" Garner shouted, his voice too hoarse and cracked to be heard above the tortured howl of the rotors. He closed his eyes and clenched his teeth as the helicopter spun them around, shuddered through a weak attempt to climb, then dropped back toward the inlet. Sliding free of the line, Garner spun across the floor of the helicopter toward the open door before catching himself on the winch footing.

The helicopter was still out of control. . . .

Falling . . . falling . . . then—

Leveling out.

The engine regained its regular pitch. Garner felt the return of normal gravity and opened his eyes.

"Like I was saying . . . about flying," he croaked.

From the opposite side of the cabin, Zubov grinned at him. "Son of a bitch, we did it!"

Garner looked around, puzzled. "Where's Sweeny?" Garner asked, then followed Zubov's indication over the side. Far below, frozen into the surface of the colony just behind the *Kaiku*'s hull, they could see the bloodied remains of Sweeny's containment suit.

"Knot tying," Garner said, regaining his breath. "That guy needed a good course in knot tying."

"Captain Porter on the line for you," the crewman said.

Garner took the headset the pilot handed him. "The stage is yours, Captain Porter. Let's see you light it up. . . ."

30

From the Coast Guard helicopter, the spectacle below was surreal.

The *Kaiku* remained in its upward-pointed direction, its starboard stern settled the lowest in the water, submerged nearly to the base of the A-frame. A greasy black slick of leaking fuel stained the pristine white surface of the inlet behind the ship, enveloping the remains of Sweeny's freeze-dried corpse.

"Someone should really get him out of there before the fireworks start," Zubov commented.

"Someone should've gotten Freeland, too," Garner said. His eyes were fixed intently on the inlet. *Come on, Porter. What are you waiting for?*

"Confirm targeting of the *Kaiku* and fire when ready, Captain," Jakes's voice came over the radio. Porter relayed the status of the *Whale*'s weapons systems.

"Target lock confirmed," Porter said.

"Conn, weapons," came a second voice, that of the *Whale*'s weapons officer. "Tubes one and two flooded. Torpedoes loaded and armed."

These conditions were relayed through the communication channel between the ships.

"Weapons, conn," Porter said. "Firing on my mark."

Come on, come on . . .

"Mark, fire one," Porter said.

"Fish is gone," the *Albany* confirmed. "The first torpedo is in the water. Bearing one-seven-seven."

"Fire two," Porter said.

"Second torpedo is in the water," the *Albany* confirmed. "Bearing one-seven-five."

From their vantage point above the eastern fringe of Port Gamble Bay, neither Garner nor Zubov could see the *Whale,* much less its torpedoes. As the radio fell silent, the wait seemed interminable. Garner knew the torpedo would be set to allow at least a thousand yards to arm itself. Accelerating to its top speed of 50 knots, it would take nearly another minute for the torpedo to reach the *Kaiku.*

"Closing," the *Whale* confirmed. "Seven hundred yards."

"Seven hundred," confirmed the *Albany.*

"There!" the helicopter's crewman said, pointing to the north.

The first torpedo struck the edge of the colony and burst through it, shearing a channel for itself in the frozen mass. From the helicopter, the torpedo's progress could be seen clearly, then behind it, the second. Shards of the crystallized water were broken from below and thrown into the air as the twin furrows streaked through the solidified colony.

"Here we go. . . ." Zubov said.

Seconds later, the first torpedo struck the *Kaiku,* ramming the vessel directly astern. The torpedo ripped into the metal plating and exploded, instantly igniting the cache of fuel inside the hull.

The explosion lit up the entire inlet. A massive fireball erupted from the rear of the *Kaiku.* Then the second torpedo hit its mark, slamming into the sandbar itself, the explosion lifting the *Kaiku* slightly up, then rolling it over into the frozen colony. The rest of the fuel ignited with a loud *whump,* sending a river of flames slipping across the top of the colony. The air itself crackled angrily as the ammonia of the aerosol was burned away. A third and final explosion ripped the *Kaiku* completely apart, peeling back the sides of the hull and throwing pieces of the superstructure into the predawn sky.

The explosions rippled through the frozen mass, enveloping, then obliterating the suspended growth of cells. For a moment it seemed as though the entire surface of the inlet lifted with the force of the firestorm, then shattered into microscopic crystals as though made of glass. Flames shot upward from the inlet as a single, enormous fireball raced through the remaining aerosol cloud, devouring ammonia and metabolic toxins. Over nearly two square miles, the air crackled and snapped with the aerosol's incineration, the ignition erupting from the sea's surface like reverse lightning.

In less than thirty seconds, the firestorm had passed, consuming its fuel and extinguishing itself. As hoped and provided for, not a single water-drenched tree was ignited on the shore.

Garner was immediately on the radio to the *Exeter*. "How does the data look?" he said.

After a pause, Carol answered him. "It looks great, Brock," she said. "There's a hell of a mess down there, but I'm not picking up *any* residual flow."

Garner told her they would return to the *Exeter* immediately to confirm the data, then the cleanup of the inlet could begin. He signed off and slumped back against the wall of the cabin.

"Relax," Zubov said with a chuckle. "We win."

"Yeah," Garner said, allowing himself a smile. "We win. Bugs lose."

"Man, you should see your face." Zubov grinned. Behind the Plexiglas face shield of his containment suit, rivers of sweat coursed down Garner's face, and bruising had begun to color his cheeks and forehead, souvenirs from his return trip to the *Kaiku*. "You look like you've been through a war."

"We all have. Let's get out of here," Garner told the pilot, banging on the cabin wall to show his urgency.

"Where to?" the pilot asked.

"Just *down,*" Garner said. "The ground, somewhere. Anywhere will do."

————

True to her assurances, Margaret Porter withdrew the *Whale* from the area and returned to Bangor in time for breakfast. As dawn broke, Garner dispatched a small army of technicians to the inlet to confirm the destruction of the slick. One by one, the reconnaissance teams returned word that there was no trace of the *Pfiesteria* cells. The reports from Medusa showed none of the dinoflagellate's life stages in the plankton, and several core samples of the inlet's sediment revealed no cysts of any kind.

"Victory?" Zubov asked, as he stood with Garner on one of the Navy's launches.

Garner set down his field kit and unzipped the hood of his containment suit. Around him, several of the technicians he had recruited stopped what they were doing and watched him.

Garner slipped off the hood and breathed deeply, drinking the fresh air.

It tasted good.

He smiled.

One by one, the cleanup team members around him peeled off their biohazard suits, letting the bracing air revitalize them. A few of them even let out a whoop and tossed their hoods or gloves into the air like mortarboards on the grandest of all graduation days. Then, looking toward Garner and his fantastic grin, they began to applaud. The applause grew slowly at first, then built to a strong encore that rippled across the entire surface of the inlet.

"Victory," Garner confirmed with a wink to Zubov. "And it isn't even raining."

Further searching through the rest of that day revealed no sign of the slick, beyond scorched fragments of the fractured *Pfiesteria* cells. As the shore, sediment, and water column of the inlet were examined using Medusa, Betty, and a score of more traditional samplers, these areas were marked off on a large grid kept on a chart on the bridge of the *Columbus*.

Although the full environmental cleanup of the bay would take several more weeks, the Navy and USAMRIID removed the disaster area designation within hours. It was now well into the first day of September and, befitting the Labor Day holiday, Jakes radioed the remaining vessels and granted their crews the rest of a well-earned day off as soon as their field reports were issued and cleared. Nowhere was this dry-witted news better received than on the *Exeter*, where the remaining crew had by now exhausted nearly all of their scheduled leave.

Zubov collected the last of his personal gear and prepared to return to the *Exeter*. As he waited on the landing platform of the *Columbus* for the Navy launch to arrive, he was joined by Garner, Carol, and Ellie. Carol threw her arms around the big man and kissed him on the cheek. "Thank you, Sergei," she said. "The rumors were true: you're the best there is."

Zubov started to shrug off the compliment, then reconsidered. "Yes," he said with a smile. "I *am* the best there is."

"Thanks for the overtime," Garner added, shaking Zubov's hand. "Now go home and get some sleep."

"None of us will be able to sleep until you get that problem child of yours off our deck once and for all." Zubov laughed, clapping a hand onto Garner's shoulder.

"I'll send FedEx for it in the morning," Garner promised.

"Good. That way McRee and I can still use it as a piñata at tonight's docking party."

"Just remember to save me all the pieces. I have a dissertation to finish with her." Garner gingerly touched the bruises on his face. "Maybe not today, but eventually."

As Zubov stepped down into the launch, Garner shouted after him. "Hey!"

"What?"

"I'd take the view, too."

"You're full of shit," Zubov shouted back, then was gone as the launch rounded the end of the *Columbus*, headed toward the *Exeter*.

Jakes returned from the bridge and joined them on the landing platform. "I just got off the phone with Admiral Lockwood," he said. "And I still have all of my ass."

"I take it he's pleased?" Garner asked.

"I'm still employed," Jakes grumbled. "Which is more than I expected. As for you, I think Lockwood's going to replace his wife's picture on his desk with yours. He also wants me to talk you into returning to naval intelligence. I'm sure we could find a permanent posting to your liking."

"Thanks, but no thanks, John," Garner said. "I'm more of a freelancer these days."

"Then how about some contract work?"

"If the past two days is your idea of 'contract work,' I think my asking price just went up."

"Name it," Jakes pressed. "Anything you want."

"Coffee," Garner said. "A good cup of coffee. Do you think there's anyplace in Seattle to get one?"

"One or two, I'd say." Jakes chuckled.

"And my boat," Garner added. "I haven't seen the *Albatross* since the storm hit."

"Already taken care of." Jakes nodded toward the west.

Sailing in parallel, the *Albatross* and the *Pinniped* passed Point Hannon, each piloted by one of Jakes's men.

"You do good work." Garner nodded.

"So do you," Jakes replied, taking a card out of his vest and handing it to Garner. "Here's my number. Let me know if I can buy you that coffee." As the launch returned from the *Exeter,* Jakes said his good-byes and retreated to the *Albany.*

Moments later, the *Albatross* and the *Pinniped* were brought alongside the *Columbus.* Garner, Ellie, and Carol helped to moor the vessels together and began loading whatever remained of their personal belongings into the two sailboats.

"I think these hulls survived the storm better than any of the others," Garner observed.

"Or us," Ellie agreed.

"I guess bigger isn't always better," Carol said, giving Garner a sly smile. "With boats, at least."

"You sound just like my ex-wife," Garner teased.

"And you bear a remarkable resemblance to my first husband," she said, embracing him. She held her face to his chest for a long moment, her eyes closed. "Thank you," she said. "Thank you for coming. Thank you for everything."

"Anytime. Just call."

Carol wiped her eyes and smiled. "Well, it's time for me to get going, I guess." She had loaded her gear into the *Pinniped,* while Ellie and Garner put theirs in the *Albatross.*

"Where are you headed?" Ellie asked.

"I don't know." Carol shrugged. "Many places, I hope. The first stop will be Helby Island. Daddy and I have some catching up to do. I'm going to get the whole story of his involvement in this, even if it takes the rest of my patience and all of his whiskey to do it. Then I can deal with the paperwork from all this."

"Sounds like a good idea to me," Garner said. "Let me know the story from wherever you land."

They embraced again and said their good-byes. Garner helped untie the *Pinniped* and tossed the lines to Carol. She donned her sunglasses, gave them a hopeful wave, then turned toward open water.

Garner and Ellie stood alone on the landing platform next to the *Albatross.* Above them, a pair of seagulls playfully circled the mast of the *Columbus,* then swooped low over the water, looking for food.

"Ghosts," Garner mused, watching the birds for a long moment. "Mariners used to believe seagulls carried the ghosts of dead seamen. An escort of such birds could be considered an omen of things to come."

"Good or bad?" Ellie asked.

"I suppose that depended on what eventually came," Garner said. Even as he spoke the words, the prospect of an uncertain future seemed less daunting to him than it had, even a few weeks ago. Randomness, it seemed, could hold great promise.

The birds, already a half mile away, glided up into the western sky, where the sun had begun to set behind thick clouds. The fading light, assisted by the lingering haze from that morning's firestorm in Port Gamble Bay, slowly turned the sky a breathtaking shade of scarlet.

"Red sky at morning, sailors take warning," Garner murmured, a distant memory of the Junkman pulling him momentarily into the past.

"Red sky at night, sailors' delight," Ellie responded, kissing Garner. She slid her arms around his waist, gently pulling him toward the future.

"It looks like we're the last to leave the party," Garner said, returning to the moment with a wry smile. "Can I give you a ride somewhere? Back to your hospital, Dr. Bridges?"

Ellie pondered the question, tilting her head in a way that suggested they both already knew the answer. "No, I don't think so, Commander Garner," she said. "In fact, I think the hospital will be getting my two-week notice of resignation, back-dated to two weeks ago."

"So where does that leave you?" Garner asked.

"Rootless and restless," she said. "With a strong desire to see the San Juan Islands," she said. "I hear the natives there are rather friendly. Driven, but friendly."

"Really?" Garner mused. "Then maybe you'd better see if those rumors are true."

Garner wrapped his arms around her and drew her close. When their lips finally parted, Ellie smiled and let her breath out slowly. "Wow. What's the projection on *that,* Commander Garner?"

"Two exposed, zero fatalities."

"Chance of affliction one hundred percent," she added. "At least it's safe for human consumption."

Pressing his lips to hers, Garner consumed her again.

As the day faded into twilight, they untied the *Albatross* and headed north, following the gulls toward home.

EPILOGUE

The black oystercatcher, *Haematopus bachmani,* was commonplace among the rocky promontories guarding the coastlines of Pacific Rim National Park. Smaller and easily distinguished in appearance from a crow or raven, the bird's black feathers possessed a duller, matted sheen. Its beak was thin but sturdy, effectively designed and subtly arrogant with its orange coloration. Befitting their name, oystercatchers fed predominantly on the shellfish and sparse vegetation in the highest portions of the intertidal zone. The birds were typically found in flocks of several dozen, their collective group of eyes more effective at finding potential feeding grounds in the ephemeral and rugged terrain they frequented. By the end of summer of this year, however, their population had decreased markedly, without apparent cause. Though few people who visited the area would notice, it was increasingly common to see an individual or small, struggling squadrons making their way around Barkley Sound, their flight path low to the water and close to the shore to increase the possibility of locating food.

A single female oystercatcher glided down from the slate-gray September sky and settled on a rocky bench, just out of reach of the waves crashing against the shore below. Fully grown, she had a wingspan of only sixteen inches and weighed a pitiful 300 grams. She was undernourished and extremely thin for this late in the year. Her feeding grounds had been increasingly devoid of interesting food for several weeks, despite even the reduced competition from other birds.

It was late in the season. Though the water remained unseasonably warm, the air had cooled considerably. She could feel the coming change of seasons in her thin, hollow skeleton, feel it in the way the small digestive stones in her gizzard ground against one another, awaiting sustenance.

She waded tentatively into a shallow splashpool high on the shore, clipped off a few strands of tubular seaweed with her beak, then drank from the water, siphoning a few dozen microscopic crustaceans into her stomach. The exoskeletons of the tiny *Tigriopus* copepods were rich in fatty acids, which would give her energy and help to insulate her against the cold. The water in the pool tasted stagnant and burned in her throat, but the festive reddish coloration of the minuscule crustaceans added to the aesthetics of her meager dinner.

Clearly, the early birds had long since claimed their timely rewards, but it seemed too soon in the fall for there to be so little food. The weather was cooler, but certainly not lethal. Yet, as she browsed a little farther, there was disappointingly little life in these pools. The vegetation was sparse, and the coastal plankton had been depleted. Whatever shellfish remained here tasted bitter and rotted; she had noted the same elsewhere along this particular section of coastline. Perhaps it was time to move on, to follow the rest of her reduced flock in search of warmer climes and more plentiful food. Without either, she certainly could not stay in the area.

A mink scampered down to the rocks from its perch in the nearby forest, its moist brown eyes fixed on her. She raised her head, watching it with caution and poised to take flight. She expected the mink to be especially emboldened by the continual opportunities to pillage tourists' campsites during the recent summer. Ordinarily, the sleek animal wouldn't hesitate to make a lunge for her—this one looked hungry, too—but instead, it kept a mindful distance. Perhaps it had grown too lazy to chase its food. As she watched, the mink circled around her, sniffing at the air. After a moment it returned to the protection of the forest, clearly distraught. It seemed to dislike something in the water.

The beaches no longer smelled as strongly of the visitors who came to the park over the summer months, but neither had the land returned to its natural maritime fragrance. This year the air had instead grown noticeably foul. It lingered unpleasantly in the bird's nostrils, especially since she had settled in the pool.

Although the bird would have no way of knowing it, the outcrop on which she was foraging was adjacent to the isolated mud bank where David Fulton's daughters, Caitlin and Lindsay, had filled their bucket with clams not quite a month previously. (Though only Caitlin had been immodest enough to wade knee-deep into the thick, squishy sediment.) Despite its proximity to several popular campgrounds and exposure to the open ocean, the shoreline here was relatively isolated and free from disturbance. Life could continue here of its own accord, inevitably finding a way to subsist, to adapt, to survive.

A shore crab, no larger than a quarter, scurried past her feet in the shallow water. She made a half hearted stab at the intruder, which was hardly worth the effort. Nearly half its carapace had been eaten away, leaving its tissues exposed within a peculiar, crescent-shaped wound. Slightly indignant but nonetheless ravenous, the bird continued dipping her beak into the water, searching for anything of potentially nutritive value.

Though she could not yet detect it, the pool in which she was foraging contained a dense seed bed of dinoflagellate cysts.

The species was *"Pfiesteria junckersii"* to some, "Batch 9" to others.

The microscopic cells floated passively into the warren of her plumage and the webbing of her feet, unfettered by the meager assortment of mites, tenacious parasites, and dried zooplankton carried there. Kept away from the warmth of the bird's body temperature and the tantalizing aroma of her blood, the *Pfiesteria* cells were dormant and might remain that way indefinitely. Clinging to their convenient avian carrier, kept dry and unstimulated in the air, the cells would be transported along with the bird wherever she traveled. Rehydrated in a warm body of water with the promise of adequate nutrients, they would begin their vegetative reproductive cycle once again.

If their unsuspecting host chose to remain nearby, or succumbed too quickly to their infestation, the colony could easily find any number of replacements. The nondescript shoreline was situated on the migratory route of at least two dozen avian species, a corridor that extended from the Aleutian Islands to the Baja peninsula.

As long as the cells remained dormant, the bird could remain indifferent to her infection. But in time, as the mildly acidic membrane of the cysts began to irritate her, she would try to preen them from her plumage. Once ingested, the conditions in her digestive tract would be ideal for the genesis of a new colony. The cysts taken into her belly would smell her blood and sense its warmth. Within hours, they would be roused from their semi-hibernation and begin to feed. Within days, the bird would be dead, with half its flesh eaten away and the remainder hemorrhaged beyond recognition.

Given the time of year, she would soon begin her winter migration in earnest. She would leave behind this comparatively isolated sanctuary and fly south.

Over Seattle.

Then over Portland.

Then over the entire coast of California.

She could be hundreds of miles away from this place by the time the *Pfiesteria* cells claimed her. As the colony lay waiting, their accommodating host would explore countless coastal waterways. She would bathe often in the warm water of shoreline pools, forage wherever food could be found, and rest whenever the need arose, wholly indifferent to her proximity to human settlements.

She would live on the resources available to her, surviving on the graces of luck, the lessons of experience, and the benefit of acquired skill.

Subsisting in moderation in the way that nature typically does.

Surviving only until the predator she carried awakened once again.

GLOSSARY

ABIOTIC STASIS: A fictional "hole in the ocean"; literally, a permanent or semi-permanent condition of zero organic content or activity. Real-world homologies to this condition are sometimes called DEAD ZONES.

AEROSOL: Particulate matter dispersed into the atmosphere. Natural aerosols may include sea salt, sediment particles, or fog.

A-FRAME: The main boom on the afterdeck of a research vessel, via which sampling equipment and instrumentation is moved over the stern.

ALBANY: With the *Columbus,* one of two Whidbey Island Class Navy LSDs that provide military support to the containment operation.

ALBATROSS: Brock Garner's live-aboard sailboat and a "twin" of the *Pinniped.* The single-masted, fiberglass-hulled boat is 35 feet in length.

ALGAE: Single-celled or colonial aquatic phyta possessing chloroplasts for converting light energy into chemical energy (PHOTOSYNTHE-SIS). Though often considered primitive "plants," they lack vascular tissue, leaves, and a proper root system.

ALGAL BLOOM: Rapid or excessively dense growth of algae, usually due to high ambient levels of nutrients.

AMBERGRIS: Thick, waxy protective secretion found in the digestive tract of whales. Toothed whales, such as the sperm whale, have an abundance of ambergris, which is thought to protect the lining of the gut from hard or sharp prey items.

AMPLIFICATION (BIOAMPLIFICATION): The exponential growth or reproduction of a biological or chemical agent, either within a host (such as a virus) or throughout an ecosystem (such as a pollutant).

ANHYDROBIOSIS: Life or suspended life in the absence of water. Organisms exposed to periodic drought or desiccation benefit from the ability to survive brief periods in such a state of animation. Usually restricted to simple, microscopic organisms with a small body volume.

ATOC: Acoustic Thermography of Ocean Climate. Method and research program to investigate fine-scale ocean temperature and transoceanic communication using LFA (low frequency active) transmitters.

BETTY: Brock Garner's fictional prototype for the Medusa sampler.

CBDCOM: Chemical and Biological Defense Command, the U.S. Army's primary research and development center for chemical and biological defense technology, engineering, and service, headquartered at the Aberdeen Proving Grounds, Maryland.

CBW: Chemical and Biological Warfare.

CDC: Centers for Disease Control and Prevention. The civilian counterpart to USAMRIID, headquartered in Atlanta, Georgia.

CFB: Canadian Forces Base.

CILIATE: Taxonomic class of Protozoa characterized by having threadlike projections (CILIA) for propulsion during at least part of their life cycle, as well as a double nucleus in the cell.

COLONY: General designation for the accretion of *Pfiesteria junckersii* ("Batch 9") cells, both above and below the surface. The mucoid secretion of the colony that allows intercellular communication is fiction.

(Such secretions are not typical of this dinoflagellate, nor of most plankton species.)

COLUMBUS: With the *Albany,* one of two Whidbey Island Class Navy LSDs that provide military support to the containment operation.

CTD: Abbreviation for Conductivity, Temperature, and Depth. Used to describe the sampling method or device that records these parameters.

CYPRID: With the *Zoea,* one of two submersibles aboard the *Kaiku.* Named after the juvenile life stage of a barnacle (the juvenile itself is known as a CYPRIS).

CYST: The dormant or over-wintering life stage of a dinoflagellate. Also, any fluid-filled sac.

DEAD ZONE: A region of the ocean devoid of life. Although dead zones may be extremely large, they are usually ephemeral. Many dead zones result from depleted oxygen in the water due to over-nutrification and an abundance of microbial respiration.

DINOFLAGELLATE: One of more than 2,000 described species of micro-organism having a shell made of cellulose and two whip-like flagella for propulsion and steering. These flagella allow some dinoflagellates to swim up to 1 m/hr in their motile, planktonic life stage. Cell diameter is typically up to 0.2 mm (0.008 inches) at maturity. Dinoflagellates also have a dormant cyst stage, which sinks out of the plankton into the sediment. As members of the Kingdom Protista, many species possess the characteristics of both plants and animals, feeding either via photosynthesis or by consuming other organisms. Most produce some kind of toxin as metabolic waste or as a chemical defense. Dinoflagellate populations may double in size every 24 hours by asexual or asexual reproduction. They prefer warm, stable conditions, and may encyst if exposed to turbulence or temperature extremes.

DoD: Abbreviation for the United States Department of Defense.

DOWNWELLING: Downward movement of a water mass due to an increase in its density or a "piling up" of water on top of it.

DRAFT: The depth of water required to float a vessel; the maximum depth of the hull below the waterline.

DROPSONDE: An instrument for measuring atmospheric conditions with altitude, including wind conditions, moisture, and temperature. DROPSONDES are deployed from aircraft; RAWINSODES are carried to the upper atmosphere by balloons.

EL NIÑO: A measurable change in the circulation of the ocean's surface waters, literally named "The Christ Child" by the Spanish in recognition of its appearance near Christmas. Produced by a periodic west-to-east flow of warm Pacific Ocean surface waters following a disruption or reversal in the trade winds, especially strong El Niños can raise the mean sea surface temperature by as much as 12° C (22° F). Evidence of the phenomenon has been noted since at least the late 1800s and is seen to recur at irregular intervals of three to seven years. A single event may last only eighteen months, but the global pre- and postcursor events may extend this interval to as long as three years.

EXETER: Fictional United States research vessel assigned to the JGOFS program and other oceanographic duties.

GPS: Global Positioning System. Navigation aid that uses a network of satellites to determine a vessel's location with extreme precision.

HEPA: High-Efficiency Particle Absorbing. Descriptive of the filters used in biocontainment facilities and some biohazard suits.

HOT DECK: A fictional device used to heat large pockets of water or the metal hull plating of vessels trapped in polar ice.

JGOFS: Joint Global Ocean Flux Study. International research program to study the cycling of organic and inorganic constituents in the sea.

KAIKU: A fictional converted Hunt Class minesweeper/minehunter. The Nolan Group's research flagship.

LFA: Low Frequency Active. Descriptive of the transmitters used for ATOC.

LSD: NATO STANAG abbreviation for landing ship, dock. A multi-purpose vehicle, equipment, and troop carrier with a length of approximately 600 feet and a displacement of 15,000 tons.

MEDUSA: The semi-fictitious plankton sampler designed by Brock Garner. While Medusa samples all the typical scientific aspects of plankton populations, measuring their various parameters is currently assigned to an array of instruments.

METAZOAN: A multi-celled organism.

MICROBE: A microscopic organism.

MOTILE CELL: Descriptive of a cell able to move by locomotion using flagella or cilia.

NOAA: National Oceanic and Atmospheric Administration. Government agency responsible for the study of the ocean, the atmosphere, and global interaction between the two. Headquartered in Washington, D.C.

NSF: National Science Foundation. Government agency responsible for funding scientific research and education, principally at colleges and universities. Headquartered in Arlington, Virginia.

ORGANELLE: A functional constituent of a cell.

PAPA: Cartographic designation for JGOFS sampling station P24, located at 50° 0′ North Latitude; 145° 0′ West Longitude.

PATHOGEN: A disease-causing agent, such as a parasite.

PFIESTERIA: Taxonomic genus of dinoflagellate first described in the early 1990s and found in the Gulf Stream waters of the Atlantic Ocean. *Pfiesteria* prefers warm, brackish conditions and has been linked to seasonal fish kills in nutrient-laden estuaries of the U.S. mid-Atlantic states. It consumes other algae, sometimes using their chloroplasts for photosynthesis. The organism has been described as having up to 24 distinct life stages and produces at least two toxins that act offensively rather than as a passive deterrent. One, a water-soluble neurotoxin, is used to stun prey, while a second, fat-soluble toxin ulcerates and destroys tissue. *Pfies-*

teria piscicida (= piscimortua) is a real species; *Pfiesteria pacifica* and *Pfiesteria junckersii* (a.k.a. "Batch 9") are fictional.

PHYTOPLANKTON: Plant plankton.

PINNIPED: Mark Junckers's sailboat, a twin to the *Albatross*. Named for a subgroup of marine mammals including seals and sea lions.

PLANKTON: Classically, *plankton* referred collectively to all living or nonliving material found passively floating in the water. Today, *plankton* generally includes only living material floating in the water. Diatoms, dinoflagellates, copepods, and jellyfish are major constituents of plankton. By definition, plankton is moved by wind and wave action; organisms large enough to actively resist such transport (e.g., fish, whales) are called NEKTON, while nonliving organic material is today called TRIPTON (= DETRITUS). Plankton can be further categorized by cell size, taxa composition, and location in the water column.

POLYGON: Semi-fictitious military computer software for calculating and forecasting/predicting the fallout of chemical and biological weapons.

RACAL: Brand of containment "space suit" consisting of a full bodysuit and a pressurized helmet. HEPA-filtered air is blown into the helmet from a portable, battery-powered forced-air respirator or "blower."

SATO MARU: Fictitious Japanese ship of opportunity where the slick was incubated. A general-purpose freighter 900 feet in length with a displacement of 30,000 tons.

SLICK: The *Pfiesteria* colony as it is spread across the surface of the water. *Pfiesteria* is able to photosynthesize its own food; therefore, it will attempt to spread itself as flat as possible against the ocean's surface to maximize the number of cells exposed to the sun.

SOSUS: Sound Surveillance System. An array of NATO-sanctioned passive listening devices developed to track Soviet submarines.

SSN: NATO STANAG designation for submarine, attack, nuclear.

TYVEK: Dust- and water-resistant material used in some biohazard suits. Tyvek is a product of the DuPont Company.

UPWELLING: Upward movement of a body of water, usually due to a divergence of the water above it.

USAMRIID: United States Army Medical Research Institute for Infectious Diseases. USAMRIID is the military counterpart of the CDC, headquartered at Fort Detrick in Frederick, Maryland.

VIRUS: Submicroscopic agents consisting of a nucleic acid (DNA or RNA) wrapped in a protein coat. Viruses typically turn the host cell into a manufacturer of other virus particles, increasing in number until disease is manifested. Viruses themselves are typically unstable under intense heat or UV light and usually require a host in order to reproduce.

WHALE: The United States nuclear attack submarine SSN-638.

ZALOPHUS: Taxonomic genus of sea lions including the California sea lion.

ZODIAC: Inflatable boat of various sizes, consisting of a pair of pontoons joined at the bow and a flat bottom. Also, the manufacturer of such vessels.

ZOEA: With the *Cyprid,* one of two submersibles aboard the *Kaiku.* Named for the larval stage of a crab.

About the Author

As a biologist, oceanographer, and adviser to several environmental agencies, James Powlik, Ph.D., has walked many of the same footpaths as Brock Garner, in Barkley Sound, the San Juan Islands, and elsewhere.

Dr. Powlik has been a consultant to science and education projects for the National Science Foundation, NASA, the U.S. Department of Commerce, government and school programs, nonprofit organizations, and public attractions. He has researched and published articles related to such timely biological issues as global warming, plankton sampling and population dynamics, the exploitation of exotic fish stocks, the effect of pollutants on coastal waterways, and the consequences of ecosystem destruction, including the increased influence of microorganisms such as *Pfiesteria*.

Born and raised in western Canada, he currently resides in Arlington, Virginia.